Dedalu

THE BALLAD O

For thirty years Hugh Lupton has been a central figure in the British storytelling revival. He tells myths, legends and folktales from many cultures but his particular passion is for the hidden layers of the English landscape and the stories and ballads that give voice to them. He has written several collections of folktales for children.

The Ballad of John Clare is his first novel.

THE BALLAD OF JOHN CLARE

by Hugh Lupton

Dedalus

Published in the UK by Dedalus Limited
24-26, St Judith's Lane, Sawtry, Cambs, PE28 5XE
info@dedalusbooks.com
www.dedalusbooks.com

ISBN printed book 978 1 915568 46 5
ISBN ebook 978 1 907650 99 4

Dedalus is distributed in the USA & Canada by SCB Distributors
15608 South New Century Drive, Gardena, CA 90248
info@scbdistributors.com www.scbdistributors.com

Dedalus is distributed in Australia by Peribo Pty Ltd
58, Beaumont Road, Mount Kuring-gai, N.S.W 2080
info@peribo.com.au www.peribo.co..au

First published by Dedalus in 2010
Reprinted in 2011, Retro Edition 2023

Printed and bound in the UK by Clays Elcograf S.p.A.
Typeset by Marie Lane

For Elizabeth McGowan, with love.

Contents

…While the mice in the field are listening to the Universe, and moving in the body of nature, where every living cell is sacred to every other, and all are interdependent, the Developer is peering at the field through a visor, and behind him stands the whole army of madmen's ideas, and shareholders, impatient to cash in on the world.

Ted Hughes

1

Rogation Sunday 1811

There is nothing of the parish of Helpston that I cannot see and hear. Like the bees whose skeps nestle against the churchyard wall and who have been busy in the April sun, I scatter myself across the parish and return at dusk burdened with happenstance.

And so it must be until he who keeps me from sleep joins his loam to mine.

At eight o'clock this morning the bells swung and filled the air with such sound as sundered the people of the parish from breakfast or kitchen or stable or yard and out to Butter Cross where Parson Mossop waited upon their coming. Almost every soul was there, for who among the hungry would not tread a few miles for the promise of meat and ale? And who among the prosperous would not gloat upon their charity?

The Turnills were there, the Crowsons, Closes, Wrights, Dolbys, Bains, Wormstalls, Bullimores, Royces, Samsons, Bellars, Farrars, Clares, Burbridges, Billings, Turners, Dyballs…every one of them buttoned up tight against the damp. The air was racked with sounds of coughing, of scolding mothers, murmured talk and stamping feet. There was a thin drizzle and the air was chill.

On the steps of the cross Jonathan Burbridge and Samuel Billings waited. Jonathan sat with his bass-viol enclosed entire in its canvas sack between his knees, only the spike jutting out beneath and stirring the wet turf at his feet. A few wood shavings, that any wife would have brushed away, clung to his beard, betraying that he had been at work upon the Sabbath. Sam Billings, who is as fat as Jonathan is lean, hammered wedges beneath the cords of the great bass drum that had grown slack with the dampness of the air. He looked up from time to time at the gathering crowd, his eyes shrewd and blue as corn-flowers.

Then Dick Turnill pushed forward from the crowd and sat between them, screwing together the three parts of his flute and blowing it clear.

Parson Mossop pulled the watch from his pocket, studied it, shook his head and slipped it back. He whispered to Sam:

"You promised me the full village band Mr Billings, and there are but three of you."

Sam turned his pink face to the parson, frank as the full moon:

"They'll come sir, I give you my word, they'll come."

The clock was creeping upon the quarter hour when they came, all three at once.

"Here are your fiddles, sir."

"Ah," said Parson Mossop. "Three sheep that have wandered from the fold. But no doubt they can bleat as well as any."

Leading the way came Old Otter, his white beard spread square as a spade across his horn-buttoned jerkin, bright-eyed as a robin. He had the smell of an old ham that has been long smoked in the chimney. He stepped down the street jaunty as a jackanape, his fiddle tucked under his arm. Behind him trailed the other two who had tried to match him pot for pot the night before. John Clare and Wisdom Boswell dragged their feet up Woodgate, past the Bluebell towards the waiting congregation.

The curled crown of John's head, lowered as though a little heavy for its neck, fell short of Wisdom's shoulder. Broad shouldered, high of forehead, shaped a little as a circus dwarf though with legs that are in proportion and comely, John stands dimute and small, being some five feet tall from head to foot. His mouth is full and red and wet as though he would lift the rim of the world to his lips and gulp it down. Few in the village can get the measure of him. He is bookish and solitary and cannot seem to set his hand to any trade. One minute he will be muttering to himself and crouching beneath a hedge or inside a hollow dotterel scribbling onto a scrap that he holds against the crown of his hat, the next he will be picking a quarrel with some village Hickathrift. Around his neck he was wearing a scarf as yellow as gorse.

Wisdom Boswell cut a very different figure. Dark where John is fair, thin where John is stocky, tall where John is squat. He has the restless, hungry, gangling stance of an unbroken colt. His sharp, high cheek-bones are softened by a dark down that has never known a razor. He is one of the Boswell crew that camps on Emmonsales Heath, and as close a friend as John has got. Though he's seen no more than seventeen winters there's more he could tell of the roads and lanes that snake beyond the parish bound than most who have lived here a life-time. But such knowledge counts for little. He and his kind are considered little better than vermin by most in the village, for even the poorest of the poor know their place and must find some soul to hold in greater contempt. Wisdom, though, because he can scrape such a reel from his fiddle as'd set the dead to cutting capers, has won a place in the village band.

John and Wisdom stepped gingerly up to Butter Cross, their bedraggled coats drawn across their shoulders, their fiddles held beneath. They were greeted with a tutting and a muttering and a shaking of heads from the waiting crowd.

Bob Turnill whispered to his wife:

"There's Parker's boy going to the devil again, and keeping company with tinkers."

Parson Mossop nodded to the churchwardens, who tapped the stone of Butter Cross with the foot of the processional cross. Sam Billings began to beat a steady measure from his drum. The bells fell silent and the congregation made its way along West Street following parson and churchwardens towards the open fields. Each kept to his own. Farmers walked ahead with their wives or aged parents on their arms. Tradesmen walked with their families. Apprentices and housemaids bantered and gave each other the eye. There were babes in arms and toddlers clutching mothers' skirts. There were children squabbling and laughing and weaving in and out of the crowd, some bare-footed and others with shoes to their feet. Labourers and their families came next. Those with a few farthings to spare had brightened their working smocks with ribbons or printed cotton scarves to their bonnets or throats.

Last of all came the parish paupers, the old and sick, some with their feet bound with rags, eager for the promise of food. They clicked and clacked their sticks and crutches, they coughed and cursed and called upon the rest to slow down. When the village houses were left behind they broke from the procession and turned away from the crowd. They made their hobbling, shuffling way straight to Snow Common to wait upon the Rogation feast.

The rest of the procession followed the road westwards, with Heath Field lands all fallow to the south and speckled with sheep and cattle. To the north the long furlongs of Lolham Bridge Field, with their new growth of wheat and barley, made a patchwork of dark and paler greens.

When King Street came into view the children - all at once - surged forwards with a sudden shout and raced towards the meer-stone that marks the parish bound. The first of them to beat the bound and strike head to stone receives some sweet token. They ran full tilt, their heads back, gasping at the air. The little ones were quickly left behind. It was Tom Dolby who first butted the stone and he will not forget it, for he was rubbing his head still when Mrs Bullimore caught up with him and popped the sugar plum between his lips that made all well again.

The churchwardens tapped their cross against the stone and Parson Mossop lifted his Bible and read from the book of Joel:

"Be not afraid, ye beasts of the field: for the pastures of the wilderness do spring, for the tree beareth her fruit…and the floors shall be full of wheat, and the vats shall overflow with wine and oil… and ye shall eat in plenty and be satisfied."

"Ay," whispered Parker Clare, "Ay, if you be a parson."

"Shush." Ann Clare put her hand across his mouth.

"We will sing psalm one hundred and four."

High above the parson's head a lark spilled its melody out upon the air. The band, all but Wisdom Boswell who knows nothing of hymns or psalms, lifted their instruments and played the opening phrase. The crowd broke into song.

A little apart from the rest of the congregation stood a cluster of farmers with the breakfasted look of those that keep a well-stocked larder. There was John Close, churchwarden, and his wife and daughters. There were Mr and Mrs Bull, Ralph Wormstall, churchwarden also, with his wizened mother. And there was the recently widowed Mrs Elizabeth Wright and her brother Will Bloodworth. All sang with heads thrown back as though each word might bring profit pushing up from the quickening earth. Will Bloodworth, though, is no farmer. He is a keeper of the game at the Milton estate, visiting his sister this Sabbath, and dressed in the livery of the Earl of Fitzwilliam, a claret-coloured frock coat with crimson lining. He stood in contrast to the brown and lawn jackets of the farmers with their cocked hats. His clear tenor rang out above the other voices with the easy confidence of one who believes the world to be in his thrall and pliable to his will, though he was by far the poorer member of the company.

Wisdom Boswell had settled himself on a stile. He pulled a lump of yellow rosin from his pocket and set to rubbing it up and down his fiddle bow. A cluster of children gathered round him, a little shy for they had been told over and over to steer clear of gypsies. He looked down at them and grinned. Tom Dolby took courage, he came closer and reached out his arm, he uncurled his fingers. He was holding a stone with a hole clean through the heart of it. He offered it to Wisdom and whispered:

"Riddy Riddy Wry Rump."

Wisdom took it. He knew the game.

"Have you got any string?"

"Ay."

Tom handed him a piece of twine. Wisdom threaded it through the stone and tied it tight. He winked at Tom:

"Who?"

Tom Dolby turned back to his friends. They stood in a circle their arms about each other's shoulders whispering fiercely. Then Tom broke away. He pointed with his finger.

"Him!"

Will Bloodworth was standing a few paces from them, his back towards the stile. He was holding the hymnal high for his sister to read.

Wisdom Boswell knotted the end of the twine into a loop. The children watched as he crept behind Will as quiet and subtle as a cat. He knelt on the grass and gently drew the loop over the two tin buttons at the back of Will's jacket. Then slowly he lowered the stone so that the weight of it would not be suddenly felt. The children smothered their laughter with the backs of their hands. The twine was hanging like a tail, the stone just behind Will Bloodworth's knees. Wisdom edged away from him and back to the stile.

But though Will had seen nothing, his sister had. Mrs Elizabeth Wright had watched Wisdom from the corner of her eye and seemed to take little pleasure in what she saw.

As soon as the psalm was spent John Clare and Old Otter struck up 'Jockey to the Fair'. Sam Billings beat his drum in time. Dick Turnill blew his flute, his parents frowning that he should have fallen so far into the clutches of mammon as to know such a tune, let alone blow it upon the Sabbath. Jonathan Burbridge sawed his bass viol. And Wisdom lifted his fiddle to his shoulder and joined them. The churchwardens held up the cross and set off striding towards Lolham Bridge, the congregation trailing behind. The rain had eased and the warm April wind seemed to have blown away all aches and cares.

Will Bloodworth pulled a little clay pipe from his pocket and filled it from his pouch. He took a tinder box and struck flint to iron. Soon he was puffing smoke and smiling, the pipe clenched between his teeth, with that tight drawn smile of a man who enjoys his tobacco. His sister took his arm and they joined the crowd. The children had been waiting for their moment. They began to dance behind him:

"Riddy Riddy Wry Rump
Riddy Riddy Wry Rump!"

Will strode on all innocent that he was the butt of their laughter.

"Riddy Riddy Wry Rump!"

Then his sister tugged his arm. He stopped. She leaned across and whispered into his ear. The children held their breath and watched as he reached behind himself. His fingers closed around the twine. He lifted the stone into his hand. Suddenly they were dancing round him again:

"Riddy Riddy Wry Rump!"

He pulled the pipe from his mouth and turned. There was no easy smile on his features now:

"Which one of you little varmints has made a mock of me?"

The children scattered and threaded through the crowd, soon they were running ahead. There had been something in the measure of those whispered words that had told them their game was over. His sister shook her head:

"'Twas none of them Will." She said, "'Twas the gypsy whelp. I saw him with my own eyes."

The band were still playing at the meer-stone. Will looked back towards Wisdom Boswell who drew his bow across the strings of his fiddle mindless of all but the swelling melody that filled the air. A shadow fell across Will Bloodworth's face. He pushed the stone into his pocket, turned on his heel and strode on in silence.

****

All morning I followed the village congregation as it circled the bounds of Helpston as though it edged the very rim of the world. Every sod they trod I know as familiar as my own face, more so since flesh has folded into clay. With scripture and song, with tune and meer-stone and sugared plums they came to Lolham Bridge and followed the stream that skirts the fen. Where the stream marks the bound they threw sweets into the water and the children plunged in, for now the sun shone and the air was sweet as the very first morning. Then all of a straggle they came round by Green Dyke and Rhyme Dyke and Woodcroft Field, with Glinton spire pricking the sky beyond, where the furlongs are sprouting with beans whose green leaves break the loam and swallow the sunlight. And as I followed their compass I was at the edge of all knowledge, for beyond the parish the world begins to sink away into reaches and distances that are beyond my naming.

Meer-stone followed meer-stone and the church clock had long struck noon when the crowd reached Snow Common. The parish paupers were standing waiting, shivering by the lane-side. By now there wasn't a soul that wasn't bone weary and ready to sit and take its ease. Parson Mossop lifted up his frock coat and rested himself upon a tussock. Churchwardens followed suit and soon all were settled, all but a few children and dogs that ran and shouted and barked as tireless as the first swooping swallows.

The crowd had not been waiting long when there came the sound that all had been straining for. The clattering of a horse's hooves, the rattling of a cart, the "Whoaa" and "Easy" of the driver and then above the tops of the bushes three heads appeared: Farmer Joyce, his daughter Mary sitting beside him, and the black ears of his mare Bessy. They made their way along the track towards the congregation. Farmer Joyce, who is churchwarden at Glinton, reined in, swung down from his seat and tied the horse to a post.

The waiting crowd cheered and there was a surge towards the cart, as men, women and children clambered forward and would have scrambled up had not the churchwardens moved between the cart and congregation.

"Now, now, stand back! Easy! Bide your time!"

The churchwardens pushed some backwards so that they sat suddenly on the turf at the track's edge and they stood in a row as sentinels before the cart.

The cart was filled with victuals and small ale and sweetened water that had been paid for by subscription by the people of the parish according to their means. Farmers had thrown in their shillings, tradesmen their thruppences and the rest their thin farthings. There were pies, meats and conserves, there were loaves, nuts and dried fruits, free to all however great or modest their contribution.

The parson opened his Bible to Deuteronomy and tapped the iron shod wheel of the cart with his cane:

"Blessed shall be the fruit of thy ground and the fruit of thy cattle, the increase of thy kine, and the flocks of thy sheep. Blessed shall be thy basket and thy store."

He snapped the Bible shut as the village answered "Amen".

The parson was the first to tuck a handkerchief under his chin. The churchwardens parted as he poured himself a pot and sank his teeth into a pie. Others followed according to their station. They clustered round the cart, helping themselves and carrying armfuls across to families that were waiting on the tussocked grass. Farmer Joyce and Mary passed and poured and made themselves agreeable to all. When everyone else had taken their fill the churchwardens stood aside and the parish paupers pushed forward and grabbed their share. Charlie Turner pressed bread and pastry with his fingers into his half-wit daughter's mouth, as though he was some hedgerow bird that has hatched a cuckoo. Like the birds of the field the village paupers filled their crops.

All hearts and minds were on the food except for one. John Clare sat a little apart, upon a stump and so still it was as though its timber had spread through him and he was himself wood from head to foot. No one paid him any mind for he is often considered strange. When Old Otter pressed a pot into his hand he took it but did not sup. He sat like one amazed. His eyes were fixed on Mary Joyce who stood waist deep among ragged children pouring sugared water from a jug.

His eyes were fixed on Mary, who he remembered as a child in Glinton vestry school, as shy and quick then as a wild thing, and bold besides, and as nimble to scramble up onto the church roof and scratch her name upon the lead as any. And now she was become a woman. John's mind was quick with calculation, if he was seventeen then she was three behind. And she was grown lovely. Her hair was dressed in ringlets and covered with a lace cap, and over it a wide brimmed hat. Her cotton gown was yellow as a cowslip and underneath it the firm shapely rounding of her breasts, and loose over her shoulders a russet cloak...he shook himself from his reverie, supped his ale for courage, straightened, and casting all thought of station aside walked across to the cart.

"Mary."

She turned to him. He saw that her face still had something of the impishness he remembered as a child, but there were other layers beside, of thought and sorrow, and then a soft kindness about the eyes that was beyond her years. John remembered that she had lost her mother a year since.

"Mary, have you forgot me?"

She broke into a smile and a new light seemed to shine

from her face.

"John Clare!"

"Will you come and sit with us Mary?"

He offered his hand and she took it, light as a bird, and sprang down from the cart.

"Of course I've never forgot you John."

They walked across to where the band was gathered on the grass. John unbuttoned his coat and threw it down for her.

"Here's Sam and Jonathan, Old Otter who the whole world knows, Wisdom who you have not met before, and Dick who you've met a thousand times."

She laughed and kissed Dick Turnill on the cheek, for she had schooled with him too, which made him blush and which in turn made the rest laugh out loud. And she shook hands with Wisdom. Then she sat on the coat and gathered her knees up to her chin.

"'Tis two years since last I saw you John."

"I've been away Mary."

John suddenly found himself awkward at a divide that seemed to him to have grown between them. She smiled:

"Seeking fame and fortune in the French war?"

He shook his head and said nothing.

"A trade then?"

"Hardly, though my parents would wish it so."

"Well, here you are, and home again, and I for one am glad of it."

She broke a piece of twig and flicked it at him. There was quiet between them for a while.

"Do you recall John," she said, "the time that Mr Merrishaw put a question to the class and I put up my hand to answer and he said 'Yes Mary', and I mouthed the words and made no sound. He picked up his ear trumpet, d'you remember,

'Speak up child' he said and I did mouth again. And he said 'I cannot hear thee, is there anyone can give me the answer as can speak up like a man?' And you put your hand up. 'Yes John Clare,' says he. And you mouthed the words as well. And old Merrishaw frowned then and put down his trumpet and made his way out of the church. And we all climbed up to the windows and we could see him among the gravestones poking a rag first into one ear and then t'other. When he came back we were sitting in rows as though we had not shifted.

'Now then John Clare,' says he, 'as you were saying.' And he lifts the trumpet to his ear once more, and you stood up and shouted the answer so that he jumped clean into the air, but said no word thinking as he'd cleaned his ears of all obstruction."

And John laughed and nodded and delighted in her as she was this day, sitting beside him. And he delighted in memories of how she had been. And in his mind he was forming a design on how things might be one day between them, though he could not bring any word to his tongue to express it.

Her talk turned first one way and then another.

And then, suddenly, it was interrupted.

"A word if you'd be so kind."

They looked up and Will Bloodworth was standing above them, swaying a little, for the farmers had been sweetening their small ale with a flask of French brandy. His pipe was smouldering in his left hand and his right was drawn tight into a fist. His voice was raised, as one who has drunk over the odds, and on hearing him the congregation quietened.

His sister, sensing trouble, called out to him.

"Come and sit down Will."

He paid her no heed.

"I want a word with our gypsy friend."

Wisdom got up to his feet as though nothing in the world

would hurry him. He met Will's gaze with a wry lop-sided smile, with nothing in it of fear or servitude. If Will had been master and Wisdom apprentice, that smile would have been rewarded with a wallop for its cock-sure cheek. Will whispered:

"What's your bloody name?"

"Will! Sit down!"

Wisdom's brown eyes looked steady into Will's.

"Wisdom Boswell."

Will raised his voice:

"Ah. One of them as camps out on Emmonsales and helps himself regular to what ain't his."

There were muffled grunts of assent from all sides. Wisdom said nothing. And Will, grown bold with the ready sympathy of the crowd, carried on:

"Well I've heard as you 'Gyptians, for all you're a pack of thieves, can read the future in tea leaves or the lines on a body's hand. If I was to give you sixpence what could you read of me?"

There was laughter and old Miss Nelly Farrar shouted out:

"Ay, and ain't I still waiting for that handsome devil I paid Lettuce Boswell thruppence for?"

Will smiled with his mouth, though there was little of a smile in his eyes. He uncurled his fist and held out his hand palm upwards, there was a silver sixpence lying on it.

"Come on Wisdom Boswell, unravel for me all that is writ in the stars."

It was clear he meant to make a mock of Wisdom. And every face was on the two of them now as Wisdom reached across and took Will's hand into his own. He picked up the coin and pocketed it.

"It's the women as usually do the dukkering, but I'll tell

you what I can."

He stroked the palm tenderly with his thumb and looked down upon it with a great attention. Will Bloodworth turned to the crowd and raised his eyebrows.

"It ain't often I hold hands with a damned gypsy."

There were titters of laughter again.

The children did not laugh though, for since the riddy stone Wisdom was as a native chief to them, and they his tribe. Nor did Sam Billings, who watched Wisdom with a bright, shrewd eye, knowing more of the Boswell crew than most.

Wisdom traced the lines on the palm with the tip of a finger. Then he spoke in a whisper, loud enough for all to hear and filled with portent, his face fixed as though staring beyond Will's hand into some world no one else could see.

"I see rivals in love. I see two as both nurse a tender affection for thee in their secret hearts."

Will turned and winked at the crowd.

"Two you say?"

"Ay, two there are, and each would have thee to husband. And if they knew as they was rivals in love there would be such a scratching and a shrieking as would shame a cage of cats."

Will made as if to yawn:

"And both of them beauties I've little doubt. One dark perhaps? One fair? "

He threw his pipe onto the grass and thrust his other hand under Wisdom's nose so the blunt fingertips caught his chin.

"Come on sir, be plain!"

The crowd's mocking laughter echoed Will's mocking grin, but Wisdom did not change his tune.

"Ay, one is dark right enough," he whispered, "But no stranger to you Will Bloodworth, for she has rolled you in her arms full many's the time."

"Tell me more!"

Wisdom lifted his voice to a tremulous note.

"I see her stand before me now....she is ninety and nine years old with leathery dugs as a spaniel's ears and one black tooth to her gums....and the bits and the bobs that dangle from her tail would muck an acre."

There was a pause when all the air seemed to hold its breath, and then the cackling, guffawing, shrieking, barking laughter began. Wisdom raised his voice above the din:

"And as to the fair one..."

But no one heard more of her for Will Bloodworth had seized him by the collar and would have struck him where he stood, had not John Close stepped forward and put his arm about Will's trembling shoulders. He whispered:

"Easy Will, this ain't the place to settle scores."

Will Bloodworth shook Wisdom, then let go. He turned away with his shoulders hunched and his fists knotted. John Close steered him back towards the clump of tussocks where his sister and the other farmers' families sat.

The children danced behind him:

"Riddy riddy wry rump! Riddy riddy wry rump!"

And no scowl of Will Bloodworth's could stop them now.

The parson, seeing that decency had been thrown into confusion, tapped his stick against a cartwheel, Sam Billings took up the rhythm with his drum, and the crowd began to carry all the empty wooden platters and horn mugs back to the cart.

But as the congregation made ready to move, the children, grown wild now with laughter and too long sitting, tipped over a basket of walnuts and began to throw them in all directions. There was such a shouting and dodging, with mothers scolding, fathers clipping ears, the old swinging their sticks at ducking boys, and the shrill voice of the parson trying to call order that Jonathan's drum was drowned.

Little Henry Snow flung a nut that caught John Clare upon the chin. John picked it up and threw it hard back again. It was at that moment that Farmer Joyce called:

"Mary!"

She jumped to her feet and caught John's nut full in the eye. She let out a sudden little cry and lifted up her hand, and though she was nine parts woman the tears came spilling down her cheeks. John froze, he was become wood again, and knew neither what to do nor say to make amends. He looked at her. She looked at him. They stood for a moment in all the confusion like mawkins in some storm-tossed field. Then Farmer Joyce called out again:

"Mary! Come now. Glinton calls."

She turned and ran back to the cart, climbed up beside him, and with a flick of the reins they were trundling along the track. Her hand was still lifted to her eye when she disappeared from sight. And John Clare stood frozen, as though a terrible weight bore down upon his heart.

It was the first psalm of the afternoon that seemed to wake him from himself. He pulled out his fiddle and picked up the tune that the band had launched upon.

The procession made its way around the skirts of Snow Common. Old Otter's squat rose up above the blackthorn blossom with its mottled canvas, its stacked turf and its white trickle of smoke rising from the smoke-hole as familiar to the crowd as the twisting line of stunted willows that follows the stream.

Round the edge of Oxey Wood they went, the children racing from one meer-stone to the next, butting head to hard barnack. Wherever the stone was gone and there was but a mere-pit left, one child or another would be lifted by its feet and lowered down until the crown of its head was awash with muddy water, and then lifted to its feet and a fistful of sweets thrust into its pocket. So it is we remember for all time the bounds of our native place.

Round Emmonsales Heath they went, where all the gorse was showing gold. Then they skirted Langdyke Bush where the Boswell crew were camped. Little could be seen of the gypsies save smoke and the brightly coloured rags of clothing that were stretched across the thorns to dry in the sun. Even their dogs were hushed as the village congregation passed, peering in among the thickets but seeing nought.

Wisdom Boswell touched John's shoulder.

"I'm away bau, I'll see ye soon. Be good!"

He turned and ran, zig-zagging among the scrub and thorn towards the rising smoke. Something flew through the air behind him, trailing a thread as a comet trails its tail. It struck him hard against the small of his back. Wisdom stopped and turned. Lying on the ground at his feet was a stone with a hole through its heart, a twine was threaded through and tied to the end of it a slip of paper. He turned it over between his fingers and peered at it. He pushed it into his pocket and ran on to join his family who were squatting among the scrub, smoking their pipes and waiting for all the hubbub to die away.

From the height of Helpston church I watched the congregation make its circle true. From Emmonsales to the Kings Road, and then past the quarry at Swordy Well and along the side of Heath Field, where Jim Crowson and Sam Wood were rounding up cattle from the fallows. And at last the bounds were beat and the late sun sent the shadow of Butter Cross stretching towards Glinton and all the day's journey was complete.

****

And now the evening grows chill and I have rubbed the fine, dusty pollen of happenstance from myself. The parish is returned to quiet, each family separating at Butter Cross and trudging home in its little weary cluster. Windows are lighted up and chimneys send their smoke to a darkening sky. Parson Mossop lifts a glass of claret to his lips and stretches his feet to a banked fire. Mrs Elizabeth Wright and Will Bloodworth sit down at the oaken table to a cured ham. Old Otter dips his ladle into whatever hollow meat Kitty has added to the pot. Tom Dolby and his brothers nibble hunks of dry bread and sup on the memory of Snow Common. And in his hovel behind the churchyard wall Charlie Turner and his half-wit daughter wrap themselves in their damp rags and go early to bed.

In Bachelors Hall Sam Billings and Jonathan Burbridge tap a barrel and fill their horn mugs to the frothing brim. Jonathan drinks and wipes the foam from his beard:

"Sam, I've been thinking today, as we was walking with all the multitude, as I've a mind to wife."

Sam Billings raises his eyebrows so that his glistening forehead folds into wrinkles of surprise.

"A wife! Jonathan, think again, 'twould be farewell to all sweet freedom."

"I've two lads working under me and an apprentice, and not a coffin nor joist in Helpston or Glinton as ain't felt the touch of my saw or plane....and now I'm a man as can hold up his head I've a yearnin' for a welcoming bed and maybe a clutch of little Burbridges to fill the air with their prittle-prattle."

"Who d'ye have in mind?"

"No one, though I've a vision in my head..."

"Ay?"

"I see one as ain't so young but still comely, fine grained like, but not sawn so thin as she'll bend this way nor that, like a hardwood I reckon, that ain't stood too long, and with a shapely curve to it."

"Well Jonathan," says Sam, "I reckon I've got the very lass for thee."

"Who?"

"She'll make you a tidy little wife."

Sam Billings disappears into the next room and comes back with a piece of broken shelf. He drops it onto Jonathan's knee.

"She's fallen for you already my friend. I'll get old Mossop to read the banns next Sabbath."

****

The Clares are gathered round the fire cooking eggs in a skillet that hangs from the chimney hook. Little Sophie stirs them with a wooden spoon. Ann slices hard bread upon the board and John and Parker warm their knees before the flames. No word is spoken between them as the food is spooned onto plates and eaten. John pours some water from a wooden jug into his mug.

Ann breaks the quiet:

"Ay, water tonight John, no frittering your wage on ale."

John drinks.

"Now Sophie, mop the yolk from your platter, 'tis time for your bed!"

They climb the wooden steps and Ann tucks Sophie snug beside the little cot where once poor Bessie slept. Downstairs

Parker has thrown some more sticks on the fire. He and John watch the smoke as it's sucked up the chimney. Ann comes down and picks up her knitting, the ball of coarse woollen yarn on her lap.

There's a sudden knocking at the door. Ann puts down her needles. She goes across and lifts the latch. The light of fire and candle shows Wisdom Boswell standing on the threshold. She frowns:

"Away with ye! You gypsies are steering our John to the bad. There'll be no drunken capers tonight! There's them as have to be up wi' the dawn and earn an honest wage. Away with ye!"

Parker calls out:

"Twas only the frolicsomeness of youth Annie, let him in for God's sake. What are you after lad?"

Ann still bars the doorway. Wisdom calls past her shoulder.

"It's nothing of the ale Mr Clare, I swear on my mother's grave."

Then he looks at Ann with a tender pleading:

"'Tis a matter of scholarship, Ma'am, your John bein' a por-engro and master of his ABCs, and none of us Boswells havin' the skill."

Wisdom has struck a tender place, for it is a source of pride to Ann Clare that she should have set aside shillings enough to give John a few months schooling each year when he was a heedless boy. And his skill at mouthing aloud the silent markings of the printed page is a wonder to her yet.

She sighs and stands aside. Parker beckons to him:

"Pull a stool up to the fire. Warm thyself."

Wisdom fetches a stool and sits down beside John. John turns to him.

"What is it you're after?"

Wisdom hands across a scrap of paper.

"That game-keeper from Milton, he flung it after me this afternoon, tied to the riddy stone, there are words on it but I cannot unfathom them. Read it for me."

Parker Clare chuckles:

"Will Bloodworth, the man with two sweet-hearts."

John holds the scrap with its pencil scratchings to a rush candle:

"Tis writ in capitals and reads thus:

'I SHALL HAVE SATISFACTION OF THEE

NO GYPSY WHELP MAKES MOCKERY OF ME'."

John passes it to Wisdom who scrunches up the paper in his fist and throws it into the fire. Parker looks across at him:

"I fear you've made an enemy Wisdom Boswell, and of one better left uncrossed."

Wisdom shrugs.

"I meant no harm. 'Twas all in jest. And now he's tippoty dre mande. And to tell you the truth of the matter, there were lines on that man's hand that were better left unread."

2

May Day

This fortnight last John has worked the gardens of John Close's farm. Thistle, campion, poppy, fumitory, yellow charlock, pimpernel, groundsel, all must yield to the hoe before they bloom and seed and overwhelm, for all they're the common flowers that he loves best. But a man must work and John must sentence them as weeds and condemn them to have their green grip upon the soil scratched away. And having served his time as executioner, must trudge back to Close's yard, clean his hoe and take his place in line to receive his paltry wage.

And now, his pocket lined with pennies, he sought his solace.

Once inside the woods and shaken free of the ceaseless gossip and the women's shrill laughter and the hacking cough of poor Jem Farrar. Once he was free of the tireless scratching of iron to stony soil and the day's slate had been wiped clean by sweet solitude, John Clare set his mind to the next day's holiday.

From the willows bordering Round Oak Water he cut slim withies and wound them together into a loop. From the may at the wood's margin he found sprays that were breaking into early white blossom. He cut away their thorns and wove them into the loop. He took primroses from a bank that caught the afternoon sun and a fistful of early blue-bells and fixed their stems between the twisted withies until the garland was bright with pale yellow, creamy-white and blue flowers. He worked until the day's light began to grow dim in the wood. Then he shouldered his garland and trudged home.

Sophie Clare, her face pressed to the window glass, watched John hiding his garland in the lean-to where Parker stores his garden tools. She slipped out of the back door and stood quiet behind John as he pushed it among the shadows. He was startled by her voice.

"It ain't no good, John."

He turned to her.

"I know what you've made and it ain't no good."

Sophie was looking at him, her eyes so solemn and worldly-wise in her face that John had to smile.

"What d'you mean it ain't no good?"

Sophie pulled the garland from its hiding place.

"Everybody knows a garland's gotta have some pear blossom."

She ran across the garden, climbed up into the pear tree and broke a spray of white blossom from it. She brought it back and thrust it into John's hand.

"Pear for fair."

John nodded and wove it into the garland. Sophie watched him with disdain. It was clear to her that John knew nothing about the ways of the world for all he was seven years older than her.

"And where's the yew?"

"Yew?"

"Yew for true of course. Every girl in Helpston knows that."

"All right, I'll go to the churchyard and fetch some yew."

Sophie turned to run back indoors. John caught her by the shoulder. He pushed his finger to her lips:

"Shhhhhh. Don't tell!"

She nodded fiercely, shook herself free from his grip and ran into the house.

It was nearly dark as John made his way past Butter Cross and over the road to the churchyard wall. He cut a long sprig of yew, brought it home and wound it onto the garland. Now it was ready. He put it back into its hiding place and went indoors.

His mother was lighting the candles.

"Where's Sophie?"

"She's gone to bed, John."

John climbed the steps. He leaned over her bed.

"It's done."

He could see her pale face searching his in the shadowy room.

"Good."

He kissed her forehead.

"Goodnight Soph'."

"You know what to do. Hang it on her door."

John nodded:

"Ay."

She whispered:

"Who is she John?"

John stood up and turned away.

"That's for me to know and you to ponder upon."

"Who is she, or I'll run downstairs and tell..."

"You wouldn't dare!"

She jumped out of bed and made towards the stairwell.

John seized the hem of her shift and pulled her back towards the bed.

"All right."

She climbed under the blankets. John bent down and whispered in her ear. She peered at him with the doubtful look of a craftsman who is about to send some new apprentice out upon a task, and wonders whether he has the gumption to see it through.

"You'll need to wear your yellow scarf, and is your shirt washed? And money enough for the May fair. And she'll want to hear gentlemanly talk, John, and don't sweeten your breath with onions because look here, I've got something as I took from Farmer Close's kitchen when I was helping mother, for I had a notion you was courting."

She pressed a little screw of paper into John's hand.

"Chew these John, cloves."

She lowered her voice to a tiny whisper:

"Then your mouth'll be sweet for kissing."

She began to laugh and pushed the blanket into her mouth to quieten herself.

John cuffed her gently and bade her sweet dreams. He dropped the cloves into his pocket and went downstairs.

He'd not been down for long when Parker Clare lifted the latch and came in through the garden door. He'd been shutting up the chickens for the night. He put his hand to John's shoulder:

"That'll win her John, whoever she is! Though I'd sooner you hadn't broke those blossoms from the pear."

John sighed. There is little privacy to be had in either cottage or parish. He picked up a candle and reached into his cubby hole. There his precious volumes lean side by side: Thomson's *Seasons*, Watts' *Hymns and Spiritual Songs*, Abercrombie's *Every Man his own Gardener*, Burns' *Poems*.

Alongside them his chap-books are stacked: *Robin Hood's Garland*, *Tom Hickathrift*, *The Seven Sleepers*, *The King and the Cobbler*, *Old Moore's Almanack*. And tucked into all of them are his own precious scribblings on shop paper and pages torn from old copy books.

He pulled one out and settled down with it.

****

This Mayday morning John was up and dressed in clean linen shirt and yellow scarf before the church clock had struck four. He ate a hunk of bread and washed it down with water. He took his garland from the shed and slung it across his shoulder. Then he made his way out of the village and across Woodcroft field towards Glinton, following the stony track between the furlongs. The sky was bright with spring stars. The young beans stuck their dark green heads out of the tilth and seemed to glister with all the silver dews of Eden. The knee-high barley brushed his breeches and soaked them through.

The first light of morning etched Glinton steeple against the sky and the cockerels of both villages began to call out their clarion. A barn-owl, quartering the field, shrieked close and sudden and John's heart raced, for he is easy frit. When he came to Glinton he cut through the churchyard and along the street to Joyce's Farm.

He came between the gateposts into Farmer Joyce's yard, that is always swept clean. The last of the ricks loomed high above him. In the kitchen garden to one side all the birds were singing now, pigeon, robin, starnel, sparrow, finch, the shrieking swifts were swooping low across the yard and the rasp-throated rooks busy about their nests high in the elms. The chickens were scratching outside the barns, and inside the stables he could hear the horses snorting and shifting in their stalls.

Then the mastiffs in their kennel began to bark at John and alerted Will Farrell, Joyce's stockman and groom. He pushed open the stable door and came sauntering across the yard, his breeches tucked into his boots, his grubby smock tied at the waist with a piece of twine, his bald head seeming to mirror the sky. For even though it is a holiday the master's horses must be fed, and they must shine at the fair too, combed and brushed and sleek as chestnuts. Will looked John up and down with a knowing smile.

"What do you want?"

John reached into his pocket.

"Two pennyworth of ale, Will, if you'll tell me which is Mary's bedroom window."

Will looked at the Mayday garland and laughed:

"Here comes John Clare sniffing at Mary Joyce's door like a dog that scents a bitch on heat. You're wasting your time boy, she'll never give ye the time of day, she's way above your station."

John rubbed the two coins together and Will shrugged.

"It'll do you no good."

He took the two pennies and dropped them into the pocket of his breeches.

"'Tis the casement window above the front door Johnny, but you won't thank me for telling ye."

John went round to the front of the farm house. Its barnack stone glowed yellow-gold with the first rays of the sun and the windows on the easterly side blazed with reflected light. He hung the garland from the iron knocker on the front door and, thinking it was a little early yet, sat down on a mounting block and waited. He could hear the clatter of milk pails as they were carried out to the barns swinging on their yokes. He could hear the 'Whoaaaa' and 'Get along there' as Nathan Cushion drove the milk cows along the lane and into the yard. Downstairs Kate Dyball was pulling the shutters back from the windows. The church clock was striking the half hour after five when John reckoned his moment had come. He picked up a handful of gravel from the path beside the lawn and threw it at the window above the front door. And then he launched into the old song:

"I've been rambling all this night
And the first part of the day,"

He flung up another fistful of stones.

"And now I'm come to your own front door
To make you the Queen of the May."

Above his head John could hear the sound of the shutters being pulled apart. And then the casement window was thrown open. John shouted:

"Will you be my Queen of the May?"

"The Devil I will John Clare."

John looked up and saw Farmer Joyce's head, bleary-eyed, unshaven, the nightcap dangling over one ear, squinting down at him.

"And I'll thank you not to come caterwauling at my front door before the church clock has struck six of the morning on this or any other cussed day of the year."

The window slammed shut. And from the corner of the yard John heard what seemed to him at first to be a sneeze. He turned and saw Will Farrell and a couple of milkmaids peering round the side of the house with their fists in their mouths, rocking with stifled laughter.

Then from behind him came another sound. A peal of clear laughter that he recognised at once, laughter that seemed to spring out like a rill from behind the yew hedge.

"John!"

This was too much for him, to be the mockery and laughing stock of all Glinton. He lowered his head and walked towards the gate vowing, in that moment, never again to show his face at Joyce's farm.

Mary, in her nightdress with a blanket tucked about her shoulders, ran after him. She stood in front of him her head tilted in mock reproach.

"What John Clare, are you come to black my other eye?"

He could see she still bore a purple stain where he had struck her. He looked at her dumb-founded. Mary tugged at his arm and pulled him back towards the farmhouse.

"I was up for the dawn John, washing my face in the dew, and I saw you come round to the front door, and I hid behind the hedge, and you sat and so I sat.... and then you sang your song to father...."

And she filled the air again with her clear laughter so that John was part mortified and part filled with exaltation. She led him back to the lawn, then broke away and ran along the gravel path to the front door. She lifted the garland in her hands and studied it carefully.

"Here's pear for fair, and a sprig of yew..."

Then she turned to him, her face suddenly solemn:

"Yes John, I'll be your May Queen. I'll be your Queen of the May today."

And soon afterwards John found himself sitting at the great table in the farm-house kitchen. Mary had run into the dairy and fetched a jug of whey. She'd poured him a cupful.

"Wait here, while I dress myself for the fair!"

He'd sat and supped while Kate Dyball, Lizzie Tucker and Hope Farrell bustled about the kitchen and put food upon the table. They were full of high spirits, for as soon as breakfast was done they would be free to take their holiday. The great iron skillet over the kitchen fire sizzled with ham. The pewter plates on the shelves against the wall glistered in the flickering light like so many battered moons. Above them, on the top shelf, the rows of brass candle-sticks stood, cleaned of their grease and put away until the autumn draws its dark hours in again. It seemed to John that he had set foot in the land of Cockayne, where the rivers run with buttermilk and the barns are thatched with bacon.

At seven o'clock the household sat down to breakfast. Nathan Cushion and the milk-maids came in from the milking shed shaking the straw from their shoes. Will Farrell left his stable boots at the door and sat down. John Fell and his dog came in from shepherding by the fen. Mary sat down beside John, wearing the yellow dress that he had first seen at Rogation.

When Will saw John with Mary beside him he raised his eyebrows in surprise but knew better than to speak his mind. Then Farmer Joyce returned from his early morning inspection of the stables.

"Well, well, good morning, the horses are well brushed Will, they will not disgrace us. What time did ye feed 'em?"

Will Farrell got up to his feet:

"The clock had not long struck five."

"Good, good. Sit down Will for God's sake."

Farmer Joyce was dressed in holiday attire, blue frock coat and yellow swansdown waistcoat, his breeches tucked into top-boots. He sat at the table and cut himself a lump of bread from the loaf. No sooner had he lifted food to mouth than all the household set to eating. Then he became aware of John. He looked across at him with the shrewd, quizzical air of a farmer at market.

"Mary, you've brought your sweet throated throstle in from the garden I see."

Will Farrell and the milk-maids chortled into their cups. Farmer Joyce continued:

"Ay, and you're welcome at this table John Clare, for Mary's often talked of thee."

He held out his hand and John shook it readily.

"I remember she said as you was the best scholar in old Merrishaw's class."

John shrugged and reddened.

"Yes, you were John," said Mary, "he was always holding up some page of yours as an example to the rest of us."

Farmer Joyce poured himself a mug of small ale.

"Well, book-learning's all very well as far as it goes."

He looked along his own table, spread with bread, butter, cheese, conserves, ham, hard-boiled eggs, a plate of steaming bacon and jugs of whey and ale, as though it was itself a tidily writ page. For a moment it seemed he would say more, but then he stopped his mouth with cheese and bacon. But his thoughts, for all they were unspoken, were clear enough. He was weighing, as a chandler in some corn-hall, his precious daughter's happiness this May holiday against the prospects of a Helpston lad without land or trade. But, for all his rumination, he ate with relish enough, pausing from time to time to mop the corners of his mouth with a handkerchief. All the household ate with him and for a while no word was spoken. Then he rapped the table hard with his knuckles.

"Away to Helpston Fair with the pair of you, for we're only young once and John Clare is as good a lad as any, for all he owns no more in this world than his breeches and a brain-pan full of Merrishaw's clap-trap!"

He had swapped his scruples for Mary's bright face as she jumped to her feet, ran round the table, put her arms about his shoulders and kissed his cheek. And it seemed to him a fair trade.

Later he watched them through the open door as they set off across the farmyard. With his inner eye he was watching his own courtship twenty years since. It seemed to him, for a moment, that the two of them were ghosts as they walked between the gateposts and made their way side by side along the lane, John's garland across Mary's shoulder. Then they entered the churchyard and disappeared from sight.

He turned back to the table, lifted his mug and tipped the last of the small beer down his throat. He strode out of the house and across the yard to the stable.

****

All day John Clare and Mary Joyce were swept up in the rigs and the jigs of Helpston Fair as though they were part of some fevered dream that had been conjured by poppy-head tea. They wandered among stalls where children tugged at their mother's arms or stood solemn-eyed staring at the bright-coloured array of sugar plums, brandy-snaps, barley sugar, candied lemon and gingerbread. They paused among the beer shops and food stalls where farmers laughed loud and bit into hot pies that spilled gravy upon their shirt-fronts, and lean-faced labourers counted out their farthings and weighed a pint pot against a loaf of bread. They haggled with hawkers over ribbons and chapbooks. John dropped a penny into Charlie Turner's cup where he sat on the roadside. His half-wit daughter rolled her eyes.

Mary flung her garland over the coloured rags of bunting that stretched from eave to eave and John ran to catch it. They danced before the maypole while the village band sawed out the old tunes with their hats set on the pavement for coppers. John waved to them as he passed. He swung Mary so that both her feet were lifted from the ground. And she, in her yellow dress, part woman, part child, laughing and dancing at his side, held him in her thrall.

"We'll take the long way home." He said.

With the last of his pennies they bought a gingerbread milk-maid, and a gingerbread coach and horses and nibbled at them until Mary's milk-maid was one-legged and John's horses headless, and then giggled as though they were children at Glinton School.

They followed Maxham's Green Lane towards Snow Common.

"If you weren't fighting Boney John, and coming back a bold hero to sweep me off my feet, with a star on your breast and a purse-full of prize money for all them galleons you'd sunk, where were you these two years?"

And John picked up a stick, tucked his arm into his coat, closed one eye and lifted the stick to his closed eye.

"I see John Clare at Burghley Hall working in the garden."

Mary curtsied to him.

"Gardener to the Marquis. Then I am walking out with a gentleman of quality."

"Well, to tell ye the truth Mary, apprentice to the master of the kitchen garden."

She curtsied again:

"Then I am walking out with the breeder and bearer of the Marquis' turnip."

John bowed low to the ground.

"At your service, Ma'am."

And he told her of the great walled-kitchen garden, and how, on first arriving, his master had sent him out for liquor late at night, and he had become fearful and lost his way in the park and slept beneath a tree and woken up half white with frosty rime. He told her how, weary with ill treatment, he'd run away to Grantham and worked in an orchard under one George Cousins who could recite the best part of the Bible word for word and knew more ghost stories than any man.

"Tell me one of his stories John."

And John told her about the 'Hand of Glory', that cut from the arm of a hanged man will burn like candles at the finger tip and cast a household into sleep, so that the robber who carries it can take purses from pockets and rings from fingers without waking a soul.

"And why did you come back?"

"I was so far from home that I could not tell from which quarter the wind blew, Mary. It seemed to me that even the sun's course was altered, and I longed for the sight of the steeples."

Soon enough they drew close to the edge of Snow Common. It was as though the world was holding its breath after the hustle and the bustle of the village street. It was early dusk now and the blackthorn bushes and hazel trees stood dark against the fading sky.

"It's lovely here." She said.

"Follow me."

They wound between the bushes, lifting their feet high over the moundy tussocks.

"No one's been here before, that's how it feels."

"Shhhhh."

They sat on the trunk of a fallen tree, side by side. She reached down and picked daisies, laid them on her lap and made a chain. She lifted it and hung it around John's neck.

All of a sudden from a tangle of bramble and thorn the wild strain began:

"Chew-chew, cheer cheer cheer."

The notes grew higher and shriller:

"Cheer-up, cheer-up."

Then they dropped down to a low sliding:

"Teeeeee, jug jug jug."

She whispered:

"A nightingale."

John nodded. They sat together silent as stone as the song cascaded and fell, a silver rain of sound:

"Wew-wew, wew-wew, chur-chur-chur-chur, woo-it, woo-it."

Mary leaned towards John. He could feel her warmth beside him.

"Tee-rew, tee-rew, tee-rew, will, will, grig-grig-grig-grig."

She slipped her hand into his hand, curled her fingers around his fingers, light and delicate as a leaf.

****

Mr Ben Price, the stout bailiff of the Milton estate, was hammering a notice onto Helpston church door.

Out in the street the fever of the fair had cleared, the stalls were being packed away onto carts, the farmers shifting allegiance from small ale to strong beer. And the village constable, Mr Bullimore, was hurrying all chapmen, pedlars and beggars that weren't of the village out across the parish bounds.

Ben's horse was tethered to the church gate, and he'd attracted little notice 'til now. But the hammering began to draw a crowd. People pushed into the porch, peering over his shoulder.

"What's this Mr Price?"

People are always civil to Ben Price, though it is through fear rather than respect, he being the chief collector of rents and tithes for the Milton estate, and having little less than power of life and death over them.

He lowered his hammer and turned to them. His grey eyes looking through them rather than at them, and the flickering twitch at the corner of his mouth, much imitated in the ale-houses of Helpston and Glinton, sending little ripples across his plump cheek.

"'Tis the settlement for the enclosure. Now, if you'll be so kind as to let me through, I must ride to Glinton and perform the same duty there."

The crowd parted. As soon as Ben Price was gone they pushed forwards.

"It's too dark to see, fetch a lantern."

A lantern was brought and held over the parchment. Richard Royce, at the front of the crowd, peered at it and frowned. Someone shouted:

"What does it say?"

"The devil a word can I read, 'tis no more to me than a bird's footprints on wet clay."

"Then make way for someone as can."

"Look, here comes the parson."

Parson Mossop, disturbed by all the noise, had wandered across the churchyard to see what was amiss. The crowd let him through. He pulled his spectacles from his pocket and planted them on his nose. He drew his breath and began to read aloud:

"*In this year of Our Lord 1811 an Act of Parliament has been passed allowing for the Enclosure of lands in the parishes of Maxey, Northborough, Glinton, Etton and Helpston in the County of Northampton.*

Whereas some Part of the Arable, Meadow and Pasture lands are intermixed and inconveniently situated for the respective Owners and Occupiers thereof, and the Commons and Waste Grounds yield but little Profit, it shall be very advantageous for the said Arable, Meadow and Pasture lands, along with the Commons and Wastes to be enclosed and allotted to the several Persons interested therein, in proportion to their respective Estates, Rights and Interests."

The parson turned back to the crowd.

"There we have it."

He pointed to the second notice.

"And here we have the map of the enclosure awards."

News travels quick in the parish, word had already reached the more substantial village farmers. Ralph Wormstall, Mrs Wright, Mr Bull, Thomas Bellar and John Close were approaching the back of the crowd, keen to see how they'd been served by the award. The parson was pushed against the door by a surge forward that grew stronger and stronger. He lifted the latch and it swung open, spilling the crowd into the cool of the church, the parson ahead of the rest like the cork from a bottle that has been too much shaken. And now the churchwardens stepped forward:

"Easy. Easy. Stand aside, one at a time please."

****

When Mary Joyce came home to the farm it was dark. She went to the kitchen. Her father was sitting at the oak table poring over a parchment that was pinned down at its four corners by brass candlesticks, each one with its flickering candle. He was bent over it and so engrossed that he did not hear her enter. As she drew closer she could see it was the parish map he was looking at. His thick fingers were tracing the various furlongs and lands he rented on the three great village fields. She put her hand on his shoulder. He looked up suddenly.

"Ah, Mary my sweet-heart, so young John Clare has brought you safely home."

If it had not been dark he would have seen that she blushed.

"Ay Father."

He reached up and patted her hand.

"He's a good enough lad but don't be getting over-fond, you're young yet and there's plenty more fish in the fen."

She said nothing.

"And besides, Mary, we'll be turning you into a young woman of quality soon enough."

He stabbed the map with his fingers.

"Ben Price nailed up the enclosure award this evening, and it treats us very kind."

Mary drew up a chair and sat beside him. She looked down at the map. She could see Maxhams Green Lane. And there was Snow Common. Where the fold of the map crossed the lane would be the very place that she and John had sat.

"Ay, very kind Mary. All the scattered furlongs are brought

together into one nice compact piece of land, and a tidy piece of grazing common has been thrown in for good measure. All shall be fenced or hedged with quick thorn. And the streams straightened and the marsh dyked so that the tilth may give of its best. Yes, soon enough it'll be squires as'll doff their caps to you Mary, or maybe the Earl of Fitzwilliam's boy hanging his Mayday garland from your front door."

"And I'll curse him, just as you cursed poor John this morning."

Her father threw back his head and laughed.

"Well spoken Mary, for he's as sallow a youth as I've ever clapped eyes on...but there'll be others with tidy fortunes that are trimmer than him, you mark my words...the times are changing and we're going up in the world. God bless this new legislation."

****

When John came home he found his parents and Sophie sitting before the fire. Ann was busy with her knitting needles. Sophie sat crossed legged with the cat upon her lap, she looked at him most careful, she marked the wilting daisy-chain about his neck and smiled. John seemed to her to be showing some promise, the real test would have to wait 'til later.

"There's cold potatoes under the bowl."

John fetched some food, pulled up a stool and stretched his feet to the heat, with his wooden platter set upon his knee. Parker smiled:

"We saw who wore your garland John."

Ann nodded.

"She's a lovely girl is Mary Joyce."

John didn't answer. He could still feel the press of her hand as she'd turned to run the last of the lane to her father's farm.

Parker carried on:

"And Joyce is a decent enough sort when he's in temper, and never spares the ale at harvest home nor the goose at Christmas, and there's none that works for him as complains of his pitcher or his pipe bein' empty...unless they've crossed him... ay, you could do a sight worse than Mary Joyce."

"But be careful John," said Ann, "I wouldn't want you burned, and I'll warrant Mr Joyce has his eye on someone with a few more prospects than what you've got, Mary being an only child and all."

Parker reached into the fire and lifted a burning stick to the bowl of his clay pipe. He sucked in until the tobacco glowed red in the darkened room and the air was thick with fragrant smoke.

"Ay John, and I'll wager as old Joyce is clapping himself on the back and shaking his own hand and drinking a glass to his own good health tonight, if the enclosures in Glinton have gone the same way as the enclosures here in Helpston."

Ann shook her head:

"Ah, it's a shame for us all."

John put his platter onto the floor:

"I'd heard the award map was up."

"It is John, and it tells an old story."

Parker leaned forwards on his stool, his eyes bright above the high cheek-bones that are tanned red and finely webbed with veins from long hours in sun and wind.

"The rich grow richer and the poor grow poorer. The enclosure favours them as have plenty of lands and spits in the face of us that have none. The big old fields are to go, as are the wastes and heaths and commons. All will be fenced and hedged and will become the sole property of some body or other. Them with plenty gets plenty. Them with a little gets a little. And them with nothing gets less than nothing for all our ancient rights are gone. We can no longer go out upon the common for firewood or withies or rushes or hazel for hurdles. We cannot gather brushwood or mushrooms or berries. We cannot snare coneys or net birds or put our pigs and geese out to graze. We will be trespassers to be prosecuted on the very land we have trod since ever time was and our only wealth will be the penny in our pocket."

"And what about Old Otter and Kitty," said Ann, "who squat upon Snow Common with nought above their heads but canvas and turf, and bear the world no malice for all they are poor as the birds of the hedgerows? Where will they go when the commons are took? And what if the harvest fails, as it did those years after John and Bessie was born? Where would we have been without the commons then, to keep us fed in the hollow months, for the devil a penny we had in our pockets those winters? Ay, and every farmer happy enough to get us, reduced to paupery as we were, working his furlongs for next to nothing… with the parish paying two parts of a wage that barely bought a loaf of bread."

"And there are still those that play that game!"

"And what about Wisdom," said John, "and all the Boswell crew that are camped at Langdyke Bush?"

"It is a sorry day," said Parker. "And a man will no longer call to his neighbour across the furrows however-so-many acres he does or does not farm, for there will be hedges and fences between, and such lofty notions as make strangers of us all."

They fell into silence for a while. Then Ann turned to Sophie suddenly, as though she'd clean forgot she was there.

"What, still up miss, when tomorrow's work starts early. Up to bed with ye!"

John stood and stretched.
"And I'll go too, for it's been a long day."

****

John's boots were under the bed, his breeches and shirt upon the wooden chest beside it, the daisy-chain hanging round the bed-post, his cheek to the pillow and him drifting into slumber, when he heard a creaking of floor boards. He opened his eyes. Sophie had slipped into the room and was standing beside the bed. She had a candle on a saucer. She set it on the floor and took his breeches. She slipped a hand into the pocket.

"What are you doing Soph'?"

She looked at him and said nothing. She pulled out the twist of paper from his pocket and tipped the cloves onto the saucer. She counted them in a whisper.

"One, two, three, four, five, six, seven, eight, nine, ten, eleven, twelve, thirteen, fourteen, fifteen."

She looked at John in disbelief.

"There was fifteen when I give them to you John. You never even kissed her did ye? You never once even kissed her."

"What if I didn't."

She widened her eyes and shook her head, picked up the saucer and tip-toed out of the room.

"What'll we do with you John Clare."

John reached above him to the bed-post. He felt the withered daisies between his fingers and smiled into the darkness.

3

Bird Nesting

Tom Dolby always has hunger gnawing at his belly and like any growing boy will find as many ways to ease it as he can. Clearing stones, scaring crows, running errands, anything to put a few pennies in his mother's apron pocket. He knows well enough that little of his father's labouring wage will ever reach the table. It is whispered throughout the parish that Joseph Dolby would sooner see his children starve than forsake his pot of ale.

So yesterday, when word reached Tom's ears that the keepers on the Milton estate were paying sixpence apiece for buzzards eggs, he set off alone to Oxey Wood. He'd seen a nest in the fork of a great oak and he was determined to get to it. He found a woodman's ladder and set it against the tree, but when he reached the top the birds swooped down on him and tore his face with their claws, and in the struggle the ladder slipped. It was some hours before Sam Billings heard him whimpering on the ground. Sam carried him in his cart to Snow Common where Kitty Otter cleaned his face and bound his arm into a splint.

In the taproom at the Bluebell that evening Joseph Dolby, in his cups as ever, lifted his squint-eyed, straggle-bearded countenance, sunk into its shoulders like some ill-used fairground bear, and told Tom's story. John Clare and Wisdom Boswell leaned forward on the plough-bench and listened with intent. They'd been sitting a little apart making a penny pot of ale last an evening. When Joseph had fallen silent Wisdom nudged John and whispered:

"That's the end of you an' me bein' bi luvva John. How many eggs are there to a buzzard's nest?"

John shrugged:

"Three...four maybe. There was one I saw in the quarry cliff once at Swordy Well, it had three chicks to it."

"Four is a florin! That's a shilling each John, that's twenty four penny pots of ale! And there ain't many trees as'll get the better of me."

****

This morning, when the greater part of the parish was on its knees and muttering its prayers, or opening its throat in psalms and hymns, John Clare was making his way to Oxey Wood. Wisdom was waiting for him beside the Ufford Road. He was sitting in the grass with his back to a tree, there was a coil of rope on the ground beside him, he was holding one end of it in his hands. He'd bent it over and was fastening it into a loop. He looked up as John drew close:

"Here's the boy for the job John, I borrowed it from Ismael, and God help me if I don't get it back to him safe an' sound."

John squatted down beside him. Wisdom nodded to the road.

"Look, there's the marks in the road where Sam Billing's cart stopped...and there's the gry's shit, look, where he stood and waited while Sam went into the wood."

Between the trees they could see the bruised and flattened

bluebells where Sam had trodden.

"He's left us an easy trail to follow."

John smiled:

"Sam Billings was never the man to walk on his tip-toes."

When the loop in the end of the rope was tied tight, Wisdom coiled it over his shoulder and stood up.

"Come on."

They entered the wood. The trail of flattened flowers led to the clearing. There was a scene of devastation. Bluebells, campions, and white deadnettles had been trodden into the soft earth, there were heaps of wood chippings and every leaf was white with a layer of sawdust like flour in the workings of a mill. The air was full of the smell of sap and bruised greenery.

"The woodmen have been hard at it."

Two great oak trunks, pale and stripped of bark, lay side by side the length of the clearing, like the naked legs of a felled giant. Lying across them were the drying, curled lengths of their bark.

John stroked them:

"Brandy-snaps for Tom Hickathrift."

Wisdom sniffed them:

"Ay, but wanting in sweetness."

The fallen ladder was lying at the foot of a huge oak whose trunk rose twenty feet before its first branch jutted out from it. Thirty feet higher again it divided into two great knotted, gnarled boughs. John and Wisdom sheltered their eyes from the sun. In the crutch between the boughs they could see a ragged, slovenly nest of sticks and stems.

"There it is."

John whistled between his teeth.

"Tom Dolby must have been hungry if he reckoned he

could climb up there."

Wisdom peered up through the leaves.

"Ay, but an empty belly will go to any length to fill itself, John."

And John nodded, for he remembers well enough the hard times when a slice of bread and some dripping begged from a farm-house kitchen was all the comfort he had.

Together John and Wisdom lifted the ladder and leaned it against the trunk. The top rung was level with the first branch. John picked up a stick with a spray of wilting leaves at the end of it.

"You'll need something to keep the birds away."

Wisdom took it and tucked it into his belt.

Overhead there was a sudden shrill, melancholy mewing.

"Peeeeio......peeeeio."

From high above the tree-tops of the wood a buzzard was flying downwards with slow, measured flaps of its wings. It glided across the clearing to the nest with something yellow hanging limp and bloody from its talons. They could see the ribbed markings of its fanned tail feathers.

"Peeeeio."

Its mate answered from the nest.

John whispered:

"Leave them one egg."

Wisdom took off his boots and laid them side by side at the foot of the tree. He adjusted the rope over his shoulder.

"Ay, I'll leave them one brother. Now, hold the ladder steady."

He climbed the first rungs and as soon as his feet were at eye-level John stepped forward to grip the sides of the ladder. When he'd got to the top of the ladder Wisdom swung the rope and threw the looped end over a branch high above his head.

He fed the rope upwards until he could catch the swinging lowering loop again. He threaded the end of the rope through the loop and pulled it tight around the branch. Then he climbed the rope, with his curled toes to the rough bark, putting one hand over the other until he came to a branch below the one his rope was secured to. He curled a leg over the branch and pulled himself up so that he was sitting on it. Then, gripping the bark with his fingertips and the branch with his feet he pulled himself upright.

He loosened the rope. He unthreaded the loop and threw it over a higher branch. He threaded it and pulled it tight. Again and again he scrambled from branch to branch. John watched him disappearing and reappearing among the green leaves as he clambered higher and higher into the tree.

As Wisdom drew close to the nest the mother buzzard shrilled with alarm. She beat her wings and flew up. She circled the tree, mewing with agitation.

John stepped back into the clearing. He could see Wisdom more clearly now. He was standing on a branch just below the divide of the two boughs.

The nest was at shoulder height. Wisdom could see into its soft hollow, lined with grass and wool and lichens. And lying snug in its shallow cup there were four streaked and mottled eggs. He lifted an arm and reached into the nest.

It was then the birds attacked, swooping and shrilling. With one hand Wisdom pulled the stick from his belt and waved it in the air to keep the buzzards at bay. With the other he lifted the eggs. They were as big as chicken's eggs and warm against his palm. His knees were gripping the trunk of the tree. One of the birds screeched into his face. He pushed the eggs into his shirt, teetered backwards, dropped the stick and seized a branch to steady himself. Talons sharp as needles tore at his forehead. The blood poured into his eyes and blurred his sight. He punched the bird away. He had three eggs.

He swung down from branch to branch, the furious birds circling and crying and worrying him with sudden swoops and sallies. But it was hard for them to get close now that he was enfolded in greenery.

He dropped the rope to the ground. Soon his swinging legs met the top rung of the ladder. He broke another branch and held it ready, but the buzzards were circling the tree, crying most pitiful.

John came forward to hold the ladder steady. By the time Wisdom reached the ground the mother had settled on the one solitary egg that had been left to her.

John looked at his friend. Wisdom's black hair was tousled and tangled with twigs and leaves. The blood was trickling down his nose. He pulled a rag from his pocket and wiped it away. Then he looked at John, his brown eyes shining beneath blood-caked eyebrows, and grinned a lop-sided grin of such deep merriment that John could not help but laugh aloud and punch Wisdom's shoulder.

Wisdom lifted his fists.

"Easy John."

Then he patted the bulge beneath his shirt above his belt.

"Be careful where you put your punches."

They both sat down on the end of one of the pale stripped trunks. Wisdom dipped his hand into his shirt and when he pulled it out his fingers were curled around an egg. John cupped his hands and Wisdom put it gently into the nest of pink calloused skin.

"One....two...three..."

John felt their smooth, warm strangeness against his palms. He studied the red-purple mottlings on the white shells that had the faint green of a duck's egg. He soaked in their beauty.

"Now put them back!"

He was speaking only half in jest.

It was Wisdom's turn to punch.

"That's one and sixpence you're holding in your hands bau, that's eighteen penny pots of ale. We shall get ourselves chirping merry tonight."

"Ay, give me your rag."

John slid off the trunk onto the ground. He set down the eggs. He pulled up some moss. He stretched out Wisdom's blood soaked rag. He cushioned the eggs with moss and wrapped them up. Wisdom took the soft bundle and put it back into his shirt. He hid Ismael Boswell's rope under a tangle of ivy.

"Let's go to Milton Hall and claim our prize."

****

All along the Marholm road they were chewing lumps of dry bread that John had brought in his pocket. After a while they came to a beech tree that threw its shade across the rutted road. They pulled the soft new leaves from it and laid them on their crusts. They bit leaf and bread together and chewed until their mouths were sweetened with the sharp nutty flavour.

At the edge of Hayes Wood there was a scrubby heath of broom, hawthorn, hazel, whin and blackthorn, tangled with brambles and briars.

John turned to Wisdom:

"How would you like to see something not many clap eyes on?"

Wisdom winked:

"What, naked women John, takin' a plunge and then

running to dry themselves, then lying in the sun...and lovely Mary Joyce spreading her legs in the middle of 'em...?"

"What squit you talk."

"What then?"

"Put the eggs safe, here on this tussock."

Wisdom took the bundle from his shirt and set it down in the long grass.

"When I was at old Merrishaw's I found it here one afternoon when I cut free from school...and year after year they seek the same solitudes, I'll warrant it's here yet."

"What are ye rabbiting on about John?"

"Shhhhhh."

"It'd better be good."

John got down onto his hands and knees and Wisdom followed. They pushed through the scratching blackthorn into a waste of dead leaves. They crawled on until a wall of hazel blocked their way. John parted the branches and clambered through.

"John, you didn't tell me you've been hob-nobbin' with boggarts and todloweries. Well, they say they brew a fierce ale...."

"Shhhhh."

There was thin grass beyond, and a cluster of cuckoo-pints with their spotted leaves. John turned to Wisdom, crouching like a creature in his lair.

"A body could die here and never be found."

"Now I understand John, you plan to cut my throat and keep all them eighteen pennies for your own good self…"

He loosened the neck of his shirt, gulped and whispered:

"Spare me John Clare, I only buttered her once…and that was by mistake."

John laughed. Wisdom looked about himself. John could

see writ on his face that the place didn't hold much allure for him, save only if he needed somewhere to lay low from the law.

"Hey John, you could pass a happy day here – racing pismires."

Suddenly above their heads there came a song of alarm. A small brown bird was hopping from branch to branch. John smiled:

"Ah, there she flits, we ain't far away."

John crawled forwards and the bird's song stopped as sudden as it had started.

"We must be close, she always holds her breath when someone draws close."

He lifted his arm and pointed to a pair of rotten whitethorn stulps, pressed side by side, surrounded by tall grass.

"What?"

John crawled closer. He pulled a tangle of brambles to one side.

"Look."

Between the stulps there was a cluster of dead oak leaves. It was only when Wisdom came close and looked down from above that he saw, deep-bedded inside there was a nest of moss and wool and grass....and lying at the bottom of it six little eggs of a deep green-brown. John whispered:

"Nightingale."

Instinctively Wisdom lowered his hand to scoop up the eggs, but John gripped his arm.

"Leave these ones be."

Wisdom looked into his friend's face and saw a resolution he would not mock nor challenge, for in it he saw what he loved in John Clare.

"Ay brother."

He lifted his arm and turned from the nest.

"I understand thee."

They made their way back between the hazel branches and through the thorn, and as they did so the mother bird began to sing again as though it was melody not air that she breathed. As though she had held her breath until she could hold it no longer and now was gasping in lung-fulls of song.

Once they were back on the road Wisdom put the buzzards' eggs into his shirt and they continued through Marholm and then turned their faces southwards towards Milton Hall. When they reached the western gate at Stamford Lodge Wisdom stopped.

"I've played my part bau, the next is yours."

He handed the eggs across to John.

"I'll be waitin' for you."

He sat himself down at the edge of the lane and pulled a broken clay pipe from his pocket.

"I'm made uneasy John, by that Wishengro as wishes me ill. You'll fare better on your own."

He pulled out a tinder box and struck a flame. A curl of smoke rose from the bowl of his pipe.

"Good luck brother."

John nodded. Wisdom, in a cloud of smoke, slipped behind a clump of trees, patted down the grass and stretched out on the ground.

John, with the bundle in his hands, made his way across the wooded park towards Milton Hall.

****

"It's Bill Henderson you'll be after."

One of the grooms pointed towards a broad door that stood

half open beyond the stables. Nailed to it, with their wings stretched out, were the dried up carcasses of a heron, a couple of kites and a barn-owl, remnants of the last season's keeping. John crossed the cobbled enclosure and knocked. The stiff carcasses rattled and whispered with the strike of his fist.

The Head Keeper, William Henderson, was cleaning the Earl's sporting guns. He was sitting in the sunlight with one of them laid across his knee. The others lay side by side on a wide wooden table. He was still dressed in his Sunday best, with an old leather apron over his claret livery. Beside the guns his prayer book sat on a corner of the table. Behind him row upon row of traps and snares were hanging from iron hooks on the wall.

He lifted his grizzled head, took off his spectacles, and nodded to John:

"What are you after lad?"

John held out the bundle he was holding in his hands:

"I've brought some buzzard's eggs."

Bill Henderson got to his feet. He laid the gun down beside the others, as tenderly as a mother might lay a new-born babe in its cradle.

"Let's be havin' a look then."

John set the bundle gently on the table and began to unfold Wisdom's blood-stained rag. Bill Henderson waved his hands at him:

"Now, now, you keep your filth away from these guns... take them up to the far end of my table."

John lifted them and set them down again. When he'd unfolded the rag and revealed the cluster of three eggs wrapped in moss, Bill Henderson picked them up and weighed them in his palm. He put them down and put his spectacles back onto his nose. He leaned forwards and peered down at them.

"Ay, these have the look of buzzard's eggs...but we must make sure of it before I part with the Earl's money. First we'll put them under the pump to ascertain that you ain't painted a clutch of hen's eggs...for I've had village lads try that caper afore...then we'll set them against the Earl's collection and make certain-sure. Follow me."

John followed him to the stable pump.

"You work the pump arm I'll watch the eggs."

John moved the pump arm up and down and as the water glugged and spurted Bill Henderson held each egg in turn under its torrent. The colours stayed firm.

"Good, good. Now come with me."

He put the eggs into the pocket of his apron.

John followed him to the back of Milton Hall. They made their way through the kitchen. Bill Henderson pushed open a door and suddenly the stone flags of the floor gave way to carpeted corridors. There was a wooden box full of leather slippers.

"Boots off lad, stocking feet from here onward."

John pulled off his boots.

"I ain't got any stockings."

His bare feet were stained brown from the leather and were black with dirt between the toes. Bill looked at them and shook his head most sorrowful."

"These won't do at all....they'll have to be washed. Back to the pump lad."

They went outside again. This time Bill Henderson worked the pump and John held each foot in turn under the chill water.

"That's more like it..."

They went back to the kitchen. Bill nodded to the great open fire.

"Dry them off."

John sat on a wooden stool and stretched his feet out to the heat as the cooks bustled about on either side of him. All around him copper pans of all shapes and sizes hung from the walls, polished as bright as mirrors and reflecting the flickering light. As soon as John's feet were dry Bill threw him a pair of slippers.

"Try these for size, they'll fit you close enough I reckon."

John pulled the slippers over his feet and followed the Head Keeper through a maze of corridors. They came to a white door with a polished brass knob. Bill turned it and the door swung open.

In front of him John saw a great hall, and at the far end of it a curving staircase of polished oak. Portraits of men and women in gilded frames were hanging from the walls, their eyes stern or solemn or amused in equal measure. He stood dumb-founded, in amaze, as though he had stumbled into the court of Queen Mab, or had entered the pages of one of his chap-books: *Beauty and the Beast* perhaps, or *Mister Fox*. This was beyond all he'd ever known. For a moment he could not move.

"Come on lad."

Bill Henderson broke the enchantment. He strode across the hall and climbed the stairs. John followed.

Suddenly there was a commotion. Two little children with long curling hair, both dressed in linen smocks so that it was hard to tell whether they were boys or girls, burst out of a room and chased one another headlong down the stairs. Behind them came a harassed woman dressed in fine rustling silks. She hurried towards John, who stood aside to let her pass. For one moment she paused and looked him up and down with such an expression of distaste writ upon her features that John wished, for all the world, that he was anywhere in the world but here. Then she tossed her head and was gone.

At the head of the stairs there was another door, Bill Henderson pushed it open and disappeared inside. John followed. Wonder followed wonder. He found himself in a study with great windows looking out across the park. There were shelves lined with leather-bound books, more than John had ever seen in the bookshops of Stamford where he has pressed his face to the glass many times and felt the hollow promise of a labourer's wage mocking his ambition.

It was to a polished wooden chest of shallow drawers that Bill Henderson made his way. Each drawer was marked with a letter of the alphabet. He took the little ivory handles of the drawer marked 'B' and slid it open. Beneath a sheet of glass there were birds eggs in rows, laid in nests of green felt, each with its label. Bill ran his finger down the glass:

"Bittern, blackbird, black-cap, brambling, bullfinch, bunting...buzzard. Here we are lad, now then..."

He reached into his apron pocket and pulled out one of John's eggs. He laid it on the glass. The two matched perfectly.

"Ay lad, there's no denying it. 'Tis a buzzard and you shall be paid according."

John looked down at the rows of eggs, every one of them was known to him, but he'd never seen them laid in rows before, like soldiers outside the barrack gate.

"Who collected these?"

Bill Henderson's face softened.

"When the Earl was but a boy it was his passion. Every spring when we was on our rounds we'd keep our eyes open and take note of any nests we found. And the old Earl, God rest his soul, would send him out with us, I can see him now skipping alongside us, and we'd help him take the eggs himself, as long as he were'nt put into too much danger. Ay, and he'd blow them too, and cook would make him an omelette of their meat. By the time they sent him away for his schooling he'd collected most of the common-place eggs, and the old Earl had this little chest o' drawers made for him special, for his ninth birthday as I remember. But look here..."

Bill pushed the drawer to, and pulled open another marked 'N'. He ran his finger down the glass again.

"See here. This empty place. This waits on the nightingale. It was the one nest we could not find...and haven't yet. The Earl is in his forties now and with sons of his own, and he ain't forgotten. We'll be out shooting and he'll turn to me: 'What about that nightingale's nest Mr Henderson?' he'll say, and I'll have to own that of all the songbirds 'tis the most cunning concealed."

He pushed the drawer gently in.

"I reckon he'd pay a florin apiece, two shillings an egg, to any as could bring a clutch of 'em to Milton Hall."

He turned to John:

"I don't suppose it's a nest that you've ever clapped eyes on?"

John shook his head.

"I never have Mr Henderson, nor know of any as have."

Bill Henderson looked the squat, awkward village youth up and down: the tousled hair, the thick neck, the greasy smock and tattered breeches. He remembered the caked boots that lay beside the kitchen door and the filthy unstockinged feet beneath them. He shook his head and said, kindly enough but not without condescension:

"No lad, I don't suppose you have."

****

Half an hour later John found Wisdom. He was stretched out fast asleep in the place beneath the trees where he had left him. He shook his shoulder:

"Wisdom!"

Wisdom sleepily opened his eyes, then sat straight up.

"John. How did ye fare?"

"Look."

John reached into his pocket and scooped out eighteen pennies. He cupped them in his hands and rattled them under Wisdom's nose. Then he dropped the fat coppers onto the ground one at a time. Each of them struck the moist earth with a soft thud.

Wisdom grinned his lop-sided grin and punched John's shoulder.

"Good work bau...did you see Bloodworth?"

"No, only Bill Henderson, the Head Keeper. He seemed a kindly old soul."

Wisdom shook his head:

"Not if you're a Romany he ain't. King Boswell reckons we ain't no better than stoats or foxes to him, and he'd be happy to see us swinging from a keeper's gibbet."

He divided the pennies into two piles.

"Here's good work though, God bless the Earl of Fitzwilliam for these. Nine for you and nine for me."

He dropped his nine pennies into his shirt.

"Did you sniff out any other ways that we might earn a few coins?"

John shook his head:

"No."

He shoved his coins into his pocket.

"Come on, let's get ourselves to Bachelor's Hall and drink the Sabbath dry."

4

Sheepshearing (Day)

Bright June has come, and the barley's silken beard grows long and green, and on Lolham Bridge Field it nods and dances to every shifting whim of the wind.

From dawn to dusk the frantic bees wallow in fox-glove and bean flower as though no glut of labour or journeying could fill their store with honey enough for all. And from dawn to dusk, when the sun shines, the mowing teams are out upon Heath Field. The swish of their curved scythes is the sound of June breathing and the rasp of the whet-stones against the iron blades is the sound of June coughing. For sickness and health are as rain and shine, and all men know that for every week of fine weather there will be a debt to pay in slanting showers. And a closer look betrays the rotten teeth, the small-pox scars, the twisted spines, the swollen joints and all the curses that hard labour and a scant wage bring.

Parker Clare swings his blade in the mowing line, as ready as any though stiffer than some. From time to time he calls a halt to mop his face. Around him the cut swathes sweeten the air. Behind him the raking women turn and toss yesterday's labour and at the far end of the field the lifted hay-cocks wait upon the wain.

On Woodcroft Field Ann and Sophie Clare have been gathering and shelling beans with the other women in John Close's employ, Sophie's ears acute to the rise and fall of the gossip that surrounds her, gleaning what she can.

John has joined a shearing team, working his way from farm to farm these last five weeks.

Such is the timeless round of summer labour upon the face of the parish, an old, hard, familiar melody. But there is a new sound alongside the sighing of the scythe, the bleating of the sheep and the rising and falling of the talk. It is the sound of posts being hammered into the ground and measuring chains pulled tight between. The sound of ropes being stretched across fields and commons where new boundaries will fall, of men shouting from mark to mark where roads will be cut or streams straightened, of splashes of red paint being daubed onto trees that are to be felled. The Earl of Fitzwilliam has sent surveyors out to mark the lie of the land for enclosure. Slowly, from day to day, a new pattern of squares, fine as the web of a net or a snare, is set across the looping, winding limbs of the parish.

But John Clare, moving from farm to farm in the accustomed way, has been too busy to pay it any heed. There are nine in all in the shearing team: Jack Ward is Captain. There are seven Lieutenants. And John, who catches and carries and folds up the fleeces, is Corporal.

Last week they worked for Ralph Wormstall, and were given a shearing supper of such pinch-purse, nip-cheese paucity that they had to spend their own wages at the Bluebell when it was done in order to feel their bellies comfortably lined with food and ale.

This week they have worked for Farmer Joyce at Glinton and their hope has been for kinder treatment and fuller fare at the week's end. From Monday to Thursday they laboured in his threshing barn, stripped to the waist in the June heat as John Fell brought the sheep in from the fat grass at the fen margin. Yesterday was the fifth and last day and they had high hopes of Joyce's hospitality, for he is known to be open-handed.

John was up before the dawn and when he had eaten a crust he made his way out of the cottage and along Heath Lane. The first birds were stirring and moistening their throttles. As he passed Snip Green the song began in earnest. He followed the stream across Heath Field, where the hay, cut and uncut, was too soaked with dew for any early mower to venture out. A family of hares were gambolling across the furlongs, stopping to lick the dew-fall, then dancing, squatting, loitering like happy thoughts. He walked on, past Swordy Well with its worked facing of yellow stone. Behind him the first smoke began to rise from the village chimneys and the bustling clatter of the village farmyards made itself distantly heard. There were no bounds to his exultation, though he gave it no more mind than did the singing birds.

When he came to Langdyke Bush there was smoke before him as well as behind. Lettuce Boswell was leaning an iron snottum over the flames and hanging a kettle from it. She looked up at John and nodded towards a cart.

"That's where you'll find him chal."

John squatted down beside the cart and whistled between his fingers. There was a stirring from beneath it. A rustling of dried bracken and straw. Wisdom, wrapped in blankets, poked his lean head out into the morning. He looked up between the shafts and blinked blearily at John.

"What do you want brother, it's scarcely dawn?"

He wormed his way from his sleeping place and they both walked across to the fire and sat side by side, holding out their hands to the heat.

"There is to be a shearing supper tonight, Wisdom, at Joyce's in Glinton. His table will be groaning with frumity and ale and good vittles. Bring your fiddle and I'll warrant he'll find a place for you…or if he won't Mary will."

Wisdom shook his head.

"I can't John, not tonight."

"Why not?"

"There are other plans afoot."

He lowered his voice to a whisper.

"I tell you but I'd tell no other. There will be a full moon and…."

"Tel te jib!"

From behind the door-flap of an ancient, patched, military tent that bordered the fire came a voice as gruff and abrupt as the bark of a mastiff. Wisdom fell suddenly silent. The flap lifted and King Boswell's ancient head appeared. Two dogs that had been dozing placidly jumped up and danced about John, snapping at his ankles. King Boswell lifted one of his huge hands and waved it at them.

"Shhhhhh."

They quietened and lay down again.

He looked at John, his eyes sharp as a hawk's beneath great shaggy over-arching eyebrows, his face as wrinkled and brown as an old dish-clout, his hair jackdaw-black.

He uncurled a finger and pointed it at him.

"Ja! Ja! Go!"

He looked at Wisdom.

"Tell your boshomengro friend to keep to his own."

He looked back at John.

"And mind to his own, and ask no more questions…and we shan't have to tell him no lies."

He disappeared back into his tent. Wisdom rolled his eyes and shrugged, and John could see that there was nothing he could do to make things otherwise. He nodded and got up to his feet.

"I'll see you another time Wisdom."

Then he remembered a phrase he'd heard King Boswell use before.

"And the luck of the blessed be with you."

From inside the tent he heard King Boswell's rumbling voice again, as though it came from beneath a pool of phlegm in the deep of his belly:

"You're a good boy John Clare, for all you're a gorgio, now piss off and keep your own council!"

John made his way back across the fields. The village had wakened now and Jack Ward and the rest of the threshing team were waiting for him at Butter Cross. Together they trudged along the track through Woodcroft Field to Farmer Joyce's threshing barn.

****

The sheep were huddled tight into a corner of the barn, fenced in with hurdles. The shearing platform was laid out ready upon the floor as it had been these last four days. As soon as they had sharpened their shears against the whet-stones the team started work. Jack Ward, as Captain, set the pace.

John dragged a ewe across to him from the holding pen. Jack seized her, flung her onto her back and clipped the tresses of wool from her forehead, neck and shoulders, then, with his knee on her head, he opened up the front as though he was unbuttoning a waistcoat. He cut away the wool down to her back legs where it hung thick. Then he sat the ewe up on her backside and clipped the fleece away from her flank. He spun her round as though she was his partner in some dance that was not of her choosing and did the same to the other side. With a final flourish he snipped the last of the wool from the top of her tail so that the whole fleece fell away from her like a coat.

There was no mark or cut upon her body for the gentils to get in by, she was pink as a babe. For a moment she stood in amaze, then she bleated and trotted back towards the rest of the flock. John seized her, lifted her up in his arms and carried her over to the empty pen where the tar pot was waiting.

Farmer Joyce stood watching Jack with an indulgent eye. He came forwards and clapped him on the back and filled his mug with small ale from the barrel against the wall, he pressed it into Jack's hand. Jack grinned and nodded his thanks and drank.

As Jack worked, so with varied skill did his lieutenants in the shearing team. Wherever they nicked or cut the creature's hides with their shears John had to staunch them with tar, so the sheared sheep in their pens bore a speckled testament to the skill – or lack of it – of their barbers. It was John's job too to roll and tie the fleeces, and to stamp the new-shorn sheep with Farmer Joyce's mark 'JJ'. So he laboured and sweated in the June heat as busy as the rest of them.

Slowly the long day passed, the barn echoed with grunting and clipping and bleating, and with every five sheep shorn there would be the pause for a 'pull up and sharp' when shears were whetted and thirsts quenched. As the afternoon dwindled, so did the sheep still wearing their ragged, slomekin fleeces.

There were only a few waiting in the pens when young Jim Crowson cut the best part of a ewe's ear off with his shears. It was his first season with the team and he was tiring. His hand slipped and the damage was done. The ewe cried most pitiful and the platform was awash with blood.

"What the devil!"

Farmer Joyce strode forwards.

"I ain't paying you to butcher my flock."

He seized the shears from Jim's hands and finished the job himself without doing any more damage to the ewe, but by the time he'd finished he was daubed with blood from head to foot like a butcher. He turned to the shearing team and grinned:

"There, I ain't altogether lost the knack boys."

He nodded to Jim, who grabbed hold of the ewe while John staunched the blood as best he could.

"You leave the shears to the old hands now."

The work continued. Jim helped John. As the clock struck five the last of the sheep was dragged onto the polished platform. By six o'clock the threshing barn had been cleared of all but its heap of tied fleeces.

John and the rest of the team wasted no time. They washed away the dirt of the day under the pump in the yard. They piled their greasy smocks against the barn door and pulled clean shirts over their shoulders. Bone-weary and famished they made their way round to the back of the farm house.

Farmer Joyce was waiting for them, scrubbed and fresh-dressed. The great kitchen table had been carried out onto the lawn and covered with a clean white cloth. Benches had been set to either side of it. John Fell the shepherd, Nathaniel Cushion, Will Farrell and a few other farm-hands were already seated. The shearing team sat down beside them. Farmer Joyce turned on his heel and strode into the house. Soon he returned carrying in his hands a large beech-wood bowl filled with frumity. He set it down. Mary Joyce and Kate Dyball followed with pewter bowls and horn spoons, one to each of the team.

The men at the table cheered. John tried to catch Mary's eye as she hurried past him but she seemed to pay him no heed. Farmer Joyce served his men with his own hands, ladling the sweet, thick, spicy, creamy mixture into the bowls

They supped it down in silence.

Then a great steaming rack of lamb was fetched and set on the table, with fresh bread, onions, new potatoes, peas, beans, cabbage and thick gravy. The tap was opened on a barrel of Joyce's strong beer,

"Let it run like a well," said Farmer Joyce, "and not be staunched 'til it is dry."

Pewter mugs were filled and filled again. Plates were piled with food. More and more was brought to the table: cheeses, hams, bowls of strawberries and redcurrants. Little was said, the sound of the scraping of knives and forks against pewter and the chomping of jaws was a conversation all its own.

From inside the house the women watched the men through the window.

"Just look at 'em," said Lizzie Tucker shaking her head, "the flower of English manhood!"

"Heads down, tails up, like porkers at the trough," said Hope Farrell. "And if the Frenchie come, what then? They'd only have to show this lot a ripe cheese and they'd be kissing Boney's arse afore ye could say 'bonjeer'."

Mary Joyce stood at the window too and smiled. She was watching John Clare, who she's barely seen these five weeks of the shearing, and waiting for her moment. She'd been out that afternoon when there was a lull in the cooking and had gathered a Clipping Posey from the garden: pansies, roses, sweet-peas, honey-suckle, snap-dragons, pinks, fox-gloves, lavender. She'd tied them with a ribbon and hidden them among the shadows by the pantry door.

Her secret had not passed unnoticed, though the other women had bitten their tongues and said nought. But now, seeing Mary's fixed attention on the table Lizzie Tucker raised an eye-brow:

"What Mary? Has one of them fine beaus caught your eye?"

Mary didn't answer but blushed.

"Is it the one wiping its mouth against its shirt sleeve I wonder, or the one that's licking its plate?"

Then Hope Farrell nudged Mary:

"I'll tell you what Mary, steer clear of any that ain't Glinton men, for you know that what they keep in their breeches is the same as what they keep in their belfries."

Then the two chanted the old rhyme together:

"Helpston cracked pippins, Northborough cracked pans,
Glinton fine organs, Peakirk tin cans."

When at last even the heartiest eater had pushed his plate away and loosened his belt, Lizzie, Mary and Hope gathered up the empty vessels and carried them indoors. Now that the cooking and serving was done it was their turn to sit down at table.

"It'll do the dirty dishes no harm to stand awhile," said Lizzie, "and there's plenty of good lean left on the lamb yet."

Outside Jack Ward got up to his feet and struck the table with his fist. He lifted his tankard and began to sing in a voice that proved that whatever Helpston men may keep in their breeches there is some truth in the old rhyme when it comes to their throats.

Farmer Joyce called for pipes and tobacco, that were a little slow in coming, the women being loath to leave their table. And song followed song, the choruses filling the fragrant air and growing more raucous as the evening darkened and mugs were emptied over and over again.

A full moon was sliding up through the hedge and the horn lanterns were being lit and set upon the table when Mary seized her moment. She grabbed the posey from its hiding place, slipped out of a side door and ran behind the yew hedge that divided the lawn and flowerbeds from the orchard. She lowered her head and followed it to the woodbine arch, halfway along its length. She peered through. The men were singing still, her father at the head of the table, John at the near end, his back to her.

"Old Reynolds finding shifts in vain
While hounds and horns pursue,
Now leaves the wood to try the plain,
The bugle sounds a view…"

And now came the chorus. She knew their eyes would be half-closed, heads tipped back. She darted forwards, quick as a fish.

"This day the fox must die
Brave boys,
This day the fox must die."

John's belly was full, his head was swimming with ale, his muscles aching with the day's exertion…and he was lost in a sweet oblivion of song. Suddenly he felt something cool being thrust between his fingers. He looked down and saw the bright nose-gay. Its strong scent filled his nostrils. He turned his head and glimpsed Mary disappearing behind the hedge. His head cleared as though it had been thrust beneath the spurting pump in the yard. Here was a Clipping Posey in his hand. A pursuit was demanded and expected of him. He clambered to his feet. He put his hand on his neighbour's shoulder and stepped over the bench. He left the song behind him.

He ran behind the hedge. There she was! Slipping through the little wicker gate in the garden wall. He followed her, a trifle unsteady on his feet. He pushed open the gate and ran through. He looked to left and right. She seemed to have vanished. He started forwards…

"Well?"

He stopped and turned and saw that she was standing behind him with her back pressed to the wall.

"Ain't you going to kiss me then?"

Suddenly shy despite the beer, John paused, then he leaned forward to kiss her decorously upon the cheek, but Mary turned her face so that their lips met and lingered. For the first time they kissed.

"There." She said.

Then she threw her arms around his neck and they kissed again, drinking of each other as though there was no slaking their thirst. And there they would be still if John hadn't heard his name shouted from beyond the wall.

"John Clare!"

The song had finished and Farmer Joyce was calling him. They broke away from each other.

"John Clare!"

"You'd best go John."

He ran through the gate and back along the hedge to the table. The Clipping Posey was still in his hand. Every eye was on him as he climbed back on to the bench and sat down. Farmer Joyce was standing at the head of the table. He looked at John for a moment, savouring his discomfiture and the mingled laughter and envy in the eyes of the other men.

"Well John Clare, you sang to me like a throstle on Mayday morning...but they tell me as you can scrape a passing tune from a fiddle as well."

A fiddle was passed down the line of men to John. He took it and looked down at it, a little sheepish:

"Ay, I play a little. What tune would you favour?"

"Well, we've seen that you're a fair hand at 'Off She Goes' and 'Come To The Bower' and 'Kiss My Lady'...but what the devil else can you play?"

John, his blushes hidden by the night, tucked the fiddle under his chin and played a horn-pipe. The lilting melody rose and fell upon the beat with such a sweet, skipping enchantment that soon every tankard was striking the table in time to the tune.

And Mary Joyce, behind the hedge, unseen by any, had lifted her skirts and was stepping the dance with no partner but the moon.

5

Sheepshearing (Night)

The shearing supper was done. The shearing team had taken their wage from Farmer Joyce. As they were staggering home through Woodcroft Field, another line of men was making its way out of the parish. They were crossing Emmonsales Heath in the silver moonlight. They were skirting the fields north of Castor. They were climbing the stone wall of the Milton estate and threading their way between the oaks and beeches of the park woodland.

The light of the moon shining through the leaves made it easy for them to find their way. King Boswell was leading. Behind him, in single file, five men followed. Their feet cracked no twigs. They were silent as their own shadows. A soft breeze was blowing into their faces.

King Boswell sniffed it and smiled to himself. The night was perfect. He was thinking of the cooking pots filled with simmeno and the dogs cracking bones. He stopped and turned. The other men froze. He nodded. Ismael Boswell was carrying a bag on his shoulder. He swung it onto the ground and pulled out a net woven from dark twine. King Boswell held two corners and Ismael unfurled it. They stretched it to its full length and tied it between two smooth-trunked beeches. Each tied one corner to his own height and one at ground level. The other three men squatted on their hunkers and waited. In the silver-shadowed wood the net, as it was drawn tight, seemed to disappear from sight.

When all was ready, without a word or sign, the men followed King Boswell along the wood's edge. Suddenly he lifted his fingers to his mouth and whistled. They turned and angled into the wood, running through the trees. They fanned out, with no caution now, crackling leaves and twigs beneath their feet. The soft wind, blowing at their backs, carried their scent forwards. There were perhaps a hundred paces between King Boswell and Ismael, the other men ran between.

In a clearing in the wood a little herd of deer were grazing. Long before any of the Boswell crew came close they'd lifted their heads and sturted away, leaping over bushes and between trees. The men quickened their pace. King Boswell and Ismael at either end closed the fan inwards so that the animals were driven towards the stretched net. The frighted deer bounded before them.

Then the moment came. Some of the herd, sensing danger, swerved to the left or right. But two were caught. A stag and a doe. Their forelegs were tangled in the twine, they were kicking and struggling. Wisdom Boswell put his arms around the shoulders of the doe and dragged her back, the net was pulled from her kicking legs. King Boswell studied her, he reached forwards and with his big, scarred hands he tenderly felt her swollen belly and swelling teats.

"Cambri." He whispered.

Wisdom opened his arms and she bounded away into the shadows.

King Boswell nodded to the stag, whose antlers were now entwined. The terrified beast was tearing the net and tangling himself more and more tightly in his trap, like a bluebottle struggling in a spider's web:

"Chin his curlo."

Ismael pulled a long knife from his belt. Two men seized the flailing antlers and drew back the head. With a swift, deft movement of his arm he drew the blade across the animal's throat. With a shudder it gave up its life. The dark blood spurted and the body staggered and folded onto the forest floor, the clean red slit in its throat like a gaping grin.

Following their old, familiar routines the men unfastened and rolled up the net. Ismael slipped it back into its bag. They tied the fore and hind hooves of the stag together and pushed a pole between the legs. Two men, one at the front, one at the back, lifted the pole onto their shoulders. They hurried through the wood to the high estate wall. They clambered over. They heaved the stag up and rolled it over and down on the other side. They crossed the road. There was a knot of hawthorn bushes on the far side. In the middle of it there was a little leafy clearing. They hung the stag from a branch by its hind-hooves, its antlers resting gently on the ground, and butchered it. They skinned it and cleaned it and cut the joints of meat. King Boswell took one of the steaming kidneys and popped it into his mouth, he chewed and swallowed. He smiled and gave the other to Ismael. They divided the joints between them, dropping the rich flesh into leather bags. One of them rolled up the hide and slung it onto his back. They flung the bones and the steaming, quivering entrails into a bramble thicket. Ismael winked at Wisdom:

"Mr Reynolds can have the cocalor and vennor."

By the time the first light of dawn had broken the sky all the Boswell Crew were safe home to Langdyke Bush and sleeping fast. The women were stoking the fires and cutting the meat for stew, those joints that hadn't been neatly set aside for selling in the village to those who could be trusted to hold their tongues.

****

If the moon had not been so strong Will Bloodworth would not have seen the blood. He was making his nightly round, following the inside margin of the estate wall, his ears and eyes tuned to anything untoward. Something had alerted him half an hour before, some sound, but it had been faint and far away. He'd paid it no great mind. But now he was not surprised to find blood on the wall. He put down his musket and dipped his finger into a little pool of it that was held in a cup in the stone. He licked his finger. The blood was fresh. He picked up the gun and scrambled over the wall. There was a trail of dripped blood across the road. He followed it to the hawthorns. The smell of the butchering was still strong. With the barrel of his gun he pushed aside the brambles and saw the stag's head with its antlers sawn off at the root, the white, curved, bloody bones of the spine like a notched bow. He saw the hooves and lower legs, the purple of the stomach and the grey tangle of the guts. He reached down and touched them. They were still warm.

By the light of the sinking moon it was easy to see the path the poachers had followed. The long grass was broken where they'd skirted the edge of the Castor fields. He followed, keeping low, running as fast as he could with his head and shoulders held below the height of the bean stalks. It was as he approached Emmonsales Heath that he caught his first glimpse of them. There were six in all, they were more ambling than hurrying. They were carrying bags on their backs. Will snorted.

"We all know what's in those, by God ."

He ran forwards again and crouched low behind a clump of gorse. He could see the last of them clearly in the moonlight. He was carrying the rolled deer-hide on his back. Will leaned forwards to look more closely. The shift of his weight snapped a twig beneath his foot. The poacher turned at the sound and glanced over his shoulder. Will Bloodworth, in that moment, saw his face as clear as day: the black hair, the long face with its quick, dark-lashed eyes. It was the gypsy whelp. It was Wisdom Boswell.

There was a grim resolution writ upon Will's countenance that bordered on contentment, as though something beneath his skin that had twisted him into mis-shape had been laid straight again. He crouched behind the gorse bush until the Boswell Crew were out of sight. Then he turned and ran back to the estate.

The moon had set now and the sky was bright with stars. Will knew where he was going. He crossed the road and as he approached the estate wall he lifted his gun to his shoulder and fired it into the air. Then he re-loaded, ramming the new shot into place, tamping it with wadding. He fired again. He reloaded a second time. He clambered over the wall and ran between the trees and across the open parkland towards Milton Hall.

Soon he heard the sound he'd been expecting:

"Hulloa! "

Dark figures were approaching him.

"Who goes there?"

"'Tis I, Will, Will Bloodworth."

"We heard shots."

Will drew up to them, panting for breath.

"Poachers, six of 'em."

"Did ye stop them?"

"No. They stopped me. One of them turned his damned musket on me."

"What! Are ye hurt?"

"No, they missed by a whisker, I felt the wind of it against my cheek."

"Thank God for that Will, what did they take?"

"A buck. They were climbing the wall with it when I first clapped eyes on them."

"Go back to the hall Will, you'll be shook up. We'll see if we can't catch 'em."

They began to make their way towards the wood.

"I saw his face," Will called over his shoulder, "I saw the face of the one with the gun, I saw him as clear as day, 'tis etched on my memory."

"Ay Will, and if we can catch him we'll see him swing."

The keepers tramped into the shadows and were swallowed by the trees. But without a moon there was small chance of them finding the trail that Will had followed. By dawn they'd returned to the hall empty-handed.

****

Morning is come now. Will Bloodworth is being shook out of his short slumber by one of his fellow keepers.

"Will, wake up!"

He sits up and rubs his eyes.

"The Earl of Fitzwilliam has sent to Helpston for the constable. He is come, Will. Get dressed. Come downstairs."

Will pulls on his breeches, shirt and boots. He rakes his fingers through his hair. He makes his way from his little room in the servants' quarters, down the wooden stairs and outside to the courtyard. Bill Bullimore, the village constable is waiting, his hands behind his back, whistling between his teeth and staring up at the great brick chimneys and the roof of the hall with its seeming acres of grey slates and red tiles. Behind him his horse is being led to the trough. As Will approaches he brings his gaze down to the level:

"Morning Will."

Will nods.

"I've heard your story. I'm told a buck has been killed, shots taken, and you've seen the face of the varmint that fired the gun."

"Yes, I have."

"Was it a face you knew?"

"It was a face I'd seen before."

"The Earl has sent orders to press charges. Could you lead me to him?"

"Ay, I could."

****

At the same time as Will wakes, Wisdom is being shaken to wakefulness by King Boswell. He beckons with his thick finger.

"Avata acoi, chal."

Wisdom pulls himself out from the warm blankets under the cart and follows, pulling on his clothes. The air is thick with the smell of smoke and bubbling stew. The dogs are happily crunching bones.

King Boswell thrusts the deer hide into Wisdom's hands.

"Rig the stannyi mutzi to Kitty Otter."

Wisdom nods. He can see that Ismael and Lettuce are out to the villages, and guesses that already they're knocking on back doors and selling the meat. If any gorgios come to the camp prying and asking questions there will be little for them to find.

King Boswell smiles, showing his white teeth.

"And when ye come back, chal, ye can dip a spoon into the stannyi simmeno and sup."

Wisdom swings the rolled hide onto his back and makes his way across the parish to Snow Common.

Kitty's geese, with their grey goslings in tow, stretch out their necks and hiss as he approaches her squat. Kitty lifts the door-flap and pokes her wrinkled face out into the light. She looks to left and right, her head jutting from the bowed, blackened canvas like a tortoise from its shell. When she sees Wisdom she cackles:

"Ah Wisdom, good boy, d'ye have the hide? Bring it inside, bring it inside."

Wisdom pushes through the flaps, he ducks beneath the woven baskets of rush and willow, the tied clusters of herbs and the cured skins that hang from the roof. His nose takes in the strange, strong smell of the place: the sweet herbs, the tickling smoke, the wet canvas and something sharp and fetid like the lair of a wild animal.

"Old Otter ain't here, he's away at the hay-making."

Wisdom passes her the bundle and she unfastens the twine with nimble bony fingers. She spreads the dappled hide across the floor.

" 'Tis a good one. A buck."

She pinches it.

"Ay, 'tis a good one. There's boots here, or a jerkin…when 'tis scraped and salted…"

She looks across at him sharply.

"Did ye bring me a cut o' meat?"

Wisdom reaches over and folds back the neck of the hide to reveal a cut of red meat tucked inside. She sniffs it.

"Good boy, good boy. We'll dine like kings and queens tonight Wisdom."

She picks up the meat and drops it into an iron pot.

Wisdom turns towards the flap:

"Mutzi and meat are payment Kitty, for the mending of the net. King Boswell thanks you from his heart. 'Twas torn again last night though, and will need more mending."

"'Tis fair payment, ay, 'tis payment fair enough. Bring the net and I'll fix it for ye again Wisdom."

She puts her hand on his shoulder, Wisdom turns and she winks at him with her shrewd, sharp eye, blue as a dunnock's egg.

"And we'll do business again, no doubt, when the time's ripe."

She rolls up the hide.

"We ain't so different, you an' me."

She tucks it into the shadows.

"Only you Boswells journey far and wide and me an' Otter stay where we've allus been…an' you're brown as Turks an' old Otter pink as any porker."

She squeezes his arm. He pushes out into the sun and breathes deep of the clean June air. Then he sets off back to Langdyke Bush.

****

It was past midnight when John staggered home from Glinton, giddy with ale and the taste of Mary's kiss. Her Clipping Posey hangs limp now from the pocket of his coat that is thrown across the chest at the foot of the bed.

It is a shaft of sunlight shining through the little window in the eaves that wakes him. He opens his eyes. He remembers the shearing supper and the joys of the evening and smiles to himself. He looks up at the dancing motes of dust caught in the sunbeam and he blesses every one of them. He blesses his aching head, his aching limbs. The whole world seems blessed to him this bright morning. He rolls out of bed and pulls on his breeches. He blesses the rattle of his shearing wages in his pocket. He pulls on his shirt and makes his way down the steep stairs.

Ann Clare is stirring a pot over the fire. The room is full of the savoury smell of meat and herbs. John sniffs.

"Ay, John, it's a treat for supper tonight. Your father wouldn't have it otherwise. When you was sleeping we took a few pennies of your wages from your pocket to pay for it, I hope you ain't vexed."

She lowers her voice to a whisper:

"Though it pains me to press money into a gypsy's fist… we didn't think you'd begrudge us a taste of venison."

Ann pulls the pot away from the flames.

"There, now I must leave it to simmer awhile, for Sophie will be waiting for me on the bean field."

She looks at John.

"How was the supper last night? Old Joyce served you better than Mr Wormstall I'll warrant? And was Mary there?"

John smiles, and in his smile is all that his mother needs to know of the night before.

"Ah good. And I hope as you and Jack Ward and the rest of 'em didn't get into your altitudes and make donkeys of yourselves."

John is just about to answer when there's an urgent rapping at the back door. Ann Clare pulls it open. Lettuce Boswell is standing on the step. Her bright shawl is drawn over her shoulders and she's breathless from hurrying the full length of the parish.

"What do you want? Away with you! Two visits in a morning!"

Lettuce's words come spilling out before the door has swung shut in her face:

"Wisdom is took! For pity's sake they've took poor Wisdom as a felon. They've manacled him up in chains and took him to Peterborough and he's to be brought before the poknies..."

She gasps for breath and then covers her face with her hands and sobs.

John runs forwards and pulls the door open again.

"Wisdom took?"

Ann steps aside with a sigh:

"You'd better come inside...sit yourself down. John fetch a stool."

Lettuce sits down and composes herself.

"They come this morning, not long after I returned from the village, seven of 'em from Milton Hall, pointing their guns this way an' that way. They searched the carts and tents but devil a scrap they found of what they was lookin' for, for all their pokin' and pryin'. 'Hare' we told 'em when they lifted the lids of the pots, 'Hollow meat', and I wouldn't have ventured as they believed us but they said no word...and they loitered and would not let us be until Wisdom come running back through the gorse from Kitty Otter's Squat. 'There he is!' shouts one of 'em."

Lettuce whispers beneath her breath:

"O bengte poggar his men."

She pulls a handkerchief from her pocket, mops her cheeks and carries on:

"'There he is! He's the murderous varmint that would have shot me dead!' They seized poor Wisdom then and had him bound in irons in the blink of an eye. King Boswell came forward and held out his hands: 'We have no firing piece, I swear to God, you've searched the camping ground and found nought.' But one of the keepers, that Bill Henderson, curse his soul, leaned forward and spoke into King Boswell's face: 'The youth will hang for the pack of ye...we know venison when we smell it sir.'

And then with Wisdom chained and the rest watching, they took our dogs and shot them. One after the other they put their muskets to the creatures' heads and showed no mercy, throwing them in a heap at King Boswell's feet. And he saw his own two precious bitches, that he has trained so that they read his thought, lying dead before him... and then the damned wesh-engros were gone, pushing Wisdom ahead of 'em."

Lettuce falls silent awhile, and neither John nor Ann speaks a word. Then she stands and takes Ann's hands in hers:

"I know you and the rest of 'em think low of my kind, for we are little understood...but your boy, bein' thick with Wisdom, should know the truth before it's rendered lies by wagging tongues."

She squeezes Ann's hand, then she lets it go, and in a swirl of her shawl she's out of the door.

"But why Wisdom, of all of 'em, why the chal?"

And she's gone, round to the street and away through Royce's Wood.

"I reckon as we know why." Says Ann.

John nods, and all the bright, blessed promise drains away from the day, and the smell of the stew seems to have lost its savour.

6

July Storm

The Boswell crew have for some weeks been cutting rushes from the streams, leaning forward from the river banks and slicing the long leaves with blades that are tied tight to wooden poles. They have bound them into bundles and carried them to town. From door to door they have been mending rush-seat chairs for a few coppers a time. Housewives have gladly brought their chairs out onto the street and there's few of them can fault the tight-wove work that their fingers bring to bear on them.

With a careful-put question here and there the Boswell Crew have pieced together all they need to know of Wisdom's whereabouts. They have learned that he is held in the Bishop's Gaol and that he waits for the September assize where he must stand trial before Judge Ashurst.

"There's nought between him and the gallers..."

A plump housemaid from one well-appointed household was mardling to Ismael Boswell as she watched him weave his rushes.

"Save only a prayer...him shooting a keeper in cold blood... and didn't he shoot again despite all pleas for mercy...and they say he shows no remorse...these are the times we live in... an' all for a taste of another man's meat...an' him the Earl Fitzwilliam..."

Ismael had had no qualms about slipping his fingers into her pocket when she took the chair into her fat hands and turned to carry it indoors.

The Boswell crew have been to the Bishop's Gaol, they've pleaded and cajoled for a glimpse of Wisdom, but all to no avail.

"He's locked away," the turn-keys at the Minster Gate told them, "and none may see him until he's brought to justice... least of all you."

John Clare, hearing where Wisdom is kept, has spent a portion of his shearing wage on bread and cheese and cake and carried it to Peterborough.

The turn-keys were happy enough to take the food from him.

"God bless you for your charity sir, but it is not allowed for any but officers of the law to visit the accused in his cell. We will deliver the vittles into his hands and doubtless he will thank you for them."

And John knew from the eye they cast on his parcel that there was small chance of any crumb reaching Wisdom's lips.

****

Day follows day as June slips towards hot July. The gypsies are suddenly gone. They've upped-sticks and disappeared beyond the circling orison vowing they'll return for the assize.

These long summer days the ragged village boys play by the hedgerows as they mind the cattle. Tom Dolby turns to the others:

"Who am I?"

Barefooted he walks across the grass with a studied self-regard, stands on a molehill and makes the sign of the cross with a finger.

"In the name of the Father and the Son…"

"Parson Mossop!" The others shout.

Then he pushes out his belly and waddles to the branch of a tree, he pats it as though it was the neck of a horse:

"There, there Billy…"

"Sam Billings!"

Then he strides along the hedgerow, his head drawn down to his shoulders, his legs bowed as though he would shrink himself further, and with a look of abstraction writ upon his features he speaks to himself so that the others cannot hear the words but only the pattern of them:

"I put the pudding in the pot to boil…and seed the grimey goose upon the hedge…"

He stops suddenly and bends to examine a leaf, then carries on muttering:

"And farted all the way to kingdom come…and told her how it happens in the hay…"

The other boys were falling about with merriment:

"John Clare! John Clare!"

Poor John. He is the creature of his joys and sorrows. He's one moment thinking of Wisdom and fancying the rasp of the noose about his throat, the next remembering Mary, and then all of a sudden some text or tract will come into his mind, and then some sharp sound will startle him, and then he will be soothed by a line of verse he's learned. All day he is at the mercy of his wayward thoughts and at night he tosses and turns and finds but little rest. He is unsettled, and though he works at the hay harvest with the other men and women - mowing or raking or helping build the stacks – he swings with nervous thought like the weather-cock on Glinton Spire, turning with each interior wind. His eyes and ears, by habit so fine-tuned to all sensation, are drawn inward. He does not take his accustomed delight in the horses, their heads bowed as they pull the wains to the yards, the loaded hay rising up behind them like new-risen loaves; or the fly-crazed cattle flicking their tails; or the sudden regiments of purple-headed thistles grown shoulder high by the hedge-rows.

And sometimes, forgetting himself or thinking himself alone, he mutters his monologue aloud, to the delight of any village boys who chance to hear him.

John's one stay and anchor is Mary Joyce. She is become his solace. Every Sabbath when the village is at prayer he walks to Glinton and waits at the lych-gate.

This last Sabbath past when Mary came out of the church porch she whispered a word into her father's ear, pushed her prayer book into his pocket and slipped away across the churchyard. She ran to the lych-gate and took John's arm. They followed North Fen Lane to the bridge over Brook Drain. It was a hot, close morning and the warm wind that they could feel on their faces as they stood on the hump of the bridge was a sweet relief.

"I have pleaded with Father on Wisdom's account, John. And though he is no lover of gypsies he will not tolerate an injustice. He has ridden out to all the farmers who were at the Rogation feast whose word would carry some weight at the assize. He has spoken to Mr Bull, John Close, Thomas Bellar and Ralph Wormstall…"

"And how do they answer?"

"They laugh in his face that he should consider bearing witness on a Boswell's behalf. And anyway, because it is the Earl of Fitzwilliam that is bringing the prosecution, they would not dream of standing against him…he being their landlord."

"What does your father say to that, Mary?"

"He calls 'em damned cowards, but I can see that he is torn himself, for all his living hangs on the Earl's good will."

"Will he stand witness then?"

"I am trying to persuade him."

"And what about his farm?"

"He has paid rent and tithe as regular as the sun, and the Earl stops off particular to order his cheeses and hams if he is passing close by, and to drink a glass of his ale…and admires his husbandry above all his tenants…I have told him he should not fear for his farm…though he is not so sure as I."

She wrapped her arms around John and pressed her cheek against his cheek.

"There is nothing more we can do…Look here," she pulled away from him, "look what I've brought from the orchard, they've been in my pocket all through the morning service."

She tipped a handful of cherries onto the palm of her hand.

John picked one up and popped it into his mouth. The sweet, fresh, sharp taste dispelled, for a moment, all fears. He took the other cherries from her and laid them in a row on the stone bridge wall.

"Eat them without using your hands."

Mary leaned forward and picked one of them up between her teeth. She pushed it into her cheek with her tongue. She lifted her head, turned to him and smiled:

"Eat it without using *your* hands!"

She put her hands onto his shoulders and kissed him, as their lips met she pushed the cherry into his mouth. He chewed it and spat the stone into the stream.

"Now it's my turn."

He leaned forward, picked up another cherry between his

teeth. They kissed again. She took it from him and pressed the red flesh against the roof of her mouth with her tongue. She spat the stone at John. It struck him just above the eye.

"There, now we are even!"

Then came a rumble of distant thunder and with it the old disquiet returned as sudden as it had disappeared. He looked up at the sky. It was piled high with clouds that were the bruised purple-grey of a pigeon's breast.

Mary pressed herself against him again.

"And now I must go to Sunday dinner John. Father has invited the parson."

She pressed her lips to his cheek, broke away from him and ran away along the lane.

John set off towards Woodcroft Field.

There was a flash, and almost on the instant a crash of thunder. He ducked down. His shirt was wet with sweat. The first fat drops of rain began to fall. He straightened again and hurried onwards along the stony track.

As he walked a storm-dread was gathering that he felt in every fibre, for the fears of childhood run deep as marrow-fat. The rain grew heavier and the dust danced at his feet and then turned to mud. Soon he was soaked from head to heel.

At last he reached Woodgate. The cottage was empty. Though the rain was pounding heavy against the thatch and running in rivulets along the street, it was still hot indoors. He pulled off his shirt and hung it over the back of a chair. He was oppressed by the quiet and wished with all his heart that he had company. There was another crack of thunder. Maybe he should pray. With a trembling hand he reached into the cubby hole and pulled out the chap books and horn books and battered volumes and scraps of scribbled paper. All of them seemed vanities to him. And he could not lay his hand on the one book he sought. He rummaged again, and then he remembered that he'd given his prayerbook to Sophie. She liked to carry it to church and make as if to read. And not being book-learned she would hardly have noticed the tables of lessons and moveable feasts that John had torn out to light his fires…nor the forms of prayer to be used at sea…nor the form and manner of ordaining and consecrating Bishops, Deans and Deacons. All were ash now.

When the knock on the door came he started. Uneasily he walked across and lifted the latch, half expecting the Ghostly Enemy to be standing on the step. It was Dick Turnill, the water dripping from his coat.

"John, do you have an hour or so free?"

John was relieved to have a distraction.

"Ay."

"Parson Mossop drew me aside after church this morning and thrust a sheaf of tunes into my hand, asking if the church band might learn them. For he does prefer hymn to psalm… even if it be penned by them as favour Methody…I know you ain't regular in your churching John, but you're more regular than Old Otter…and Wisdom never comes…so you're as close to a first fiddle as we've got."

In the ordinary run of things John might have been reluctant, but this afternoon Dick seemed like a visiting angel, and John saw in his request some divine intervention and sign.

"Ay Dick, come in out of the wet while I fetch my fiddle."

He bounded up the stairs two at a time and returned with his fiddle under his arm. He pulled his wet shirt over his head.

"Where are we to play?"

"In the parlour of my house. The others will be waiting on us."

John grabbed his coat, tucked the fiddle and bow underneath

it, and the two of them ran out into the storm. They splashed down West Street to the Turnill's farm.

It is a modest yard. The new thatched haystacks and the last of the ricks loomed above them as they ran through wet straw to the farm-house door. The farm dogs barked but did not run out into the rain to greet them. In the centre of the yard there was a pile of tarred fence posts, and against the stable wall row upon row of tarred wooden slats were stacked. In front of the house lines of quick-thorn seedlings, their roots wrapped in sacking, leaned towards the wall. Once they were inside the house Dick waved his arm at the yard:

"They are for the enclosing of our entitlement, John, and have cost us very dear."

In the steamy kitchen Mr Turnill was sitting at the table with a huge Bible open before him. He was reading aloud, his finger following the text. Beside him his wife listened and studied the page as though even the pattern of the type might reveal some unfathomable mystery. His face, tanned like old leather from long hours in all weathers, was furrowed with Sabbath concentration; while Mrs Turnill's face, pale and round as a dumpling, nodded, beneath its linen cap, in solemn agreement with each word uttered. The rain lashed the windows, and drops fell down the wide farm-house chimney and hissed in the embers of the kitchen fire.

When they became aware of Dick and John entering the room Mr Turnill fell silent. Husband and wife looked up at them.

"Ah, John Clare, parson was asking for thee again at morning service. He's compiling a list of them that are church-shy and you're on it."

John looked at the ground and scraped the toe of his boot against the stone flags of the floor.

Mrs Turnill shook her head:

"And 'twas not only Parson Mossop that was asking for thee. Our Lord and Saviour – as sees and hears all – did not hear your voice raised in prayer, and it pains him John, it pains him sore."

"Think on it," said Mr Turnill, "For I do fear for thee sometimes. If your own father won't rule you on this then I will."

There was a long silence. All four of them knew that Parker Clare, even though he takes his place in his pew every Sunday, has only a scant regard for Parson Mossop, and leans towards dissent.

"Come on, John."

When they were out of ear-shot Dick said:

"I'm sorry John, they are anxious. We are waist deep in debt for the fencing of our fields. They are both preyed upon by fears of ruin and it feeds their zeal."

When they came to the parlour the rest of the band were waiting for them. Sam Billings filled a wooden armchair with his bulk, his drum set on his knee. Jonathan Burbridge drew his bow across the strings of his cello so that the candlesticks rattled, he was fingering one of his fancier melodies and had one eye set on the third member of the party, a woman John had not seen before. Sam Billings pulled himself up to his feet.

"Ah John, here you are, here you are at last, good."

He gestured towards the woman with one hand:

"Meet Mrs Betsy Jackson, who is recently come from Stamford as cook to John Close."

Betsy smiled. John remembered his mother speaking of her. Her husband had been a cobbler, had died of consumption and left her penniless. But though she is a widow and had been married for some fifteen years, she is scarcely two and thirty years of age. John saw a plump, well-featured woman, good natured with full cheeks and eyes that liked to laugh and did not dwell upon the past. She was wearing her Sunday clothes: a printed gown, a white apron, and a linen cap edged with lace and tied about with a pink ribbon. Her brown curls spilled out beneath it. There seemed to be something untroubled about her that in turn lifted John from his turmoil. He shook her hand.

"What do you play?"

She reached down and picked up an oboe that lay between the feet of her chair. She waved it in the air.

"I blow upon the horse's leg!"

She laughed a peal of shrill, easy laughter. Jonathan nodded his head up and down in appreciation.

"Very good, very good."

Dick Turnill untied the ribbon from the parson's sheaf of manuscript papers with the tunes pricked out upon them and laid them on a table. The band gathered round, adjusted themselves so that they were ready to play.

Sam Billings beat the time:

"One two three and...."

They began in a ragged way. First they struck up 'Morning Trumpet', then 'Thy Soul-cheering Presence', then 'Come all ye Faithful Christians', 'Windham' and 'Idumea'. And though it was but the tunes they played, in John's mind the words of the hymns shouted their admonitions and certainties into his trembling thoughts.

He found his fingers suddenly sticky with sweat so that he was scarce able to play. And then he looked up and saw Betsy Jackson's face, red from blowing, with cheeks puffed out and her breasts rising and falling, looking like the wind in the corner of a mariner's map. He saw Sam Billings beating time on the drum that rested on his belly, lifting each stick with a flourish as though he played for a battalion on the march. He saw Jonathan Burbridge's studied frown as he played with all of his art, his fingers trembling on the cello's neck as though he'd been brought before the crowned heads of Europe. And John found himself suddenly smiling, and all his fear was, for a little while, eased by the comfortable, familiar world of the farm-house parlour.

They were mid-way through 'Sound, Sound your Instruments of Joy' when Old Otter appeared at the farm-house door. Mr Turnill was still reading from the Bible. The strains of the hymn tune could be faintly heard from the back of the house. Otter threw a hare onto the table in front of the Bible.

"Kitty sends this with her kind regards."

Mr Turnill looked up from his text:

"They that are after the flesh do mind the things of the flesh..."

Otter has long since, as far as Bob Turnill is concerned, thrown in his lot with the Devil.

"And they that are after the Spirit do mind the things of the Spirit...Ye'd do well to ponder upon that Otter...I didn't expect to hear you playing hymns upon the Sabbath, but I welcome it with all my heart."

"A tune's a tune Bob, and my fingers was itchin' to play."

Mr Turnill picked the hare up by its hind legs. He looked it up and down.

"I hope and pray as Kitty hasn't been labouring on the Sabbath."

Old Otter grinned, his eyes bright between the white thatch of his hair and the white tangle of his beard.

"She set the trap yesterday eve, though whether Wat here was at his labours and sprung it before or after midnight I couldn't tell 'ee."

Mrs Turnill laughed. She reached across and patted the hare's head.

"If he was transgressing then he has been punished for it, and we are beholden to ye both."

She took it from her husband and carried it through to the dairy. She put it in the cool shadow under a stone table.

"And he's a beauty, Otter."

Old Otter nodded and made his way through to the parlour. Sam Billings raised both sticks above his head and drummed a roll.

"Here's Old Father Time!"

Otter shook Betsy's hand, and they played the tunes through to him so that he could learn them. And then he pulled his battered fiddle from under his jerkin and they played them again together, filling the pantry with fiddles, oboe, flute, cello, drum. And they played with such a full accord, with such a rhythm, that even Mr Turnill in the kitchen found himself beating time with his feet as he read, so that they were as good as dancing under the table. His wife put her hand on his knee and whispered:

"It is not proper, Bob."

When they'd played the tunes over and over and they were lodged in their memories, Old Otter put his fiddle down onto the table.

"Call me an old sinner if ye will…" He said.

"You old sinner!" said Sam Billings and clapped him on the shoulder.

"…But it seems to me that the one that Parson Mossop has called 'Thy Soul Cheering Presence' is only a whisker away from 'Rosin the Bow'."

He lifted his fiddle to his chin and played.

"See!"

He played again, and instinctively the others joined in.

In the kitchen Mr Turnill's feet started dancing again under the table, more vigorous than before.

Mrs Turnill seized his arm.

"Bob! Listen!"

In the pantry the musicians played and played, lost in the rise and fall, the twists and turns of the tune, oblivious to all but the pleasure of playing.

Suddenly the door crashed open.

Mr Turnill stood framed in it, shaking with rage.

"How dare ye? On the Sabbath, under my roof!"

They stopped and stared at him, as if woken from a dream.

"What! D'ye mistake my parlour for the snug at the Bluebell? Away with ye! Go on, out with the lot of ye!"

He waved his arms at the village band until they gathered themselves, pulling on coats and picking up instruments. They hurried out of the parlour, through the kitchen, where Mrs Turnill was standing, her hands on her hips, glaring at them, and out into the damp evening. Only poor Dick was left behind,

"And Dick! We bring ye up godly and for what? For old Otter to lead ye down to damnation!"

The rain had eased now, there were distant rumbles and grumbles of thunder somewhere beyond the orison. When the band reached West Street it was Old Otter who broke the silence:

"Where's the damage in a little tune that never done harm to man nor beast?"

Sam Billings, a little breathless from their hurried departure, nodded:

"There's them as wear their Sabbath breeches too tight."

Jonathan Burbridge, with his cello in its canvas bag slung

across his back, turned his attention to Betsy.

"Too tight by half...Well, I'm away now to tuck old grandma up for the night."

He reached behind himself and patted the cello. Then he bowed to her:

"'Twas a pleasure to meet you Betsy, if I may call you such, and to hear you play...we'll meet again on Sunday next...if not before."

Betsy Jackson, with her oboe in one hand and the other lifting up her Sabbath gown so that the hem stayed clear of the puddles in the road, smiled:

"Elizabeth, Elspeth, Betsy or Beth, 'tis one and the same to me...anything save Widow Jackson for that won't do at all."

She laughed then, and there was in the rise and fall of her laughter the note of one who has learned to put good humour over the ill-usages of fortune.

"A very good evening to ye all."

She splashed away towards John Close's farm.

Old Otter turned to the rest:

"'Tis a grand tune is 'Rosin the Bow', but I felt the lack of young Wisdom, he'd ha given it a lift that'd have had Bob Turnill and his missus capering on the kitchen flags, Sabbath or no Sabbath."

Sam Billings nodded

"Ay, there's no arguing with that."

And the village band went their different ways. Sam winked at Jonathan. Old Otter waved his fiddle in the air and strode down Crossberry Lane. John nodded his farewells but said no word.

****

John was not the only one to fall asleep troubled last night. Will Bloodworth came back to Milton Hall soaked from waist to foot from the dripping grass of the estate. It was two hours short of the dawn when he climbed the steps to his little garret room beside the great chimney above the kitchen. He lit a candle, took off his sodden clothes and spread them out as best he could against the warm brick. He rubbed himself dry and pulled a night-shirt over his head. He lay down and pulled a blanket over himself. But though he was dog-tired he could not sleep.

Will Bloodworth knows that he has lied. And he knows with equal certitude that he cannot renege upon that lie. And so there is a part of him that lies to himself about the lie and would have it truth. And there is a part of him that knows that by doing so he locks himself in a double falsehood. There is a part of him that would gladly see the gypsy swing. And there is a part of him that shrinks from having blood on his hands. Contrary thoughts trouble him and give him no peace, writhing in his mind like maggots in a wound. And deep beneath them all he harbours a terror that he is damned.

Few would read these troubles in his features during the day-time though. Will's narrow, clean-shaved and freckled face with its brushed side-whiskers is given to smiling often, but not so that it can be read in his eyes. He moves briskly from task to task and has won the respect of many, but is loved by none. And though he is five and thirty years old, he is a bachelor yet.

7

Harvest (The Assize)

It was the day before the September assize, Thursday last. All through August John has felt a growing weight of forboding. Five times he has walked to Peterborough and tried to get some account of Wisdom from the turn-keys at the Bishop's Gaol, but all to no avail. He knows the torment that a stone ceiling would afford to one who has lived his life beneath the sky. And in his mind's eye he has seen all too clearly the rank straw, the stinking flea-ridden blankets, the overflowing bucket of piss and shit that spills its slops onto the floor.

All these were preying on his dreams when he was woke at first light by a shrill note.

'Paaaaaaaarp. Paaaaaaaaarp.'

Richard Royce has been chosen as this year's Lord of the Harvest. He was making his dawn circuit from street to street, blowing the harvesters awake with his hollow hemlock horn.

Soon enough the sound of the stirring of every household and farm filled the air. John got dressed. He and Parker ate a chunk of rye bread apiece and washed them down with water. Ann and Sophie packed their baggin. They walked to Close's Farm to collect their scythes. They slung them over their shoulders, put their whet-stones in their pockets and set off, tramping the stony track towards John Close's furlongs on Lolham Bridge Field like foot-soldiers. His were the last furlongs still standing upon the great field. The rest was stubble now.

The rhythm and hard labour of these harvest days have been a sweet relief to John. They have rendered him too tired to think. All morning the team of men, in smocks and wide-brimmed hats of rush or straw, worked together. They swung their curved blades in the easy accord that their health depends upon, for to be out of rhythm is to cut flesh to bone of the man alongside. From time to time they stopped to sharpen their blades, drawing the whet-stones along the curved blades, two strokes below and one above. The scythes rang out like cutlasses. Then they'd return to their harvest, Richard Royce leading, the others falling in behind, like fiddlers in a band with their bows rising and falling in perfect time.

The women followed, Ann Clare and Betsy Jackson amongst them. They gathered the fallen swathes of wheat in their arms and lifted them up, as though tending the fallen. They tied each sheaf with twisted straw. They leaned the sheaves together, six at a time, into stooks. Behind them row upon row of lifted stooks stood, each like a cluster of tousle-headed prisoners of war bound together back to back. Overhead a fierce September sun beat down upon bent backs.

On the other side of Lolham Bridge Field, where Mr Bull's and Bob Turnill's stooks had stood three weeks in bright sunshine, two great carts had been drawn to the edge of their furlongs. One man stood in each and built the load, six more forked the sheaves up to them as they worked. The waiting horses stamped in the heat.

Beyond them, where the stooks had all been taken, Kitty Otter, Sophie Clare and a gaggle of other girls, old women and village paupers were gleaning the stubble for spilt grain.

When mid-day came, it was to the shade of those two carts, piled high now, that the men retired. They crawled between the high wooden iron-shod wheels and patted down the sharp stubble. Some lit pipes, some unwrapped their baggin. All of them filled mugs from the harvest barrel that had been lifted onto a corner of the cart. They washed the dust from their throats. John and Parker shared the bread and cheese and apples that had been wrapped for them. When they had eaten they stretched out in the shadow of the load and rested.

The women ate apart. They went down to the willows that leaned over Green Dyke at the edge of the field and settled there. They dipped their feet into the cool water and brushed away the flies with withies as they talked.

When the hour was over and Richard Royce called them back to work the men made their slow way across the field to their scythes that lay alongside the uncut corn. As John was drawing the first stroke of his whet-stone against the blade he heard his name being called:

"John Clare."

He turned and saw Betsy Jackson. She was with the other women, coming back from the stream's edge. Her face was in shadow under her wide brimmed straw bonnet, but he could see she was smiling at him. She beckoned.

"Come here John!"

He put down his scythe and wandered across to her.

"Us musicianers must stick together John, so I've made ye something special."

She fished beneath the cotton cloth that covered her basket. He could see the yellow stains of dried sweat under the arms of her cotton blouse.

"I've made ye a mutton pasty."

She pulled out a golden brown pastry with pinched edges

and handed it to him.

"You'll enjoy that I reckon."

John thanked her most civil and took it. He went back to where the men were waiting, broke it in half and shared it with his father. Parker turned and waved at Betsy, he touched his lips with his fingers then opened his hand. She laughed and waved. But it was John she watched as he sharpened his blade and set to work with the reaping team. It was John she watched, and then, as though she had thrown water into her own face, she shook herself so that her brown curls bobbed, and hurried forwards to catch up with the other women.

And John, oblivious of her scrutiny, bent his back to his work and tried not to think what tomorrow morning might hold in store.

****

At the same time, under the same bright sun, Farmer Joyce was overseeing the reapers at work on his furlongs in Glinton parish. They had stopped to whet their blades for the third time when he heard a horse approaching across the stubble. He turned and saw Ben Price, the bailiff.

Farmer Joyce raised his hand:

"A fine harvesting day Ben, and the dew gone from the ground by six o'clock."

Ben Price reined in his horse and climbed down from the saddle. The two men shook hands.

"Ay, John."

He reached down and broke an ear from one of the stalks of wheat. He rubbed it between his hands, blew away the chaff and tipped the grains into his mouth. He chewed in a slow and considered manner, the flicker at the edge of his mouth giving his milling rumination something of a pained air.

"Good," he said, "'tis a good grain John."

He wiped his mouth with the back of his hand.

"But 'twas not to discuss grain that I have ridden out this afternoon. The Earl's secretary has pressed me most urgent to put this into your hands."

He opened his jacket and reached into the pocket. He pulled out a letter sealed with wax.

"I am told to tell you to give it your most considered attention."

Farmer Joyce took the letter. Ben Price climbed up into the saddle, reined his horse around and set off at a trot across the dusty stubble. As soon as he was gone Farmer Joyce broke the seal and unfolded the letter. He read it once and then he read it again.

"Damn him."

He stuffed it into his pocket.

"Damn him to hell."

He strode across the field to where his mare was tethered in the shade of a stand of sycamores. He untied her and rode to the village. When he came to his yard he handed the horse to Will Farrell and strode into the sudden dark shade of the house.

"Mary!"

She was in the bake-house with Kate Dyball.

"Mary, where are ye?"

She came running into the parlour where her father was pacing up and down. She ran forward to him.

"What's amiss?"

"Mary, I cannot stand witness at the assize…"

"But you promised that you would…."

"Read this."

He pulled the letter from his pocket and thrust it angrily into her hand. She unfolded it and read aloud.

Sir
It has come to the attention of the Earl of Fitzwilliam that you intend to stand witness in favour of one against whom the Earl presses charges for affront to his Property, Game and the very Life of one of his most trusted Keepers. He wishes you to know that should you continue in your Folly no cheese, ham or husbandry will assuage his displeasure. He wishes also to remind you that your Land and Living, your Rents, Privileges and Entitlements are entirely at his Discretion.
Yours
Robert Smethwick
Secretary to the Earl of Fitzwilliam

Mary looked at her father:
"You must stand true to your conscience."
He shook his head.
"And risk losing all that I have worked for, and my father before me and my old grandsire, bless his soul... and all that I might pass on to you Mary. And put all these other lives in jeopardy that depend upon me for their living, Will Farrell, John Fell, Nathan Cushion, Kate, Lizzie and Hope….all for the sake of a gypsy I have only once clapped eyes upon…'tis too high a price."
Mary was silent. She looked down at the floor so that her hair fell forwards across her face. He took her hands. He whispered:
"I'm sorry Mary, I know this injustice hurts you very sore… but you will not prevail."

She nodded.

He turned and left the room. She stood a long time alone in the parlour.

****

In the Bluebell after sundown it was the same story. The fear of the Earl's displeasure was too strong a medicine for any to swallow save Old Otter.

"I'll come with thee John, for what have I to lose by telling God's truth?"

From the rest there was nought but a shaking of heads. He was only a thieving gypsy after all, and if innocent of firing the gun there could be no denying the poaching. Even those who knew Wisdom shook their heads. Jonathan Burbridge feared losing his carpenter's shop and half his custom. James Bain feared for his forge. Sam Billings feared the loss of his carting business. Even Parker Clare feared for his cottage, though he saw but little danger in John standing witness.

"You say your piece, son, for we know who's at fault in the matter and the truth must be spoke according to your conscience and even the mighty stand naked before the law."

Sam Billings stood then and raised his mug.

"Here's to Wisdom Boswell."

Most of the tap room ignored him, but one or two raised their mugs in response:

"Ay, Wisdom Boswell, poor sod, and may his neck be spared."

But there was a despondency, a dullness in the pitch and cadence of their toasting that did little to engender hope in John's heart for the next day's verdict.

****

Yesterday the dawn broke clear. The village woke to Richard Royce's horn. But as the rest were shouldering their scythes John was making his way first to Old Otter's squat on Snow Common, and then to Langley Bush where King Boswell was camped again.

The three of them walked the dusty road to Peterborough: the two old men and John. From behind, seeing them silhouetted against the early sun, any watcher would have been hard pressed to discern which of them was old and which young. Otter was on the left, with his lifting-falling lope; King Boswell on the right, thick-set and broad as a bare-fist boxer in the Fancy, with two pups dancing at his heels; and between them John, shorter by a head, dimute and small, though with little narrowing where head meets neck. But from the front, with the sun shining strong upon them, their faces told a different tale. John fresh-faced, with the bloom of boyhood upon him still, clear-eyed and holding the world to its promises. The others, one dark-haired, one white-bearded, each in his own way carrying his burthen of experience upon his features.

Barely a word had been spoken between them as they drew close to the outermost edges of town. The yellow stubble fields were giving way to tanneries and ware-houses when John heard the steady hollow ringing of a horse's hooves striking the dry stones and baked earth of the road behind them.

"John! John!"

He turned and saw Mary. She was sitting side-saddle on Dobbie, her dappled cob. She sprang nimbly down and ran forwards with the reins in one hand, the horse trotting beside her. She slipped the other hand under John's arm. She pressed her lips to his cheek. King Boswell stood aside and bowed most gentlemanly. He looked first at Mary in her striped gown, her petticoat of blue printed cotton and her ribboned hat, then at the mare, that was as pretty a coloured cob as ever he'd clapped eyes upon. For a moment Wisdom was forgot in the double loveliness that beguiled his eyes.

But John and Old Otter could see that Mary was not herself. Otter was the first to speak:

"What troubles thee Mary Joyce?"

She shook her head.

"Father will not come. He has received a letter from the Earl. He risks losing all if he stands witness."

There was quiet for a moment. Then John said:

"And he has let you come alone to the assize?"

"I did not ask him. He was out upon the harvest. I took the mare and slipped away."

"He'll be unhappy when he finds you gone."

"Happy or unhappy, I'm coming with you John. I've writ him a note, though chances are he shall not find it. He lets the business of the farm over-ride his conscience, for he knows clear enough who is innocent and who guilty and would speak plainly if he dared."

****

The Sessions Court was three-fourths filled when they entered, though there was still a full hour before the Judge would make his entry. John, Old Otter and King Boswell registered themselves to the clerk as witnesses, giving names and places of residence. They found a bench in the gallery and sat and waited. The crowd pushed in through the court doors until the room was packed. And there was a clear divide between those that had come to see their own kin stand trial, and those that had come for a day's diversion; for there were some that sat quiet and said but little, and some that peeled oranges and talked merry. Mary entwined her fingers with John's. His palm was damp with sweat. The room grew hotter and hotter and there was a greasy smell that pervaded the air, of clothes too long worn, of rotten teeth, of unwashed children and shit besmirched leather. In front of them the jury's bench, the judge's seat, the witness box and the caged dock for the accused stood empty.

Then at last came the ringing of the bell. First the jury took their place, though they would be of little succour to poor Wisdom, his being a Game Case and punishable by the judge alone. They sat down upon their bench with that air of dignified self-import that signals small-mindedness and fair-play in equal measure. Then the Court Room fell quiet as Justice Ashurst made his entry. Solemn and stately in his scarlet robes lined with ermine and his full bottomed wig, his chin still greasy with breakfast, he walked to his seat. Behind him the mayor and aldermen of the soke of Peterborough took their places along the front row. They took off their tri-corn hats and rested them upon their knees.

A woman, the daughter of some gentleman, stood and curtseyed to the judge and put a nose-gay of scented flowers upon his desk to sweeten the air.

The first of the accused was brought forward. He stood chained in the dock, his head bowed. When his name was spoken he lifted his head and glowered at the room.

"William Samson. Aged thirty five. You stand accused of feloniously assaulting Luke Rowbotham between eleven and twelve in the night in a field near the King's Highway and stealing from his person three promissory ten pound notes, eight or ten shillings in silver, one silver stop-watch and various other chattels."

The case was heard. Witnesses for the prosecution said

their piece. Witnesses for the defence claimed that he was on a pauper's wage with five children to feed. The jury found him guilty.

And then the second of the accused took his place. Elizabeth Firth, aged fourteen, stood trembling before the judge, accused of 'twice administering a quantity of verdigrease powder with intent to murder Susanna, the infant daughter of George Barnes of Market Deeping.' She was found innocent, her weeping mother ran forwards to embrace her but was pushed back to her seat and told to await the afternoon.

Then came James Moody, aged twenty eight, charged with 'committing the odious and detestable crime and felony called sodomy'. He was found guilty.

Wisdom was the last to be brought up to the dock. John could see, by the rough way that the turn-keys pushed him into the cage, that he did not rank as a favourite amongst them. And when he lifted his head and looked at the judge it was with the same insolent directness of gaze that had so enraged Will Bloodworth. He is like some dog that will not be kicked into submission and refuses to be cowed. John shook his head at Wisdom, willing him to show some contrition, but it was clear that he could not see him in the ocean of faces.

If Wisdom had been thin and stringy before his arrest, he is like a skeleton now, the skin drawn tight across the bones of his face. His cheeks and chin have sprouted a first beard, as silky and raven black as his cropped hair. In his eyes there is a new smouldering light that seems to be equal parts hunger and anger. His coarse prison canvas hangs loose from the angles of his body. He is a boy no longer.

The judge tapped his gavel: "Wisdom Boswell. Aged seventeen. You stand accused of trespassing upon the Property of the Earl of Fitzwilliam, of trapping and killing one of his bucks, and of the attempted murder of a keeper of his game. How do you plead?"

Wisdom spoke quiet, but his voice carried clear to the back of the room:

"Innocent."

"On all counts?"

"I took the buck, but I fired no shot…I do not have a gun."

King Boswell stood up:

"That is the truth by God."

"Order, order! You shall have your chance to speak in due course Sir."

Then the witnesses for the prosecution were called to the box. First came the keeper who had heard the shots and met Will Bloodworth on the night of the incident, he swore his oath and said his piece. Bill Henderson spoke of Will's good character and long and steady service to the Earl. Then Will Bloodworth himself stood and rested his hand upon the Bible and swore to tell the whole truth and nothing but the truth. With a steady voice and his eyes fixed almost unblinking ahead of him he unravelled his lie, as though he knew that the pebble he had set rolling down the slope of Swordy Well had loosened another that was rolling beyond his control. As though he knew that nothing could be put back into its former place, or reneged upon. And this gave a resignation, a slow sorrow to the rise and fall of his voice that seemed to make his story ring all the more true.

As Will spoke John could feel King Boswell trembling, like a pot that is brought to the boil with its lid too tight fixed.

When he'd finished his story Will added in a whisper that seemed to hold some forlorn hope of his own redemption:

"'Twas but a small buck your honour, and when all's said and done, the bullets went wide of their mark."

"You seem inclined to give your murderer the benefit of the doubt sir, very generous-spirited for one so seriously aggrieved."

Will Bloodworth lowered his head to acknowledge the compliment.

King Boswell leapt to his feet and roared like a bull.

"Damn him for a liar! The wesh-engro will roast in Hell for this!"

The Judge pounded his gavel again.

"Order in the Court! Take him out! Take him out by God!"

From the back of the room a dozen militia-men waded through the crowd and seized King Boswell. He kicked and struggled, flailing with his arms, his dogs yapping at the ankles of his assailants, but soon they overpowered the old man and dragged him through the doors. He turned and shouted over his shoulder.

"Kiss my blind cheeks. There'll be a reckoning for this. No Boswell forgets a lie."

When order had been restored the judge turned to Will Bloodworth again:

"Do you have anything to add?"

Will was trembling like a leaf. King Boswell's interruption had woken his secret terrors and he suddenly felt the weight of his own damnation. It was as though it was he that was condemned and Wisdom the accuser.

"Don't hang him your honour..."

The Court Room quietened. Will's voice was cracked so that it slipped into a high falsetto:

"He's but a boy when all's said and done..."

Judge Ashurst looked him up and down:

"And you fear for your soul, perhaps, having lied under oath and committed perjury?"

He turned to the Aldermen and whispered:

"I've seen it before, by God. I've seen it before."

Will pulled himself together, seeing his own liberty hanging in the balance before him:

"No, no your honour, I have spoke truth…"

He swallowed and turned to the judge:

"I ask only for clemency."

The judge raised his eye-brows:

"Most affecting, sir. Most affecting to be sure."

Will stepped down from the witness box. Bill Bullimore took his place and told how Wisdom had been arrested in the camp on Langdyke Bush. The picture he painted of the Boswell crew was not a pretty one, and was given substance by the rage of King Boswell that still hung in the air like a thundercloud. He ended his testimony:

"For my part I firmly believe, your honour, that this tribe of wandering vagabonds should be made outlaws in every kingdom."

The judge sighed and lifted the nose-gay to his face, then mopped his forehead with a handkerchief.

"There is one more testimony I understand."

Robert Smethwick, secretary to the Earl of Fitzwilliam, stepped forward then, dressed in the Earl's livery, wigged and spectacled. He swore his oath and then unfolded a piece of paper.

"I have this, your honour, from the Earl of Fitzwilliam: *'William Bloodworth has worked as a trusted keeper upon my estate for full twenty years, he has executed his work with skill and I have never had reason to doubt him.'* There we have it."

"Do we have any witnesses for the defence of the accused?"

John Clare and Old Otter got to their feet and came forward. Each in turn entered the box and said his piece, telling in his own way the story of Rogation Day, each testifying to Wisdom's character, each swearing that he had never possessed any fire-arm. The heat in the Session Court, as the morning approached full noon, was near unbearable now. The judge fanned himself with his sheaf of papers. Old Otter spoke plain and forthright and very loud as is his custom, being one who is used to talk across furlong and common. John, overwhelmed by the eyes fixed upon him, talked down into his shirt so that only those in the first rows could follow him, but for those that could catch his drift it was a testament as to how he considered the race of gypsies to be misunderstood and unfairly maligned and Wisdom more so than any, he being young and strong and never shy of work nor play.

When John had finished, the judge spoke:

"We have two sides of an argument here. I hold the scales of Justice in my hand and into one pan I put the testimony of two keepers, a constable and the Earl of Fitzwilliam. Into the other I drop the words of a squatter upon the common, a landless labourer and the intemperate ranting of an old gypsy who had needs be dragged from the Court. Is it any wonder which carries the greater weight?"

He banged his gavel and looked across at Wisdom.

"I have no hesitation, Sir, in finding you guilty on all charges."

He looked into the Court Room and smiled.

"Now Ladies and Gentlemen we will adjourn for luncheon and I will return this afternoon to pass sentence."

****

It was two hours after noon that Justice Ashurst returned to the

Sessions Court, refreshed from his luncheon and the several glasses of claret that had washed it down. Every eye was on his hands as he made his entrance. Would he be wearing the spotless white gloves that signalled a Maiden Assize? He was not. He took his place at the desk. He cleared his throat:

"It is the King's earnest desire, as well as his truest intent, that all his subjects be easy and happy. He places his greatest security and glory in the preservation of the laws of his kingdom and the liberties of his people. Without order how miserable must be their condition? Without order surely every man's lust, his avarice, his revenge, his contempt for property and his vaunting ambition would become a law unto itself. It is with these thoughts in mind that I ask the officers of law to bring in the accused."

The four prisoners were brought into the cage. The judge looked at them. There was a long silence. And then he spoke, his voice momentous.

"Elizabeth Firth... you have been found innocent and blameless and I hereby acquit you with no besmirchment upon your name or character and I do set you free."

There was a clicking and rattling as the turn-keys unfastened the manacles from the girl's wrists, the door of the cage was opened and Elizabeth Firth ran sobbing into her mother's arms.

"Sam Moody....you have been found guilty of a filthy and despicable act that would shame even the beasts of the field. I do therefore sentence you to twelve lashes, twelve hours in the public stock and seven years transportation."

"Oh Sam, no!"

From the gallery Sam Moody's mother keened out her shame and sorrow. Two men led her from the Court.

Then the judge reached down and picked up the black cap.

A deep silence filled the Court. He passed it solemnly from hand to hand.

"There are transgressions that are unpardonable upon earth."

He turned and fixed his eyes upon the accused, waiting until every last echo of his words had left the room.

"William Samson and Wisdom Boswell, you both are found guilty of an assault upon property and an attempt upon life - that most sacred and sweetest of gifts.

That neither of your victims perished is due to providence rather than intent. Were you guilty of mere theft, whether of game or monies, I might have been more disposed to mercy. That Luke Rowbotham crawled bloodied from his assault and raised the alarum; that William Bloodworth felt only the wind of the shot that was intended for his heart, does nothing to soften the gravity of your wicked and sinful acts. Greed for gain and contempt for life have conspired, in both your cases, to bring you before me, and were I to spare you 'twould make an example that would spread a contagion of lawlessness throughout the land."

He paused and took a breath.

"But because of his youth, and because of the heart-felt pleading of his intended victim on his behalf, in the case of Mr Wisdom Boswell I have stepped back from the ultimate sanction."

He turned to Wisdom:

"It is ordered and adjudged, that you shall be transported upon the seas to such a place as His Majesty shall think fit to direct and appoint, for the term of your natural life."

He lifted the black cap, then, and fitted it carefully to his head.

"And as for you, Mr William Samson, poverty can be no

excuse. On Wednesday next you will be taken to a place of execution and there hanged by the neck until dead, so help me God."

William Samson crumpled to the floor and sobbed like a child. The turn-keys jerked him to his feet again. Wisdom merely opened his mouth as though to speak. Then he closed it and turned away from the silent eyes that scrutinised him.

****

On the outer edges of the Milton Estate Will Bloodworth walked briskly homewards along the ride beneath the dappled shade of the beeches that were beginning to turn to their autumn browns and yellows. There was an ease in his manner, a lilt to his stride that had eluded him these last months. He knew that he would be ribbed by Bill Henderson for pleading on a gypsy's behalf. He knew Bill wanted Wisdom and his kind to swing like stoats and weasels on a keeper's gibbet. But for Will Bloodworth the verdict was neat and trim as a well sewn seam. He settled down on a stile and scraped his pipe clean with a piece of twig. He filled it from his pouch, struck fire and sucked it to life. Yes, the damned gypsy youth had been properly rewarded and there was to be no hanging to trouble his conscience. He blew a mouthful of smoke into the warm evening air and got up to his feet. Life was sweet again and he its master, and the cold dread of the court-house and his glimpse of damnation all but forgotten.

8

Harvest (Horkey)

Farmer Joyce had been overseeing the thatching of the last of the ricks in his yard. He watched the four men on their ladders that were set against the round bastion of straw. He watched them as they passed the coils of sisal rope from one to the other and pulled the knots true, fastening an intricate web and weighing it with stones so that the rush thatch was held firm over the precious corn until the time came for threshing. As they climbed down he surveyed his fourteen golden ricks, like round towers with conical rooves, a testament to the labours of the year. Behind them stood the green-grey rise of his hay stacks. And behind them the steep point of Glinton church spire rose up against the sky, its pale barnack stone yellow in the afternoon sunlight. To Farmer Joyce rick, stack and steeple seemed all of apiece.

He was uneasy. He knew there was a chance that the Boswell youth would be hanged. He'd seen the gifts that are bestowed upon visiting judges by the gentry: the sides of venison, the beef and carp and pheasant that fill their coaches on their return to London. He did not cling to any great hope for clemency. He was uneasy, too, that he had incurred the Earl's displeasure. Out loud he addressed his men:

"We've done our best lads, and the best can do no more... We'll call it a day now."

As the men went their ways he put his hand to Will Farrell's shoulder.

"Will, could you spare me a few more minutes?"

Will shrugged:

"Aye."

"Would ye do me the kindness of reaching into one of the ricks and breaking off an ear of wheat."

Will Farrell thrust an arm shoulder-deep into a rick. He felt for an ear and twisted it. He pulled it out and held it on his palm as though he had guddled a little golden fish from a deep stream.

"Bring it to the kitchen Will."

The two men made their way to the farm-house kitchen. The fire was smouldering as always, despite the heat of the day. Farmer Joyce crouched down and with the iron fire-shovel he scooped up the smouldering embers and threw them to the back of the fireplace. He swept the front of the hot red-brick hearth clean with a brush. Then he straightened himself, went to one of the shelves against the wall and took a piece of paper and a goose-feather quill. He did not notice Mary's note that had lain unread all day upon the kitchen table.

"Now Will, I'll show ye a secret that my father showed me, and his father showed him before. Break the ear apart and blow the chaff away."

Will rubbed the ear between his hands just as Ben Price had done the day before. He blew away the chaff so that there was a little cluster of grains against his leathery palm.

"Say no word of this to the Parson Will, for it has a savour of witchery to it...but my old Grand-Sire swore by it. Now, take one of the grains and throw her onto the hearth. She's for

September see."

Will threw the grain onto the hot brick, it lay for a moment then leapt back towards them. Farmer Joyce dipped his quill into an ink-pot and scratched some words onto the paper.

"That means the price of grain will rise in September. Now, throw October down."

The grain lay still and did not move.

"October prices will stay steady."

Another grain was dropped.

"As will November."

December's grain jumped towards the fire.

"They'll drop in December by God!"

Another.

"And rise in January!"

Grain after grain was thrown onto the hot bricks and each prediction noted down.

Will had just dropped June's grain onto the hearth when the door was thrown open and Mary came running into the kitchen. She spoke no word but ran to her father. She pressed her face into the familiar, smoky, sweaty, stiff linen of his shirt. He could feel the wet warmth of her breath and tears through the cloth and against his skin and he held her firm.

"There, there child."

His forehead was folded into a frown, his voice was but a whisper. A sign his workers knew well and marked with caution:

"The last of the grains must wait Will."

Will Farrell tipped the last of the yellow grains carefully into a saucer and set it on the mantleshelf. He tip-toed out of the room.

Farmer Joyce pressed his lips to the top of Mary's head. She whispered:

"I went father, I went to the assize..."

"I feared as much...what was the verdict Mary?"

It was a while before she pulled her face away from his shirt and found the words:

"He is to be transported...for ever...for life...we shall never see him again."

For a moment Farmer Joyce was of one accord with Will Bloodworth, a sweet relief flooded over him. Then a sense of the cruel gravity of the sentence dawned on him, the terrible journey to the ends of the earth, the endless years of hard labour that sooner or later would break body and spirit.

"It is a harsh sentence Mary, a harsh sentence."

Outside in the yard Mary's mare, Dobbie, untied and dusty from the road, stooped her head to the water trough. Will Farrell took her reins and led her to the stable.

****

Today has been the last of the harvest. The day broke with but one small stand of wheat still waiting on Lolham Bridge Field. But though it should have been a day of ease and joy with the promise of largesse and horkey writ large in every heart, it was a sombre village that woke to the harvest horn.

Sorrows rarely come singly, and as the news of Wisdom Boswell's sentence was reaching the village yesterday afternoon and casting its solemn shadow, the Turnills suffered a setback that has cost them dear.

Dick and Bob Turnill had been leading a loaded cart back to their yard from Lolham Bridge Field when the bank beside Green Dyke gave way and the piled load lurched out of true. The cart tipped its grain into the dyke and one of the horses fell with his full weight upon his collar. He was struggling so fierce that none could get close enough to cut him free. Soon he was strangled, his tongue lolling between his teeth. Many had rallied to rake the soaked straw from the dyke and lay it to dry again, but a broken cart, a dead gelding and half a wagon-load of corn are a higher toll than Bob Turnill can afford to pay, as all the parish knows. It is a harsh God that he prays to so avid.

And there is a third sorrow too in the fence-posts and quick-thorn seedlings that wait on the moment when the harvest largesse is finished and autumn comes riding across the fields in her russets and ochres, red as the leaves of the dock and brown as its steeples of seed.

John and Parker Clare walked silently out to the field this morning. The other men were muted too, avoiding John's eye. For although most believed that the gypsy had reaped his just deserts, the transportation of a known man puts a quiet on the busiest tongue. There was not the usual babble of talk among the women either, rather a whispered, subdued gossiping. The children, though, ran and whooped as oblivious to care as the barking village dogs.

When they reached the stand of wheat the old rhythms of harvest that have governed these months of high summer were a balm to John's heart, for they demanded no more than the song of whet-stone to blade and the mindless drudgery of hard labour. Yesterday's sharp sorrow was numbed by an aching shoulder and a sweating back. Slowly and steadily as the morning progressed the wheat diminished in front of him and the stooks gathered behind.

It was mid-morning, when the wheat was all but taken, that a hare leapt out from between the stalks and dodged between the legs of the men. It was one of this year's leverets, full grown but gangly still, sleek and brown, its black-tipped ears tilted back against its shoulders. The reapers' dogs, lying under the stooks, jumped to their feet and set to barking.

Richard Royce dropped his scythe and dived across the stubble. He caught the creature by a hind leg. He scrambled to his feet laughing. The hare, its eyes bulging, crying most pitiful, kicked and struggled beneath his red fist.

"Here's supper lads!"

John has seen this a thousand times. Coneys, hares, maybe a fox or a marten, bolting from the stands of wheat or barley, have been fair sport for reapers since harvest first began. But this morning the sight of the hare twisting and whimpering in Richard's grasp was more than he could bear. He dropped his scythe and stepped forwards to him.

"Let it be, Richard."

Richard Royce looked at him and laughed.

"Let it be jugged, John Clare!"

John's voice was trembling, on the edge of tears.

"I'm asking you to let it be, set it free Richard."

Richard Royce cocked his head to one side:

"Just because your gypsy pal should've pissed when he couldn't whistle, it don't follow that the rest of us go hungry."

John clenched his fists.

"Set…it…free."

Richard Royce looked down at John. There was no laughter playing on his features now.

"I'll break its fucking neck, then I'll break yours."

John's voice was a whisper.

"Set it free Richard."

Parker came across and put his hand to John's arm, but John shook his father away.

"Set it free."

"Alright John Clare. I'll set the fucker free."

He put his other hand to the leg he was holding and with a sharp crack he broke the hare's leg. He flung the shrieking creature to his lurcher, who had its neck between his teeth and was joyfully shaking its life away in moments.

"How d'ye like that?"

"This much!"

John's first punch caught Richard Royce so hard and sudden on the chin that he bit through his lip. A second smashed against his neck and sent him reeling. All John knew was white blazing rage. He jumped forward and began to pummel Richard's chest with his fists. Richard had caught his balance now. He seized John's hair with one hand jerked his head back and with the other fist smashed him on the cheek below the eye. Then he grabbed John's throat and hurled him so hard backwards that he staggered across the stubble and crashed into a stook of corn. As John tried to scramble to his feet Richard ran forwards and kicked him with a boot to his temple. John fell back and the stook collapsed on top of him. Richard Royce lifted his fingers to his mouth and whistled. His dog ran forwards with the limp hare swinging from his mouth. He took it in his hand and held it high.

"Nothing comes twixt me an' my supper."

He turned to the women and grinned, blood spilling from his lip and dripping from his chin. They stood and looked at him, and there was not one of them that returned his smile.

"My missus will vouch for that."

Sally Royce shook her head ruefully.

"There's none as'll argue with that Richard."

Richard returned to the stand of wheat and picked up his scythe.

"Back to work lads. The harvest's damn near done. We

could have the Old Sow down before dinner."

The men, without a word, sharpened their scythes and set to work. Not one of them, not even Parker Clare, looked over his shoulder to where John lay under the sheaves, curled up like a child, his hands covering his face. Each of them knew well enough that the world often takes the form of a hard fist, and there's no words can soften that understanding.

The women also worked around the fallen stook as though John wasn't there. Their seeming indifference was, in truth, a sort of kindliness, for no dabbing of handkerchieves could mend this hurt.

Only Dick Turnill came to John. He crouched beside him with a leather bottle of water in his hand.

"John."

John peered out of the wheat straw. Already two purple bruises were spreading across his temple and his cheek.

"Have a sup John."

John crawled out and shook the straw from his hair and shoulders. He took the bottle and drank, then he tipped some water over his throbbing face. Dick whispered.

"I heard about Wisdom."

There was a silence between them. They sat for some minutes and watched the men swinging their scythes.

"'Tis a harsh injustice."

John drank some more.

"And I heard about your gelding, Dick."

Dick Turnill lowered his head and sighed.

"Ay. Father was on his knees all night. Like Job."

"There's injustice and there's bad luck and I ain't sure where one bleeds into the other."

The two friends got to their feet and set the stook upright. The women watched them without reproval. And Betsy

Jackson, her arms wrapped around a sheaf, looked upon John with a new tenderness, for she had heard of his sorrow, and she had seen that he did not lack courage, and she had seen that he was hurt, and now she saw him brush his hurt aside. And all conspired in her breast to a soft affection that ached to rock him in her arms.

And then the shout went up:

"Old Sow! Old Sow! Old Sow!"

The last stalks of wheat were standing naked in the field.

John Close, catching wind that the work was nearly done, had ridden across the field to the men. He pulled a tangle of bright ribbons from his pocket, climbed down from the saddle and bound the stalks together. Then Richard Royce, the Lord of the Harvest, his shirt stained with dry blood, swung his scythe and brought the last stand toppling down. The men and women gathered in a circle around him and cheered. He lifted the ribboned sheaf high above his head:

"I have it! I have it!"

The final sheaf of the long months of harvest was cut at last.

****

And now it is the Horkey in John Close's barn. The parish settles itself down to eat and drink as food and ale are set beneath the nose of every man and woman.

At the end table closest to the door, John Clare sits with Parker, Ann and Sophie. Old Otter and Kitty have joined them, and she has put a compress to the side of John's face that is so swollen now that he is lop-sided as a three-quarter moon. Dick Turnill sits with them too. Old Otter looks across at John from time to time and shakes his head most sorrowful, his voice booming out above the other talk like a bittern upon the marsh:

"We done what we could Johnny, we done what we could."

The other villagers fight shy of the Clares.

When all have eaten the paupers are called in to take their fill. From the high table there comes the call for a dance. I see Old Otter look across at John and raise an eyebrow. John shakes his head:

"Not tonight."

Betsy Jackson, Jonathan Burbridge and Sam Billings take their places on the tumbrel at the end of the barn. Then Old Otter climbs up beside them and pulls his fiddle from beneath his jerkin.

John turns to Dick:

"Don't mind me Dick, you play if you've a mind to."

So Dick Turnill, a little uneasy, climbs up and takes his place beside them, not liking to think of himself playing reels while his parents pray and his friend nurses his bitter hurt, but not liking either to miss the chance of a tune.

When the parish poor have crammed the left-overs into their mouths, the boards and trestles are pushed back against the walls and the dancers begin to mill about on the floor and wait for the band to strike up the first tune. Old Otter raises his hand to the crowd:

"Cast your mind back a year friends. We had a fiddler with us then as could lift a tune for dancin' like no other… you'll all know who I'm speakin' of, and would that he was here with us tonight."

All evening Richard Royce, on his throne at the high table, with the ribboned Old Sow swinging above his head, has been downing mug after mug of harvest ale. Now he stands unsteady and bellows back:

"Ay, and if there was any justice he'd be dancing the Tyburn Frisk come Wednesday!"

An uneasy silence falls on the barn. There are nods from many, while on the tumbrel Sam Billings and Old Otter tighten their fists. There is a moment when it seems the harvest accord might fall apart and a fight begin. But then Sally Royce pushes through the crowd to the high table, she stands before her husband and, with every eye of the village upon her, she lifts her hand and slaps him hard across the face.

"There. We've all heard enough of your prattle for one day."

He looks at her in astonishment then slumps back onto his throne and from the tumbrel at the far end of the barn the band strikes up 'Drowsy Maggie'.

John Clare sits as the band plays and the dancers step their measure. His head is leaning against the stone of the barn wall, one eye watches but the other is half sealed with the swelling of cheek and brow. Not even the harvest ale can ease his hurt. Parker moves along the bench and puts his arm around John's shoulder.

"Come on son, let's get thee home."

The two of them get up to their feet. Ann Clare catches Parker's eye and nods. Father and son slip un-noticed through the barn door and make their way along the village street. The autumn constellations are clear overhead: to the east the Tailor's Yard-band, to the north Charles's Wain with its three bright stallions and high above the orison the Shepherd's Lamp shines its solitary light, all innocent of the flickering and dimming of human lives.

9

Michaelmas

Yesterday was Bridge Fair in Peterborough, and for those that have been promised another full year's employ and are secure in their appointments, it was a high holiday.

On Joyce's farm each man and woman in turn was called into the parlour - Will, John, Nathan, Kate, Lizzie, Hope and the rest - each hand was shaken, a silver florin pressed into it, and each of them was taken on for another year. It was a similar tale in John Close's farm house, though 'twas but a shilling given. But poor Bob Turnill has laid off all his men, for he knows he does not have money enough to pay even a pauper's wage. For them, as for many another, it was the Michaelmas hiring that drew them to the Fair.

For the Clares it was a cheerful morning. Ann has promise of work at Close's Farm. Sophie has been taken on in his dairy. Parker has sold the pears from the tree that spreads its shade behind the cottage and made up his Michaelmas rent. And John and Parker were easy in the knowledge that the enclosure work would provide for them this winter. The day of the Fair stretched before them with all its bright promise.

They set off early. Dressed as fine as they were able, with Ann and Sophie in bright cotton gowns and aprons and ribbons in their hats, and John and Parker with new handkerchiefs about their throats, not to mention John's new winter boots that he has bought with his harvest fee.

Sam Billings stopped his cart and offered them a lift to town, and they were happy to climb up and hunker down on a heap of sacks with their backs to the rattling barrels he was delivering.

"Wheeee-up Billy!"

As they trundled along the Peterborough Road, Ann put her arm around Sophie's shoulders and sang softly to her.

Behind and before them a thickening throng was making its way to Peterborough: some on foot, some on horse-back, some in gigs or carts, carriages or phaetons. The air was full of the clatter of hooves and the rattling and splashing of iron-rimmed wheels over the muddy tracks. And from all sides came the sound of voices lifted in expectation of all that the day might hold, men's voices, women's and children's calling deep and shrill to one another as they left the fields behind and made their way through the city streets to Town Bridge and the meadow beyond.

When they reached the fair John and Parker thanked Sam Billings for the ride.

"Good luck friends," Sam twitched the corner of his mouth and winked, "I hope Mr Ben Price is feeling kindly disposed this morning."

They climbed down from the cart and cut straight across the meadow to the Hiring Fair where they knew Ben would be looking for labourers. They wound between clusters of shepherds, farriers, cow-men, house-maids, grooms and milk-maids, all of them seeking appointments that would fetch a few pence more than those they left behind; each of them, with crook or whip or pail, carrying some token of their trade.

In the far corner of the field a crowd of men was already gathered. There were many that John and Parker knew from Helpston, Glinton, and the villages close-by. But there were others that they'd never clapped eyes on before, for there are those that follow the enclosures from place to place and settle only as long as the work lasts.

Ben Price, in the Earl's livery, his hands clasped behind his back, was standing beside a polished table. Seated, with his legs tucked under the table, was a clerk with his eyes fixed upon a ledger and a wooden box inlaid with brass. Ben shook a little bell and as it tinkled all fell quiet.

"The Earl of Fitzwilliam offers his employ this winter, from October to April, to any able-bodied man as'll assist with the enclosure of the parishes of Maxey, Northborough, Glinton, Etton and Helpston. The wage will be one shilling and six pence per working day. And each man that commits himself shall receive from the Earl, as an earnest of his good faith, one silver florin. And any that breaks his bond will be brought to Court and fined according. Now then, now then, make a tidy line please gentlemen that we may choose them most fitted for the task at hand and take down names and full particulars."

John and Parker joined the line, and being tanned and muscled from the long labours of the summer, they were duly taken on. The clerk opened his polished box, gave them each their florin and scratched their names into his book.

"John Clare, aye, of Woodgate, Helpston. And Parker Clare of the above. Good, good."

Ben Price shook them by the hand.

"Monday next, and not a minute after seven."

Then he caught a glimpse of the mending bruises on the side of John's head.

"You ain't been fighting have ye?"

"'Twas a horse Mr Price."

"Good. 'Cause we'll have none of that caper in my teams."

Behind them in the line was Jem Farrar, Ben Price took one look at him and turned him away.

"What, are you making a monkey of me! I doubt you could lift a mallet let alone crack a stone!"

"Have pity Mr Price, you're all that stands between me and the parish."

"Pity be damned, Jem Farrar, is the Earl running an estate or an alms house? Away with ye!"

As John and Parker pocketed their florins and turned away they saw Dick Turnill waiting in line.

"Dick. What are you doing here?"

John looked into Dick's face.

"You look spent."

"I'm doing the same as thee John."

"But why? You've got your father's fields to farm? He'll need you more than ever this autumn."

Dick shook his head:

"He'll need this little pinch of money more. He borrowed over the odds to enclose his entitlement, and he's borrowed again to buy a new gelding…he vows he can plough his fields himself. And though the wheat that was raked from the dyke is spoiled he reckons there's enough in the ricks to see him through the winter, and he blames his past sinning for all that's gone amiss…and when he ain't working he's on his knees."

Parker put his hand to Dick's arm:

"'These are hard times for poor Bob, but maybe his God'll see him through Dick."

"Maybe he will but..."

He looked at them both most candid:

"...To tell ye the truth, I'd sooner be shifting stones and planting hedges with you boys than watching him and poor mother breaking their backs...and giving thanks for it."

"Ay." Said John with a sigh.

"And if I work six days that's nine shillings a week, and they'll need every penny of it for already their creditors are hammering at the door."

"True enough, they will," said Parker. "But Dick, today's a holiday and soon you'll have a florin tucked into your palm...you'll allow yourself a little of the rigs and jigs of Michaelmas...you'll join us for a penny pot and a chop... it'll give you strength for tramping home, and the rest will be rattling in your pocket yet."

"Ay Dick," said John. "That's two bright shillings over the odds!"

He laid a gentle punch to Dick's shoulder and Dick grinned. He has always looked up to John as to a brother. And, in truth, they are of a kind, both being book-learned and candlelight scholars.

John and Parker made a winding, looping progress through the fairground. They passed blacksmiths, cart-builders and wheel-wrights with their displays of ploughs, tumbrels, wains and wheels of all sizes. They passed horse and cattle dealers. Parker paused to buy a ginger-bread for Sophie. John leaned over a table of old books, chap-books and ballad sheets. He picked up a battered leather-bound volume that spilled its pages as he lifted it. He read the spine aloud:

"*Paradise Lost.*"

The bookseller looked up at John, a little surprised to see a labourer, of an age to have an eye for little but ale and wenches, turning such a book over in his big hands.

"It has fallen apart by Book Twelve....but the best of it's

over by then my friend."

John pushed the pages back between the covers.

"How much?"

"Thruppence."

John looked at Parker, who shrugged. He handed his florin across and took the change. He slipped the book into a pocket.

They wandered on past gypsies, past tea-stalls and coffee stalls, past ale benches and roasting hogs. Parker is as short of stature as John, but stiffer in his gait and bald of head where John's brown curls spill down beneath his battered hat. And if you were to look close into their faces you'd see that Parker's mouth is thinner as if resigned to the hand of twos and threes that fate has dealt, while John's is full lipped and eager to play his trump and sup his winnings down.

They lingered for a while at a sparring match. Five gold sovereigns were on offer to any man who could stay five rounds in the ring, bare-fist fighting with Johnny Jones, a blackamoor giant with fists the size of coal-scuttles. They watched two swarthy country boys go down with bloodied noses and cheered the victor, for both John and Parker have a taste for the Fancy.

"Here's the man for Richard Royce!"

"Ay!"

They passed a velvet curtained booth in which could be viewed, for sixpence, the fattest man in Europe.

They passed cobblers and clothiers and drapers. They passed tables laden with glass lanterns, cracked crockery and cutlery. John bought a little pocket knife with a horn handle.

They found Ann and Sophie by the bird stalls. The wicker cages were swinging from a long pole and filled with canaries, goldfinches, linnets, warblers, all manner of pigeons and doves, ornamental pheasants and peacocks. And lined on a perch beside them, hooded and fastened, were falcons for sporting gentlemen.

Sophie ran to meet them with a fistful of bright feathers she'd gathered from the ground.

"Look at these! Ain't they lovely?"

Parker stroked her cheek with the back of his hand.

"Aye, they're lovely pet, but would be lovelier yet if all these doors were opened and every bird was free to the wind."

For Parker is of a mind with John concerning caged birds.

Sophie turned to John:

"Do you remember Tom, John?"

John nodded.

"How you did whack poor puss upon the nose whenever she came close to him until she fought shy, and Tom would perch upon my finger tip and take crumbs from my hand and flutter free about the house."

"Ay," said Ann. "And he never knew a cage, and then when poor puss had her kittens drowned she took him as her own and caressed him most kind and pressed her nose to his red breast."

"And she brought him mice," said Sophie. "And laid them at his feet, and he would flutter up and sit upon her head."

They turned away from the cages.

"Poor Tom," said John. "And we never found out who it was killed poor Cock Robin…though I reckon he took some other cat to be as mild as our puss."

They walked away from the caged birds and stopped at a stall where they bought food and ale and sugared water for Sophie. Dick Turnill joined them. Parker passed him a hunk of mutton on a crust:

"Don't be chastising yourself Dick. Get that down your

neck....and buy yourself a pot of ale."

As they were finishing their meal and wiping the grease from the corners of their mouths, Farmer Joyce strolled past with Mary on his arm. When Mary saw John she tugged at her father's arm:

"John! Papa, here is John Clare and his family!"

Farmer Joyce was dressed in his accustomed best: frock-coat, swansdown waistcoat and breeches tucked into polished top-boots. He turned his red face towards the Clares. On this high holiday he was determined to bear the world nothing but goodwill.

Ann Clare, flustered and discomfited, got up and brushed the crumbs from her lap. She curtseyed. Parker shook the farmer's proffered hand.

"A very good day to ye both…and to you John Clare."

John shifted uneasily from foot to foot.

"Good day sir."

"We'll have no sir-ing here John...there's too much damned sir-ing in this world already, what do you say Mr Clare?"

He turned and fixed his eyes on Parker.

Parker Clare met the farmer's gaze.

"Ay, that is my opinion."

"A man can make his money, by God, without expecting every other soul to fawn before him like a frightened dog. We are all the sons of Adam after all. There ain't much to choose between us."

"Ay."

Farmer Joyce leaned forwards and patted the battered book that was jutting out of John's coat pocket.

"My Mary tells me your John has a good head on his shoulders, for all he comes with his pockets stuffed with hokum-pokum."

Ann Clare curtseyed again:

"He's a scholar, is John, and can unriddle any page you put under his nose."

"Good, good, I'm glad to hear it, but a little cleverness never filled a larder. A good head ain't worth a straw without stout arms and legs to do its bidding, what do you say John?"

John nodded uneasily and said nothing. The farmer turned to Parker again.

"I judge a man by what he can bring to table, for there is the true measure of his good sense."

Mary pulled her father's arm then:

"Papa, can I show John the French prisoners?"

Farmer Joyce gestured with his hand:

"Very well Mary, away with the pair of ye!"

When they were gone he lowered his voice:

"Ay, there's the measure, and your John, for all his ABCs, must add some pounds to his ounces before I give him countenance…I don't mind him at my table, but he's a long mile to travel has that youth, a very long mile… though I grant he showed some pluck with the Boswell boy."

Parker nodded:

"It was a harsh verdict."

The farmer's voice dropped to a whisper:

"A few lashes might have been in order for taking the sixth part of a buck…but the gypsy has paid an over-heavy price. Transportation is a bitter journey and there's many don't survive it, let alone what waits beyond. But at least he still has the breath in his body, and he's young and strong. The law is an ass Mr Clare, and there are times when we should treat its loud hee-haws with the contempt they deserve..."

Then he raised his voice again:

"But the day is fine and all the fun of the Fair awaits us.

There's a bull that has been bred at Holkham that I would dearly love to let loose among my cows...I must show it to Nathan Cushion...I'll bid you farewell."

****

"Have you seen them? There is such a display! Come!"

Mary steered John through the Fair.

"They have been brought, all chained and manacled, from Norman Cross, poor things. But John, they have made such carvings from wood and bone as you would not believe."

They pushed through the milling crowd to a corner of the Fair he had not seen.

A great display had been made of the three French prisoners. They had shackles to their ankles that were joined to iron chains that were bolted to heavy iron balls. These in turn rested upon a tattered French flag that lay, mud-besmirched at the prisoners' feet. They were sitting at a table with the Union Jack flapping on its pole over their cropped heads. To either side a soldier stood guard, dressed in the full regalia of the Northampton militia, with musket and sword at the ready.

The prisoners were dressed in old canvas shirts and trousers, with wooden clogs to their feet. The scene would have struck fear into the heart of any Boney-loving traitor, were it not for the friendly ease with which victors and vanquished shared their tobacco, and filled the air with sweet smoke.

The people of Peterborough were not so kindly disposed, and the babble of talk around the stall was thick with shouted insult, for there's many have not come home from the French Wars. And Boneparte still struts his bold tyranny as cock-sure as ever you please.

But the prisoners took no notice of the crowd, they eyed

the girls, whistled, waved, made faces and held up their wares to any that lingered. John and Mary pushed to the front of the crowd.

"Look John!"

The table was covered in wonders. There were woven flowers of straw and coloured wood. There were tiny ships of bone, fully rigged with cotton sails. There were carved eagles. There was a likeness of Peterborough Cathedral fashioned from different shaded woods. There were children's toys: spinning tops, painted soldiers and chickens that pecked the ground when they were tilted forwards. There was a tiny guillotine with a blade that fell and chopped off a man's head so that it rolled into a basket.

One of the soldiers waved his pipe in the direction of the table and shouted at the crowd:

"All the work of Frenchie prisoners. Roll up and see. Every item for sale."

Mary pointed to a man and woman made of bone who stood facing each other on a little wooden platform. One of the prisoners picked it up by its handle. He looked at Mary and smiled:

"L'amour!"

Underneath the ground the figures stood upon, a wooden ball hung on two threads. As the prisoner swung it from side to side the little bone man bent forwards at the waist and kissed the woman, then, as the man straightened, the woman bent forward and kissed the man. Backwards and forwards they kissed and kissed again: click clack, click clack.

Mary laughed out loud with delight:

"Oh John, look!"

John took it and tried it himself. Again and again the little marionettes met lip to lip: click clack.

"How much?"

These were words the Frenchman understood.

"Deux...two...two sheeeling."

"Two shillings," said a soldier. "But it's yours, today, for the knock-down price of one silver florin."

It was more than John could spare, but he had the last of his harvest fee in his pocket, along with all that was left of his advance. He pulled the coins from his pocket and counted them out onto his palm.

"Here you are."

He handed four sixpences across the table.

"Merci."

The prisoner looked up at John and Mary and his eyes misted for a moment with tenderness. Then he winked.

"Un moment."

He picked up a sharp little knife and started scratching words onto the wooden ground at the feet of the little woman in beautiful, curling, tilted script. He lifted the wood to his lips and, as though he was kissing it, blew away the dust.

"Bon."

The other two prisoners peered across at it.

John took it from him and showed it to Mary. She read aloud:

"AMOR VINCIT OMNIA. I have enough of Merrishaw's Latin to understand that."

She looked at the Frenchman and smiled such a sweet smile that for a moment he glimpsed a memory of sunlight through the endless cloud of English imprisonment. Then she whispered shyly:

"Love conquers all."

The prisoner jumped to his feet and bowed setting the iron shackles rattling and clanking beneath the table. The other prisoners laughed, but he turned to them and raised both his hands:

"C'est vrai...c'est vrai!"

He took the carving from her, wrapped it up with a great display of tenderness and tied it with string. He gave it back to Mary.

John and Mary turned from the stall and walked away arm in arm. They bought a bag of apples, found a quiet place and sat down on the grass. Mary rested her cheek on John's shoulder and munched an apple as he untied the string and unfolded the coloured cloth that wrapped the carving. He pulled his new knife from his pocket and with the point of it scratched into the ground beneath the feet of the little bone man, in letters more crude of manner than the Frenchman's flourishes: JCMARY♥1811

"There."

He passed it to her.

"'Tis for thee, Mary."

She wrapped it up and put it carefully into the little bag that hung from her shoulder.

"I shall keep it always."

She kissed his cheek.

"And now I must find my father."

"And I must find mine."

She kissed him and turned, he caught her hand, pulled her towards himself and they kissed again. She laughed:

"Click clack."

She ran into the crowd and quickly disappeared.

John walked towards the bridge. He was thinking to himself that from that vantage he would be able to look down on the mass of people and maybe catch a glimpse of Parker, Ann and Sophie. He climbed the slope of the bridge, leaned on the stone parapet and looked back at the jostling crowd with its myriad shifting colours. He listened to the strains of fiddles and pipes, the shouts and the deep murmur of babbling talk, the whinnying of horses and the lowing of prize bulls, the shrieks of children and the flapping of canvas. All the sounds mingled in John's ears and became a strange music that he both longed to be a part of, and at the same time longed to be far away from – deep in his own sweet solitudes. He closed his eyes and enjoyed the tugging contradiction of his secret heart, basking also in the thought that somewhere in the swirl of sound was Mary's voice.

Suddenly his reverie was broken by his own name:

"John Clare!"

He turned and saw Betsy Jackson tripping up the bridge behind him. She was dressed for the Fair with her fitted jacket drawn tight about the waist so that her breasts – under their striped neckerchief – swelled above it, and her hips – under their white petticoats – swelled ripe and rounded below. Her curls spilled out from under a lace cap. She was a little unsteady on her feet. She drew closer to John than good manners would allow on any other day of the year. Her voice was loud:

"I've been celebrating with the girls John, for John Close has took us all on for another year and has added five shillings to my wage."

John could smell the gin on her breath. She reached out and steadied herself on the parapet of the bridge with her strong, working hand.

"Was that your little sister I saw you with just now?"

John shook his head, innocent of her design.

"No, that was Mary Joyce."

Then he added with a certain note of pride for he had never spoke it aloud before:

"She is my sweetheart."

"Oh, but she seemed such a little shrimp of a thing John. And now she is run back to her Papa."

Betsy reached forward and stroked John's coat with the back of her hand.

"And you are left here all alone John…as am I."

John shrugged.

"And it don't do, John, to be on your own at Bridge Fair... it don't do at all."

John's heart was so full of Mary he still did not read her. She leaned forward and whispered:

"Walk me home John, walk me home to Helpston."

"We shall all be walking home in a while Betsy…me and my family…and you are welcome to walk along with us on the road."

She looked at him, her head tilted on one side, as a parent might look a little disappointed at a child, but there was such a lack of guile on John's face, and his heart shone out of his eyes so clear that she suddenly laughed out loud:

"Ay, you go with them John Clare. I shall no doubt find company…"

She turned on her heel and walked back down the bridge towards the Fair.

****

It was late afternoon when the Clares walked home. The red of the sinking sun drew the redness out of the stubble fields, the soil, the ricks, the bricks, the turning leaves…so that half the world seemed to glow as though it was made of flesh and blood. And across the fields the piled heaps of dung that waited on the plough steamed quietly in the autumn air.

They had been walking silently for a while when Parker turned to John:

"Give us a page of your new book John, something to shorten the road."

"Oh, go on John!" Said Sophie.

John pulled the battered volume from his pocket.

"Ay, all right then…though it might not be altogether to your liking."

"Spit it out boy, 'twill pass the time one way or t'other."

John opened it and read aloud:

> "Sweet is the breath of morn, her rising sweet
> With charm of earliest birds; pleasant the sun
> When first on this delightful land he spreads
> His orient beams, on herb, tree, fruit, and flow'r,
> Glist'ring with dew; fragrant the fertile earth
> After soft showers; and sweet the coming on
> Of grateful ev'ning mild, then silent night
> With this her solemn bird and this fair moon,
> And these the gems of heav'n, her starry train…"

John paused, as if for a moment a sharp draught of some strong liquor had warmed his blood. Then he said:

"'Tis Eden see…I heard something of it from Merrishaw."

"Ay," said Parker. "'Tis fine enough writ, though a little gentlemanly for my taste. I doubt he's ever blistered his fingers with a spade."

10

All Hallows' Eve

There is a big bowl that Ann Clare has been keeping beside the fire since September, covered in a muslin cloth that is stained with dark red splashes. Beneath the muslin there has been such a bubbling and frothing as has filled the cottage with a yeasty savour. Her elderberry wine is her pride and the toast of the neighbourhood. Last week she strained it and poured it into earthenware jars where it will stand until Christmas when, with ginger and cloves and mulling irons, its moment will come.

There has been a fermentation too in the mind of John Clare, a fever almost, a frenzy of scribbling. Since first he learned his ABCs he has scratched with his nib at whatever scrap of paper he could lay his hands upon. Most have been scrunched in his fist and thrown into the fire. Some he has folded most careful into the pages of his few precious books. But since Bridge Fair he has writ as one possessed. Whether it was that tattered volume that woke in him something that had long been slumbering. Or whether it is to sharpen and sweeten his tongue for Mary. Or whether it is merely to take his mind off poor Wisdom, who languishes still in the Bishop's gaol waiting on the convict ship that'll take him to New Holland. Whatever his reason, when he's not labouring he is either dipping his pen into ink or hunched over one of his volumes muttering the words aloud to himself as though it was a book of devotions. If he was an earthenware pot he would have long since popped his cork.

Each morning, along with the bread and cheese in his dinner bag, he must carry his paper and pencil stub. When the other men rest from their fencing or hedge-setting or stone-breaking and settle down for their baggin he sits apart and sets down the rhymes he has whispered to himself as he laboured. There are those that mock, and those that shrug, and those that say 'Good luck to ye', but John is indifferent to them all. He is in an amaze of words that will not let him be, they come spilling and rhyming from his tongue and he delights in the pictures they summon. And then, when a poem is done, he will doubt it also. And there's many a verse as has served no higher purpose than to wipe his arse behind a hedge.

And now October is gone and November gathers her dark skirts and the bracken on the heath flattens beneath her feet.

Five days ago John and Parker came home soaked to the skin by the cold rain. Ann had been sweating since before first light in John Close's kitchen. She'd brought home a cut of salt bacon and she'd boiled some potatoes, which they all ate with relish. When food was done Parker threw some twists of whin onto the fire so that it blazed. John took one of his books from its cubby hole and leaned over it, devouring the words. Ann was spinning thread with her rockie, from the pile of combed wool on her knee. Parker dozed. Sophie, wrapped in a blanket at her mother's feet, talked idly of this and that, snatches of gossip she had garnered from the dairy. Suddenly Parker woke with a start and turned to John:

"All the world has been watching thee John, worrying pen to paper as though you'd ease an itch...but no one's heard a word of it. Read us something, one of your poems, if poems they be, for I've always had a taste for such."

"Ay John", said Ann kindly. "It would be a treat for us."

John looked up from his book, reluctant. He pulled a piece of paper from between the pages of it and unfolded it slowly. He is shy of any audience but the nodding of Ann and Parker urged him on and gave him courage.

"My mind has been turning on the Boswell crew of late and I penned this with them in mind:

To me how wildly pleasing is that scene
Which does present in evening's dusky hour
A group of gypsies center'd on the green
In some warm nook where Boreas has no power
Where sudden starts the quivering blaze behind
Short shrubby bushes nibbl'd by the sheep
That always on these shortsward pastures keep
Now lost now shines now bending with the wind
And now the swarthy sybil kneels reclin'd
With proggling stick she still renews the blaze
Forcing bright sparks to twinkle from the flaze
When this I view the all attentive mind
Will oft exclaim (so strong the scene pervades)
'Grant me this life, thou spirit of the shades!' "

There was a pause, then:

"'Tis well enough," said Parker. "'Tis well enough writ and tidily rhymed John, though to tell you the honest truth, it will never do."

"Ay," said Ann. "'Twas prettily spoke John, but not so as any but us would give it the time o' day."

John's heart was sinking to be kickshawed so harsh.

"The trouble of it is," said Parker, "you do too much ape the gentleman in your words, they do not speak true as a ballad speaks true."

"Ay," said Sophie. "And why say sib…sub…"

"Sybil." Said John.

"Sybil," said Sophie. "When all the world knows you mean Lettuce Boswell…though I saw her clear enough John, worriting the fire."

"And what's wrong with wind, John, for the love of God, it's a word as has served our fathers well enough, and their fathers before 'em. These fancy words are like dancing monkeys at a fair, that bow and scrape with little tri-corn hats and silken breeches. Speak common speech or not at all."

John folded up the page and tucked it back into the book. All his malingering doubts seemed now to be well-founded.

"Now read us something from one of your books John, so we can hear how such a job o' work is truly done and set 'prentice against master."

John shrugged and leafed through the book, it fell open at a place where he'd tucked a piece of paper between the pages earlier in the year.

"Now grey ey'd hazy eve's begun
To shed her balmy dew –
Insects no longer fear the sun
But come in open view

Now buzzing with unwelcome din
The heedless beetle bangs
Agen the cow-boys dinner tin
That o'er his shoulder hangs

Now from each hedgerow fearless peep
The slowly pacing snails
Betraying their meandering creep
In silver slimy trails

The owls mope out & scouting bats
Begin their giddy rounds
While countless swarms of dancing gnats
Each water pudge surrounds."

"By God, that is the real thing," said Parker. "That's what ye should be aiming for John, though I doubt you'll ever hit the target so fair on the bulls-eye as our man here."

"Ay John," said Ann with a sigh, "keep trying and who knows but one day you shall be ranked alongside such a one as this…what is his name?"

John closed the book and pointed to the stained spine:

"*Poems* by Robert Burns."

His parents nodded.

And it was only a short while later that John climbed the stairs to his bed. Soon he was beneath the blankets hugging himself and chuckling into the darkness at his deception, and at the thought that even them as cannot read are held in thrall to the printed page.

****

November is come. The church bells have rung for All Hallows.

Although the fences are not yet up for the enclosure, the land is being farmed as though they were. Charles Knight's allocation at the eastern edge of Helpston parish is being ploughed by his men. Each pair of horses lower their shaggy heads as the iron blades lift the turf and the mouldering yellow stubble of the baulk gives way to the long lines of dark turned earth, dipping and rising with the folds of the land above the fen, where once the patchwork of furlongs met side to side.

All along the old track there are teams of men digging ditches, planting hedges, breaking and setting stones for what will one day be the Helpston-Glinton Road.

Mary rode Dobbie along the track and watched the seagulls following the ploughs and plundering the soil for riches. As she drew close to the village she saw there was a team of twenty Helpston men working together on the new road. John Clare was amongst them.

"John!"

She called aloud and John looked up, as did nineteen other men.

One of them whispered:

"Now I understand his scribblin' an' scratchin' by God… damned if he ain't pennin' sweet nothings to old Joyce's Mary."

"As would I if I had the gift and 'twould make her wriggle out of that riding jacket and settle down upon my knee!"

John straightened and wiped the dirt from his hands against his smock. He walked towards her and she climbed down from the saddle with her basket on her arm.

The foreman, Will Mash, winked at the men:

"Ye've two minutes John Clare, afore I starts dockin' your wage."

Mary thrust the basket into John's hands:

"Here's liver and onions John, for you and your family. We've more than we can manage."

As John took the basket she pressed his hand:

"And shall I see you on Sunday?"

"Of course you shall!"

And she was up-saddle and away.

John, red-faced, turned back to his spade, he put the basket down on the verge and was just setting to work when Jem Johnson broke the quiet. He looked at John most solemn:

"Tomorrow, John Clare, I shall speak and you shall be advised and scratch it down upon the page word for word like a magistrate's clerk."

He put his finger to his palm and made as if to write:

"Dear Mary," he said. "Meet me tonight at Langley Bush."

Someone else shouted:

"In one of them hollow trees…"

"In your nightdress…"

"At midnight…"

"And there you shall make the acquaintance of Mr John Thomas…upstanding gentleman of this parish…"

And Jem, who has got the measure of John more than most, raised his eyebrows then:

"And together, Mary, we shall hunt the cuckoo's nest."

And there was laughter then, even Will Mash guffawed, and poor John stood and grinned and stared at his boots most discomfited. Then Jem began to sing:

"Give me a girl as'll wriggle and'll twist…"

And all the rest joined in:

"At the bottom of the belly lies the cuckoo's nest."

"All right, all right, back to work." Shouted Will Mash.

John filled his spade with soil and flung it at Jem, who clapped him on the shoulder.

****

It had long been dark when John got home with one cut of liver in Mary's basket.

As he drew close to the cottage he saw there was an unaccustomed light flickering in the window. It was a turnip lantern. Sophie had hollowed it out and cut eyes and teeth and set it on the window-sill with a candle inside. John pushed open the door and showed his mother the basket.

"The Joyces are pig-killing and have more than they can eat."

Parker shook his head and grunted:

"While others go hungry… 'tis an old story."

John patted his father's shoulder:

"Go easy… get off your high horse. I gave a piece to Mrs Dolby. They'll go to bed with their stomachs full tonight."

And Ann carried the liver into the pantry:

"I'd heard Jo Dolby was gone on the parish… maybe that'll cure his thirst… but how will he ever feed those boys on a pauper's pittance? And no doubt Ralph Wormstall has taken him into his employ."

"Ay," said Parker, "like the angel of death."

Soon the black cooking pot was hanging from its iron hook in the chimney and the smell of liver and onions mingled with the smell of scorched turnip from the lid of Sophie's lantern. Ann tapped the pot with her wooden spoon.

"We shall eat like kings and queens tonight."

Parker had his habitual theme like a bit between his teeth and would not stop worrying at it.

"Joyce, I'll grant you, has a good enough heart when he ain't crossed…but look at the rest of 'em, Wormstall, Close, Wright…lining their nests at the poor man's expense…And think on poor Wisdom…what d'you suppose he's sinking his teeth into this evening…no pig's liver for him I'll wager."

Ann snorted:

"As if that gypsy hasn't swallowed enough of our time... he has his life and that's a blessing..."

But then her face softened:

"But I do think of him languishing there...maybe we should keep some meat aside."

"Ay," said Parker, "and give the turn-keys a treat."

He spat into the fire.

"There's little we can do for Wisdom this side of the law... but there are other laws beside the law of the land, Ann... there's God's law...natural law...and the weight of one must be weighed against the weight of another if a man is to rest a-nights with an easy conscience."

He pulled a glowing ember from the fire and lit his pipe.

****

When the Clares had eaten their fill of the liver and onion stew and had mopped the gravy from the wooden platters with lumps of bread. And when the platters had been swilled clean beneath the pump, the family settled down again before the fire, all but Parker who walked across to the window, stiff and solemn. He lifted the lid from Sophie's lantern, and gently blew out the flame.

Sophie cried out with indignation:

"Why did you do that?"

Parker's voice was little more than a whisper:

"Sssssh, because all this shrieking Hallowe'en lark of ghouls and ghosties is wrong-headed Sophie. We don't want to frighten away little Bessie this night o' the year."

Sophie fell silent and lowered her head. John looked into the fire.

Parker returned to the fireside and sat down again. His eyes were wet. He turned to Ann:

"Did you bring a jug of cream from Close's dairy?"

"Of course I did."

She went to the pantry. She poured the cream into a bowl. She cut some honeycomb, dropped it in and stirred it. She cut some fingers of bread from a loaf. She set bowl and bread onto a platter, carried them back and put them down carefully on the hearthstone.

"There. Sophie, put puss outside! Ay, 'twas always her favourite, bless her. I can see her now dipping her chubby little fingers into the cream and licking them clean."

Parker smiled:

"Ay, and dipping the crust in and sucking it, and what a mess she'd make o' herself."

There was silence for a while, then John said:

"Tell me more about Bessie, for I have forgot her."

Ann laughed:

"You and she come sliding an' slithering an' yelling an' kicking out into this world, one a-hind the other like two puppies into a basket. Kitty Otter was there as handywoman, and when you was washed she tucked you up side by side in the one cradle."

"And from that first day," said Parker, "you was never apart, but tugging at your mammy's bubbies, one to left and one to right, or laying side by side and a-kicking of your legs, and later on crawling and toddling together as though 'twas an idea shared betwixt and between."

"And she was such a bonny thing," said Ann. "Such soft yellow curls that would lift and fall to the breath of my nostrils… And then come that winter of ninety-six when so many went to pauperdom, and we was a-queuing for a few pitiful pence, and

John and little Bessie grew so perishing thin…ay, there was no dipping fingers into cream that winter…and then she took the fever. And how we did dab her forehead and wipe her cheek, and borrowed money for a doctor, and Kitty came as well and done what she could…but all to no avail. We had to lay her in the ground that winter in her little coffin that Jonathan Burbridge made and would take no money for."

Parker and Ann were weeping now.

"And little John so quiet. He shed no tear but was like a lost thing, for a full six month he was in a daze as though he was himself half-gone, and we did fret that he would follow her."

Parker put his hand on John's shoulder:

"But then the summer came and you did wax like the moon into a sturdy little fellow…and then we was blessed with Sophie…and our sorrows was eclipsed…but never altogether gone, for a soul does not forget."

Ann turned the wooden platter on the hearthstone so that the bowl was evenly warmed. She called in a voice that was soft and sad and tender in equal measure:

"Come little Bessie Clare, on this night when the dead can walk, come and drink your fill."

One by one, with no word exchanged they climbed the wooden steps to bed, leaving the food on the hearthstone.

And this morning, Ann came downstairs early, took the platter outside and set it on the cottage steps while it was still dark. Soon enough puss came winding between her legs and lapped up the cream, then Richard Royce's dogs chased her away, swallowed the bread and licked it clean a second time. When Parker, John and Sophie came downstairs no word was spoken of the night before. But on her way to John Close's dairy Sophie gathered a little posey of berries – hip, haw, sloe and early holly – and when she came home at the end of the day she climbed the stairs and laid them tenderly in the little wooden cot where Bessie did use to sleep.

11

St Thomas' Eve

Christmas draws close. A wet November has given way to frost and all leaves are gone save only the few brown rags that cling to the oak, for he is always the last to let go of summer. The toiling ploughs still churn the earth. Poor Bob Turnill is out every day, alone with his team, working his allocation and praying with every breath to make good his debt with the sweat of his back and the depth of his devotion.

Charlie Turner's half-wit daughter Isabel is fallen sick. Every morning he's in Royce's Wood gathering wet sticks. He mixes sawdust with flour for the grey scones he bakes in the ashes, and pulls leaves and grass and begs an onion to make her a bowl of thin green soup. Jem Ferrar limes the hedgerows with trembling hands for little birds to give meat to his broth. And Joseph Dolby drinks away his wage and sleeps in one of Ralph Wormstall's lambing sheds while his wife and boys lift stones in the fields.

Parker, John, Dick Turnill, Jem Johnson, Will Mash and all the enclosure team, after four weeks cursing the bitter, slanting rain that soaked their clothes and turned the soil to mire; now curse the cold frost that stiffens earth to stone.

And there is a new sound that echoes and redounds across

the parish – the sound of axe to wood. All the streams are to be straightened into dykes and drains, and the willows and alders and dotterels that border Rhyme Dyke and Green Dyke and Round Oak Spring and Eastwell Spring and all the winding river banks are to be felled. The water must run now to the constraints of the ruled line.

With every stroke of iron to timber there is a sudden veering in the flight of a bird; a sudden start in the winter-sleep of badger, hedgehog, mole; a sudden shift in the deep droning note of the bees in their skeps against the church wall. The parish is set a-quiver and every fibre trembles. John knows it too, whose strings are tight-tuned to all sensation, though he is asleep to its cause and knows only a hollow ache of sorrow as the felling troubles his ears from across the fields as he works.

****

Last night was St Thomas' Eve, when every woman who is not wed hopes to catch a glimpse of her true-love.

In John Close's farm house there are two suppers. One is eaten in the front dining room, where he and his wife and their two daughters sit down to a mahogany table and pick and click upon china plate as though they were lords and ladies. The other supper is eaten downstairs in the kitchen when all has been cleared away above. All those that have lodging in the farm sit down together and eat and gossip – as much as they dare – about them upstairs.

Last night it was the same as ever. And when all had been cleared away and 'good-nights' had been bid, Betsy Jackson was brushing the crumbs from the table when she heard her name whispered:

"Betsy."

She turned, and there was the elder of the Miss Closes, standing in her nightdress with a flickering candle.

Betsy curtsied, for the Close girls are strangers in the kitchen:

"What can I do for ye Miss Elizabeth?"

"Betsy, peel me an onion."

Betsy smiled to herself, remembering suddenly what night it was, remembering the old custom and how she'd done the same herself before she was wed. As she turned to cut a red onion from the string that hung from the kitchen beam she found her cheeks were moist with tender memory. She carefully peeled the onion, put it onto a plate and gave it to Elizabeth Close, wiping the tears from her eyes with her sleeve. Elizabeth took the plate.

"Don't tell Papa, he thinks 'tis only a stupid fancy."

Betsy smiled at her and sniffed.

"I won't tell."

"Are those real tears?"

"No, just onion tears."

Elizabeth walked away.

"Goodnight."

When she had disappeared up the stairs Betsy looked at the string of onions.

She cut another one and peeled it with quick strong fingers.

"'Tis only a stupid fancy but…"

She smiled through her tears, took a last look at the empty kitchen, blew out the candles, crossed the tiled hallway and made her way upstairs to her little cupboard of a room against the chimney. She slipped the onion under her pillow, undressed and climbed beneath the blankets. She had barely closed her eyes when she fell asleep.

****

And now it is St Thomas' day, when the night's hold is strongest upon the day. This year it has fallen upon a Sunday.

At Joyce's Farm it was only when Mary's tasks had been finished that John's Sunday visit could begin in earnest. She put on her coat and woollen hat and scarf. They walked out into the yard and round to the frosty garden. When they were behind the yew hedge and out of sight of the house, John said:

"Turn around Mary."

She turned her back to him. He pulled down her scarf, pressed his nose into her hair and sniffed the back of her head.

"I smell onions!"

She turned and looked at him and blushed and smiled:

"Maybe you do John."

"Did you dream?"

"Maybe I did John."

"Of me?"

She shook her head:

"No…first 'twas of old Charlie Turner, for I like a man with no teeth…then I saw Merrishaw, for a scholar needs a wife and I like a man with spaniel breath…and then 'twas…"

John put his hand over her mouth and he could feel her soft wet laughter against his palm.

"Tell me the truth!"

She pulled his hand away and looked into his face:

"I saw thee John, as plain as day."

She pressed herself against him, tilted her head and they

met lip to lip.

For all that was left of the afternoon they walked and talked, but not for as long as is their custom. When Glinton church clock struck four he said:

"Now I must go."

"Already?"

"Ay, we practise the Morris play tonight."

He pressed a piece of paper into her hand.

"This is for you. 'Tis but a trifle…something I wrote."

She unfolded it and read aloud:

"Sweet is the blossomed beans perfume
By morning breezes shed
And sweeter still the jonquils bloom
When evening damps its head
And perfume sweet of pink and rose
And violet of the grove
But oh – how sweeter far than those
The kiss of her I love."

She took his hand so tender then:

"And I do love thee John Clare."

She pressed her lips to his cheek and turned back towards the farm house. Then she stopped and called across the lawn:

"And sweet the smell of onion juice
Upon my true love's hair!"

She ran through the front door and was lost to sight.

And John strode the track through Woodcroft Field, warmed against any cold the mid-winter evening might bring.

12

Christmas

It was dusk on Tuesday afternoon when the guisers acted out the Morris Play at Butter Cross. The four of them, in their bright ribbons, stood in a row on the steps of the cross, while John, Dick and Old Otter kept out the cold as best they could with their music.

Saint George and the Turkish Knight were dressed in smocks that were so festooned and tangled with rags and ribbons that scarce a glimpse of canvas or breech-cloth met the eye. Each wore an ancient tricorn hat on his head that was stuck all over with curled wood-shavings from Jonathan's workshop and strips of coloured paper that dangled over the eyes. Each had a belt drawn about his waist and a wooden sword thrust into it that reached to the knee; St George's was straight and the Turkish Knight's curved as a scimitar.

The Fool had a hunch between his shoulders that rucked up his ribboned coat at the back. He had a leather tail that dangled behind his legs. He wore a clown's pointed hat that was wound about with coloured cloth and bright ribbons. Over his shoulder he carried a wooden club, and hanging from the end of it a pig's bladder, blown up and tied tight, on a twine.

The Doctor wore a tall hat, a long coat to his ankles bright with rags and ribbons, spectacles of twisted woodbine upon his nose, and in his hand an ancient leather bag.

All the players, musicians and guisers, had their faces blacked with grease and soot from James Bain's forge.

The villagers gathered around them, tapping their feet to the tunes. The four guisers watched them, still and solemn as four rooks upon a fence.

Then, all of a sudden, the music stopped, the fool stepped forward, and the play began.

> "Gentlemen and Ladies I'm glad to see you here,
> Soon and very soon our actors shall appear..."

The play followed its accustomed course. St George fought the Turkish Knight with a rattle and a clatter of wooden swords, the fool skipped around them, urging them on, swinging his club and walloping them with his pig's bladder. The musicians shouted:

> "I am the blade
> That drives no trade
> Most people do adore me.
> I will you heat
> And I shan't you cheat
> And I'll drive you all before me..."

And the old story played itself out. The villagers huddled together in the cold like a herd of cattle, their breath steaming in the frosty, darkening air. The guisers spoke the familiar lines, in part to entertain the crowd, but in part as a job that must be done, just as wheat must be threshed and fields ploughed. For the Morris play is one of the stations of the year and cannot be neglected.

When the play was finished the Fool went round with his hat and gathered his thin crop of farthings. Then the company made their way round the bigger houses of the village. They performed for Parson Mossop, for John Close, for Mrs Elizabeth Wright, for Mr Bull and Ralph Wormstall, and were rewarded with ale and food and coppers for the Fool's hat.

It was drawing close to midnight when they returned to Bachelor's Hall to lay out their instruments and costumes ready for Christmas Eve. Sam Billings warmed a pan of water over the fire so that they could wash the black grease from their faces.

When the musicians had set their instruments beside the guisers costumes, Sam put down a dirty cloth bag with its draw-string tied in a knot:

"John Clare," he said, "you'll bring this an' all, won't ye."

John reached forward and felt the tight fiddle-strings beneath the cloth. He stroked them so that they sounded, and tapped the hollow wood. He smiled:

"Ay."

When all the company had cleaned themselves as best they could and were wiping their faces with a piece of cloth, Old Otter took Sam Billings by the arm and drew him aside.

"Kitty sends you this with her kind regards."

He pulled a little bottle from his pocket.

"She says mind her instruction."

"Ay, it is not forgot."

Then Sam raised his voice to all the company:

"Tomorrow, at Farmer Joyce's farm, at two of the clock gentlemen, and not a moment later. And a very good night to ye all."

****

It was at three o'clock on the afternoon of Christmas Eve that Farmer Joyce's haywain trundled through the streets of Peterborough towards the Minster Gate. Sam Billings, in Doctor's coat and hat, held the reins and Joyce's two great shires lifted their feathered feet and snorted into the frozen air. Huddled in the back, horse blankets drawn about themselves, their faces dark as blackamores, the rest of the Helpston players, musicians and guisers, watched the thronging shops and stalls with pink-rimmed eyes.

When they came to the market Sam reined in the horses and tied them to a rail. He threw blankets across their backs.

"There my sweet-hearts, we won't be gone for long."

The company crossed the market place, that was teeming with revellers, and stationed themselves in the archway of the Minster Gate. Straight away the musicians began to play 'The Devil among the Tailors' with Dick blowing his flute, John and Old Otter sawing with their bows as though they could make fire with them. Soon a crowd began to gather, drawn by the music and the four guisers standing behind in their solemn row, bright with ribbons, barely blinking. On and on they played until the crowd stood fifteen deep in a curve before them, children pushing forward to the front so that they could see.

And then a studded door in the wall of the Minster Gate opened, and a turn-key peered out of the entrance to the Bishop's Gaol to see what all the noise was about. Out of the corner of his eye John saw him beckoning with his arm and then heard him shout:

"Guisers!"

Another one appeared in the doorway:

"It's only Christmas once in a damned year. What harm in watching? Ned, come an' have a look! Guisers. Bring out some chairs."

A third turn-key came out carrying three wooden chairs. They settled down side by side on the great stone doorstep. Behind them John caught a glimpse of their little office with its fireplace and black kettle singing on the coals, and behind that the locked iron door that led to the honeycomb of cells.

The music stopped. Parker Clare, the Fool, stepped forward:

"Gentlemen and Ladies I'm glad to see you here,
Soon and very soon our actors shall appear,
Though our company is but small
We'll do our best to please you all.
To get your love and gain your favour
We'll do the best of our endeavour."

And then it was the Doctor's turn, in a new twist to the play that had never been spoken before:

"In comes I, a Doctor merry,
That has such remedies as'll make you cheery,
As'll strengthen the blood and redden the cheek,
As'll give courage to the humble and stomach to the meek."

He pulled a bottle from his bag:

"Here is the elixir as turns a beggar to a dandy,
Truth to tell 'tis nothing but the best French...."

The crowd roared: "Brandy!"

"Is there any here among you as'd like a little sip,
To gladden the heart and keep out the winter's nip?"

"I will!"

Shouted someone from the crowd.

And with a flourish the Doctor pulled the cork from the bottle and offered him a mouthful. He took a swig and sighed:

"Aaaaah."

The crowd laughed.

"Me too!"

Shouted another.

When four or five had drunk from the bottle the Doctor dropped it back into his bag.

"Now the time is come to start our play
So I'll step back and let the others have their say…"

He turned to the three guisers behind him, and then suddenly stopped, he swung round to the three turn-keys sitting in the doorway:

"What about you my friends, will you not have a sup,
And welcome in the season by tipping the bottle up?"

He reached into his bag again and pulled out a bottle. The turn-keys looked at one another and shrugged.

"I'll take a drop for good cheer."

One of them took the bottle lifted it to his lips and gulped down a mouthful. He looked at the others, winked and wiped his mouth.

"So will I by God."

The second one drank and passed it to the third. He took a

swig, gave it back to the Doctor and grinned:

"A merry Christmas to ye!"

The crowd cheered. The Doctor stepped back and Jonathan Burbridge stepped forward:

"In comes I, Saint George, a champion bold,
And with my bloody sword I won three crowns of gold..."

And the play followed its time-honoured pattern. First came swaggering George, and then James Bain as the Turkish Knight, and then the fight with the rattling of sword to sword until the Fool, dancing in and out, was struck his mortal blow. As he dropped to his knees and rolled onto his back the fiddles and flute struck up such a plaintive air that the crowd sighed.

Then Saint George roared:

"Is there a Doctor to be found
To cure this deep and deadly wound?"

And all the children at the front of the crowd pointed at the Doctor:

"There he is!"

Some ragged boys ran forwards and pulled him across to the stretched body of the dead Fool.

Sam Billings looked down at the Fool and up at the crowd:

"Ay, there's a Doctor to be found
As'll cure this deep and deadly wound!
I'm a Doctor pure and good,
With my right hand I'll staunch his blood."

Then Saint George and the Turkish Knight together put the old question:

"Where have you come from, where have you been?"

"From Italy, Titaly, High Germany, France and Spain,
And now am returned to old England again."

"What can ye cure and what can't ye cure?"

"All sorts of diseases,
Just what my physic pleases,
The itch, the pitch, the palsy and the gout,
Devils within and devils without,
And I've got a little bottle down the side
Whose fame has travelled far and wide!"

He pulled out a bottle and waved it in the air. The crowd cheered. Someone shouted:
"That'll do the bloody trick!"

"The medicine in here's called Alicumpane,
It'll bring our Fool to life once again."

He pulled out the cork and poured a splash onto the Fools lips, and another onto his chest.

"A drop to his head, a drop to his heart,
Rise up bold fellow and play your part!"

Fiddles and flute slid slowly from their lowest note to their highest, and as they did so the Fool stirred, opened his eyes, sat up, stretched and stood up on his two feet. Then, suddenly,

John, Dick and Otter broke into a jig and the Fool danced, swinging his club so that the bladder bounced to left and right, and all the crowd clapped in time.

When the dance was finished the Fool, a little breathless, bowed to the crowd:

> "Ladies and Gentlemen a-sleeping I have been,
> And I've had such a sleep as the world has never seen,
> But now I am alive, not in my grave a-laid
> Fair's fair when all is said and done – the Doctor must be paid!"

He took off his hat and held it out to the crowd:

> "It's your money we want and your kindness we crave,
> Then we'll play ye a tune and take our leave."

Parker stepped forward amongst the audience who flung farthings and ha'pennies into his hat.

"Thank you sir, thank you madam, thank you kindly and a merry Christmas."

The band struck up 'Tom the Piper's Son' and then 'Speed the Plough'. And nobody noticed that where there had been two fiddlers there were now three, their blackened faces almost melting into the gathering night. And only the musicians noticed that the music had a new lift, a lilting swagger that it had not known for half a year.

****

When the players reached Joyce's farm no word was spoken of what had taken place at Peterborough. Will Farrell helped Sam bring the horses round to the barn where they were unharnessed from the wain. Will led them across to the stable. Sam helped Will to towel and brush and feed them. They left them with blankets over their backs and their noses to their mangers.

The rest of the company was welcomed to the kitchen. The great table had been pushed to the wall and all the household were waiting for the Morris Play. John, Dick and Old Otter played tunes and as soon as Sam and Will came into the warm Parker stepped forwards:

> "Gentlemen and Ladies I'm glad to see you here,
> Soon and very soon our actors shall appear..."

When all was done and the hat had been passed about, Farmer Joyce stood up and clapped his hands.

"Very good, very good indeed. And now, as it is the Christmas season, let's drag out the table and put a ham to it... for what could be the harm in having one for the eve and one for the day."

Kate, Lizzie, Hope and Mary went out to the bread oven where ham, parsnips, potatoes, carrots and onions had been roasted and now were keeping warm. All were brought to the table, with ale and bread, and all the company and household sat down, elbow to elbow, and ate together.

It was as the gravy was being mopped from plates with chunks of bread that there came a great commotion in the yard, a clattering of hooves and all the farmyard dogs barking. Then there was a hammering at the farm-house door.

"Open up in the name of the law."

Kate Dyball went across and lifted the latch.

Two town constables pushed into the hot kitchen, followed by several militia-men, all of them flushed and short of breath having galloped hot-foot from Peterborough.

"We are seeking the Helpston guisers."

Farmer Joyce got up to his feet.

"And here they be gentlemen, every man-jack of them, still blacked up and dressed in their ribbons as you can see."

The constables looked across at them. The guisers sat impassive at the table, their faces unreadable beneath the soot and grease. One of the constables went across to Farmer Joyce:

"There has been an escape, a break-out. A Boswell. A condemned felon, waiting on his transportation. Broke out of the Bishop's Gaol this evening."

Farmer Joyce shook his head:

"Then none of us are safe by God. He'll have gone back to his own… have you not searched the Boswell camp?"

"Yes, we've ridden to Langdyke Bush…they've broke camp and vanished."

"And what about the turn-keys, why weren't they doing their damned job?"

"We can get no sense from them…one cannot put two words together before he must stare at some piece of fluff upon his jacket as though 'twas a crown jewel. One sees vipers in every shadow, and the third jibbers like an ape."

Old Otter pulled out a piece of rag and blew upon his nose.

"In short sir," said the constable, "they have been drugged."

Farmer Joyce turned to his household.

"This is an outrage, Hope, Lizzie, make sure all doors and windows are barred tonight...but what has any of this to do with our guisers?"

"The escape was made sir, while they did strut and swagger

their Morris Play beneath the Minster Gate."

James Bain sucked in his breath:

" 'Tis the first we've heard of any escape."

Sam Billings nodded:

"Ay, we was just collecting a few coppers for Christmas cheer."

The constable rapped the table with his fist:

"But that's not the end of it...we have been given to understand, from several reliable witnesses, that the prison warders drank of a bottle that you did offer them."

"Ay, the alicumpane, and several others drank of it as well," Sam Billings lowered his voice, " 'Tis nothing but brandy and water, Sir, with a little sugar to sweeten it."

"Where is the bottle?"

"It's in the Doctor's bag."

Sam Billings pointed to the leather bag that was lying on the floor beside the fool's club and bladder, and the discarded wooden swords.

One of the militia-men picked up the bag and passed it to the constable. He reached inside. He pulled out a bottle. He pulled the stopper from the neck and sniffed.

"It smells harmless enough...but I'll be damned if it ain't drugged."

Farmer Joyce put his hand on the constable's arm.

"The proof of the pudding is in the eating, my friend."

He went to a shelf and picked up a horn cup.

"Fill this from the bottle. Get one of these guisers to drink it...and soon enough you'll discover whether they be innocent or guilty."

The constable smiled.

"Ay, and if none will drink, we'll arrest the lot of 'em, and they shall all be taken."

He turned to the militia-men:
"Go and fetch the manacles."
The kitchen door opened and closed.
"Now, is there a man here as'll drink of this?"
He poured the liquid from the bottle into the cup and held it up.
Parker Clare got to his feet, his leather tail still dangling behind his legs.
"Ay, I will."
"Very well. It shall be the Fool."
The cup was passed across. Parker lifted it to his lips and gulped it down. He wiped his mouth. The militia-men returned from the yard and threw the manacles and chains onto the kitchen floor. The constable nodded to Parker:
"Watch him like a hawk."
"Ay," said Farmer Joyce, "'tis the only way. Now, how long should we allow for the physic to take effect?"
"Not more than twenty minutes," said the constable, "for the Morris Play, I'm told, lasts barely fifteen from start to finish."
"Time enough to take a glass. Come through to the parlour fire the pair of ye and we'll open a bottle of claret. There's a comfortable settle there. Come through, come through."
And Farmer Joyce ushered the two constables out of the room.
In the kitchen Parker sat, with a soldier to either side of him. He enjoyed the warm flush that spread from his belly to every fibre of his body. No word was spoken around the table. It was as mute a Christmas gathering as ever sat down to table. And the militia-men looked uneasy, as though they were on the edge of some joke they could not fathom.
Mary, Lizzie, Hope and Kate gathered up the empty plates

and scrubbed them clean at the sink. From time to time Mary caught John's eye but, like all the others, he gave no sign.

From the parlour the voices of Farmer Joyce and the two constables could be heard rising and falling in good-humoured conversation.

At last the door opened and the three of them returned, a little flushed from the claret and the fire. One of them came forward to the table and peered down into Parker's blackened face. Parker looked steadily back at him.

"He's not moved from his chair?"

"No sir." Said the soldiers.

"Nor supped?"

"Not a drop beyond what was in the mug sir."

"Hmm, the eyes seem clear enough."

He nodded to Parker:

"Stand up."

Parker stood.

"Walk towards the fire."

Parker walked.

"Hmm, steady too!"

"Question him," said the second constable.

"Ay. What is your name? Where do you live?"

"My name is Parker Clare. I do live in Woodgate in the village of Helpston."

The constable looked quizzically at Farmer Joyce. He nodded:

"Plainly spoken and true."

"What year is it and who is our sovereign King?"

"The year is eighteen and eleven, and our King is George, and the third to bear that name, though it is his son the Prince Regent as has taken the reins."

"Ay, there's no gainsaying that. And 'twas a sounder answer

than His Majesty would have give himself. And with whom are we at war?"

Parker smiled beneath his grease:

"Jean FRANCE-wah…"

"Ay, ay. And how many hundred-weight to a ton?"

"Twenty… and shouldn't I know it, having broke my back oft' enough beneath a hundredweight sack."

"Now, now, we'll have less of your lip, answer me straight. How many pints to a gallon jar."

"Eight."

"And a half of eight is?"

"What! You would take four of my pint pots from under my nose and leave me with only four!"

The room filled with laughter. The second constable raised his eyebrows.

"He's no more addled than a new laid egg. We'll try one more test though."

He stepped forward and pulled a piece of printed paper from his pocket:

"Read me this."

Parker shook his head:

"I can't neither read nor write."

Farmer Joyce stepped forwards:

"No more he can, though not for lack of wit."

He turned to the constable:

"Surely there can be no argument. His head is clear as daylight and he has proved himself and all his company innocent as babes."

The constables looked at one another and shrugged:

"So it would seem."

The militia-men picked up the manacles and made towards the door. The first constable bowed to the Company:

"Please accept my humble apologies, gentlemen, for disturbing your meal, and the best of the season to ye all..."

Then he turned to Farmer Joyce:

"But how that cursed Boswell youth broke free is a mystery to me, and him only spared the gallows by a whisker..."

Farmer Joyce ushered them to the kitchen door:

"Ay, 'tis a curious thing..."

He stood in the icy air and watched the constables and soldiers mount their horses and ride away between the frosted ricks and out of the farmyard gate.

"Goodnight gentlemen, and a merry Christmas to you all!"

When he returned to the kitchen, the guisers and musicians were pulling on their coats and making ready to leave. He stood and blocked the doorway:

"No soul will stir from my kitchen until the grease has been washed from your faces. Kitty, put the kettle on its hook and fill a bowl with hot water. We can't have you straggling into Helpston like a company of imps and devils...you'll give poor Mossop his death of fright...and Richard Royce will think you've come to fetch him home."

He went to the side of the fireplace and pulled a big earthenware jug from the shadows. It was filled to the brim with ale and spices – cinnamon, nutmeg, cloves. He pulled a glowing iron poker from the heart of the fire and thrust it into the jug, there was a rush of steam and the ale hissed and bubbled.

"There. Mary! Fetch some mugs."

The mulled ale was poured and passed around.

"Now, who'll lead us in a carol? Parker, if you ain't too fuddled with alicumpane! I'm told you're a man with as many songs as there are days to the year."

Parker Clare stood.

"Ay, I'll give you a verse or two of God rest ye Merry Gentlemen."

As he sang, one by one, the Helpston players knelt over the bowl of steaming water that had been set on the hearthstone and washed the black grease from their faces. When the carol was finished and the mugs were drained they made their way out of the warm kitchen and across the yard. Farmer Joyce walked them to the churchyard gate.

One by one he clasped their hands.

It was only when he came back to the kitchen that he discovered that not all the Helpston company was gone. John Clare sat fast asleep in one of the wooden chairs before the kitchen fire. His coat was on. His head was slumped backwards wearing its hat. His mouth was open and his legs stretched out before him.

"None of us had the heart to wake him," whispered Lizzie Tucker.

Farmer Joyce looked down at him:

"Ay, leave him be."

Then he added, half under his breath:

"The days are short, but this will have been a long one for John Clare."

****

It was not until the Glinton church clock struck three of the morning that John woke, and then only because he was disturbed. He opened his eyes and for a moment was unsure as to where he might be. He looked about himself. He cast his eyes on the glowing embers of the kitchen fire, on the moon that shone through the window and filled the room with silver-grey light and dark shadow. And then, with a sudden jolt of wakefulness he knew he was not alone. He turned his head and saw Mary. She had pulled a chair close beside him. She was dressed in her nightdress, with a blanket drawn across her shoulders. And she was holding his hand to the warmth of her body. Her eyes were closed, but he could see by her upright posture that she was not asleep.

He whispered:

"Mary."

She opened her eyes and turned to him:

"John."

There was silence for a while between them, then she said:

"John, is he really away? Is he safe? I could not sleep for thinking."

John nodded:

"He is away…to the north."

"Thank God. And shall we ever see him again?"

"Who knows Mary…I doubt it…but would we have seen him again had he been transported? Or hanged? He is alive and has his sweet liberty..."

"And I pray he can keep it…or it will go hard for him."

She pressed his hand, then lifted it to her lips and kissed it.

"John, come with me. I have something for you."

She stood up and tugged him to his feet. She led him to the doorway where the kitchen opened onto the parlour. A sprig of mistletoe was hanging from it, its berries like little moons in the silver-grey light. When they were both beneath it she wrapped her arms around him and hugged him tight, her face pressed to his collar, her breath warm through the coat he was still wearing. Then she pulled away and lifted her face to him and their lips met. John could taste the salty wetness of her tears upon her mouth as they kissed.

"There," she said. "That was all. Merry Christmas, and I

love you John Clare."

"And I love you Mary."

"And maybe one day we shall be wed."

"Maybe we shall."

They crossed the kitchen and pulled their two chairs to the edge of the hearthstone. Mary threw some kindling onto the embers. As the flames danced and reddened their faces they sat side by side, holding hands and saying nothing.

Then John whispered:

"Mary."

"Ay."

"We could be betrothed, you and me."

She shook her head vigorously:

"Father would not hear of it. He thinks me too young, and he sees no prospects in you. He bears you no malice, John, but he sees in us some childhood courtship that is innocent of all the trappings and settlements of a marriage…we must wait, bide our time."

They were quiet again for a while. Then John said:

"But what if it was a secret, Mary…just between you and me…what if it was an understanding that no others knew of? Then, in the fullness of time, when I have made something of myself, we could announce it to your father and my father and all the wide world."

She turned to him and smiled:

"Ay John, we could do that, we could keep it secret."

She leaned across, curled her arm around his neck, and whispered fiercely, like a child:

"We must make a pledge, a secret one. I must pledge myself to you and you to me, formal-like and sincere, and no breaking it…cross my heart and hope to die."

John grinned:

"Ay."

"Name a time and a place."

John thought for a moment:

"St Valentines day…the fourteenth day of February…at Helpston church porch…at nine o'clock in the morning…I shall be there come snow or hail."

"And so shall I."

She pressed her mouth to his, tugged the blanket over her shoulders, ran out of the kitchen and up the stairs to bed.

John got to his feet, picked up his fiddle, tightened his scarf, and set off for home.

****

And now it is nine of the clock, the Helpston bells are ringing full swing and Sophie is shaking him into wakefulness:

"John! Merry Christmas! Wake up! Wake up!"

He sits up and rubs his eyes.

From downstairs Ann shouts:

"Wake up John, the band will be tuning their music even now!"

"Ay John," says Sophie, "And you a slug-a-bed…" Then she lowers her voice. "And I heard you creepin' upstairs as the church clock struck four, where had ye been John?"

He pushes away the blankets and stands.

"And still in your coat!"

Then, from downstairs:

"I've warmed a pan of water for you!"

He stumbles down the stairs and splashes the water over his face and neck.

"And there's your clean shirt over the chair."

He unbuttons his coat, tugs his old shirt over his head and

pulls on the clean one. He seizes his fiddle that lies on the chair where he'd dropped it five hours before. There's a bowl of wrinkled winter apples on the window-sill. He grabs one and bites into the soft sweet flesh.

"Take another one in your pocket, John."

Ann pushes an apple into his coat pocket, then hands him the coat. She kisses his cheek.

"There'll be more to eat soon enough."

John runs along the street, pulling on his coat as he goes, passing his fiddle from one hand to the other as he pushes in his arms. He runs past Butter Cross and through the churchyard, dodging the first of the congregation who are making their way towards the church porch dressed in their Christmas best.

Already the church band are midway through 'Christchurch Bells'. John tightens the tuning pegs, lifts the fiddle to his chin and draws the bow across the strings. When the tune is done Dick Turnill leans across to him and whispers most urgent:

"Have ye heard the news?"

"What news?"

"About Will Bloodworth?"

"No."

"He is vanished."

"Vanished?"

"Ay. Last night. He was passing Christmas with his sister. When supper was done 'tis said, he went upstairs to bed…and when she brought him up a cup of spiced wine as a cordial… Will Bloodworth was gone."

John stares at Dick:

"How d'ye mean, gone?"

"Gone John. She called and searched the house and yard and could find no sign. She raised servants and neighbours who helped her… but they have found nothing. She is quite beside herself they say."

"There is no clue?"

"No sign of a struggle, no mark of a ladder to the window-sill, his bed-clothes still folded on the pillow. There are no footprints, the ground being frozen. She sent word to Milton Hall but they have not seen him. He has quite disappeared."

"Shhh."

Parson Mossop coughs. Sam Billings taps the time on the edge of his drum and the band strikes up 'While Shepherds Watched'.

Slowly, steadily, the congregation fills the church. And in every pew, from mouth to muffled ear, it is the same story whispered.

13

Plough Monday

Twelfth Night is over and Plough Monday is past. Now it is Tuesday and work resumes and hard labour wastes no time in wiping the slate clean of the sweets of holiday and all the misrule of the day before, leaving only the aching limbs, the numbed fingers and the harsh coughs of winter.

Yesterday, Plough Monday, is the day that custom dictates that all men return to work and the season of ploughing begin. But custom is long-since beggared by usage, for the ploughs have been working the fields since October. And there are few men under thirty who, on Plough Monday, have their eyes on anything but the pint pot and the pie?

All is white with snow, and has been since Christmas night when the sky opened and the snow settled like feathers on the frozen ground, so that every battered, tattered, familiar place is become strange and beautiful, softened by the white fall that has folded its cold bright coverlet over thatch, stack, stable, street and field. The Earl of Fitzwilliam has given a sack of coal to every pauper that's on the parish, and even so there is a rash of new dug earth against the churchyard wall.

Mrs Elizabeth Wright has knocked on every door in her slow relentless search for some clue as to Will Bloodworth's whereabouts. The ice at Lolham Bridge has been broken and the river dragged. But all to no avail, and the village is agog with gossip and speculation. Everywhere the same conversation is played out:

"I put it down to that damned gypsy."

"Ay, when all's said an' done, 'tis more than chance."

"That Boswell youth breaking free on the very night…"

"And him with a grudge, for was it not Will Bloodworth as apprehended him?"

"Ay, the youth tried for his life once, and now he's doubtless tried again."

"And if he didn't hang for it the first time he shall now, by God."

Every rumoured hiding place has been probed and pulled apart. The Clare's cottage has been searched as has Old Otter's squat but nothing has been found. The Earl of Fitzwilliam has sent militia-men riding north and south on the Great North Road, but all have returned empty-handed.

****

As the red sun rose over the white orison on the morning of Plough Monday the streets and lanes were already busy. From every cottage and farm house the young men of the parish, buttoned up against the snow that crumped beneath their feet, were all tramping towards James Bain's forge.

James had thrown new coals onto the fire and put the bellows under, so that as each new man arrived he could stretch his hands to the heat and feel the fire upon his face, even as the winter chilled his back. There was a circle of warmth, and soon there was a circle of men marking its outer edge.

In the hot and chill air there was a quickened mood of

expectation. A barrel had been broached and James was heating the sooty pokers among the coals and thrusting them into jugs of ale. Behind him the forge, with its black iron tools hanging from their nails, lightened and darkened every time the bellows reddened the coals. The jugs were passed around the circle.

John Clare and Dick Turnill, much against his father's pleasure, were there. Dick had brought two leather harnesses glinting with horse brasses. He gave one to John. They slung them around their necks. When all the team were gathered they dipped their fingers into a bucket of axle-grease and smeared their cheeks. They scraped soot from the chimney of the forge and sprinkled it onto their faces until they were striped as savages.

Then from the open doorway came a roaring voice:

"Only two bollocks between us…and both of them mine!"

Richard Royce beamed at them, with the gap-toothed grin of one of the snowmen in the street. The Lord of the Harvest is always Ploughman come winter, with six youths before him as Plough Bullocks.

He went forwards, dipped his hands into the grease, and rubbed them across his face as though he was washing himself at the pump. He stuck his head into the chimney, and when he pulled it out he was black as pitch. He grabbed a jug from one of the lads and emptied it with one long gulp.

"Aaaaaah!"

Some of the men who were to be Plough Witches were stuffing straw into the backs of their smocks to make hunch-backs, they had besoms and ladles filled with sooty grease to smear any poor soul that crossed their path.

The rest were Bullocks. When all were well greased and sooted they made their way out of the forge. Lying on the ground was a pole with three short cross-pieces that had been lashed and tied with rope. Joined to the end of the pole by a piece of frayed leather was an ancient wooden plough without share or coulter.

The Plough Bullocks, in pairs, took their places, three to either side of the pole, each behind a cross piece. Dick and John were side by side. They lifted the pole. Richard Royce got between the stilts of the plough. James Bain brought a jug of ale to each bullock in turn and lifted the spout to his lips so that he could gulp it down. The ale splashed into their faces. Already the team was half cut.

"Our team must be fed and watered!"

"And so must their ploughman…come on you tight-arsed bugger, I'm dry as a witch's tit."

James came and lifted the jug to Richard's lips, but as he drew it away Richard grabbed it from him and emptied it.

He lifted his whip and cracked it over the team's heads:

"Whoaaa!"

The Bullocks set off at a trot, drawing their rattling burden through the village street, shouting and whooping with the Witches dancing and staggering alongside waving their besoms and ladles in the air. And Richard Royce followed behind, waving his whip and swearing with drunken abandon at any face he recognised: elderly spinsters, farmers or their wives, parson, pauper, constable.

All the world is turned upside down this one day of the year.

It's a day when doors are locked and bolted and few venture out into the streets. When those waiting in their houses hear a knocking at their doors they will pull back the pins and give ale or bread and cheese, for they know well enough that there's a penalty to be paid if the Plough Team isn't kept happy. Shoe scrapers will be pulled up. Gate posts will be pulled out. Even it has been known for a share to be fitted to the plough and a front lawn churned and turned over as though it was a field.

Yesterday was the same as any. All but the young stayed indoors. All decency and decorum disappeared in a rough, drunken circus of Bullocks and Witches, with Richard Royce like the Devil himself whipping his imps to mischief. Anyone who strayed from home on any errand was chased the length of the street and smeared with grease from the ladles. Any who wandered too close to the Bullocks was charged. Only the children ventured freely abroad, pelting the team with snowballs and wearing their grease marks proudly like battle scars. The air was full of their hoarse, shrill shouting and the roaring of the Ploughboys.

By the time morning turned to afternoon the Plough Bullocks were so drunk they could barely stand. They stopped at the Bluebell, leaving the plough in the street outside, and spent their pennies on pies that had been baked in expectation of their visit.

As they were eating and warming themselves there came a shouting from outside. A snowball smashed against the window and cracked the glass. Little Tom Dolby came running into the inn, his face and clothes smeared with grease and soot. He was dancing from foot to foot with outrage and excitement:

"It's the Glinton Ploughboys. It's the bloody Glinton boys! They've took your plough!"

Richard Royce stuffed the last of his pie into his mouth. He bellowed:

"Fuckers!"

He ran outside with all the Helpston Bullocks and Witches behind him and there followed such a battle in Heath Road, such a hurling of snowballs, such a wrestling and fist-fighting, such a smearing of grease, such a shouting of profanities that even the stout-hearted were obliged to sit behind their locked doors with fingers to their ears, resolved, as ever, to draw up a petition that would put an end to these Plough Monday antics for good and all.

By the time honour had been restored and the Helpston Plough Bullocks were back in their team with their Ploughman behind them between his stilts, and the Glinton Ploughboys staggering home shouting insults over their shoulders, the afternoon was darkening to evening. A thin scattering of snowflakes was fluttering down from the heavens. They found themselves, with no very clear idea of how they had got there, in John Close's yard.

****

All through the Christmas season Betsy Jackson has worked in the Close's kitchen, sweating over the roasting, the baking, the steaming, the broiling of all that was served upstairs at their table. This weekend past they've given her three days off to go home and see her people in Stamford. Early on Saturday morning she mounted the coach, handsome in her starched cottons, with baskets of pastries and pies on either arm.

On Monday afternoon she returned. She found a lift to Helpston in a tradesman's cart. As dusk settled she made her way to John Close's farm with her empty baskets. As she drew close she heard the shouting of Richard Royce and the Plough Bullocks. Knowing which day it was and not wanting her best cottons and shawl to be smeared with sooty grease from a Witch's ladle, she followed the fence and then walked behind the stables so that she could slip un-noticed through the kitchen door.

Out in the yard the Plough-boys had drunk John Close's ale. It was the last call of the day. The Bullocks put down their pole and Richard Royce stepped out from between the stilts. He put his hands to his mouth and bellowed up at the house:

"Give us a bloody rope will ye!"

Inside the drawing room Mr and Mrs Close were sitting with their two daughters. Mrs Close lifted her fingers to her ears:

"Oh that horrid man, however did he get chosen as King of the Harvest."

"Because," said John Close, "he'll do twice the work of any other. He's strong as an ox. No one can match him."

He called down to the kitchen:

"Give them a length of cart-rope!"

Mrs Close shuddered as though all her sensibilities had been offended.

Outside in the yard Richard Royce was enjoying himself.

"We'll finish the day with a tug o' war! Witches against Bullocks."

A rope was thrown out into the snowy yard.

"Come on! Stand to!"

Befuddled with John Close's strong ale, the Bullocks staggered to one end of the rope and lifted it. At the other end the Witches were throwing down besoms and ladles and conferring, there was a shout of laughter. Then they lifted their end.

Richard Royce unfastened the handkerchief from his throat and tied it to the middle of the rope. He scraped two lines into the snow with his heel.

"There…pull it across your line and you've won."

He raised his arm:

"Take the strain!"

The rope tightened between the two teams.

"Heave!"

The tug began. Iron-shod heels dug through the snow into the frozen muck of the yard below. Every man was leaning his weight against the other team, but the handkerchief was moving slow and steady towards the Witch's line.

Richard Royce turned to the Bullocks:

"Heave you useless sods!"

The handkerchief was almost over the line when Richard seized the rope and joined the Bullocks. He leaned backwards and grunted. The handkerchief began to move the other way. The Witches were being pulled forwards and slowly, inch by inch, the handkerchief drew close to the Bullocks' line.

"Heave…heave…heave…"

The team was working to Richard's rhythm.

Then Jem Johnson whistled and all the Witches opened their hands and let go of the rope.

The Bullocks staggered backwards across the yard. Richard Royce crashed into the iron pump and fell senseless to the ground. The others collapsed in drunken heaps. The Witches, laughing, pelted them with snowballs.

John Clare, holding his balance longer than most, was loosed like a stone from a sling. He staggered backwards across the yard into the shadows by the stable wall.

There was a woman's voice:

"Careful!"

Then he was aware of colliding with something and falling into a softness that was warmer than snow. He was on his back, laughing, and tangled up with another. His head was against the stiff cotton of a woman's lap. He opened his eyes and looked up at her.

Betsy Jackson had pulled herself up into a sitting position, her baskets half buried in the snow to either side of her. She peered down into the Plough-Bullock's face, smeared with soot and grease, and in the moment she would have pushed him aside and cursed him for his drunken antics she recognised him.

"John Clare!"

Before John had time to answer her lips were soft and warm against his mouth.

"How does that feel John?"

John was filled with a drunkard's oblivion to all but the sensation of the moment. He smiled up at her and she kissed him again, loosening the buttons of her coat and blouse and lifting his hand to one of her breasts. John could feel her nipple between his fingers. She recoiled and then relaxed at the sudden coldness of his touch. She kissed him again, more urgent, and John was lost to all but the prompting of his blood and the sweetness of sensation… for he had never run his hand across a woman's naked skin before. She whispered:

"Come with me!"

She scrambled to her feet, took his hand and pulled him upright.

"This way."

Unseen by any she pushed open the door of the stable. They went inside. It was dark. The air was full of the sweet, musky smell of horses and hay, and the sound of snorting and the scraping of hooves against the stone floor. She led him to the corner of the stable where some coarse woollen blankets had been thrown across a heap of hay. She threw herself down onto them.

"John…"

She pulled his hand and he fell down against her. Their lips met again. As they kissed she reached down and unbuckled his belt. She reached inside.

"How does that feel, John Clare?"

She did not need to hear his answer for she could feel in her hand how he wanted her now. With her other hand she pushed his fingers against her breast and for a long moment their mouths were pressed together, drinking thirstily and gasping against each other.

Then she hitched her petticoats up to her waist and drew him atop of her.

"John…"

But he silenced her mouth with his kisses, and for that little while that seems to be both an eternity and but a few short heartbeats they clung to one another as though all life depended upon it, as though all else before and after was lost in some faint mist that could only be dispelled by the quickness of their breath. And then with a sudden shudder and a cry she lifted her knees and drew him to her, and he lowered his mouth to her neck and folded against her, and she held him in her arms like a child.

Outside the Helpston Ploughboys were still shouting. Betsy lay back under John's weight and listened. As time passed the voices began to grow fainter. One by one they were leaving the farmyard and making their way home through the snow. John had fallen asleep. She eased him gently onto his side and pulled away from him. She folded a blanket over him. She climbed down from the hay-pile and brushed down her petticoat and gown. She buttoned up her blouse and coat. She made her way across the stable and pushed open the door. The night air was cold against her face. She picked up her two baskets and shook out the snow. The last of the Ploughboys was staggering out of the yard. She crossed quietly to the kitchen door, lifted the latch and pushed it open.

Elizabeth Close was standing in front of the fire pouring hot water from the kettle into a china pot.

"Oh Betsy, good, you're back at last…"

Then she gasped:

"Oh Betsy! Those horrid Plough Witches! They have smeared your face all over with their awful filth."

She put down the pot, poured hot water onto a cloth, ran across and dabbed Betsy's cheeks with it.

"There should be a law! Mother says so and I agree with her. It is a barbarous custom."

Betsy sat down on one of the wooden kitchen stools. Her body felt alive with a sleepy, triumphant song. She enjoyed the busy sensation of the cloth against her face. She smiled:

"'Tis an old custom, Miss Elizabeth…and I have never seen any great harm in it."

14

St Valentine's Day

Snow has given way to rain again and everywhere is mud. In the fields the men at their ploughs, or hedging and ditching, curse the cold wet that lashes their faces and the cloying mud that clogs their boots and drags them to a standstill. The shepherds set their backs to the wind as the winter lambing begins. The enclosure teams, at their fence-setting and stone-breaking, listen for the chiming of the church clock and count the hours until dusk when spades and hammers can be dropped and forgotten. The women, hurrying from dairy to coop, from kitchen to midden, lift their gowns and scold the wet that soaks their feet and the puddles that stain and bedraggle the hems of their petticoats. They curse the splashing horses and carts that throw up their stinking mud from the street. Only the ducks and geese in the yard-ponds rejoice at the wetness of the world.

Under the trees in the skirts of Oxey Wood and Royce Wood and beneath the blackthorn bushes on the commons the nodding snowdrops are come, that with the first crying lambs signal that the winter season is beginning to slacken its hold.

John Clare has told no soul his secret. In the weeks since Plough Monday maybe those who know him best – Dick Turnill, Parker, Ann, Sophie, Sam Billings, Mary Joyce –

maybe they have noticed some slight, subtle shift, some new turbulence in his inner weather that they cannot put a name to.

He cannot lie down to sleep at night without his thoughts turning to Betsy. He knows it would take only a word, a sign, a note slipped into her hand after the village band had played, and she would meet him, and all that had happened before would happen again. His body aches with desire for her, every drop of blood urges him to creep out of the cottage to John Close's yard and throw a stone at her window, if only he knew which window it was.

And then he remembers Mary.

Then he remembers Mary Joyce and his heart wakes up and his head sinks back against the pillow. He remembers her in every detail: her lovely, wild spirit; her tender, funny, kindly ways; her trusting, soft, bold kisses. And he hates every part of himself that could entertain the thought of betraying her.

Every Sunday John and Betsy have played together in the church band, without any word or glance being exchanged between them. As John is often silent and will stare at his boots rather than speak his thoughts, little notice is taken of his reticence by the rest of the band. And Betsy does not let John's silences keep her tongue from its cheerful chatter that gives away little of her thought.

On the third Sunday of this new year of our Lord that is 1812 she lingered in the church porch and waited for John, who himself had hung behind, hoping she was gone ahead. As he came out of the church door she called to him:

"John."

He blushed and carried on walking towards the church gate, his fiddle under his arm. She stood and walked swiftly to catch him up. The congregation was dispersed, the parson was still in church.

"John...Have you forgot me?"

The echo of his words to Mary when first he'd seen her at Snow Common made him blush deeper. They also served to harden his resolve.

He whispered:

"Let what happened be forgot. I have a sweet-heart. She is not thee."

"Not once again John?"

He felt his cock stirring in his breeches:

"Never."

He broke into a run and left her behind.

That afternoon, when the Close's Sunday luncheon had been served and cleared, Betsy Jackson asked if she might have a piece of paper and the use of one of Mr Close's quills and a bottle of ink.

"Ay Betsy," said Mrs Close. "Take what you need."

She carried them upstairs to her little room. She bolted the door. She put the ink pot on the chair. She knelt on the floor put a board on the bed and spread the paper on it. She dipped the pen into the ink.

'Dear John' she mouthed and scratched. *'You have pointed her out before. I warrant she hasn't shewn ye such sweets as I. Ay, and would again. Though I would not come between ye. Our secret is safe. Do not fear me. BJ.'*

She read the page several times over to herself, then tilted her head to one side, smiled and set the pen down on the chair. And in that smile was writ far more than her letter contained. It was sad and knowing and defiant and seemed to say to itself: 'For all that I have you hooked to my line, I will not die if I lose you, for I have known enough of love and loss to live another day without regret for what I have and have not done.' She tossed her curls, folded the paper, tucked it into the wooden box where she kept her oboe, and carried quill and ink downstairs.

The next Sunday she slipped the note to John.

It was not until he was walking the new road through Woodcroft Field on his way to Sunday luncheon at Joyce's Farm that he pulled it from his pocket and read it through. He tore it into tiny pieces and scattered them over the low hedges to the ploughed fields on either side as though he was scattering corn. There was little in the letter to ease his torment for it was clear enough that, Mary or no Mary, there would be a welcome from Betsy if he was to go to her.

But providence has been kind, for in the fortnight since the passing of the note she has not appeared in church. She has sent word that she is not feeling altogether well. And with her absence John has, at last, been able to begin to push Plough Monday to the back of his mind. He was after all, he tells himself, in his high altitudes. He was not altogether himself. And without Betsy's presence he has been able to dream that it is Mary's soft legs enclosing him, Mary's flesh against his hand.

And every Sunday he walks to Glinton and sits beside her at table and rejoices in her. He tells himself that he is shaking away the taint of Betsy Jackson and in his heart he thanks her for her absence.

****

Ever since Christmas morning, when the news reached Glinton that Will Bloodworth had vanished, Farmer Joyce has been uneasy. Every grain of evidence and every long-held prejudice point to foul play. He lies awake at nights telling himself that his willingness to testify on the gypsy's behalf and his complicity in his escape were grave misjudgements. He mutters to himself: "Maybe the Boswell youth should have hanged after all" and "Poor Mary is led astray, and I have been swayed by her". His good name is in danger of disgrace, and there is no soul to whom he dare speak his mind. He blames himself for being blind, and for letting himself be over-fond. "And was it not" he tells himself, "John Clare's influence on poor Mary that was the cause of all my distress…I should have listened to first promptings and nipped him in the bud?"

He governs his farm with an eye to every fault so that Will and Nathan are in a constant flurry of brushing and sweeping, and the women in dairy and kitchen wary of every smut.

And though he welcomes John Clare to his table on a Sunday it is clear in the tenor of his voice that his doubts have won the upper hand. Where he had been lax he feels that he must now be firm. And Mary, for her own happiness and for his peace of mind, must be made to see sense.

So it was that last Sunday, when John's visit to Glinton was ended and he was making his way out of Joyce's yard and Mary was standing in the kitchen door watching him, she felt her father's hand upon her shoulder.

"He won't do Mary."

She turned to face him.

"What d'you mean he won't do?"

"He won't do at all. I was riding home from Helpston on Friday and I saw him breaking stones for the new Glinton road with the enclosure team, and I thought to myself that he will never do for my Mary. He ain't going anywhere."

"He's a better man than any…"

"I'm not saying there's any harm to him…but think about it Mary, that's all I ask. Think about who you are and where we stand. And think about John Clare who has no land, no prospects and no fortune beyond his last week's wage…"

Mary's eyes filled with tears:

"Is that all you can think about? Is a man to be measured by the acres he owns?"

"I bear him no grudge Mary, but could he keep you? Could he make you happy? Love is blind, but marriage is a great eye-opener…"

"Whoever spoke of marriage?"

"Sooner or later you'll have to turn him down Mary. And the sooner it is the less you'll both be burned. Think on it."

****

On Valentines morning Mary Joyce was up before the dawn. No word of her father's would sway her from her resolve. Sooner or later – she told herself – he would see sense and give her and John his blessing. She had laid out her yellow dress the night before, the one she'd worn on Rogation Day and May Day, for it seemed to her that it had good fortune sewn into every seam. She washed herself and cleaned her teeth with twigs until they seemed to shine. She dressed and combed her hair. She made her way downstairs to the kitchen. Kate Dyball was already up and busy. Mary drew her into the pantry. She whispered:

"How do I look Kate?"

Kate looked her up and down. She brushed a stray hair from Mary's shoulder. Then she spoke from her heart:

"You look a picture Miss Mary. I reckon John Clare is the luckiest man in all England."

Mary laughed with delight at Kate's earnest face, and at some intimation that she spoke true. She kissed Kate's cheek.

"Listen. Here's my plan. I shall ride over early."

Mary cut a slice of bread. She cut herself some cheese. She took a mouthful.

"And I shall hide behind a tomb-stone, and when John comes he shall wait and wait and think that he's forsook. And the clock shall strike a quarter past the hour, and he'll be pacing up and down...and when his back is turned I shall creep up and surprise him from behind. What do you think o' that Kate?"

Kate's red fingers were spread out on her plump cheeks, her little eyes were round and shining and her mouth was open at the romance and the rashness of the plan.

"Oh I wish I had such notions as you Mary...but with Nathan I'd fear after five minutes he'd give up an' go home... and not see the funny side when I did jump out at him."

"But John'll wait," said Mary with conviction.

"Ay, I reckon he will..." Kate looked at Mary and smiled, "leastways he's a dolt if he doesn't."

Mary crammed the last of the bread into her mouth and winked. Kate laughed and then a shadow of concern played across her round face:

"Be careful though Miss Mary. Wrap up warm. We don't want you catching your death this day of all days."

"I have my father's constitution Kate, who has never seen a day's sickness in his life...but don't worry, I'll wrap up in cloak and scarf and bonnet."

Mary and Kate slipped out of the pantry door and crossed the yard to the stable. Together they saddled the little dappled cob. Kate helped Mary up.

"God bless you Mary. Good luck. I shall be thinking of ye!"

Mary leaned down:

"Tell no one I'm gone. If they ask I'm abed with a sore head."

"Ay. We're only scrubbing the copper for tomorrow's brewing. You shall not be missed."

Mary waved and rode out of the yard. The sky overhead was blue with high white clouds and the road beneath the cob's hooves was awash with puddles that reflected the heavens so that it seemed to Mary that she rode between sky and sky.

She rode out of Glinton and along the new road to Helpston. At the edge of the village she tethered the horse to a fence-post. The parish was astir. The labourers leading their horses out to the fields took little notice of her, nor did the enclosure teams. She walked the last half mile to the church. The clock was striking the half hour after eight as she chose a high headstone close to the church porch. She brushed the water away from the wet grass. She had a piece of leather to sit on. She spread it out and sat down with her back to the stone. She drew up her knees and looked towards the churchyard wall where the skeps stand. She pulled a hunk of bread from her pocket and munched it, rehearsing in her mind the words of the pledge that she had composed. In the February sunshine that came and went some sleepy bees were stirring. One of them settled on her cloak. She watched it picking its careful way across the woven threads as though they carried a promise of sweetness.

****

John Clare woke earlier than Mary and lit a candle. He read the pledge that he has revised so many times these last days that it is become a mess of cross-hatchings and words writ over words so that the page is more black than white. He seemed to be satisfied. He climbed out of bed, dressed, kissed it and pushed it into the pocket of his breeches. His Sunday shirt was hanging over the chair. He pulled it over his head. He tied a handkerchief about his throat. When he came downstairs Parker, Ann and Sophie were up and about and making ready to go to work. His parents looked at John with raised eyebrows to see him dressed so fine on a workday like any other.

"Where are ye going John?"

John would not be drawn:

"Here and there."

Was all the answer he would give. Then he added:

"Tell Will Mash that I shall be late this morning and shall make up my time at dusk."

Parker grunted:

"He will not like it."

"He shall have to like it."

It was Sophie, of course, who read John's intention.

"I know where he's going."

"Where?"

"To meet with his sweet-heart of course. 'Tis the fourteenth of February after all."

John blushed. Parker sighed and pushed open the door:

"Well, don't be over-long with your sweet nothings or you'll have a sweet nothing of a job."

Ann kissed John:

"He has forgot, John, the Valentines he used to bring me when we were courting."

She followed Parker out of the door. Sophie looked at John most intent. She studied his shirt and neckerchief:

"You're got up most particular smart John Clare."

She pinched his neckerchief between finger and thumb and tilted her head to one side:

"You ain't goin' to propose to Mary Joyce are ye?"

She exploded with laughter.

"Are ye?"

From outside Ann's voice came, most exasperated:

"Come on Soph' we shall be late again."

She looked at him over her shoulder with an expression of great merriment and disappeared through the door.

John was left alone. He sat down and cut himself a piece of bread, wondering at Sophie's acuteness. He shook his head, sighed, smiled, and ate the bread. He pulled out the piece of paper and read through his pledge again. He listened to the chiming of the quarters. His feet were fidgeting, tapping the hard earth of the floor. At last it struck a quarter to nine.

He pushed open the cottage door and made his way past Butter Cross to the churchyard gate. He looked across towards the porch. Mary was not there. He followed the path. He entered the porch. He pushed open the church door and peered inside. There was no sign of her. He came out again and looked to left and right. He was early. He would sit in the porch and wait for her.

Behind the headstone Mary Joyce was pinching her nose to hold in her laughter. She turned and peered over the top of it. She could see John's feet tapping the stone floor.

John read through his pledge yet again. He pushed it back into his pocket. He stood and scanned the churchyard. He took a few paces towards the gate and peered beyond it. He turned back to the porch. He sat down. The church clock struck nine. He closed his eyes. Surely she would come…

Then he heard the churchyard gate click. He heard footsteps approaching. He jumped to his feet.

"John?"

It was Betsy Jackson's voice.

"John. I thought I caught a glimpse of you as I was

passing."

John looked at her dumbfounded.

"I have been wanting to speak to you alone. We are alone ain't we?"

Her face had lost its habitual rosy-red glow. There was a wanness to her cheek and her voice trembled.

John looked to left and right and to his relief could see no one. He whispered:

"Betsy, I have told you before…"

"John, listen to me…"

She reached and took his arm. He pulled it away from her:

"Go away! Leave me alone."

"John, you have managed in one night what my husband did not in fifteen years."

She put her hand to her belly:

"I am quick John. I am with child."

John said nothing. For a full minute he spoke no word. Then:

"How do you know?"

"A woman knows. I have not bled. I am terrible sick of a morning. I know."

John's head was empty of all thought but Mary. He looked across towards the street. There was no sign of her.

"It is mine? You are sure?"

"It could only be yours."

She looked into his face, her blue eyes candid and swollen with tears.

John looked at her and was lost for any word. She seemed to have become some monstrous thing, some breasted Annis standing between him and his happiness. She took a step towards him.

"My husband always mocked me and called me barren

John, and I believed him. But it must have been he who had the damp powder…for now we have made a baby, you and me."

She pressed her face down to John's shoulder.

"Marry me John. I will make you happy."

John's body tensed. And then he was filled with a cold white rage. He pushed her fiercely away. She stumbled backwards and tripped on the grass verge beside the churchyard path.

"Never…I will never marry you…never."

Tears were streaming down his cheeks.

"I have told you and showed you that I love another. Leave me alone."

She had fallen onto the wet grass between two headstones. Slowly she sat up and pulled herself to her feet. As she did so she saw that the two of them had not been alone after all. She saw behind one of the headstones, curled over in the wet grass someone else had been party to their conversation. She looked long enough through her own tears to recognise her. It was John's sweet-heart. It was Farmer Joyce's Mary. She was lying, in her thick cloak and dress of primrose yellow, like some crumpled thing that had been crushed in someone's hand and cast aside.

His voice was hardening and lifting in strength against her like a fist.

"Never."

Betsy stood. She said nothing. She took a deep breath and turned away from him. She gathered herself against his words, against all the world and its condemnation.

"Never Betsy."

She made her way along the path and with a sharp click she closed the churchyard gate behind her and was gone.

John sat down on the stone bench in the church porch with

his face in his hands. He lifted the corner of his neckerchief and wiped his eyes. He was trembling and there was a terrible cold emptiness in the pit of his belly. He got up again, went outside and looked up at the church clock. It was only ten past nine. He sat down again. The clock struck the quarter. She did not come.

When the clock struck the half hour he was still sitting, staring at the stone floor. He could not believe that Mary had not come. He was thinking that if she would only come he would make it all right between them and the whole world would slip into rightness around them. But she did not come.

It was just before the clock struck ten that Mrs Bullimore from the shop roused him. She was carrying a change of altar flowers in her hand.

"John Clare, here you are, I've had your father asking whether I've clapped eyes on you this last hour, and Will Mash cussing the day you was born. You'd best get along or you'll be in deep water."

John pulled himself to his feet and went out into the rain. Anyone who could have read his heart would have seen, writ full clear, that the bright world had begun, one by one, to break its promises.

15

Shrove Tuesday

Now enclosure hurries on apace. The hedges and fences are for the most part in place so that each of the three great fields is divided and divided again according to the award. The farmers: Ralph Wormstall, John Close, Sam Price, Elizabeth Wright, Mr Bull, Farmer Joyce and the rest ride out and survey their entitlements with a complacent eye.

Lolham Bridge Field, Heath Field and Woodcroft Field are all but gone now, as are the heaths and commons. Where they used to be there is an ordered cross-hatching of squares and rectangles.

More men have been hired by the Earl of Fitzwilliam to complete the straightening of the dykes and to dig the drains. William Bradford at the Bluebell Inn is prospering as never before. There is nowhere a body can cast its eye but there is activity upon the face of the land.

And what choice has the landless man but to make hay while the sun shines? John and Parker Clare have been setting fences around Langdyke Bush, for it is to become private grazing for Mr Bull. The fire-pits are still scorched black from the fires of the Boswell crew, but that common will never be a camping ground for gypsies again. With the setting of fences comes a new order.

Every day Bob Turnill is out on his small entitlement. But he is not surveying it like a squire from the saddle and counting his blessings, he is between the stilts of a plough working from dawn to dusk, stopping only to munch at bread, cheese and onion and cast his eye across a chapter of scripture. And Mrs Turnill labours as hard as he does, whether it's at the milking, or the feeding, the mucking, the winnowing, the spinning or the baking. And at the end of the day, by candle-light, when their meagre supper is eaten, the Turnills pore over their accounts and pray for clement weather. Dick, whose income is all the money they have, watches helpless as they are drawn into a deeper and deeper exhaustion, and sees his hard earned wage swallowed by creditors as soon as it is laid on the table.

In Glinton Farmer Joyce has been studying his new-hedged, new-turned fields and wondering whether the soil is ready for the spring sowing. On Friday last, when there was a clear sky and a March sun and a few early larks were spilling their songs across the parish, he rode out with Will Farrell. When they were far out in the fields and out of sight of all, he climbed down from the saddle and picked up a handful of earth. He pinched it. He crumbled it in his hand. He sniffed it. He turned to Will with a sigh:

"I cannot decide one way or t'other. She seems near enough ready for seed Will…"

Will climbed down and did the same.

"Mmmm."

"There's only one thing for it. We shall have to put her to the old test."

Both men looked to left and right, and when they were sure that they were quite alone they unbuckled their belts and pulled their breeches down to their knees.

"'Tis the only way Will."

They sat backwards and lowered their white buttocks slowly down to the furrows until their swinging bollocks touched the raw earth. Will sucked in his breath. Farmer Joyce grunted. Then they stood up again and brushed away the crumbs of soil. They pulled up their breeches.

"What d'ye reckon Will?"

"I say not yet. There's a chill upon her still and she needs to dry a little more."

"By God, you have read my thoughts. Ten more days of sun like today, and we shall fill your seed-lip with corn and make a start."

They rode back to the farm. Farmer Joyce inspected the pig-sties and the cattle, who were still lowing and shuffling on trampled straw in their winter quarters. It was dusk when he came to the kitchen door. As he lifted his boot to the scraper he saw there was a folded paper tucked against it. He lifted it, squinted at it and sighed. He pushed open the door and strode into the kitchen.

"Mary."

She was cutting vegetables with Kate.

"Mary, here's another letter from your John Clare."

She looked up at him quick and sudden, and then her face froze. It was as though her recollection had overtaken her heart's first impulse at his name. She put down her knife, came across and took it from his hand. She set it on the mantleshelf.

"Thank you Papa."

"Ain't you going to read it?"

She returned to her chopping board and did not answer him. He sized her up shrewdly from beneath his bristling eye-brows:

"'Tis a few weeks since we last clapped eyes on him."

He pulled off his boots and drew a chair to the kitchen fire. He took a clay pipe from the rack and filled it with tobacco. He took an ember in the iron tongs, lifted it to the bowl of the pipe and sucked. The chimney pulled the sweet smoke up into itself.

There was a silence, broken only by the sound of knives against wood. Kate Dyball looked across at Mary, but she gave no clue as to what thought might be playing in her mind. She chopped until the job was done and then walked across to the kitchen door, she rested her hand lightly on her father's shoulder as she passed him. She ran light-footed up the stairs to her bed-chamber. It was only when she was alone that she let her countenance fall. She sat on the edge of her bed and stared out of the window. And behind her face hid a wounded thing, a mazed swift with a broken wing that sits in the hand and will take no food, or a shrew that has been a cat's plaything.

Later, when the kitchen was empty, she came quietly down. She took the letter from its shelf and threw it, un-opened, into the flames. She prodded it with a poker until it crumbled to black dust.

****

Letters were all John's hope now.

On the first Sunday after Valentine's, when church was finished, he had walked the road to Joyce's farm, treading the stones he had broken himself. He had knocked at the kitchen door and Kate Dyball had opened. She'd looked at him and called over her shoulder:

"'Tis John Clare."

John could hear the sound of the scraping of a chair and feet hurrying away. Kate had looked at him with solemn eyes and whispered:

"I don't know what has passed between you and Miss Mary, but she is become spelled and strange as a changeling. She is but a shadow of herself."

Then Farmer Joyce was standing behind her:

"Ah John Clare, come in, come in if you must."

John had followed him to the kitchen table.

"Sit down…"

He'd looked about the room. Farmer Joyce had followed his gaze.

"Ah, Mary is gone."

John had sat down beside Mary's half-eaten plate of food. Farmer Joyce had poured him a mug of ale and pushed it across the table. Kate ran upstairs and then returned to the kitchen door.

"She will not come Mr Joyce, she will not answer."

The farmer looked at John and shrugged:

"That's the way of it."

He went to the foot of the stairs and bellowed:

"Mary!"

He turned:

"It seems she'll have none of ye. She'll no more be budged than a spooked horse can be made to jump a stile."

John had gulped down his beer, got up to his feet and nodded his leave. Farmer Joyce walked him to the door.

"A very good afternoon to ye, John Clare."

John had trudged away across the yard and the farmer had watched him for a while, then turned back to the kitchen.

Mary was sitting at the table, eating her food as though she had not been disturbed. Her father sat opposite her and smiled.

"Good girl, ye've seen sense and acted on it."

Mary looked up at him like a startled deer. Then she was on

her feet and up the stairs again.

****

Since that Sunday John has vowed that he will not return until she's replied to one of his letters.

Every day he has worked until the blisters on his hands are calloused into hard skin. He has worked so that his muscles are become taut and all fat is fallen away from him. He has worked each day until the rhythm of mallet to post, of hammer to stone, have so entered his body that all thought is driven out, all aching hurt is forgot. At dusk he trudges home and all the early flowers, that he has ever loved to see, the daisies closing their bright eyes, the retiring primroses clustered on the bank, all seem only to be sharp reminders of Mary. Some evenings he drinks ale at the Bluebell or Bachelors Hall, losing himself in loud talk and song and staggering home to oblivious sleep. Sometimes he sits and scribbles letters by candlelight, throwing them angrily into the fire, or folding them and putting them aside to deliver next day at Mary's door. On such nights it can be two or three of the morning before he lies down to sleep.

And no reply comes.

He lives from day to day in hopes of finding a white envelope on the doorstep, or hearing the clatter of hooves and the sound of her voice, clear as a throstle, calling his name.

But there is only silence now where Mary had used to be.

****

Yesterday was Shrove Tuesday and all evening Betsy Jackson was pouring fat and batter into the iron skillets that hung over the kitchen fire. First she carried the piled plates of yellow freckled pancakes to the dining room where the Closes waited for their supper. The two Close daughters had their heads together at one end of the polished table, deep in talk of Lenten abstinences. Mrs Close pushed a fork into the top pancake and lifted it onto a plate. She passed it to Elizabeth:

"You could always give up chatter."

John Close lifted his glass to his lips.

"Ay, I'll drink to that."

When the family of the house had eaten their fill, and John Close had retired to the parlour and was loosening his buttons and stretching his feet to the fire, Betsy had to turn her attention to the kitchen. The farmhands and servants sitting either side of the wooden table eyed her as she worked.

"Come on Betsy, we can't hardly hear ourselves think for the rumbling of our bellies."

Betsy tapped a wooden spoon against the jug of batter.

"They're coming, they're coming... patience is a virtue. Pancakes will only fry one at a time. Now if one of you'd slice the bacon and another would be good enough to lay out the platters to the table..."

She turned back to her cooking with a sigh.

When everyone's plate had been filled she sat down herself and laid cheese and bacon onto her pancake. She ate with a purpose, and when the others had stood up from the table and gone to their rooms she cooked herself another.

"Ay Betsy," she whispered to herself as she flicked it over in the pan. "You'll need every ounce of strength you can muster this night."

When she'd finished eating she put the platters into the sink for Ann Clare to wash in the morning. She tidied and set all straight. But she did not go to bed. She took her cloak and bonnet from their hook by the kitchen door. She took off her house slippers and pulled on her stout walking shoes. She lifted the purse that hangs from her belt and tipped her few saved shillings onto the scrubbed table. She counted them and with her cupped hand swept them back into the purse again. She opened the kitchen door. Outside a strong wind was blowing, it whipped her curls against her face. She came back inside and tied back her hair. She pulled the bonnet harder onto her head.

There was a hard resolve written upon her features, as though she was acting upon some decision long-since taken. She crossed the farmyard and the street. She turned her back on the village and made her way across the fields, shunning all the houses with their bright fire-lit windows.

Heath Field is caught tight now in a taut net of straight fences and new-planted hedgerows. She climbed over one fence after another. She pushed between the quick-thorn bushes and the thorns tugged at her cloak. A fox barked in Royce's Wood. She quickened her step. The wind sang among the branches of the willows along the dyke edge. She jumped the stream, holding up her skirts. She strode with a purpose. The moon came and went behind the scudding clouds and she seemed to walk through the darkness with a possessed assurance. She did not stumble. There was a shepherd's lambing wagon at the lower end of Heath Field. She gave it a wide berth. When she came to Torpel Way she followed it westward to Maxham's Green Lane, drawing her cloak about herself.

It was only as she passed the piles of fencing slats at the edge of Snow Common that her pace slowed and for the first time she caught her foot on the rough tussocks of the common. When she saw the rounded form of the Otter's squat looming out of the shadows, dark against the sky like a tumped burial mound, she seemed to falter. She stood a-while and the moon caught her face. She watched the white trickle of smoke rising from the Otter's smoke-hole that was quickly torn to ribbons by the wind. She shook her head, turned on her heel, and began to walk away. Then she turned again, clenched her fists and boldly strode to the canvas flap of the door:

"Kitty Otter!"

She startled herself with the loudness of her voice. Inside there was a rustling and a scuffling.

"Who's there?"

"'Tis I, Betsy Jackson."

The canvas was pulled back and Old Otter's face peered blearily out of the doorway. Behind him Betsy could see Kitty Otter throwing sticks onto the fire.

"'Tis Betsy Jackson right enough." He turned and called over his shoulder. "Her as blows oboe in the church music."

Kitty nodded:

"Bring her inside, bring her inside, it's a cold night as has blown her across the common, she must be needing something bad."

Old Otter pulled the door open and Betsy entered. The sharp smells, part apothecary's shop, part smoke-house, part fox's den, took her aback, but only the wrinkling of her nose betrayed her. She sat down on a stump before the fire and pulled the bonnet from her head. Kitty looked her up and down:

"What brings you here Betsy Jackson, from John Close's farm…as once was wed to Tom Jackson of Stamford…ay, and there's more I could tell but will stay my tongue for I do not speak ill of the dead."

Betsy looked across at her, startled:

"What do you know of Tom?"

"There ain't much Kitty Otter don't know child…but she can keep a secret as fast as a stone. What's the matter with ye?"

She smiled, kindly beneath the smoke stained wrinkles. She reached across and hung an iron kettle over the flames.

Betsy looked into the fire and said nothing. There was a long silence, then Kitty turned and nodded fiercely at Old Otter. He wrapped a blanket about himself, filled his pipe, took a smouldering stick from the fire and pushed through the door-flap. Betsy watched him go.

"Won't he be cold?"

"No, he has a hollow tree, he'll be right enough."

Kitty reached across and took Betsy's hand. She patted it between her own.

"Now…"

"I am with child."

Kitty sucked the smoky air between her teeth.

"I thought as much from the moment you come through the door. But you ain't some slip of a girl as don't know what she's doin' til the damage is done, Betsy. How did you get quick? Who done it?"

Betsy shook her head:

"To tell the truth I had thought I was barren or I would've took more care… for Tom had often mocked me…"

"Let's not talk of Tom…now, what will ye do? Who's the daddy? Is he worth his salt? Could he provide for ye?"

Betsy hesitated. She looked pleading at Kitty.

"You promise to keep my secret?"

"Upon my mother's grave."

Betsy leaned forward and whispered into Kitty's ear.

Kitty stared at her.

"John Clare."

She dropped Betsy's hand and got up to her feet.

"John Clare!"

She turned away from the fire, then turned back again.

"There ain't much can shock Kitty Otter, but you have shocked me this night Betsy Jackson. Little John Clare as is courtin' Mary Joyce, and them in each other's thrall as though each was witched by the other?"

Betsy nodded.

"Why, I have seen them walking on this common not long since, and it seemed to me that they had drawn a circle about themselves that none could enter…and now 'tis you as carries his babby?"

Betsy nodded again.

Kitty sat down, as though overcome with weariness, she shook her head and her grey hair fell down in straggles across her face. There was silence but for the crackling of the fire. Then Betsy reached across and touched Kitty's knee:

"Sometimes a body can't help herself…it was Plough-Monday, John fell into my arms, and I did ache for him."

Kitty's voice turned fierce now:

"Ah, a Plough-Monday bastard…and it won't be the first… and him as drunk as a new-dropped calf I shouldn't wonder."

Betsy hung her head and said nothing.

"Have ye told John Clare? Has any word of this reached Mary Joyce's ears?"

Betsy was careful with her answer:

"I have told John only, and he will have nothing of me."

"And what of the babby?"

For the first time Betsy shed tears. They trickled down her cheeks and she wiped them away with her sleeve.

"Why else would I have come to you Kitty…"

She put her hand to her belly.

"Though, God knows, for ten years I did yearn, and Tom did mock, and nothing came…and now where there should be joy there is only shame."

Kitty's face softened. She took Betsy's hand again.

"Ay, 'tis best it goes…'tis best old Kitty twines it from ye, or God spare us the consequence. You're strong and young enough to bear more when the time is ripe."

Betsy nodded.

"Must you work tomorrow?"

"No, John Close has give me Ash Wednesday free."

"All well and good."

Kitty lifted her hand to her lips and whistled through her fingers, piercing and shrill. Soon Old Otter was pushing through the door. She winked at him, but without any flicker of a smile.

"'Tis the old affliction. We'll need to fill the tub."

He nodded. Without a word the two of them took kettles and pots from the shadows and lifted them to the doorway. Kitty pulled a blanket over her shoulders and fastened it with a bronze clasp.

"We're away to the stream to fetch water. You stay here and sup on this while I'm gone."

She reached into the roof and pulled down a poppy head, a dried stalk of white hellebore and a stem of penny-royal. She dropped them into a wooden bowl, pounded them with a stick and poured boiling water from the hissing, spitting kettle onto them. She put the bowl into Betsy's hands.

"This will be a harsh night for ye Betsy Jackson, but it will pass with the dawn and soon enough will be forgot."

Betsy lifted the bowl to her face and sniffed the bitter steam.

Kitty threw more wood onto the fire then turned back to the door:

"Come on Otter, there's work to be done."

With a clattering of pot to kettle they disappeared into the darkness. When they returned they raked out the fire and set the water over the glowing coals to boil. Old Otter pulled a wooden tub from the shadows. Whenever a kettle came to the boil the water was emptied into the tub and filled again from the stream. Again and again the pots and kettles were filled and brought to the boil and emptied into the tub. Kitty, Old Otter and Betsy were glistening with sweat. The squat was so filled with steam that even the fire disappeared in the hot, stinging mist, and every hanging plant and skin dripped sharp and fetid moisture onto the floor.

Kitty dipped her hand into the tub. She whispered to Otter and he pushed through the flap with an empty kettle in either hand.

"Take your clothes off Betsy Jackson and climb inside."

Betsy's face was streaming with moisture. She was gasping as though she could drown in steam. Her eyes were half-closed and her thoughts already fevered with the poppy-head tea. Kitty helped her unbutton and unfasten herself. She held Betsy's hand as she climbed into the tub. The water was so hot that Betsy gasped.

"It'll do ye no harm. Settle down and drink some o' this."

She pressed a bottle into Betsy's hand. Hoping for cool water Betsy lifted it to her lips and poured it into her mouth, she found herself choking on gin.

"Ay, you'll have tasted that before I shouldn't wonder."

When Otter returned with the kettles Kitty seized them from him and put them onto the fire.

"That's enough of water…now skin me some withies."

The canvas flap dropped and he disappeared again into the night.

The willows, pollarded since time ever was, have been

marked for felling with streaks of glistening red paint that seemed to shine like open wounds as the moon rode out from between the clouds, and then close again as it disappeared. Old Otter reached up into one of them, chose two long supple withies and cut them with his knife. He sat down on a stump and skinned away the bark so that the whip-thin clean white wood was laid bare, as pale as Betsy's flesh. He carried them back to the squat and whistled. Kitty's claw-like hand pushed out through the side of the door flap. He pushed the withies into it. She pulled her hand inside.

"Now leave us be."

He turned and trudged away and soon enough the sound of Betsy's retching and crying were lost in the wind. He came to his hollow dotterel and slipped through the cracked bark of its portal. Inside his little fire was glowing still. He threw more sticks onto it until it blazed and crackled. He squatted on his haunches with his back pressed to the rotting wooden wall. He took a blazing twig and lit his pipe. He sucked and spat into the hot coals. The tree was its own creaking chimney. Tobacco and wood-smoke were swept up into the night. Above his head the thin branches lashed each other in the wind and the torn clouds raced across the moon. He closed his eyes and puffed himself into contentment.

Suddenly from the squat there came a scream, long and piercing, then there was only wind again. He poked the fire with his boot and paid it no more nor less mind than he would the screech of an owl, or a vixen on heat, or a rabbit with a weasel at its throat.

****

Betsy was woken by the grip of a hand to her shoulder. She

was warm under a heap of skins. She opened her eyes and saw her clothes spread out and drying on branches in the firelight. The shadows of the squat were dancing in the flames, all steam and water was gone.

"'Tis an hour short of the dawn, time you was gone Betsy Jackson."

Betsy pulled herself unsteadily to her feet. There was a wringing pain in her lower belly. She was stark mother naked, her skin still puffed and pink from the hot water. One by one Kitty Otter handed her clothes to her and slowly she put them on, welcoming their warmth and dryness against her skin. Kitty pulled the door-flap aside and Betsy went out into the night. The wind had eased and the air was fresh and kind. Her head was still thick and throbbing with the gin and poppy-head tea, she breathed deep. Then she pulled her purse from her pocket and pressed it into Kitty's hand. Kitty neither thanked her nor opened it. She thrust it into the pocket of her leather apron.

"Here's something for thee…"

Kitty reached down and picked up a nest of soft green moss. Lying in its cup there was something that Betsy could not bring herself to look upon. She took it and covered it gently with her hand.

"Do with it as ye will…it must not stay here."

Betsy nodded and turned away.

"Go careful now, bathe again and sleep. You'll be well enough come Thursday."

Betsy turned and disappeared into the night.

Kitty dropped the door-flap and muttered to herself:

"And if you ain't you'll need more than my physic to save ye."

She lifted her fingers to her mouth and whistled, soon enough Old Otter was pushing his way into the squat to join her.

****

And now, in the last dark of this Ash Wednesday morning, with the stars beginning to fade and the cockerels stirring on their rafters, Betsy Jackson stops in Snow Common and stoops to pull primrose leaves and cover the little bundle she holds so careful in her hand. Unsteadily she treads the lanes to Heath Road, clutching it as tenderly as little children will carry some dead thing that they have found, a wren maybe, perfect in its red-brown freckled feathers, or a shrew.

She steps slow and stumbling, as though each foot-fall costs her dear, her face as blank as a statue carved in wood or stone. It is as though she sleep-walks, until some little stumble wrenches her into pain again. She is coming to the village now and stepping as quiet as she is able. She is walking up Woodgate, past the Clare's cottage that is deep in sleep. And now she passes Butter Cross and makes her way over the street towards the church. She is not going home. She is stumbling through the lych-gate and into the churchyard. Her swollen skin is ashen now. All pink has been driven from her cheek. Her lips are open and seem to be shaping words that cannot be heard.

She threads her way between the headstones and drops to her knees beside the skeps. With her right hand she is tearing at the grass against the wall. She pulls up a ragged turf and digs into the soil beneath with her fingers. She is making a hole, scooping it out and patting it smooth with the back of her hand.

Tenderly she lifts the primrose leaves. There is enough light now for her to see clearly the little glistening red kernel of flesh that would have been her child lying on its soft green bed. She leans forward and lays the nest of moss in its tiny grave. Her tears drop into the hallowed soil. She lays the leaves tenderly on top of it and covers it with earth. She gently puts the turf on top of it and pats it down. For a while she looks at the place, as though trying to hold it in her memory. Then she pulls herself to her feet as the dawn strengthens, and hurries home to John Close's farm before any soul ventures out into the day.

And no soul has seen her – save only Charlie Turner's half-wit daughter Isabel, watching with her moon-eyes from the window of the hovel against the churchyard wall. With a solemn stare she follows Betsy's back until it disappears, then turns to where her bone-thin father shivers beneath his rags and mouths words around her hanging tongue that none can understand.

16

Easter Monday

They have found Will Bloodworth at last.

In Elizabeth Wright's house the air had been shifting with his discomfiture so that old dust was lifted on her rafters, and her dogs would growl sudden and for no reason.

Now he is quiet though, having been laid properly to rest in the churchyard, and with nothing to hold him back from his ease.

It was Jim Crowson who first caught wind of him, a fortnight since. He was shovelling the steaming muck from Elizabeth Wright's midden and throwing it up into a cart to spread beneath her apple trees. Well broke-down the muck was, and sweet-smelling as muck should be to those that can read its savours. Then, all of a sudden, there came a new stench, entering his nostrils so thick and sickly that he retched at its sweet, foul odour of decay. He stepped back and looked down at the clean cut he had made with the blade of his spade, and he saw that he had skinned the back of a hand that was tombed in the dung. The clean white bones were glistening in the sunlight. And there was no doubting that it belonged either to a man or a woman.

He dropped his spade and ran to the house, as pale as a

cheese-cloth. He shouted his alarum, and soon enough a team of men with wet muslin tied over noses and mouths were lifting a corpse from the midden.

Mrs Elizabeth Wright and all her household came out into the yard and watched as the body was laid out on a board and no word was spoken between them. It was as all had feared. It was carried into a barn and washed down with bucket after bucket of water. The smell was so strong that Mrs Wright could not come close and stood in the barn doorway, the tears trickling silently down her cheeks. The warmth at the heart of the midden had half-cooked the corpse so that the blackened skin was falling away from the flesh. But it was clear enough that this was the corpse of Will Bloodworth. His sister had rehearsed the clothes he'd last been wearing over and over in her mind, and the stinking tatters that were laid bare before her eyes were Will's right enough. And it was clear to all who looked upon him how he had met his death. There was a clean cut to his throat where a sharp knife had been drawn across it.

Long before Mr Bullimore the constable had arrived on the scene, long before the coroner had been fetched, long before Parson Mossop had ridden across with his whispered consolations, or Jonathan Burbridge had begun to measure for the coffin, the village was whispering like an aspen in the wind. The gossiping speculation that had fallen into a slumber had been woken with a jolt, and was voiced urgently across door-step, street and furrow:

"It has the mark of gypsy upon it."

"Ay, if they'd hung the Boswell youth, Will Bloodworth would be living and breathing yet."

"Damn them all, I say, transport the lot of 'em."

"I knew him, he was a tricky lad, but not vengeful, I don't see his hand in it."

"I do, for their smiles run skin deep only, and think of some of them others that camped at Langdyke…"

And those in the village that know more than they will say of the rigs and the jigs of that winter's night hold their tongues and keep their council. For they know in their hearts who is innocent and who guilty.

When Bill Bullimore came to the barn he drew the same conclusion as the village, as did the coroner in his turn. Warrants were drawn up for the arrest of Wisdom Boswell on suspicion of murder. Enquiries were made across the region, but no soul has seen sight nor sign of the Boswell crew since mid-winter. Every gypsy camp between Peterborough and Stamford has been ran-sacked, but no evidence has been found beyond hostile stares, shrugged shoulders and shaken heads.

The Earl of Fitzwilliam has alerted the Bow Street Runners, and every lead is followed, but all to no avail.

****

Mrs Elizabeth Wright paid Jonathan over the odds for a lead-lined coffin so that Will could rest in her parlour the last two nights before his funeral, with candles at his head and foot. The curtains were drawn and the household dressed in its black mourning. And all day the villagers came to pay their respects, part out of curiosity, part out of pity, and part to keep favour with Elizabeth Wright.

The Earl of Fitzwilliam had sent a wreath garlanded with yellow daffodils that took pride of place upon the coffin lid.

They filed past with their grave faces, the Turnills, Crowsons, Closes, Dolbys, Bains, Wormstalls, Bullimores, Royces, Samsons, Bellars, Farrars, Dyballs and all the rest.

Parker and Ann Clare came, for Ann had known Will when

he was little more than a boy, having worked in old man Wright's kitchen. They stood a while in the dark parlour and spoke condolences and then made their way out of the farm house and across the muddy yard. It was just as they were passing the gate that Farmer Joyce arrived, sitting high in a painted gig with Will Farrell at the reins.

"Parker Clare! Rein in the horses a moment Will."

As the horses slowed to a walk he sprang down from the bench of the gig. He bowed to Ann.

"Good day to ye both…and a sorry one."

"Ay, it is."

"I wonder if I could draw you aside a moment Mr Clare for a few words in private."

He took Parker by the arm. Parker turned to his wife:

"You go on ahead Ann, I'll catch up with ye."

The two men withdrew to a corner of the yard and stood with their backs to the ricks. Farmer Joyce fixed Parker with an iron gaze:

"It seems the law is not such an ass after all Mr Clare… maybe it would have been better for us all had the gypsy hanged."

Parker shook his head.

"There is no blood on Wisdom's hands, not a drop. He did not have it in him."

Then he lowered his voice to a whisper:

"And besides he rode north with Ismael Boswell on Christmas night, as soon as ever he was clear of Peterborough… but I cannot say the same for King Boswell."

There was a silence between them, then Farmer Joyce said:

"Well, whatever King Boswell did or did not do is outside our conscience, thank God."

He turned towards the farm house.

"And now I must go and pay my respects…"

Then he lowered his voice again:

"…Though, between you and me, they are directed more to the living than the dead."

"One last thing," said Parker Clare, "before ye go…"

He looked down at his boots.

"My John and your Mary are fallen out…and something is broke in John that will be a very long time a-mending… and if it's his lack of prospects as have brought about your discouragement, then I beg you to think again."

For a while Farmer Joyce said nothing. Then:

"My Mary is like a bird that has lost all delight in flight and song and I cannot read her…but she'll get over it…she's little more than a child."

Then his voice hardened:

"I ain't so blind that I can't see there are some things as are beyond the measure of money… but marriage, Mr Clare, ain't one of them."

He turned and strode across the yard.

And Parker made his way out of the gate and along Crossberry Way.

****

On Easter Sunday Betsy Jackson came to the morning service with her oboe. When Jonathan Burbridge spied her stepping through the church door in her Sunday best he leaned his bass-viol against the pew and sprang to his feet.

"Betsy, we was beginning to despair of ye."

She smiled at him:

"I had been a little under the weather this winter Jonathan, but now am fully myself again."

He made a space for her and she sat down, opened the wooden box and fitted together the parts of her instrument. She blew a shrill note and looked round at the members of the church band: Jonathan, Dick, Sam, and John Clare.

"And 'tis a pleasure to be musicing again with you gentlemen."

When the first hymn began she lifted her oboe to her lips and blew as full-cheeked and undiminished as when first she'd played with the band, and gave no sign or indication of any secret pain.

John Clare had paled when he'd seen her come, and had passed an anxious eye over her when she was turned away from him to see how her belly swelled. But she seemed to give no sign of her condition. Indeed she seemed to him to be trimmer than he remembered her.

Prayer followed hymn, and hymn followed prayer. When the sermon came Jonathan Burbridge's head fell forwards, for he had been at work in his shop since first light. Betsy pushed her elbow into his ribs and he woke with a start. He turned to her and she smiled, he flushed and for a moment held her gaze. And in his face Betsy saw a promise of all she lacked: a kindly welcome, a safe haven, a place where she might ease her wound. And he saw in hers the cherished hope he'd nursed since first they'd met.

When the service was finished, when Parson Mossop had given his blessing and the congregation was making its way out of the door, Jonathan addressed the band, with a particular eye to Betsy:

"This afternoon is Eastwell Spring ain't it."

"Ay," said Sam Billings, "Easter afternoon, same as ever. They'll be coming from all over: Glinton, Barnack, Northborough, Maxey, Marholm…there were some came from Deeping last year."

"And some from Peterborough," said Dick.

Betsy Jackson wrinkled her rounded brow:

"What happens at Eastwell?"

"Have ye not heard of it? It is an ancient spring. They come to take the waters, Betsy. They are said to be wonderful restorative and will cure rheumatics and fevers and all manner of aches and pains."

"Ay," said Sam Billings. "The ipsy, the pipsy, the palsy and the gout, the devils within and the devils without."

"They come with leather bottles to fill, and some plunge in up to the chin. And Mrs Bullimore makes a tidy trade sugaring the water, for it has a bitter savour."

"So," said Jonathan, "I have been thinking, what if the band was to position itself somewhere by the spring, and play out some tunes, with a hat passed round for pennies…?"

"Jonathan, that's a devilish good plan," said Sam Billings. "It'll be a good crowd and all in holiday spirits. If we don't come away a few shillings the richer then I'll be beggared."

"So what say we meet at Butter Cross. At three of the clock?"

"That'll give me time to cook and clear away," said Betsy, "I'm game."

"And Old Otter is bound to be there, for he and Kitty swear by Eastwell Spring Water as the fount of all their good health…"

Jonathan turned to John and Dick:

"What about you lads?"

John and Dick nodded their assent.

"Ay, we'll be there."

****

John is grateful for any diversion on a Sunday. The hours when he used to walk to Glinton weigh heavy on him now, though the ache of Mary's absence is becoming something familiar to him. It is a pain that he is adjusting to. As Parker Clare has adjusted to his aching knee by leaning more heavy upon the other, so, likewise, John's letters are giving way to the scribbled verses that he either burns or folds and shows to nobody. And some small part of him still lives in hope.

Having nothing better to do he walked early to Butter Cross and sat on the stone step watching the slow procession making its way along Church Lane towards Eastwell Spring. Some had hired carts and filled them with those too lame to walk. Others came on horseback. Others had hobbled all day, clutching sticks and crutches. He watched Mrs Bullimore wheeling her barrow with its wooden jug and bags of demerara sugar, beaming at the prospect of trade.

Then he saw Betsy Jackson hurrying along the street towards him. His first impulse was to get to his feet and walk away.

"John!"

Her voice cut through him, it carried in it such a confliction, such twisting impulses of desire and fear, of anger and loss that he found himself powerless to move. He was still standing rooted to the spot when she reached him. She sat down and put her wooden box on her lap. Her voice was soft and resigned and not without kindness:

"John Clare you need not fear me."

She put her hand to her belly.

"I lost it…it is gone. There's an end to it."

John looked down at her. He nodded. A weight was lifted from him, but it brought him no joy. He could find nothing to say. She whispered:

"And life must carry on, John...we must take our chances where we find 'em...willy-nilly...for though the world is harsh there's no virtue in despondency."

And then, from behind their shoulders, came a beery breath:

"There was a crooked man and he walked a crooked mile..."

Betsy's face, turned towards John, bore for a moment its burden of sorrow. Then she turned and tutted with her tongue:

"Oh shush, for shame Sam Billings!"

"But look on 'em Betsy."

"They'll give you none of their crooked sixpences if they do hear you mock, Sam. Anyway, I'm surprised you ain't ferrying them in your cart."

"Oh I've already delivered a baker's dozen of 'em from Deeping...Look, here comes Jonathan with his sack of potatoes."

Jonathan Burbridge sat down on the step and leaned his instrument, still in its sack, between his knees. His beard was trimmed, his hair and whiskers combed, a bright green neckerchief to his throat, his boots polished and all sawdust swept from his jacket and breeches.

He nodded to them all:

"A very good afternoon to ye."

Betsy made as if to take him in, eyeing him up and down and drawing in her breath through her nose.

"And to you Jonathan."

At that moment Dick Turnill arrived.

"And here's Dick and now we are complete."

The village band crossed the street and made its way slowly among the hobbling pilgrims, along Church Lane towards Eastwell Spring.

As they drew close they could see that the elms and willows, that last year had made a green and shady grove around the spring, had been dragged to the saw-mill. It is a scarred and barren slope that now leads down to the little pool. The crowds were lining up to fill their leather bottles and jugs. Charlie Turner stood white and shivering, waist deep in water, pulling his ragged half-wit daughter Isabel towards him while she wailed like a lost soul. Mrs Bullimore had set her jug upon a wooden table. Children were jostling around it with farthings in their fists, eager for a cup of sugared water.

"If we was to set ourselves up here, between the lane and the spring, then we would be heard by all, and every soul must walk past us as they trudge homewards."

"It's as good a plan as any!"

They took out their instruments and settled down on the grass.

"Oooh, it's a little damp..."

Jonathan took off his coat and laid it on the ground for Betsy to sit on.

"I'm obliged to you Jonathan."

"What shall we play?"

"I say the Red Petticoat Hornpipe."

"That'll loosen their limbs!"

They played the tune several times over, then followed it with 'The Beef Steak Hornpipe', 'The Shooters Hornpipe', 'The Stony Step Hornpipe', 'The American Hornpipe'.

They put down their instruments to catch their breath.

"Go on John, pass the hat around."

"I ain't got a hat."

"Take this then."

Betsy passed him her oboe box.

It was as he was carrying it down towards the crowd that

Parson Mossop came striding past him, his cassock billowing in the breeze, to bless the water. He raised his hand over Eastwell Spring and the people fell silent:

"And John came into the country about the river Jordan, preaching the baptism of repentance for the remission of sins: 'Every valley shall be filled, and every mountain and hill shall be brought low; and the crooked shall be made straight, and the rough ways shall be made smooth; and all flesh shall see the salvation of God.' And the multitude came forth to be baptized."

"Amen."

The Parson turned on his heel to hurry back to his horse that was tied to the lych-gate, for he is uneasy with these village ways that seem to him to smack of witchery. But he had barely taken three paces when there came the sound of a voice across the hollow.

"This is the last time!"

The crowd turned their heads and saw Ralph Wormstall walking towards them, his thin face, under wig and tri-corn hat, a mask of righteous indignation. Under his arm he was holding a sheaf of printed papers.

"This is the last time."

His thin voice echoed across the spring,

"This is the very last time. There shall be no more cavorting on my land. No more taking of my water. D'ye understand? Or I shall bring down all the weight of the law upon ye. I'll give ye until five of the clock, and any as ain't gone shall be arraigned for trespass."

He began to hand out the papers, but most being unable to read were none the wiser.

Parson Mossop seized one, pulled his spectacles from his pocket and scanned it. He walked across and took Ralph

Wormstall by the arm:

"This is ancient usage Ralph. The village has always taken water from Eastwell Spring. You have no right to stop them, enclosure or no enclosure."

Ralph Wormstall turned to him.

"I damned well have Mr Mossop. This is modern usage sir, the rights are mine and I have the title deeds to prove it."

He jabbed the paper with his finger.

"I have spelled it out for you, along with the map that settles it. Do ye not have eyes to read sir!"

He turned to the crowd again:

"Away with ye!"

It was with an empty box that John returned to the band. Already the crowd was gathering its possessions and hurrying to leave. There was a scrummage at the edge of the water as people pushed forward to fill their bottles for the last time.

Betsy flicked the pages of her tune book.

"This is a sorry turn. Let's play some more to see them home."

They struck up 'England's Glory' and 'Bobbing Joan' and 'The White Cockade'. The crowd trudged and hobbled past, but they were in no mood to fling farthings into the open box.

"One more!"

Betsy played the first bar of 'Smash the Windows' and the rest fell in with her, and then it was 'Mary no More'. By the time they'd played each tune through a few times they were alone, the crowd had dispersed.

Jonathan shrugged:

"Oh well, we've Mr Wormstall to thank for thin pickings..."

"Ay," said Sam Billings. "And not for the first time."

He adjusted his drum straps.

"By the way," he looked round at the others as they were packing their instruments away, "Did anyone clap eyes on Kitty or Otter?"

"No."

"They weren't here…they'd have surely come and passed the time of day."

"That's most odd," said Sam. "They always come to Eastwell…without fail."

"I saw Otter last week," said Jonathan, "he came to my shop for wood-shavings, as he often does when I've been planing a coffin. He was fit as a fiddle then."

Sam Billings frowned.

"There's something makes me uneasy. If I didn't have to drive my baker's dozen home to Deeping, I'd ride out to Snow Common now and make sure of 'em."

He pushed his drum sticks into his belt.

"Tomorrow's a holiday though, I'll go over in the morning."

"And I'll come with ye," said Dick Turnill.

"And so will I," said John Clare, glad of any way to fill a holiday that would keep his thoughts from Mary.

"Alright then, I'll pick you both up at Woodgate. At nine of the morning."

John, Dick and Sam Billings were walking ahead now. Jonathan and Betsy had fallen behind. The Eastwell Gate was pushed shut behind them as they stepped into the lane. The church clock was striking five. They could hear the clank of a chain and the clicking of a padlock as Ralph Wormstall's cowman locked it.

Jonathan was summoning all his mettle. He swung the weight of his instrument from one shoulder to the other.

"Betsy."

She turned to him and smiled most demur.

"Ay."

"I know you and I ain't in the first flush of youth, and courtin' might seem a foolish thing as we'd put behind us long ago."

She seemed to him to blush.

"But would you consider walking out with me tomorrow afternoon. We could take a turn in Royce's Wood, or take the coach to Stamford or…"

"Thank you Jonathan Burbridge. I should like that very much…"

She smiled at him more fully, and any sense that she was rallying against the buffetings of her misfortune were most artfully concealed behind that smile.

"…Very much indeed."

****

Easter Monday broke clear and fine, for the weather seldom gives away the secrets of the day. And it was a bright spring morning when Sam Billings reined Billy to a halt outside the Clare's cottage. John and Dick Turnill had been sitting on the step awhile waiting for him.

Dick had put his arm around John's shoulder:

"You seem a little down at heart these days John."

John had shrugged and said nothing.

"It's Mary… ain't it? It's weeks since I've seen you walk to Glinton."

"Ay."

He kicked a stone.

"Did something happen between ye?"

"Yes and no."

"That don't explain much."

John sighed:

"I wish I could unfathom it, Dick. She'll have nothing of me and I don't know why."

"But that ain't like Mary...she's such an open-hearted... such a spirited girl."

John buried his face in his hands.

"Maybe it's a judgement Dick..."

"Now you're sounding like my father!"

"There are things I cannot understand, and things I cannot tell..."

It was at that moment that Sam Billings had interrupted them:

"Whoaaa...Good boy."

He looked down from the seat of the cart:

"Climb up lads!"

They climbed up and sat to either side of him. He shook the reins and they rattled along Woodgate, Sam sandwiched between John and Dick like a toby-jug between two pewter mugs on a mantleshelf. The sun warmed them. The rooks in Royce's Wood were noisy in their ragged settlements, and behind the white veils of blackthorn blossom the hedgerow birds were busy with moss, twig, wool and hair, each fashioning its own nest according to ancient custom.

John's eyes darted from left to right, for although his spirits are low he relishes the busy industry of the hedges and all the scurrying insects that follow their courses and seem to know nothing of the seasons of the heart.

As they moved away from the village the old ragged bushes gave way to fences and hedges of quick-set, and the road straightened as though a dropped ribbon had been pulled taut.

"'Tis kinder weather than when you and I last drove the cart this way, John." Said Sam.

"Ay."

John nodded, though last December's chill had held more of kindness for him than this April sunshine could ever hold.

Then Dick put his hand on Sam Billings' shoulder and stood. He sheltered his eyes from the sun and peered across the newly divided fields.

"There he is!"

"Who?" Said Sam.

"My father."

"What, today of all days, when he could be taking his ease?"

"It ain't a sabbath," said Dick, "so he's been out since first light with his seed-lip at his waist."

Sam stopped the horse and Dick stood on tip-toe:

"Here he comes look, and there's poor mother at the field's edge with a sack of corn to reload him."

All three of them stood up in the cart and peered over the hedges. Two fields away they could see Bob Turnill marching across the ploughed field towards them, his eyes were fixed ahead as though he was a soldier on parade. His step was to a steady measure. His hand dipped into the seed-lip, and then his arm swung out and scattered the grain first to the left and then to the right, then left and right again. When one hand was empty he lifted it to eye-height and dropped it into the lip just as the other hand swung out and scattered its seed.

"He'd make a steady drummer Sam."

"He would Dick...but why don't he get one of the proper sowers to do the job for him...Richard Royce or Jim Crowson or Jack Ward?"

Dick sighed:

"He has no wage to pay them."

They all sat down, Sam shook the reins and they trundled on again. For a while nothing was said. Then Sam turned to Dick:

"I hear rumours that Mr Bull has been knocking at your father's door and offering money for his entitlement."

"Ay," Dick pressed his hands to his forehead, "he was urging what he calls his 'sound proposition' upon him again yesterday after church…But you know father, he would not speak of mammon on the Sabbath...least of all on Easter Sunday…"

Dick stopped suddenly, as though he had already spoken more than he should. Sam Billings put his fat arm around Dick's shoulder:

"Don't worry Dick, old mother tittle-tattle shall bite her tongue. I'll not speak a word of it."

Dick smiled, part in gratitude and part in sorrow. They turned into Torpel Way. He looked down at his knees. There was more he could have told, but he chose to keep his council.

When they came to the edge of Snow Common Sam whistled between his teeth.

"Someone has been at work here."

The slats had been hammered to the posts. There was a new fence running along the edge of the road for the full length of the common. Inside it Mrs Elizabeth Wright's cattle were grazing on the tussocky grass.

"By God, she might have lost a husband and then a brother, but she ain't called a halt to the enclosing of the common."

They clambered down from the cart. Sam tied Billy to the fence. John ran his hand along the wood. It was new-splintered and smelling of resin.

"Look," said Dick, "there's a sign. Over there. On that post."

He pointed to the left. They strolled along the lane to take a closer look.

Sam Billings sucked the breath in between his teeth.

Each stood and read the words silently to himself. Then Dick spoke them aloud:

"Private Property. Trespassers will be Prosecuted."

"That's the sum of it," said Sam Billings, "that's the long and the short of it."

He put a hand to the sign and used it to pull himself up onto the fence. He swung one of his legs over the top. It creaked with his weight.

"Come on lads, if Mrs Wright won't forgive us our bloody trespasses there's others as will."

He trudged away over the common. Dick and John climbed over and hurried after him. The cattle followed them at a distance, skipping and sniffing, kicking the mole-hills, delighting to be outside in the fresh air after their long winter's confinement in the barns.

As they threaded between blackthorn bushes and clumps of hazel trees the clean April air began to mingle with another, darker smell. It was the smell of burning, the smell of charred wood and scorched grass. They quickened their pace. Where the rounded form of the Otters squat should have risen above the bushes there was a pall of thin, acrid smoke. They broke into a run and soon found themselves standing at the edge of a blackened circle, a round smouldering heap of black ashes. Where the mottled hill of wood and canvas, leather and turf had stood there was the last smoking remnant of a great bonfire.

"Look at this. We don't need no Boneparte to wreak his devastation, we can do it to ourselves."

Sam Billings waded boot-deep into the warm ash. He kicked it into the air. There was nothing left, just a few pieces of charred timber that smoked a little fiercer with the sudden rush of air. All the Otter's possessions, their kettles, buckets, pans, knives, baskets, sickles and the rest were gone. There was neither sight nor sign of Kitty's geese.

Sam reached down and picked up a piece of white clay pipe stem. He put it to his lips and blew through it. He dropped it into his pocket.

"Bob Turnill ain't the only one's been at work this Easter when all eyes are turned elsewhere…"

He kicked a piece of black canvas into the air. It glowed red at its margin.

"Though I reckon this was Sabbath work."

He spat into the ash.

"It's the best part of a day since this lot went up in flames."

Sam followed the well-trodden track from the Otter's doorway down to the stream that winds across the common. All along the edge of it the pollarded willows lay on their sides, felled and stretched out to show that their wounds of red paint had been mortal ones. The hollow dotterel lay shattered also, the hopeful new-budding leaves on its branches unfolding still, not having yet been told the news of their own death.

Sam washed the ash from his boots with fistfuls of wet grass.

"What about Otter and Kitty?" Said Dick.

Sam shrugged.

"Gone, I reckon. They've took what they could and flitted… the pair of 'em…God knows where."

He wiped his forehead with the back of his hand.

John Clare stood and stared and, wordless, took inside himself the pitiless devastation of it all.

Sam Billings turned his back on John and Dick and trudged

back to the cart. They couldn't see how his round cheeks were wet with an impotent and sorrowful fury. They trailed behind him. By the time they climbed up beside him on the cart every teardrop had been mopped away.

"Go on Billy!"

He shook the reins.

"Good boy!"

Then he whispered, half to himself, half to John and Dick:

"The law will hang the man or woman
Who takes a goose from off the common,
But lets the greater thief go loose
Who takes the common from the goose."

Sam Billings sighed:

"Ay."

And then he whistled the same tune over and over to his horse as they rattled back to Helpston. And there was little else exchanged between the three of them but the mindless rise and fall of 'Begone Dull Care'.

17

Rogation Sunday 1812

Three nights ago John came home unsteady with ale from the Bluebell. He was chastised by Parker and Ann for frittering his wages away, and with good reason for he has little to show for his winter's work save a new coat. He pulled a stool to the fire and nodded and waited for their thorny admonishments to cease their echoing clatter and exhaust themselves into stillness.

"Ay, think on it John," said Ann. "It's been an easy winter for you with the enclosure work, but it won't last far beyond the spring, and then it'll be back to the old story. You need to keep something for the hard times."

"And think about a trade son," said Parker, "you've a head for letters and figures. There must be a job out there somewhere... you take care or you'll find yourself like me, threshing for farthings when you're stiff and creaking with age."

He got up and cut John a slice of bread. He put it onto a wooden platter and dropped it onto John's knee.

"Get that down ye boy, it'll lend ballast to the ale."

He ruffled John's hair with his hand.

"I know you've had a peck of sorrow these months John...

but you're young and the world beckons."

He lit his pipe. Ann picked up her knitting needles.

John ate and then put his platter onto the floor. He sighed and said nothing. He went across to his cubby-hole and reached inside. He pulled out the battered volume he'd bought at Bridge Fair. One of its loose pages fluttered onto the floor.

Sophie was sitting by the fire hugging her knees. John's unhappiness seemed an affront to all her sound advice. Now she jumped to her feet and ran across the room. She picked up the piece of paper and thrust it into John's hand. She leaned forwards and whispered fiercely into his ear:

"If only you'd listened to me, John, things would have been otherwise."

He looked at her untroubled face that still had more of child than woman upon its smooth features. He squeezed her hand and whispered back:

"That's as maybe, Soph'."

There was a sharp knock at the door. Parker got stiffly to his feet. He crossed the room, pulled back the bolt and lifted the latch. At first there seemed to be no one there, there was nothing but the scrubbed doorstep before his eyes. But then, all of a sudden, a figure stepped out of the shadows to one side of the doorway and slipped into the cottage with a rustle of skirts.

"Gracious sakes," cried Ann Clare, "'Tis Lettuce Boswell!"

Lettuce put her finger to her lips:

"Shhhhh. Don't speak my name. There's no haven for any Boswell these days, for all are tarred by one brush."

"You can't stay here."

"I ain't asking to."

She pulled a stool to the fire and settled herself with her big basket between her feet. She pushed the black hair from her craggy face and pulled a pipe from her pocket. Parker offered her a fill of tobacco. Ann frowned at him and shook her head but he took little notice.

"Thank you kindly."

She pulled a spill from her pocket and held it to a candle. She put the flame to the pipe bowl and filled her mouth with smoke.

"Where are ye staying?"

She gestured with her pipe stem:

"Out beyond Bainton. On the Heath."

Parker nodded.

"Ay I know it...You've heard they've fenced off Landyke Bush?"

"So they tell me, but you won't be seein' the Boswell crew in Helpston no more."

Then Parker put the question that was forming in all of their minds:

"But you ain't all at Bainton? Not the whole crew?"

She threw back her head and cackled with laughter.

"With every hok-hornie-mush with his nose to our scent! Lord have mercy we are not. 'Tis only me and little Liskey Smith. The rest are gone across the boro pawnee...ay, an we hope to be joining them afore too long."

And John, who had been listening to every word and hoping for some news of Wisdom leaned forwards then:

"Over the water? Where are they gone?"

"They took a big bero John, two months since. They are gone to Americay. And I pray that they are safe landed for Boneyparte is still playing skittles upon land and sea, and bolder they say than ever...and that's why I've come this night...for I won't be this-aways no more...I've something for thee, chal...Wisdom give it to me to pass on to thee. He found someone as knows his letters as has writ down his words to thee."

She rummaged in her basket and pulled out a scrap of grey folded paper. She pressed it into John's hand.

He held it to the candle-light and read aloud:

"Farewell my brother who I shall not ever forget."

Lettuce Boswell nodded and got to her feet.

"Ay chal, that's the way of it, and your tears say all as needs to be said."

She picked up her basket and turned towards the door.

"I'll bid ye'all farewell."

She put her hand to the latch, then turned again.

"Oh, and I was forgetting, one thing more. We was sitting by the fire at Bainton one evening a few weeks since, and who should come a-stepping between the bushes but old white-beard and his missus as used to squat on the common."

"Old Otter and Kitty!"

"Ay, the very same, and we could not help but laugh. Each had a pole across their shoulders as a yoke, and clinkin' and clankin' from it there was pots and pans and kettles and baskets and all sorts tied with twine. And following behind them a flock of white geese stepping in a line as solemn as goslings behind a gander and his goose. Our dogs went wild, but those geese stretched out their necks and hissed and'd take no nonsense."

"Are they there yet?"

"No, we welcomed them to our fires, and they stayed one night, but were gone next morn."

She pushed open the door, turned into the shadows and disappeared.

****

Yesterday morning was the Rogation walk. John slung his

battered fiddle under his arm and made his way with Parker, Ann and Sophie to Butter Cross. The village was gathered. The bells were ringing. Sam, Dick, Jonathan and Betsy were standing on the steps of the cross clutching their instruments of music and stamping the damp chill from their feet. John joined them.

Parson Mossop nodded to the churchwardens who rapped the steps with the foot of the processional cross. Sam Billings walloped his drum and the procession set off along West Street as ever it has done.

Betsy Jackson took Jonathan Burbridge's arm. They walked close so that their hips touched and touched again. John and Dick Turnill walked side by side, a little apart from the crowd. John told Dick in whispered tones of Lettuce Boswell's visit. Dick whistled through his teeth.

"Americay…there's a journey. Maybe I shall follow him one day."

He looked around at the bustling villagers before and behind them and sighed.

"Everything has changed John, since last year, everything and nothing."

John nodded:

"Ay, there's Wisdom and the Boswells gone…and Old Otter and Kitty…and Will Bloodworth…and only this morning they've found Charlie Turner dead, and poor Isabel trying to shake him awake."

"I hadn't heard…and then there's Mary."

John kicked a stone.

"Ay, Mary too…not to speak of the enclosure."

"And soon you shall add my name to your list, John."

John turned to him sharp.

"Yours?"

Dick swallowed hard:

"Father's selling."

He nodded to Bob and Maria Turnill, who were walking ahead of them and keeping their counsel. He lowered his voice again:

"Mr Bull pressed his offer, and father was so deep in debt he could not refuse it…deeper than ever I'd guessed."

"Where will ye go?"

"They are crying out for labour in the North. Father talks of Matlock, where my uncle Ned is foreman at a mill…and him most vehement in his worship."

"And you're determined to go with them?"

"For a little while John…but, like you, I'm still at my books. Though more of numbers than words. I have ambitions…"

"I shall miss you Dick."

John took his friend's arm and kissed him on the cheek, and though there is much of prickling stubble to John's lips, and Dick's cheek is still downy soft, it was a moment that Dick has stored away and will carry with him to the end of his days.

When the crowd drew close to King Street the children began their race for the first of the meer-stones. Tom Dolby, Lucy Bain and Henry Snow led the way, running full tilt, their mouths drinking the air. Tom, running bare-foot, stubbed his toe and fell, so it was little Lucy who was the first to strike her head to the stone. Mrs Bullimore came waddling forward with her bag of sugared plums. But someone else was striding ahead of her.

"You little devils!"

Thomas Bellar swung out with his cane and struck Lucy a crack on the side of her head. He aimed at Henry Snow, but Henry ducked. He caught him by the scruff of the shoulder and gave him a thwack on the backs of the legs. Both children began to cry.

"Look what you little devils have done to my new-set hedge!"

He was shaking with anger. The meer-stone was a few paces inside his allocation. The children had trodden down his hawthorn seedlings in their eagerness to reach the stone.

Mrs Bullimore came forwards and the children ran across to her. They pressed their faces into her dress.

"There, there…really Mr Bellar, what are you thinking, 'tis only once in the year."

"Then it's once in the year too often…you're married to the constable…can't you see this is criminal damage, criminal damage I say."

Then James Bain came pushing out of the crowd.

"Nobody strikes my daughter with a cane."

The blacksmith seized Thomas Bellar by the lapels of his Sunday coat and shook him until the silver-topped cane fell from his hand. He picked it up and broke it over his knee. He flung the two halves into the green spring wheat.

"There…and don't come knocking at my door when your horses need shoeing."

There was a silence as the two men glared at one another.

Then Parson Mossop came forwards. He stretched out his arms and urged the people to step back into the road.

"Brothers, sisters, please…stand this side of the hedge. We will have the first reading."

He thumbed through his Bible to the book of Joel. Mrs Bullimore pressed sugar plums into Lucy and Henry's mouths and peace was restored. After the reading came the psalm, and then the crowd moved on in its ragged procession.

Thomas Bellar turned from the crowd. He strode into his field and paced backwards and forwards until he'd found the two halves of his cane. A peewit flapped about him, rising and dipping and calling out its alarum until he was gone through the gate and striding homewards cursing all the way. Writ in his face was a determination to pull the wretched meer-stone like a rotten tooth from its socket and break it to shards before the year was out.

Tom Dolby, limping and running, caught up with the procession. Jonathan Burbridge, with Betsy on his arm, turned to him.

"Tom..."

"Ay."

"I've a place for a 'prentice...and you have the look of a bright lad...what'd you say to taking a trade and becoming a carpenter?"

Mrs Dolby, walking ahead, overheard and turned, and in her careworn features grown suddenly bright was all the answer Jonathan needed.

"Oh, we would be so obliged Mr Burbridge, but he's a handful I warn ye, and don't mind to give him the strap when he gets too wild..."

The crowd continued along the edge of Thomas Bellar's allocation, past John Close's fences to Lolham Bridge. They walked from stone to stone. They followed the land that has been give to Mr Bull, and to Millicent Clark, and to Ralph Wormstall. They crossed the straightened drains, that had used to be Green Dyke and Rhyme Dyke, and threw sweets into the muddy water, then followed the edge of Elizabeth Wright's award to Snow Common.

Mrs Elizabeth Wright, still in her mourning black, made a great show of unlocking the gates to Snow Common, her new entitlement, and welcoming the parson. She invited the farmers to settle on tussocks and take their ease.

The rest of the village pushed in behind.

John and Dick sat down together and sniffed the air. The smell of burning had all but disappeared.

The cattle gathered at a distance and watched the noisy gathering with a slow, uneasy gaze.

Soon enough the crowd heard the eager-awaited sound of iron-shod wheels and clip-clopping along the lane. John stood up and peered over the fence. He could see Farmer Joyce high on the seat of the farm cart with the reins loose and easy between his fingers. Piled behind him were baskets and hampers and barrels and jugs, and beside him was a woman. She was young and slight, her bonneted face turned away from him. She was looking across the fields towards Helpston church. John ran forwards. He vaulted the fence and sprang down into the lane. His heart was pounding like Sam Billing's drum.

Farmer Joyce raised a hand:

"A good day to ye John Clare."

The woman turned and John saw her face, her round, ruddy good-natured face with its little piggy eyes with their pale lashes. It was Kate Dyball.

His voice gave no indication of his sinking heart.

"Good day."

He remembered Mary in her yellow gown, her lace cap, her straw hat, her ringlets, her lovely, quick eyes... and as he looked at Kate's worn, patched cotton he wondered how he could ever have mistaken her.

"Easy...easy Bessie, good girl!"

Farmer Joyce reined the mare to a halt.

John came forward and offered Kate his hand. She took it and stepped down into the lane. She smiled:

"Thank you John."

Farmer Joyce swung down on the other side. He shouted

over the horse:

"I've brought Kate to help with the ale and vittles."

Parson Mossop came forward. He opened his Bible, tapped the iron-shod wheel of the cart with his cane and read the familiar words:

"Blessed shall be the fruit of thy ground and the fruit of thy cattle, the increase of thy kine, and the flocks of thy sheep. Blessed shall be thy basket and thy store."

"Amen," said the village with one voice and fell upon the food.

John sat down on his own at the edge of the lane. He had but little appetite. Kate was wandering this way and that with two big pewter-banded wooden jugs, refilling pots and tankards. When she had emptied both she came across and sat down beside him, puffing and panting. She drew up her knees and rested her arms upon them.

"Those jugs weigh terrible heavy. I shall have two aching shoulders come tomorrow."

She sighed.

"Still it'll be Glinton's turn next week."

John turned to her:

"How is Mary?"

Kate looked down at the grass.

"She puts a cheerful face upon the world, John. But she is terrible changed…and there's not a soul can read her...I reckon only you could do that, and she won't abide even the sound of your name."

"Do you know why she didn't come, Kate?"

"What d'you mean 'didn't come'?"

"On Valentines, we'd agreed to meet, and she never came."

Kate Dyball stood up and stared at John.

"Oh but she did. She did come in her yellow dress and looking as lovely as ever you please...and her father knew nothing of it."

"No she didn't! I never clapped eyes on her."

"Did she not spring out at ye from behind a tomb-stone, for that was her fancy, to hide until the clock had struck the quarter hour and you'd begun to despair of her...and then to jump out and surprise you?"

John got up to his feet. He looked at her as though he'd seen a ghost. He put his hands to his face.

"Oh Kate..."

"And since she come home that day, not a word will she speak, to me or any other, of what happened..."

But John Clare heard no more.

He turned and ran down Maxhams Green Lane, leaving fiddle and bow behind.

His world had fallen away from him, and he had fallen from it. Though all around him the squared fields and hedges, dressed and decked in their spring array, sang out in linnet and lark more constant and true than any churching hymn, his ears and eyes knew only loss. Every hawthorn hedge and fence was become an angel with a blazing sword that would not allow him his Eden. He ran down Torpel Way, he clambered over gates and fences, he passed Snip Green and Round Oak Waters. He ran through Royce's Wood, and the song in his blood, in his pounding heart and torn breath, was one of self-recriminating sorrow.

****

In Joyce's Farm Mary sat in her bed-chamber, her legs hanging over the edge of her quilted counterpane. Her eyes were closed.

All her attention was on the chiming of the church clock. She sat and listened to it striking its quarters. She sat so still you could have thought her asleep. From noon through all the divisions of the hour to one o'clock she listened. She listened to the quarter after one, and then the half. When the half hour chime had faded into silence she nodded to herself and slipped down from the bed.

"All is closed and finished now."

She walked across to the chest of drawers beneath the window.

"'Tis a year to the minute, John Clare, since you struck my eye."

She pulled open a drawer and lifted the little package tied with string. She could feel the carved bone figures bending to her touch under the cloth, but she did not unwrap them.

"And now your enchantment is broken."

She pushed open the bedroom door. She stepped quietly down the stairs and made her way out to the garden. She followed the yew hedge to the little wicker garden gate. She pushed it open and went through.

"Here's where you kissed me first."

She knelt down on the ground and tugged up a grassy turf with her hand. She dug with her fingers, but the ground was hard and stony. She ran and fetched a trowel. She dug a hole in the ground, throwing the loose soil into a heap. When it was arm deep she dropped the bundle to the bottom of it. The carved bones rattled as they fell. She scraped the earth on top of it and stamped the turf back into place with her foot.

"There. It is finished and you are quite forgot."

****

This evening, when all were returned from the Rogation procession, Sam Billings had set his drum in its corner and was laying sticks for a fire, when there came a knocking at the door of Bachelor's Hall.

"Come in, come in!"

The door opened and Jonathan Burbridge's thin, bearded face peered into the room.

"'Tis only me, Sam."

"Ah Jonathan, come in, come in. Sit yourself down."

Jonathan pulled a chair to the hearthstone.

"Will ye take a mug of ale?"

"Thank you Sam."

When they were both settled with mugs in hand, Jonathan said:

"I minds when I was 'prenticed, Sam, to a ship-builder in Lynn."

"You mean back in the olden days," said Sam, "before King Charlie Wag lost his noddle."

Jonathan grinned.

"Before Georgie lost his any-road...when I was little more than a boy...there was this fellow in Lynn by the name of Forby, Tom Forby, who used to carve the figure-heads for the prows. By God he was a craftsman, Sam. He'd take a piece of oak and turn it into a woman...he'd paint them too, and when they was done they'd be pegged in place at the bow of the ship..."

Jonathan took a sup of his ale.

"Anyway, there was this one ship...we'd worked on her for the best part of a year, she was called the Margarita, and Tom Forby fashioned a figure-head for her..."

Jonathan whistled through his teeth.

"You'd only to look at her, Sam, to go hard as a bone. She

had a creamy-white bosom as rounded and firm as ripe apples that you longed to reach for. And her hair swept back in ringlets behind her...and her blue eyes and plump cheeks and her lips parted as if to say 'yes, yes please'."

"Now, now, Jonathan, easy..."

"It was the first time I fell in love, and I weren't the only one."

Jonathan supped again.

"Anyway, Sam, the reason I'm telling you this is that a year ago to the very day we was sitting here, and I was saying I'd a mind to take a wife, and you was acting the fool as ever, and dropped a plank into my lap."

"Ay, and I near enough had old Mossop reading the banns."

"Well it ain't no plank I'm to wed Sam, 'tis that very figure-head, 'tis Margarita with the life breathed into her."

He emptied his mug.

"The first time I set eyes on Betsy Jackson I knew she was familiar, and then it come to me: Margarita. My first sweet-heart come to life and breathing before my very eyes."

Sam Billings clapped Jonathan upon the shoulder and shook him by the hand.

"And now you're to take her as wife! Well good luck to ye, but it don't come as a huge surprise Jonathan!"

"Mind, it's taken me the best part of the year to reel her in Sam. She was awful diffident and demur to start with...but I persevered and today she said she'd have me."

"Today was it?"

"Ay. I put the question at Langdyke Bush and by Swordy Well she'd said yes. And Mossop'll start the banns next Sunday."

"And within the year I warrant you'll be rocking the cradle!

Well Jonathan this calls for a celebration."

Sam Billings went out of the room. He came back with the piece of broken shelf.

"First of all I reckon we'd better break the news to your jilted sweet-heart."

He snapped the plank across his knee and threw a piece of it into the fire.

"She was riddled with the worm Jonathan, ye made the right choice!"

Then he pushed his chair back from the hearthstone.

"And if you'd give me a hand just lifting this stone. Ay…push your chair back, and…see that dip beneath the floorboards, if you take hold of it there…and I lift here…one, two, three lift."

As they lifted the stone Jonathan Burbridge saw for the first time what he had often suspected.

"Sam Billings! For the love of God!"

There was a deep cavity where the hearthstone had been and it was filled with row upon row of dusty bottles.

They propped the stone against the fire-place. Sam reached down and lifted a bottle. He blew away the dust.

"The very best French brandy!"

"Sam I didn't know you was a…"

"Shhhhh."

"You old rascal."

"How else d'ye think I could keep myself watered and fed…"

He patted his belly.

"In these troubled times."

"You've kept it close to your chest!"

Sam put the bottle on the table.

"And how else d'you think Mossop and Close and Bellar

and Wright and Joyce and Wormstall spend their guineas and take their succour and solace. Even Robert Smethwick and the Earl of Fitzwilliam have sucked upon these paps and taken their ease…Ay, the carting's as good a cover as any…Now, if ye'd be kind enough to help me lower the stone we could drink to a long life, a full cradle, a welcoming bed and an end to all sweet liberty…and not give o'er 'til the bottle is hollow…Oh, and one last thing Jonathan, any word of my little secret and I'll let it be known across the parish as Mrs Betsy Burbridge was once an acorn."

****

Parker and Ann Clare came home carrying John's fiddle. There was no sign of him in the cottage.

"He'll be at the Bluebell."

"Ay, something's upset him, he'll be tempering his sorrows with ale again." Ann sighed. "If only he'd take a trade then his spirits would be lifted…"

"'Twill have been the sight of Joyce and little Kate Dyball…" said Parker, "poor John, I can't get to the bottom of it…him and Mary seemed so…"

"It's simple enough by my reckoning," said Ann, sharp as a blade. "It all comes down to pounds and pennies."

"No Ann, there's more to it…but I'm damned if I can unriddle it."

Sophie came home. They ate their supper. Parker tended his garden until nightfall. Still there was no John.

It was when Sophie climbed the steps for bed that she saw that John's blankets were gone. She shouted down.

"Come and look. John's flitted. His bed's stripped bare."

They climbed and saw, by the light of the flickering candle, nothing but the flattened straw-stuffed mattress. Ann lifted the lid of his box.

"All his spare clothes are here."

Sophie seized her father's arm:

"Should we raise an alarum? Shall I run to Constable Bullimore's?"

Parker shook his head.

"No, no. Leave him be. He won't have gone far. John'll be back soon enough Sophie...and he can fend for himself."

****

John had followed the Marholm road to the edge of Hayes Wood. He'd pushed through blackthorn and hazel until he came to his quiet place. He'd crawled through brambles until he found the rotted whitethorn stulps. And, even as Parker and Sophie stared at his stripped bed, he was lying on his back amongst the dead leaves, wrapped up in his blankets, and staring through the quickening branches at the sky as it filled with stars.

All night he lay wakeful and watched until the day broke into song and his hair was wet with dew. He watched as I watch. And all day his watch continued until hunger and thirst got the better of him.

It was night-fall when he rolled up his blankets and crawled back to the road. He brushed away the dead leaves and set off for home.

18

A Dream

And now John has climbed the cottage stairs and has fallen into deep sleep at last. And I look down at him in tenderness and remember the time when we was tucked up together and it seemed there was no harm in the world could touch us.

I slip behind his closed lids and find a way through to him.

In his dream he knows me instantly and remembers me, though he does not recognise me, for I am become a young woman with eyes that seem to John to speak more of beauty than the earth inherits. I seem to him to be an angel.

I take him by the hand and together we climb Maple Hill. From the top we look down and there is an immense crowd gathered at Hilly Wood and Swordy Well.

Soldiers on horse-back are exercising and ladies in their finery are gliding this way and that. Drovers are goading their cattle into pens. Gypsies are hawking, fiddlers playing, tradesmen calling out their wares. Milling throngs surge this way and that as though driven by a shared thought, like the shoals of little fishes under Lolham Bridge. Everywhere tents and stalls and diversions glitter with bright promise.

He turns to me and asks:

"Why am I brought here, when all that my heart desires is

to be alone and to myself?"

And I reply to him:

"Of all this crowd – it is you shall be remembered."

And I lead him down and through all the swirling confusion of the Fair. Here is a stall that is selling books. I take him inside and there are shelves and shelves that are stacked with volumes, leather-bound and gilt-lettered.

John follows me, a little reluctant, to the counter where the book-man stands. I lean forwards and whisper into his ear. The book-man turns to John and bows. He stands aside and points with his finger. There, on the shelf behind him, is a row of volumes inscribed with John's own name. John leans forward, astonished. He reaches and touches them with the tip of his finger.

Then he turns to me…but I am gone and he is awake in his bed with such a strong and happy recollection that he cannot doubt me, though he does not know me for his lost Bessie.

And I shall leave his bed-side now and wait for him in churchyard clay. I shall fall silent and bide my time.

Day will follow day and John Clare shall take his fair portion of all that the world gives and withholds. His share digs deep into its furrow, and could I tug at the stilts I would not change its course. He is sundered and there's only one way that he can find what's been took from him.

Ay, though every lark in England should rise up above his head and sing for him, it can only be in his art that he shall make himself whole.

Author's Note

There's a tradition among the First Nation peoples of America that any action we take today will have its full implication in seven generations time. This is a story that takes place seven generations ago. The wholesale enclosure of the English parishes rang the final death knell for ancient patterns of subsistence economy. It also displaced the small farmers and the landless poor, who became the workforce for the mills, factories and mines of the industrial north. A different relationship with the land began that we are reaping the full harvest of today. John Clare (in his life and his poetry) has become emblematic of these losses.

Very little is known about Clare's early life beyond a few bare bones in the 'Autobiographical Fragments' that he wrote for his children in the mid 1820s.

This story is in no way 'biographical'. It is an improvisation around a few of the sketchy facts that we have of his doings between 1811 & 1812 (when he was 17 and 18 years old). I have incorporated several incidents and a dream that he describes, and throughout there are traces of his poetry, but the narrative is pure fiction.

I have used many of the names of village people that Clare mentions in his poems, memoirs and letters… but in my story their personalities are entirely invented, they bear no relation to their real historical name-sakes.

Place names, on the other hand, are for the most part pretty accurate.

I have shrunk the protracted process of enclosure, which took several years, into twelve months.

Anyone wanting to find the true story of Clare's life should go to Jonathan Bate's excellent biography (Picador), or to *John Clare By Himself* (Carcanet).

And I hope that there are enough clues here as to the real emotional journey of Clare's youth, and the language that surrounded him, for any reader to go to his poems afterwards and find that they make sense in a way that they might not have done otherwise. That is the true purpose of this story.

My thanks to Ana Adnam, Ronald Hutton, Emma Thomas, Anna Magyar and Liz McGowan for careful reading, and to Eric Lane for rigorous editing.

Glossary

Alicumpane – Doctor's remedy in Morris (Mummer's) Play
Annis – Witch-like cannibal hag of East Midlands
Avata acoi – (Romany) Come here
Baggin – Pack lunch
Barnack – Sandstone, local to Helpston
Bau – (Romany) Comrade
Baulk – A ridge left by the plough
Bengte – (Romany) The Devil
Bero – (Romany) Ship
Bi luvva – (Romany) Without money
Boggarts – Malign fairies of the Fens
Boney – Napoleon Bonaparte
Boro pawnee – (Romany) Sea (big water)
Cambri – (Romany) Pregnant
Chal – (Romany) Lad, boy
Changeling – A stolen mortal child that has been replaced by a fairy child
Charles' Wain – (Clare) The constellation of the Plough
Charlie Wag – Fen nick-name for Charles 1st
Chin – (Romany) Cut
Cocalor – (Romany) Bones
Coney – Rabbit

Crop – The stomach of a bird
Curlo – (Romany) Throat
Dimute – (Clare) Diminutive
Dotterel – (Clare) A pollarded tree
Dukkering – (Romany) Fortune-telling
Dunnock – Hedge Sparrow
Fancy – The art of boxing
Florin – Two shillings
Frumity – Wheat boiled in milk and seasoned with sugar and cinnamon
Fustian – Cloth made of linen and wool
Gelding – Castrated stallion
Gentils – Maggots
Ghostly Enemy – The Devil
Gorgio – (Romany) Someone who lives in a house
Gry – (Romany) Horse
Guddle – To fish with bare hands
Handywoman – Midwife
Hickathrift – Tom Hickathrift, legendary giant of the Fens
Hok-hornie-mush – (Romany) Policeman
Holkham – The seat of Coke of Holkham, pioneer of agricultural improvement
Horkey – Harvest home celebration
Kickshawed – Criticised, put down
Lurcher – Greyhound cross
Maiden assize – An assize with no death penalty
Mardling – Gossiping
Mawkin – Scarecrow
Men – (Romany) Neck

Mere-stone – Parish boundary marker
Michaelmas shack – Allowing cattle to graze on stubble
Mutzi – (Romany) Skin
Nip-cheese – Mean, stingy
Noddle – Head
Old Sow – Last sheaf of wheat to be cut (end of harvest)
Pismires – (Clare) Ants
Poggar – (Romany) Break
Poknies – (Romany) Judge
Poppy-head tea – Tea made with opium poppy heads, taken in the Fens as a cure for marsh fever (Malaria)
Por-engro – (Romany) Someone able to write
Pricked – (Clare) Marked or written
Proggle – (Clare) Stir up
Pudge – (Clare) Puddle
Queen Mab – Queen of the Fairies
Reynolds – Fox
Ride – A track (for riding) through a wood
Rockie – Spindle
Shepherd's Lamp – (Clare) The Pole Star
Simmeno – (Romany) Broth
Sisal – Hemp
Skep – Beehive
Slomekin – Dishevelled
Snottum – (Cant) Iron pole for hanging pots and kettles over a fire
Squit – Nonsense
Stannyi – (Romany) Deer
Starnel – (Clare) Starling

Stook – A bundle of sheaves of wheat, oats or barley
Stulps – (Clare) Stumps
Sturt – (Clare) Start in a startled way
Tailor's yardband – (Clare) Orion's belt
Tel te jib – (Romany) Hold your tongue
Tippoty dre mande – (Romany) Bearing malice against me
Todloweries – Fairies of the Fens
Tumbrel – Cart
Turn-key – Gaoler
Tyburn frisk – Dance of a hanging man on the gallows
Varmint – Pest (from vermin)
Vennor – (Romany) Entrails
Verdigrease – Crystals of copper acetate
Wain – Wagon
Wat – Hare
Whelp – Young dog
Whin – Gorse
Wishengro – (Romany) Game-keeper
Withies – Thin branches of pollarded willow

Recommended Reading

If you have enjoyed Hugh Lupton's *The Ballad of John Clare* you should enjoy the historical novels by Jean-Pierre Ohl, Mr *Dick or The Tenth Book*, *The Devil's Road* and *The Lairds of Cromarty*.
If you enjoy historical novels set in England in earlier periods we would recommend:

Theodore by Christopher Harris
Wonders Will Never Cease by Robert Irwin
The Angel of the West Window by Gustav Meyrink

If you enjoy historical novels which are very different you should try the novels of the Russian writer Vladimir Sharov, *Be as Children*, *Before and During* and *The Rehearsals*, as well as Robert Irwin's *The Arabian Nightmare* set in medieval Cairo, David Madsen's Renaissance romp *Memoirs of a Gnostic Dwarf* and Sylvie Germain's *The Book of Nights* which covers one hundred years of French history.

For exotic historical fiction we recommend:
The Father of Locks by Andy Killeen
The Khalifah's Mirror by Andy Killeen

Mr Dick or The Tenth Book by Jean-Pierre Ohl

'Mr Dick is a character from *David Copperfield* and Ohl's book is in many ways a homage to Dickens. It is the story of two young Frenchmen whose lives are consumed by their obsession with Dickens' life and books and in particular his final, unfinished novel: *The Mystery of Edwin Drood.* It's a playful and highly literary detective story, like a Gallic mélange of *Flaubert's Parrot* by Julian Barnes and AS Byatt's *Possession.*' Sam Taylor in *The Observer*

'*Mr Dick* is an odd and hugely entertaining novel, full of mock-scholarship, ghosts, impersonations, forgery and murder. Dickens, both a conventional man and wild poetic spirit, would have admired the skilful mixture.'
William Palmer in *The Independent*

'The narrative Jean-Pierre Ohl's novel is flashily post-modern in technique and reminiscent of Umberto Eco's *The Name of the Rose*.' John Sutherland in *The Financial Times*

'*Mr Dick* – to whose resourceful translator I doff my hat – is an immensely playful *jeu d'esprit* stuffed full of Dickensian jokes and with some sharp things to say about literary obsession.'
DJ Taylor

'Ohl has mastered a blend of parody and vengeance that few writers can do. Except, of course, for Dickens.'
Miranda Carter in *Three Percent Review*

£9.99 ISBN 978 1 903517 68 0 224p B. Format

The Devil's Road by Jean-Pierre Ohl

'Set in 1824 England, this ambitious mystery from Ohl (*The Lairds of Cromarty*) depicts a time of monumental social change. The first railroad tracks are being laid across County Durham, much to the suspicion and displeasure of both gentry and common folk, so when workers dredging a pond near the abandoned ancestral home of the Beresford family find a woman's skeleton with a dagger through her chest, the entire project is endangered. Locals assume that the body is that of Mathilda Beresford, who mysteriously disappeared two decades earlier, shortly before her husband mounted a coach for parts unknown, never to be seen again. Investors in the railroad send dissipated, disillusioned Justice of the Peace Edward Bailey to look into the matter, with express instructions that the Beresfords be cleared of any involvement in the woman's death. Ohl offers an enjoyable homage to the world that shaped Charles Dickens, full of Dickensian characters, including a 12-year-old Charley himself.'

Publishers Weekly

'This enjoyable novel is billed as a Dickensian romp and an exposé of the issues surrounding the industrialisation of early 19th-century England. The cast includes several real-life figures (George Stephenson, a 12-year-old Charles Dickens, and even a cameo appearance by Lord Byron), as well as fictitious ones, and at least one borrowed from *Bleak House*.' *The Historical Society Review*

'Jean-Pierre Ohl's dazzling British tale with its mixture of gothic thriller and historical novel with more than a dash of black comedy lights up the French literary scene.' *Le Canard enchaîné*

£12.99 ISBN 978 1 910213 93 3 347p B.Format

The Lairds of Cromarty by Jean-Pierre Ohl

'*The Lairds of Cromarty* presents us with a thoroughly engrossing mystery as well as an intriguing collection of supporting characters such as Par the butler, or Mary's Aunt Catriona, who watches the citizens of Edinburgh through a telescope, exclaiming loudly at their behaviour. There's even a cameo of George Orwell, for reasons we won't go into here. An absorbing page-turner that defies all attempts to put it down.' Alastair Mabbott in *The Herald's Paperback of the Week*

'Jean-Pierre Ohl's *The Lairds of Cromarty* is a bulging carrier bag of a novel, a bibliophilic *jeu d'esprit*, containing the best literary rugby match since *Tom Brown's Schooldays*, a homage to the International Brigades and a convoluted love story.'

Catriona Graham in *The Guardian's Books of the Year*

'Some books are real surprise and this is one of them. What is at heart a detective story becomes in turn a love story, a tribute to friendship and courage, an ode to books and booksellers and to nineteenth-century literature... for all its Gothic twists, this is a book filled with humour, acute observations of character and place, and literary citations worthy of a professional bookseller – Ohl's other career. It has been flawlessly translated by Mike Mitchell in what deserves to become another of the latter's award-winning works.'

The Historical Novel Review

'Mike Mitchell's translation has depth and reach, with Ohl, he creates the density of a Victorian novel, but leavened constantly as the disparate parts of the complicated plot are pulled together. This wonderful, humorous, book should be displayed in all good bookshops.' Scarlett MccGwire in *Tribune*

£9.99 ISBN 9781 907650 74 1 286p B. Format

Wonders Will Never Cease by Robert Irwin

'Robert Irwin's latest novel has much in common with *The Game of Thrones*. Both are based on the gory struggle of the Wars of the Roses, both inject large amounts of magic and the occult into their narratives, and both are hugely enjoyable, fast-moving and filled with dark humour. Though Irwin uses the actual events of York versus Lancaster in 15th-century England, he is happy to change things to make a better story – and how stories are created, recycled, embellished and interact with reality is at the heart of the book. It comprises a palimpsest of fables, myths, legends, romances, chronicles and sagas.

His hero is Anthony, Lord Scales, brother to the beautiful Elizabeth who becomes Edward IV's queen, and one of the Woodville clan whose rapid and resented rise is one motor of the mayhem unleashed by these titled gangsters. We meet him first at the battle of Towton, the bloodiest in English history, where he is apparently killed. After three days of strange encounters in a limbo landscape he returns to life and continues on picaresque adventures of chivalry and horror. Often bewildered, often slipping into occult spaces, he meets people like Sir Thomas Malory, author of *Le Morte d'Arthur*, and the alchemist Ripley (believe it or not) who turns Anthony's life into a legend. As one character observes: "The real world is a poor thing compared to the stories that are told about it."'

Ian Irvine in *Prospect Magazine*

'Amply researched yet unceasingly insistent on its own fictionality, Irwin's latest novel is like an intricate medieval tapestry or multicoloured stained-glass window, promising neither truth nor falsehood, only wonder... Irwin has brilliantly refashioned medieval history as a myth for our own time.'

Andrew Crumey in *The Literary Review*

£9.99 ISBN 978 1 910213 47 6 392p B. Format

Time of the Beast by Geoffrey Smith

'It is 666AD and Athwold leaves his East Anglian monastery to became, at the age of 25, a hermit in the great marshland of the Fens. A daunting prospect in that somewhat forbidding territory even today but even more so then when there was less delineation between land and water. Athwold not only has to battle the terrain and the conflicting forces of paganism and Christianity but also his own inner turmoil when faced with love and desire. Throw a warrior-monk, Cadroc, and a mysterious otherwordly killer into the mix and the story takes on terrifying twists as it races towards a very satisfactory conclusion. This is a fascinating little book fewer than 250 pages but you might be left wishing there were more. This an excellent debut novel.' Carole Dawson Young in *Tribune*

'It's Smith's knowledge of the time that makes his story so believable, so immersive; there isn't anything here that seems out of kilter. The concept of native British shamans is beguiling, as is the notion of pockets of the country where its original inhabitants still lurk – along with people who are even more weird and ancient than them (the last Neanderthals, it is hinted at). In short, you're transported back in time, and it's the kind of book you might find yourself wishing were longer.'

Nick Lezard's Choice in *The Guardian*

'The atmosphere of the Fens in a truly Dark Age world is very effectively evoked, as is the mindset of the time. *Time of the Beast* unusually combines fine writing with a series of properly horrid revelations. Recommended.'

The Historical Novel Society Review

£9.99 ISBN 978 1 909232 36 5 236p B. Format

All the characters in this book other than those clearly in the public domain are fictitious, and any resemblance to actual persons, living or dead, is purely coincidental.

David Hamilton
6th September 2013

Dedicated to Holly
Always my Brightest Star

THE ADMINISTRATION

Book 1 of The Governor's Men

BY DAVID J. HAMILTON

3rd Edition

Author's note

I started writing this story whilst completing my Master's degree at University back in the year 2000 and finished it about a year later, after I'd started work in the West end of London.

For some reason unbeknownst to man, at the turn of the century I had a burning desire to write a science fiction novel. This is odd because with one or two exceptions, I don't love science fiction. It is not my thing. There aren't enough Orcs and broadswords for my liking. Nonetheless, I had some good ideas for a novel but trying to string a series of ideas together does not a story make. However, I was determined to complete the book, which extends to around 43,000 words; a long novella but not quite classifiable as a short novel. This period of writing served initially as a break from studying and later as a distraction from working in a job that I had little interest in because it wasn't interesting. No, not interesting at all. I've had more stimulating conversations with cheese.

The second edition of *The Administration* improved the flow of the story, which was always a little stilted by virtue of trying to connect a number of unconnected ideas! Some of the dialogue is a little corny and my own experiences at this time in my life are thinly concealed in the story, although I do not appear as any single character. I understand the correct literary term is 'self-insertion'; which sounds ominous. I trust this constitutes fair warning for what you are about to receive!

The third edition finally receives a cover make-over to coincide with the release of the second book in the series; The Resurgence. I have also made a few very minor tweaks to the text and some more corrections to the dodgy punctuation.

I do hope you find this story a worthwhile read; there are some concepts which may be of interest and keep you entertained. You will also find it's a little heavy on architectural and planning theory and terminology although I've edited this as best I can for this edition. An interesting point to note is that several of the technologies referred to in this book were theoretical twenty years ago and are now either in common everyday use, such as the rise of Electronic Vehicles (EV's) and Amazon's 'Alexa' or are on the verge of a breakthrough to the mass market - autonomous vehicles for example.

Dave
April 2021

CHAPTER 1

The room was dimly lit, clean without being spotless, functional rather than comfortable. Vil Toradon entered from the east door. A quick glance confirmed that everything was in place and wearily he ran his hands through his light brown hair and laid aside his well-worn Mark 3 utility coat before collapsing into one of the room's two chairs.

Vil voice-activated the viewscreen, which duly turned itself on and started blaring out the usual news including the Martian land reclamation programme, the protective Dome's temperature and planned weather for the following day. Vil turned the volume down by audio command and peered at the images almost vacantly. In seven hours he would have to get up, in eight he would be back at the office, administering the tax return data cards through one of the city's central computers.

'Great' he thought, wondering where his brother, Cassus, was. Normally he would be back from the city administration quarters by now. It was quiet with no-one else in the apartment, although Vil did not particularly mind. After a day spent with nothing but the background babble of busy people and the constant hum of the computers and noise of the city so close by, the quiet came as a small relief.

Vil heard the main entrance slide open in a controlled whoosh. A second later Cassus stepped into the rest room. His brother was lighter in complexion than Vil and two inches taller with a lean athletic build, "evening Vil."

"Cassus."

"Another good day at the Inspectorate?"

"Same as always. Process, process, followed by a little more process. The tax cards come in and the tax the cards are passed on to the collectors or for storage."

"I know you don't find it particularly exciting."

"No, every day is always the same. Our well-behaved city population dutifully return their details. Nothing unusual happens. Nothing ever happens at all really!"

"No, no, probably for the best". Cassus and Vil had had the same conversation countless times. "Well, it's been a long one for me too, I'm off to bed."

The brothers said goodnight and Cassus moved into the western passage and his sleeping compartment. Vil stayed sitting for a little longer before making the effort to shift himself to his own bed.

The morning dawned. The tight environmental control within the protective domes which encased the city went about its automated functions quietly and was barely noticed by anyone. The city of Acto 1 was well established and had sustained several generations of humans without any significant problems. Many of the early settlements, informally within a Federation of systems, the 'Planetary Network', had almost secured independence as self-sufficiency increased and there was less need to rely on the Planetary Network to maintain the settlements. Of course the majority of systems which had been colonised were very much within the embrace of the Network, especially the newer, more vulnerable ones. However, the older systems, including Acto, saw less and less need to maintain close relations, although formal relations were by no means strained. Self-sufficiency was one of the original aims of the colonisation programme, rightly or wrongly, following the breakthrough in interstellar travel in the late twenty-first century.

*****

Vil hastily prepared a pro-pill breakfast simultaneously kicking the helpful little wheeled utility droid out of the way in a fit of early morning irritation.

Acto had never really embraced droid technology, certainly not human counterpart level droids at any rate. The colonists took pride in the fact that the city was built on human expertise, sweat and blood. Although in the contemporary city it was dubious as to whether this tenet still held true. Still, every household owned a couple of cheap utility droids which performed basic household functions such as washing, cooking and cleaning. Many people also owned various game-droids that could interact with their human partners in various means of entertainment and manifold formats of computer games and virtual reality simulations.

Of the more expensive and competent droids there were only a few in the city. The Administration possessed a small number of course, as well as various industrialists and some of the wealthier Citizens. In general, unlike Earth and the planet Trestel, Acto had avoided a heavy dependence on droid intelligence and labour. Its technological database and city administration was largely contained within the Central Computer Department, normally just called the CCD: The most prestigious enterprise within the city.

Vil glanced upwards as he strolled the short distance towards the electric car rank at the end of the road.

Each driverless car was operated remotely by the traffic control computer that additionally operated every other form of automated transportation within the city.

At the last census the population of Acto registered some four million people and was by far the largest and most important city on Acto (upon which there were three main cities). Vil entered the vehicle and stated his destination. The car powered up immediately, with the dashboard lighting up with a subdued, soothing steady blue and set off with a low hum of power towards the Inspectorate building seven kilometres away. The city was high density and it was theoretically possible to walk to any destination of importance. However Vil's schedule was tight and the transport system was efficient, clean and cheap.

He stepped out of the car, pausing as he did so, to slot his credit chip in the port at the side of the vehicle. The Inspectorate building stood amongst several other buildings of mixed use and quality, although all conformed to the set government standard and all were over ten stories.

The super-steel and glass exterior was neither unpleasant nor exciting. Years of trying to build the 'sustainable city' back on Earth had culminated in a set of rules that every city in the colonised galaxy had followed. Personal space requirements, street patterns, building scale, function, flexibility, form and density - All were specified, all carefully calculated so as to give each individual the best working environment.

In a largely unconnected city-state, diversity in jobs was limited at best. According to theory, a city the size of Acto should be sufficiently diverse and was of high enough density to promote far more cultural activities than the city currently did, despite its relative isolation from the rest of the Planetary Network. The city was dense in population, but standardisation appeared not to have set in because of the clever dispersal of essentially set designs across the townscape. In reality there was regularity leading to maximum efficiency, with a truly deceiving veneer of diversity in building form, although the mix of uses within this quasi-architecture was real enough. Few people realised this and Vil doubted that many people really cared. The lack of honesty in the urban form bothered Vil's conscience on some level but he accepted it as being inevitable as a member of the colony.

There was also full employment but it was the council who designated jobs based on their assessment of performance of colonists throughout their education. On this world there was a need for engineers and scientists, but far less need for planners and architects - their function had been fulfilled long ago. There was even less call for dreamers and poets. Vil pondered these matters as he sauntered to his desk in the open-plan, light and airy atmosphere of the office. The computer powered on as Vil sat down and he set about flicking through the millimetre thick plastic electrophoretic cards in his in-tray which was constantly refreshed through a hydraulic system. The day began in earnest once more and Vil's thoughts were again subdued as he set about his tasks.

*****

That evening Vil decided to take a stroll to the outer zone. This was the latest zone to be 'reclaimed' from the harsh atmosphere, which contained oxygen but was too nitrous for long exposure to sensitive human lungs. As the protective dome was gradually extended through a series of sub domes the first stage of reclamation was simply to create a habitable environment. The sterile planet surface was left untouched until the terraforming process was undertaken. Vil reached the boundary of the dome in less than half an hour, his own apartment being fairly new and thereby close to the existing boundary of the city. The earth-based ecology gradually gave way to the dusty red of the planet's crust. There were few people out this far from the centre. Vil rarely saw many people on his walks at the perimeter. People were either still working, or relaxing in one of the amenities provided by the 'Recreation Bureau'.

As Vil passed the last clump of temporary buildings he did see someone, briefly, looking outwards towards the notional edge of this particular dome. The edge wasn't actually visible of course, its colour faded to black as night descended. Vil noted the figure was wearing the uniform of one of the Core's guardsmen. Vil thought it odd that a member of that organisation would be out this far, but the man paid Vil no attention and Vil was not particularly anxious to socialise. Now the natural landscape was readily visible. A few hundred yards of softly rolling redness intermingled with black outcrops of rock. The lighting was poor, but the radiance from the city's lights provided a tangible glow to the landscape.

Vil wasn't afraid, there was virtually no crime in the city, and certainly nothing that would make him fear for his health. Vil walked briskly, wearing off the effects of the day, trying to overcome the numbness of his mind. Cassus had often joked that he should leave the Inspectorate, but whilst this was possible it simply meant reallocation and Vil was fully aware that reallocation could result in a floor placement in one of the industrial centres, or worse, another bureaucratic office, so he stayed put.

It was only then that Vil realised that he had reached the edge of the dome, the silvery sides were just visible a few metres in front of him. Cold and austere, the metal surface of the interior skin beckoned to Vil to touch it and he reached out, overcome by the need of his senses to feel the texture of the material. Vil's palm pressed lightly onto the surface. It was cold, but not unpleasant, smooth and slippery but an impenetrable barrier. Vil stood, his gaze drawn upwards into the blackness, when something crashed into the wall. Vil jumped back, his arms up. There was a further series of small humps and then nothing. Silence held the air, Vil's heart hammered inside his chest but as his reason slowly returned he thought, 'there must be storm outside, a windstorm, a rock must have been blown into the wall face, and the storm passed on.' Seeing this as the only possible explanation, Vil turned, largely satisfied and began the walk home, his desire to wander abruptly quenched.

*****

Coldor watched as the civilian strolled out towards the perimeter, his shape gradually blurring and dimming in the distance. Coldor had been more than a little surprised to see anyone out here at this time. Normally people were in bed or using the recreational facilities. He had had to cover his surprise and pretend to look away, uninterested in the man, who had displayed no inclination to talk or converse with him.

In truth, the guardsman thought he knew the motive; to get away, to flee the Core and its necessities and burdens. The guardsmen knew it because he was here for similar reasons. His position as a captain of the Core security force brought him respect and a modicum of power. Coldor did not consider himself to be one of the faceless bureaucrats, scuttling about. His prime distraction was that he was bored, possibly even more than bored, he was stifled. Coldor had worked hard, he was physically strong, lean and enjoyed a reasonably high ranking within the structure of the city. However, once these had been achieved there was little left for him to do but sit and wait for his superiors to throw him their crumbs.

CHAPTER 2

The Governor leaned back in his authentic leather chair, a priceless remnant from Earth. Of course, his factory here on Acto produced imitation leather chairs and they were expensive, but Sendrick liked to think he knew the difference.

The office was vast, a glowing testament to his effectiveness as Governor. Built at the peak of the Governor's quarters within the centre of the original dome and amidst the administrative buildings, the hub of the city, was the building known as the 'monument'.

The monument was the greatest and most impressive building in the city. A few others, also in the centre, where the height of the dome was greatest, rivalled it in storeys; but none in magnificence. Upgrades had followed extensions and functionality was hidden somewhere in the building, but its prestige was the only matter which concerned Sendrick who had no qualms that the residence has come to resemble more of a palace than an administrative building.

A small ring of smoke blew into the conditioned air, illuminated by the beam of light from a standing lamp set in deep, thick carpet. The vast imitation oak desk sat staunchly in the centre of the room, facing a double entrance doorway. Smoking was officially universally banned and had been for centuries, but the Governor was so far above the ban that it didn't even register on his consciousness. A viewing point filled the whole of the back wall behind the desk. From here the Governor could see the entire city by rotating the top floor of the building. Even now the room was rotating ever so slowly, the vistas below changing accordingly.

The off-worlders' main impression of the planet was this building complex and many systems, especially the newer colonies, had little to compare. Ambassadors often asked Sendrick how he could afford such opulence, despite the obvious success of the colony. The Governor would smile and say "It is all in the prescriptive management structure we encourage, and of course the hard work of the city's citizens." The Ambassadors would then nod sagely and press for more information, by which stage Sendrick would have excused himself and left one of his adjutants to deal with the matter.

Sendrick smiled to himself. If only they knew! His eyes turned to the model on a table next to his desk. This depicted a model of the complete city which was updated every month. Idly Sendrick picked up a perfect replica of a city residential block and turned it over in his hands. He wondered which section of the city to focus on this week.

*****

Vil walked into the office, ready, in a resigned sort of way, to face the day. With neither haste or eagerness, he made his way to his desk. It had been concluded in the 21st century that people preferred their own desk rather than moving around from day to day, which caused unnecessary tension and anxiety. Vil pulled out the cheap but comfortable chair, essentially the same as a planetary shuttle chair and made by the same people. They manufactured almost all of the standard chairs on the planet. He reached for the pile of data cards and touched the cold metal of the 'in-tray'. He looked up and searched the contents of the tray. It was empty, 'That's odd,' thought Vil, slightly confused. This had never happened before! Self-consciously Vil looked around at everyone else on the floor. They were all busy working, going about their daily tasks.

Vil debated the best course of action and decided not to ask his work colleagues. If something was wrong there was no point everybody knowing about it. He would have to ask his supervisor. She was called 'supervisor' in the loosest sense, since all the employees were well trained and not very much happened in the way of change. She had reached just high enough up the bureaucratic ladder to delegate sufficiently well to do sufficiently little. Still, she was very attractive and from the few times he had spoken to her beyond pleasantries, she seemed easy going enough. Vil made his way to the office at one end of the otherwise open plan workspace and rapped twice on the thin metallic frame of the door.

“Come in”, was the business-like reply.

Lilia Zara was sitting at her wide 'wood effect' plastic desk, on the standard issue chair, her long legs crossed beneath tight form hugging black trousers and a crisp business issue white top. Her looks were exciting, dangerous even, with an angular face out of which gazed wide-set deep green eyes and full lips that turned into a broad and engaging smile when she was amused. The sort of woman whom men desired and women were jealous of; even more so on a colony. Lilia looked up, a slight look of amusement on her face at the long pause. Vil mentally shook himself, and after some effort managed to explain his problem. The woman leaned back; her frown slightly creased as she considered the predicament.

"You're absolutely sure there are no cards? They haven't been knocked to the floor or anything?"

"No. Well, I'm pretty sure they haven't." Vil answered.

"Could one of the team have hidden them, you know, for a joke or something?" Lilia queried.

"One of the team?" Vil looked confused, "Oh, I see, no, I wouldn't imagine so, they never have before."

Lilia gave a little laugh at that. Her laugh was infectious and Vil could not help a smile spreading across his face.

"I presume you're not too enthralled with your fellow employees?" Lilia asked. Then, seeing the shadow a frown on Vil's face, continued, "it's okay, I'm here to make sure that the employees do get along, if there is a problem you should come and see me. I am the authority here, and I like to think I am not too draconian?"

"No, of course not," Vil replied, "It is just, I don't often really talk that much with the rest of the Inspectors. We get along, but I feel that...." Vil hesitated and changed tack quickly, he wanted to trust her, but a sudden burst of prudence told him that perhaps he should wait.

"No Lilia. I'm fine thank you. I just don't want to sit around with nothing to do." Lilia appeared not to notice his change of heart and said, "Listen, go and get a drink and wait at your desk for the time being. I will communicate with some people, if nothing turns up, I will let you know." Vil thanked her, smiled self-consciously and returned to his desk. The door closed quietly behind him.

Vil walked slowly to the nearest refreshment station. He could see most of Lilia's office as he filled a cup with water. His eye was drawn to her as she talked on the viewscreen. He thought it was Kathryn Gad over at the Governor's central administrative quarters. Both of them looked serious. Lilia glanced his way and Vil busied himself with a refill, a concerned frown back on his face.

*****

Half an hour later Lilia left her office and found Vil at his desk. Vil looked up expectantly. "There is nothing to worry about Vil", she said, "It's a simple case of misallocation of work-loads by the central computer.

Everything will be back in order tomorrow. You should count yourself lucky!"

Vil asked, "So it's nothing bad, nothing to do with me?"

"No, of course not. This is a simple administration error, that's all." Lilia reassured him, "I have also requested permission that you are allowed to take the day off, seeing as it is the Admin's fault, not yours. You are free to go."

Vil was pleased, he had not had a weekday off in a long time. Today was a day when he would get things done; it would be a productive day. Vil smiled at Lilia and thanked her, before making to gather his few things. Lilia nodded and to Vil's surprise, perched herself on the edge of his desk "There is one condition though Vil."

"Er, yes?" queried Vil.

"Walk me to the refreshment station first. I feel the need for a nutriboost. They've just released Cheesecake flavour."

"Cheesecake? Seriously? That sounds pretty disgusting to me but if you insist!"

"So, what are you planning to do with your afternoon off?" Lilia asked.

Vil thought for a moment, “I might call in on a friend over at the Hydrodomes and see if he fancy’s a drink or two later this evening,” he mused.

“That sounds like fun. Make sure you have a good time and that’s an order!” Lilia rested her hand on his forearm briefly with the gentlest of pressure before returning to her office. Vil watched for a moment and then hastily snapped his jaw shut.

*****

Coldor's evening was discouraging. The guardroom was cold and austere. He gloomily remembered all the times he had relaxed here with friends as a younger man. Now they were all but gone, serving in other functions across the city and indeed the planet. Coldor felt a little old and certainly more than a little bored. His duties tonight consisted of organising the patrols through the administrative complex and making sure that security was maintained. It was a near pointless duty, there was so little crime in the city that sending men on patrol in an area with as many security precautions as the core was pure overkill. Normally a lower ranking officer would have dealt with this sort of thing, but surprisingly no one else was available this evening and so it had fallen into Coldor's experienced hands.

He made his way into the little anteroom next to the guardroom, which contained a set of visual displays and controls for monitoring the administrative complex and keeping in touch with all of the patrols. Coldor plumped himself down onto the chair. Earlier he had again talked to the shuttle service bureau, Acto's only off-planet transports were in the hands of the administration, largely because it was an expensive business, but also because as Coldor increasingly suspected, to keep valued members of the community from leaving and finding a better life elsewhere. He could see the logic in it although understanding the logic did not make him feel better.

Acto was still a colony, it was not inhabited Planet-wide, perhaps five or six per cent of the planet was now colonised. There wasn't a shortage of skills because of the highly organised academic system, but the state had invested a lot more in certain individuals than others; depending on their ability and aptitude and it was reluctant to let those people go. With perfect freedom certain people would leave the planet for one of the worlds where skilled personnel were treated very well indeed. This would include the smaller colonies that were still establishing themselves and possibly lacking certain key constituents, or perhaps one of the bigger more important colonies such as Trestel which always seemed to need more skilled workers and made no secret of the fact.

Acto itself was not so averse to letting in certain people depending on their ability, profession and source planet, since there were variable levels of quality within the Planetary Network. Coldor also knew of a few people who had left Acto but they had probably not been considered by the city-state to be of any importance. A man as highly trained as Coldor could make himself very comfortable elsewhere, very quickly; which was why they weren't letting him go. There were only a handful of people planet-wide who had as much experience he did in certain fields.

*****

Cassus was in when Vil finally got home, "Good evening bro. How was your evening?"

"It was superb Cassus! The first for some time I must admit." Vil grinned as he slurred his words slightly and Cassis picked up on it immediately.

"Ha! It sounds like it! If you're going to be alright I'd better go to bed, I have a meeting with the departmental heads tomorrow."

"Yeah, I'd better get the old head down as well." Vil slumped into the nearest chair and rested his head on his hands. Cassus left the room and returned a minute later with a glass of recycled water.

"Here, drink this and you won't feel so bad in the morning."

Vil swigged down some water and murmured, "Good night and good luck for tomorrow." Then he passed out. Cassus rolled his eyes and left the room. Tomorrow could be an important day and he wanted to be properly prepared.

CHAPTER 3

Cassus was deep in thought as he rose up and up in the elevator to the core of the city's administrative complex. He wouldn't be far from the Governor himself. The CCD was the body that maintained and enhanced the various central computers, which ran the city; the tax computer, the traffic control computer, the environmental control computers; there were several dozen of them each working through a unified core system. This was a mainframe quantum computer, which could be used to add processing power to each of the city computers and maintain the harmonious running of each. The mainframe was no more powerful than any of the other city computers as a central, all-powerful, fallible computer was something that had been disregarded almost from the very beginning of the colonisation process.

Each computer had a human section assigned to see to the smooth running of that hardware. Cassus was in charge of the computer that regulated the domes' temperature and humidity. This was a minor section, but one with a vital role. He had been called to a united section-head meeting in the grand chamber on the top floor of a building directly next to the Governor's quarters. This building was essentially used to accommodate off-worlders and for lectures, meetings and various similar functions and was luxurious compared to the utilitarian residential and office buildings Cassus was used to. He appreciated the whole feel of the property. He was proud to be here and felt like he belonged. What the meeting was about he didn't particularly care; he was secure in his ability and had faith in his position within the administration. The elevator reached the top and the door pinged open. Cassus stepped out into the bright, ornate and half-full chamber.

The CCD regulators stood on a platform at one end of the chamber in front of a double door reached by three broad steps. The six regulators were resplendent in their crisp green uniforms waiting for order. These men were amongst the elite of the city. Along with the chiefs of a few other sections, no one else had such good access to the Governor himself. It was a long, long ladder to the top and these six were Cassus's direct superiors. He sidled up to Kathryn Gad, a friend of his, (in his definition) although he was normally too busy for deep friendships. This tendency was not unduly irregular. Many of the city's top cadre of inhabitants were always so focused that there was only limited time for 'friends'. He certainly placed his ambitions above many other things, although he was by no means difficult to get on with.

Kathryn was thickset with immaculately managed short blond hair and inquisitive bright green eyes set in her round face.

"Any idea what this is all about?" He asked.

"Cassus! I was going to come and find you later. I talked to your brother's supervisor earlier..."

"He's not in trouble is he?" Cassus asked anxiously, partially concerned for his brother, but also for his own reputation.

"On no, nothing like that. It just seems that my computer didn't allocate him any work today, a simple mistake, that's all it was."

Cassus recognised her defensiveness. She regarded her section's computer as family and was reluctant to reveal any faults with her department. He quite understood the feeling and tactfully moved on, not wanting to dwell on a potentially embarrassing topic.

"I'm sure it was merely a system clique or something. A chance event, not anything to worry about," he said, looking at her.

"Yes, that's about it. I have checked tomorrow's allocation and everything will be back to normal."

“Anyway, do you have any idea what this meeting is all about?" Kathryn was pleased that Cassus had recognised her embarrassment immediately. Still, his ability to read these situations was why he had come so far in so short a time. Kathryn was envious of him, but not bitter. Cassus was a rising star of the core. Bright, intelligent, handsome and ambitious, Cassus had risen from a humble computer engineer to a section head of the 'Central Computers Department', one of the most skilled and specialised departments in the city.

Cassus said “no” and would have continued, but just then one of the regulators started to speak.

"Section heads," he boomed, "I am sure some of you are wondering why you are here or if there is a problem. Let me assure you that this gathering is purely social. The colony is going from strength to strength and it is mainly down to the excellent work you have put in. Today, this afternoon, will be a break from our normal routines and take some time for you to enjoy a well-deserved rest." The speaker continued for some minutes more. Cassus was surprised at this expansive level of talk, it was new to him and definitely not what he had been expecting. He recognised the speaker, it was Hal Satsuma, the Japanese heritage still visible in his features, He was small, neat and quick in his actions and his speech. He had a reputation as highly capable and very efficient. The speech continued and Cassus focused his attention on it again. He was very surprised when he picked out the last few words of the regulator's speech: "And to top it all, the Governor himself will be arriving shortly to speak with you all." The regulator stepped back and Cassus looked at Kathryn, she seemed as astonished as he was.

The Governor entered from the double doors behind the platform. He was resplendent in his formal city robes; these consisted of a deep blue gown, which flowed around his feet and a wide cream sash across his chest. The cut of the robe was loose, unlike the uniforms of the regulators. More like an ancient Roman toga than a uniform. Cassus himself was dressed smartly in his own formal uniform; a lighter green version of those the regulators wore. He only wore it occasionally, when it was demanded, unlike some of his fellow section heads. Cassus was ambitious, but not so insecure that he had to visually display his power to others. He had no need to anyway; everybody who needed to know him already knew who he was.

The Governor's sash bore the emblems of power; The Planetary Network's symbol was of the Earth, with golden yellow arrows shooting out from it in all directions to show mankind's exploration of the galaxy. Next to it was Acto's own emblem, a blood red planet glowing against a star studded galactic background. The third and final emblem was the Governor's own markings of rank, a glass dome set upon a magnificent mountaintop, a beam of pure white light rising up from the crest of the dome, shooting into the system above.

The Governor waited until the hum of excitement that he had generated died down and began to speak. The gathered heads of department listened carefully.

"Esteemed heads of the CCD and," the Governor turned to the cluster of regulators standing on the platform, "my devoted department regulators. You know you form a significant share of the top echelons of this colony. More than this, you are all members of the elite force. You control and ensure the smooth running of this city so our colonists may work hard to guarantee the expansion of the influence and living space of Acto. Our sister cities do the same, all in the name of our offspring, for the benefit of our planet and of our system." Spontaneous applause broke out from the audience and the Governor beamed down at them benevolently.

*****

The next morning was unpleasant for Vil. His head felt fuzzy and a nasty hangover pulsated through his skull. He also had to go to work. He considered contacting the office and saying he was ill, but that might cause undue concern. A medical crew might even visit just to make sure he was not diseased or contagious. Health matters were taken extremely seriously on Acto, and indeed in all of the colonies, especially the newer ones.

Though well established, Acto had never got over its concern for protecting the majority. Diseased colonists were often held in solitary confinement, even for minor ailments, so as to protect the rest of the colony. Besides, it was rare for anyone in the city to suffer from actual sickness. All infants were immunised against a vast array of diseases very early on, as such the 'illness' excuse was a poor one that people quickly learnt not to use.

Somehow Vil pulled off his sleep creased clothes and washed and dressed for work. The car rank seemed further away than normal, but he sank thankfully into the back seat and closed his eyes, thanking Cassus for making him drink the water and hoping rather fervently that someone at work had a headache cure. By the time Vil had reached his desk he felt a little better and was also relieved to see that his in-tray was filled to the brim as normal. Vil purchased a cup of real Rossian 128 coffee on the way in and tentatively sipped at it, steadying his brain for the start of the day.

One of his colleagues, Han, walked past and noticing Vil's drawn complexion commented, "Good night then Vil?" who grunted and leant over to pick up his first tax card. A shadow loomed over his arm and he looked up to his left, a little startled. It was Lilia. She looked as bright and business like as usual which irritated Vil for some reason.

"Good morning, Vil. I just wanted to check that you have received the usual allocation of work today."

"Yes, everything appears to be fine, thank you, er, how are you?"

"Fine, thank you," Lilia responded. She leant over the desk, her body only a few inches away from Vil's face and made a show of examining his computer's pop-up flat screen monitor and the data cards. As she did so she rested one hand on the desk. "Excellent. Everything would seem to be in order." She gave a cursory glance around the room, her eyes touching everyone who was close enough and appropriately they all made a show of working hard. Then she turned and walked back to her office. It was only then that Vil realised that she had left a note on his desk. Cautiously, Vil picked it up.

He did not need to worry, all heads were down or staring at monitors and holo devices, either working or at least making a good show of it. Vil opened up the message, which had been folded into a square. Two headache tablets fell onto his desk, and the message read: "Looks like you had a good time! Thought these might help'. Vil grinned inwardly, for there at the bottom of the note she had left her personal computer line code, so that he could contact her at her apartment. Vil swallowed the tablets, feeling them do their work on his lingering headache and applied himself to his work. His heart a little lighter and a small smile unconsciously playing on his face. Yet from somewhere deep inside him a nagging doubt remained. He could not place its source; it was not Lilia, that much he knew. It was something else, a gnawing gut feeling that he could not put his finger on.

*****

Cassus was circulating, making small talk here and there as courtesy required. He was popular amongst the CCD and most of the people readily talked to him. The Governor was also on the floor, making his presence felt. At the moment the regulators and some eager looking CCD heads surrounded him and Cassus bided his time, waiting for an opening. He was not going to crowd the Governor or force himself upon him. He would find him later; or the Governor would come to him.

The moment did indeed come, as he had been so sure it would. The Governor was circulating the hall, when he crossed some ten feet in front of him but happened to look his way. The Governor stopped and as such so did the half dozen hangers-on he seemed to have collected on his travels. He raised his portly head and looked directly at him. Their eyes met and Cassus could feel the intensity in that gaze, the power and energy locked away there. He almost looked away but didn't. Then the Governor smiled and said, "Ah, if it isn’t young Toradon. I have been looking for you."

The Governor walked over to him waving away all but one of his regulators, with a benign look or gesture. Cassus bowed his head in respect and took the Governor’s outstretched hand. It felt dry and hard. Cassus swallowed back his nervousness.

"My Governor, it is a pleasure to meet you at last."

"Indeed. I have looked forward to meeting one of our top men myself. Come, we have much to discuss." The Governor's tone was friendly, fraternal. Cassus was bewildered, but let himself be led away from the hall, followed directly behind by the remaining regulator, a man whom he did not know. The regulator was thin, very slender and tall. His dark hair was receding and flashed with silver, but his cruel eyes were sharp grey. His mouth was a straight thin slash across a narrow face.

He whispered into Cassus's ear, "Pay no attention to your fellow heads of section, look straight ahead and follow me closely."

The man moved in front of Cassus who promptly followed him, the Governor stayed someway behind bidding people goodbye. The trio rose onto the platform and made for the double doors, which opened automatically. The Governor turned around for one last time and waved a hand in a farewell salute. The doors closed behind them and Cassus could hear the sound of applause. He imagined the conversations that would be held about him, the whispers and the gossip. He knew that some people would be glad if he was in trouble. He didn't know where he was going or why and a frown of worry creased his otherwise smooth forehead.

*****

The two-tone grey corridors of the core security force's main barracks and training facilities remained as pristine as they always had been. A young guardsman standing outside the intelligence room snapped to attention and saluted as Coldor passed. Coldor returned the salute and continued to the commanding officer's room. He did not recognise the guard; he must be a newly trained member of the force. Coldor's commanding officer, the CO of the whole security force in the city, had a measure of influence on the Senate and access to the Governor himself.

Another guard stood outside the commander's door. He wore the triple stripes of a sergeant and was heavily built. His right hand rested easily on the thigh holster of his blaster rifle, Coldor knew the man, Sergeant Barthan, he had served in his command for some time. The guard saluted “Sir! Good evening. Do you have an appointment?”

Coldor saluted in return.

“Stand easy sergeant, the old man is expecting me."

"Very good sir, carry on." He turned and opened the door for Coldor and announced his arrival. Coldor stepped into the room, snapped to attention and saluted the commander.

"At ease, Captain," Commander Perterson said from behind a desk with crammed with an array of data cards and portable holographic displays. “Please sit,” he gestured carelessly with one hand.

The commander spoke again, "My computer tells me that you intend to take some time off captain. Is this correct?" he said.

"Yes sir, I have not had a break in a long time and to be frank sir, I need a rest from the core."

Perterson leaned back in his big imitation leather chair. His left hand stroked his moustache thoughtfully. "This would not have anything to do with you being declined permission to leave the planet, would it captain?"

Coldor attempted to look contrite, although he knew the commander would have been informed of any high ranking officer's application to leave the planet and hence the core. Before Coldor could reply the commander continued, "In fact, I was meaning to have a little mano a mano with you about that. If you had left the colony I would have lost one of my most experienced and useful men”. The CO’s eyes were hard. “Were you going to inform me before or after you had left captain?"

"Before, of course, Sir. It's not a decision I made, or tried to make, easily. However I now realise that leaving is impossible for a man in my position."

"Yes, Captain." The commander put some emphasis on the word, captain, "you are important here on the colony. That is why we will not let you go. In fact, I am surprised that you even applied. You must realise that the City-State has placed a great deal of time, effort and resources into your development. You have not made any friends applying for an off-world permit. Like it or not, you are in debt to this Government and you would do well to remember that!"

Coldor felt like snapping, his patience was strained, and, something inside him was going to break soon he was sure. With an effort he remained cool, years of training aiding the process.

"I feel, Sir, that I have given a lot of my life and all of my effort within that time to the core and therefore to the city. I have not been reticent in my application nor dereliction of my duties. However times change, I am getting older and I am a man of ambition."
Perterson stood up and pointed his finger. "You disappoint me Captain. You know you were planned for promotion in a couple of years. I doubt whether you will have that honour now in five years, let alone two, unless I specifically advocate it."

The CO scratched at his cheek, “I am not sure I am willing to do that now I have seen your apparent lack of loyalty to this force."

Coldor didn’t give a damn and that helped him. He was leaving, promotion or no promotion. He had long ago calculated that he could possibly sit in the commander's chair if he really wanted to. The rank system on Acto was simplistic at officer level. The core was small and there were a limited amount of officers. Coldor was one of only eight serving captains in the entire city. There were two ranks above him, Major, of which there were currently four, two Colonels and then the commanding officer. Looking up at the CO now merely filled Coldor with dread. He would never sit in this cold, characterless office. The power had tickled Coldor's fancy, but he preferred the thrill of freedom. Coldor's primary aim was to be at the forefront of something, a pioneering colony for example, where the action was. Not on Acto at any rate. However, Coldor tried to look suitably chastised.

The commander appeared satisfied. He sat down and watched Colder for a few moments. Continuing in a softer tone, "I am not a vindictive man. I have no wish to keep down a man as useful and experienced as you, when you could be of more help to the city in another, higher and more responsible position. You are being watched captain, but you are still in the running."

"Thank you, sir. I will not forget this," said as Coldor enthusiastically as he could manage.

"Would it still be possible to have that leave though sir?"

The commander eyed Coldor carefully, but his expression softened, just slightly. "I think that despite everything, you do deserve some time off, what has it been? Two years? Three?"

"Only two years, sir."

"That will suffice. Yes, I think that you should have time off. But make sure that when you do come back - you are refreshed and ready to contribute as much as you already have to the core, I don't want to hear any more talk of leaving. For your own sake, captain."

"I quite understand. Thank you, commander,"

The CO nodded and turned back to his desk. “You are dismissed." Coldor saluted and turned smartly. The plan was in motion.

*****

As the door closed behind him the commander looked up again, his face thoughtful. He wondered if the captain had really meant what he said. Personally he doubted it. If Coldor tried any subterfuge Perterson himself would be in trouble. It would be best to notify the authorities above him. The commander hit a button on the control pad set into his desk. An ultra-thin tray slid out of the rim of the desk. There was a direct line to the head of the secret staff. Perterson's hand hovered over the panel. Slowly he hit the access button. Perterson understood Coldor's position. He himself had tried to leave years before and had failed in the attempt. He was sympathetic but he was not about to let a subordinate succeed where he failed.

The tiny view screen on the panel popped up and displayed a narrow face, with a straight thin slash of a mouth and cruel grey eyes. The cool relaxed voice said, "this is regulator Marsden, co-ordinator of the secret staff and adjutant to Governor Sendrick. I am not available at present; leave a message it will be returned as soon as time permits. This is an encrypted line. If it is an emergency matter you will know the procedure." The regulator stopped talking and his face faded from the screen. An artificial voice said helpfully, "Please leave your message now."

Commander Perterson outlined the situation and asked for captain Coldor of the Acto Security Core to be watched, but without interference, unless the law was violated. Perterson tapped the off button and the control panel slipped quietly back into its compartment in the desk. He rested his elbows on the desk, his hands clasped. To no one in particular he said, "I sincerely hope you don't arouse the suspicions of the secret staff Coldor. You're on your own now."

CHAPTER 4

Cassus was in a state of awe. He was sitting across from the Governor in the Governor's own office, settled into a very big, very comfortable chair with a good whisky in one hand and a cigar in the other trying unsuccessfully not to cough. There were two other chairs in the room, arranged informally around a small deep black glass table at one end of the office, to the left of the double entrance doors. The Governor watched him carefully, his expression unfathomable. Cassus's shoes were almost half enveloped in the thick carpet and he had trouble stopping his gaze from staring out of the vast, absolutely clear window behind the Governor's desk. It filled the entire wall, a good twenty metres wide.

Cassus could see the entire city below him, in vistas created by the other vast buildings of the administration, which almost matched the Governor's in height. They were monuments in themselves.

'Vil would love this,' he thought. The tops of the domes surrounding the site of the original colony dome were a little way below the apogee of the central dome, which had been enlarged over the decades. The surrounding domes didn't reach down to the ground in this part of the city because their drums and haunches had been retracted as the artificial environment had been improved, until only their crown remained. There were a several segregated fully intact domes such as the hydroponics food production domes. Cassus observed these in various places far from the centre. It was an impressive site, especially as the view was always changing as the office and the whole floor of this building, slowly rotated.

The Governor spoke. “Do you like the view?"

"It’s incredible, I never realised the extent of the city, or how compact the buildings are. It’s an inspiring sight." Cassus said as he dragged his gaze away from the viewing wall.

"Don’t you find it frightening Cassus? So many people living under a series of protective domes, trusting their integrity and their own safety to a few sheets of metal alloy and super steel."

Cassus frowned, "I must admit I’d never really thought about it. The domes’ safety is taken for granted by everybody I suppose. But the sheer size of the city, the number of people, is daunting."

"My sentiments exactly. Imagine this Cassus, if you will. There are over four million people in this city, living closely together. Almost every residential building is an apartment shared with a least fifty or a hundred other people. There are no singular detached homes. There is open space and many parks, but these are, by necessity, small. There are no farms, no natural monuments to the planet. Why?"

The question was rhetorical as the Governor immediately continued, "the answer is that we lack space and the expansion programme is slow, even when running at maximum capacity as it has been for the last twenty years or more. We simply cannot afford to make mistakes with the domes; our very lifelines. The hydroponics department is running at full stretch because of the population expansion. The city is already at its limit, Cassus and it is a narrow line we walk upon. Too narrow."

"Do you mean that the population growth is out of control?"

"No, I do not. The situation is continuously being monitored and the birth control programme adjusted accordingly. We can expand with sufficient speed to cater for the population expansion and more, which is why we encourage certain people to the colony. New skills and highly trained personnel are always welcome on Acto. But, whilst we grow slowly richer we must, by virtue of the population expansion and limited space expansion programme, maintain the same standards of housing, the same size parks, the same limited entertainment, the same daily routine. Lots of work and little play. We have to work the populace so hard, my young friend, so that they don't have the time or energy to realise that their homes are in reality quite small, that their city is really quite limited and that their lives are ultimately constrained."

"But they don't know any different. I don't know any different. The people work hard, but they are by no means poor. We have advanced technological centres and some of the best industrial complexes anywhere in the galaxy. We may be small but we are a big competitor in many fields, some of our goods even find their way back to Earth! What more can we do?"

"Does the fact that the people are ignorant excuse the fact that they could have better?"

Cassus scratched his neck, "but nothing more can be done," he paused, "unless we speed up the process of expansion."
The Governor chuckled. "Cassus, this is rich colony, but it's not Earth or one of the older systems. There are only four million people in this city and only about seven and a half million in total planet-wide, have you any idea of the cost of dome construction, terraforming, soil transplants, atmospheric control, safety measures, hydroponic domes?"

Cassus had to admit that he did not know.

"And why should you? It is not your department. Let me ask you this. If there was a way in which we could immeasurably improve the quality of most of the colonists' lives - not just the current generation but the future generations; would you be interested?"

Cassus said yes without even thinking about it. He really didn't think matters were that bad but if they could be improved for him, his family and the future, then he was interested. Surely it could only be good, virtuous even, for the people and for the colony. The Governor looked pleased and began to talk again, his eyes gleaming. Cassus sat back and drank his whisky, listening intently.

****

For Vil, the day did not seem to drag for once. He had a curious feeling of well-being, In fact when his computer notified him it was actually time to leave the office, he looked up in mild surprise. He toyed with the idea of finding Lilia, but decided against it. He also needed to go home and properly sleep off the remnants of last night's excesses.

The trip home was uneventful; Vil didn't really bother to look out of the window of his electric transport as it swooped past the central transport modules. Most of the scenery was filled in by his memory as he stared vacantly, his mind drifting. The transport modules were a long, very quick and sleek form of public transport. Naturally the central traffic computer controlled them. They operated on an electric current and occupied a wide two-way lane in the middle of the one way car lanes. Vil looked right. On this side of the car lane there was a narrow lane for two-wheeled transports; the bicycle had been largely resurrected throughout the Galaxy, and on the far side of that, a pedestrian lane. From here there was easy access to the electric car ranks or the transport modules, which were slightly cheaper. The modules had good access throughout the city and there was even a passenger and freight line to the more northerly settlement of 'City Gens' and from there down to the third and final city on Acto, 'Corinthon', as it had been named. This had been a very significant engineering feat when it had been completed, but that was years ago, before Vil was even born.

The transmods tended to concentrate on the more important avenues of the city, and left the smaller, more private roads to the cars, cycles and people.

Access to the residential apartments was only through a pedestrianised passage way or by bike. These were, by necessity, fairly narrow, but not claustrophobic. Fortuitously, because of the density of the city it only took a few minutes to reach the nearest electric car rank and less than a ten-minute walk to find a transport module which ran frequently and continuously. The modules themselves were accessed from overhead ramps, which spanned the car lanes and spread themselves into small waiting platforms slightly above the car lanes and surrounded by a waist high protective barrier.

Vil realised he had reached his car rank and the car had drawn to a stop. He slid the door back and pulled himself out. The evening was still light, the artificial environment kept the day long and bright in order to promote good spirits, higher levels of activity and increase productivity.

Vil meandered down the road towards his apartment. The common ground-floor front door was activated by a thumb print recognition panel or eye retina scan. Vil pressed his thumb against the pad without even looking at the control. The red QV-LED above the panel switched to green and Vil hit the 'open' button. Beneath that was a tiny ten digit button pad, which could be used to open the door in an emergency, either by the residents of the property, or by the emergency services who used standardised and city wide computer recognised codes. The lights came on as he entered, so Cassus was either asleep or still working - probably still working since it was not quite eight o' clock yet.

He poured himself a glass of water and sat back in his favourite chair - favourite through familiarity, since it was exactly the same as the other chair in the room. Vil leaned his head against the back of the chair and closed his eyes again. He felt tired, but mostly content. However, a nagging doubt at the back of his consciousness refused to go away even though Vil had by now made efforts to ignore it.

Then there was the sound of the apartment's front door whooshing efficiently open and in from the east door to the living room bounded Cassus, a massive grin on his clean cut face. His eyes were alight and his jaw firm, a committed determination in his movements. Vil looked up. "Vil, you won’t believe it! This is incredible, but I‘ve just spent most of the afternoon and this evening with the Governor!"

Vil leapt to his feet. "What? The Governor! How? Nothing’s wrong is it?"

"No, there's nothing wrong! Quite the opposite in fact. We're going to be moving up in this city, we are going somewhere. We will take our rightful place."

*****

"The opportunity is there, young Toradon. We have the resources, and I mean that literally, to turn this colony into so much more than it currently is. The question is how to go about it."

Cassus thought for a moment. "What form of resources? I thought all of the mineral probe ships had returned showing only medium reserves of nickel and common materials and little of any other types of precious raw materials."

The Governor graced Cassus with a wry smile. "You know your history. Let me explain further. Of course, before the first pioneers even came here, a whole series of automated probes were sent out in order to map the terrain and search for minerals and so forth. This followed the standard procedure for colonisation throughout the galaxy. The conclusive reports from the probes were that the terrain was suitable for human development and construction, being stable, and was able to provide on-planet resources for construction of the infrastructure. Indeed the planet bears similarities to Mars in many respects, including atmospheric conditions and the characteristics of the mantle and crust.

However, there were only just over five hundred pioneers in the original wave and, as you probably know, they had to pay for those probes with their own money, albeit with some subsidies from the Government and advice from the Eurasian Space Agency. Anyway, funds were extremely limited, and the probes, which were certainly durable enough, still suffered from a restricted life span. As such, not all the planet was thoroughly researched at a ground level and the original mapping satellite was too basic and cheap to do much but map the topography and environmental patterns of the planet. In short, the pioneers only had partial information."

This was all dimly familiar to Cassus, the history of the quest of the pioneers and the mother planet being deemed extremely important in the educational system which had vowed long ago not to repeat the mistakes of the past that had heralded the third great dark age. A strong appreciation for their forebears ensured the colonists did not forget who they were and why they were here in the first place. It gave them a sense of identity, a sense of place and belonging. Something to be proud of and strengthen their resolve.

A thought crossed Cassus's mind. Did the average colonist feel like that at all? Did they really care? Cassus was disturbed to find that he thought they probably did not.

The Governor coughed. Cassus leaned forward to listen.

"You are probably thinking that this was all over two hundred years ago, and that by now we have thoroughly "surveyed, analysed and planned" the development of our planet, as an ancient planner from Earth would have put it. You would be wrong. One must bear in mind that for the first hundred or so years of settlement of this planet, most of the wealth creation was put into the expansion of the settlements and other infrastructure. Our ancestors, whom we can all easily trace back to the first pioneers, sacrificed any form of decent standard of living. They worked relentlessly so that their descendants might enjoy a higher standard of living and wealth. They were successful. Their hard work has resulted in all that we see around us today, something we also strive to improve. But, essentially we are still in a very similar position as the first colonists. Much of our wealth goes on the expansion of the domes. Our standard of living is sufficient and we all continue to work hard. In reality, our knowledge of the planet has only been increased dramatically in the last thirty or forty years when we first obtained the ability and reserves to afford the proper detailed planet-wide analysis of the crust. With the aid of sophisticated satellite systems, launched whilst you were probably just a child, volunteer field biologists, physicists, geologists and other scientists, we now have an almost complete knowledge of this planet and most of our sister planets in this system.

Cassus vaguely remembered the launch of the 'Explorer' satellites when in his teens, the field volunteers everybody knew about. They had not only come from Acto, but from all over the Galaxy. It was a big push forward for the scientific community on the planet and surrounding systems. The Planetary Council, which consisted of the three leaders of the three main cities on the planet and their top aides, had agreed to fund all of the original research, a rare occurrence anywhere in the Galaxy. The research was continuing even today, although it was mostly privately funded, and the results regularly published in a popular journal throughout the Galaxy.

Cassus said, "I read some of the earlier reports. They found new reserves without difficulty and even a few deposits of permafrost in the Great Northern Canyon, but there was nothing to interest the ordinary man, no life forms, no huge deposits of valuable materials, or anything like that. I seem to remember some people even called it a waste of money after a while."

"Yes they did. They were wrong. Fortunately for us, it was some of our people who found it and we were able to keep it quiet, away from prying eyes."

"What? What did they find?"

The Governor seemed pleased at Cassus's obvious thrill. He looked him squarely in the eye, his voice soft. "We found a stratum of raw materials, the most valuable material in the galaxy, it is rare, it is precious and it is ours. There is enough to drag our planet to the forefront of the Galaxy. We can compete with the best, we can rival Earth."

Cassus exhaled slowly and whistled.

"This mineral, which I presume has to be mined, what is it and how do you extract it?"

"That is where the problems arise. The site is some way from this city and far from the other settlements on Acto. We have had to improvise and find alternative methods for its extraction. At present it's mined through mechanised open cast mining."

"I see, through some form of automated heavy mining? I have not read about any new mining machinery anywhere on the planet?" Cassus asked.

"No, that would prove to be too expensive at present." The Governor eyed Cassus warily for a few moments and then continued, "I shall tell you because I know I can trust you. Indeed; you were brought here today because we have a need for a man with as many capabilities as you have displayed. Ambition, competence, efficiency, and most importantly; loyalty. I shall be blunt. The method we use is really quite simple. We take people from the city and put them to physical work."

Cassus gawked. "They're not volunteers then. You use forcible methods to induce people to work for you!"

The Governor looked up sharply. "Do not presume that you know everything about the process, Cassus, your solicitousness is not justified. It is not quite a brutal as you are probably imagine. I see I must explain a few points to you. Firstly, there are volunteers, attracted by the Core-funded marketing campaign. Unfortunately there were not enough. There are not enough. Secondly, this is a colony. The people should expect a little bit of danger, as their forefathers did. Thirdly, we do not subject these people to such terrible conditions: They are well fed, they are well looked after and, when they have completed a number of years, they can look forward to retiring and never having to work again, albeit perhaps not on this planet. Finally, they are providing a vital service to the colony and its people. Without them, we would not be able to prosper and grow as fast as is now possible. People will look back and remember that it was I, Governor Sendrick, who sacrificed a few years of, at best, under-productive citizens so that they might immeasurably add to the wealth of the planet. In the future these people will be seen as the new pioneers with their devoted Governor as the leader of a brand new and better age."

Cassus could tell by the Governor's expression that he knew he hadn't entirely convinced him. The Governor leaned forward and smoothly poured Cassus another double whisky from the glass decanter.

He paused and then continued. "We have already discussed the issues of futurity and the desirability of bringing this colony to the forefront of the Galaxy. We have pondered the duty of our generation to the next and the related obligations and hard work; just as the pioneers did for us. This provides us with the means to fulfil that obligation Cassus, and fulfil it faster and sooner than we could have dared hoped. Sooner than we imagined we will be able to use automated devices to mine the terrain. The domes will have extended to the depository and working conditions will dramatically improve. You must remember that relatively few people have volunteered for this work thus leaving us in the same position as the last generation; stagnant. A stagnating city is a dying city. I will not allow that to happen on this planet! You must remember that many of the people who work for us now do so willingly because they know that when they have completed their obligations they will be well provided for by the city state. As you know, everyone is closely monitored by the education system and, as such, we know who will be most suited to this duty, rather than any other forms of vocation. It is not so harsh a system as you possibly imagine."

Cassus thought that he could pick a few holes in the Governor's argument but he could also see, and empathise with, the Governor's position. Moreover, his long-term vision impressed him. Cassus was not without his own doubts about the Planetary Council or worse the long slow decline of the Federation.

The Governor, as if anticipating Cassus's unspoken doubts spoke once more. "You are thinking that this is all well and fine whilst those promises of the State are carried out, but if a less scrupulous successor should chance upon power, then he may abuse his position?"

Cassus had to admit that it had occurred to him, amongst other concerns.

The Governor laughed out loud. "There is, I can assure you, nothing to worry about. We will have made sufficient returns to almost fully automate the process by the end of my term in the seat and the workforce necessary after automation, I'm sure, will be volunteers. Within a couple of decades, maybe even less, I would suggest that our domes will have reached and covered all the land to the areas of deposit and the people will again have a chance to breath."

Cassus nodded once, "I think I understand, my Governor. I also trust your word, but this has all come as something of a shock."

"That is entirely reasonable. Now I have one final thing to offer to you, I would like you to work for me here, in the central tower as a personal aide on this venture overseeing certain details and generally being my number-two man on the team. You will, I can assure you, be fully compensated for the inconvenience of taking you from your position in the CCD."

Cassus eyes widened and he stammered for a reply for a few brief seconds, but there was no hesitation in his voice when he replied. "Sir, I would be honoured. This is a memorable and exciting time for the colony and I want be a part of it!" He could not imagine that the Governor would intentionally lie to him although he was no fool and realised that the truth may have been stretched a little. However, as long as no one was dying, Cassus could share Sendrick's vision. He was not so old that his idealistic dreaming had yet turned sour and here a grand and righteous opportunity had presented itself to him. He would be an idiot to refuse it.

The Governor rose and shook Cassus by the hand, after a few further details had been sorted out Cassus retired.

*****

Vil had listened intently, a few lines of concern on his face. By the time Cassus had finished retelling the events of the evening the expression on Vil's face was shock.

"What's wrong Vil? Surely you are happy for me, don't let a few minor breaks from civil liberties distract your vision from the whole picture," Cassus said, a little irritably.

"I understand well enough, Cassus. I understand the potential benefits of the Governor's plan - if he pulls it off. But it seems to me that there are considerable flaws too and I'm not impressed by the fact that the State thinks it's acceptable to pull people off the streets at will! That's more than an excessive use of power."

"It is more than justifiable for the cause. It is people with views like that who have held this city and this colony back! Never willing to take risks or push forward."

"It is easy to take a risk when you are dealing with other people's lives!"

"But the risk is minimal. The people who are selected are well cared for and well rewarded when they have completed their duties."

"That doesn't excuse the fact that they are forcibly removed and what exactly does 'well cared for' mean? Is that what the Governor told you? Obviously they are not going to starve the workers, but you remember the outbound trips at school. All the precautions because of the dangers of working outside and we were only out there for a week. How long do they keep the conscripts on for and where do they go afterwards? I bet it's not here on Acto!"

Cassus remembered the outbound trips. As colonists, the education system still deemed it to be important to train them in some basic skills such as moving in a light gravity and the operation of certain machinery and basic repairs. The trips were normally a few days long and cramped and uncomfortable. They were dreaded by most in the senior years of school when they became compulsory for all, and many pupils opted out at the earliest possible opportunity.

"I'm sure conditions have improved since then, and no, I don't know how long the pioneers have to work for. I only know the outline details, I will learn far more though in the next few weeks as I take my position on the Governor's staff."

"Let's hope then, that it's as you say."

What offended Vil most was not the vision or the possibility of immeasurably improving the colony, those things he could concur with and excited him as much as his brother. Where he differed was in the method those aims were being carried out. However, he grasped the fact that because he knew little about the Governor's methods, he was not really in a position to debate it. He decided to end the argument and quietly see what else Cassus knew, whilst he secretly decided to make some private investigations of his own.

"Cassus, look don't be angry with me, I am only sounding out the facts. I'm sure you were a little concerned when the Governor first told you, weren't you?"

Cassus was about to retort when the truth of Vil's words hit him and he paused and leaned back smiling sheepishly, running one hand through his hair. "You're correct, of course Vil. I'm sorry. My temper got in the way of my sense."

"There's no need to apologise Cassus. Let's just discuss this more carefully." Vil said quietly. He let Cassus talk on about the afternoon, letting go of some of the nervous energy he had accumulated during the day. Vil half-listened and nodded and grunted in the right places, but his mind was elsewhere. The Citizens of Acto are being watched. Am I being watched right now? Vil thought. He looked around uncomfortably. He gulped back the sour tasting phlegm which had suddenly formed in his mouth, grimacing as he did so.

*****

At work, Vil's newly found unexpected friendship with Lilia continued to develop as he found himself spending more and more time with her during his free moments, either at the refresh station or the recreation zones. His awkwardness had started to thaw as Lilia made it clear even to Vil's obtuse blindness concerning women that she at least wanted to be friends, if nothing else.

"Vil, how many times do I have to tell you....? I hate the berryfresh flavour!"

"Whaaaat?" exclaimed Vil in mock surprise as they loitered by a vending booth at the end of the working day, "You do? You should have mentioned it before Lil! Well, it's a good job it's my favourite," he said as he took it back from a mildly exasperated Lilia.

They walked slowly back to one of the quieter recreation zones, walking closely side by side but not quite touching. Lilia paused by one of several miniature fruit trees dotted around and idly stroked one of its leaves as she turned to face Vil.

"Vil, this might be a little forward but I wondered, if you were free if you wanted to meet outside of work one day? Perhaps dinner?"

Vil raised his eyebrows, somewhat taken aback, but yes, damn it, he would take her out. She was beautiful and intelligent and Vil could do with some timeout. "I would love to" he answered,

"Good. When I say one day, what I really mean is today! Meet me here at 1900 hours?" Lilia said, half demanding, half questioning.

Vil laughed, "You're the boss! No problem, I'll see you later."

Lilia left then, having graced Vil with a private sweet smile and Vil headed towards the nearest exit, nodding goodbye to a few of his colleagues on the way out. For the first time in a long time he felt content. Not merely adequate, but really pleased with himself.

The rest of the afternoon passed quickly. Vil busied himself with various things he had been meaning to do for some time. By 1830 hours he was ready, after leaving a voice-note for his brother Vil headed towards the office, wondering why she had asked him to meet her there. After the short ride, Vil paid the vehicle and instructed it to wait for him. The sleek silver electric car obediently powered down to standby mode, waiting expectantly.

The street was quiet. There were a number of lights on in the office and Vil suddenly felt a pang of sincere gratitude, that one of them was not his own desk light. Vil was a little early and so leaned back against the car, relaxed, looking forward to the evening. A few minutes later Lilia arrived in a light blue, short cut dress.

Vil drank in the sight hungrily. His mouth was dry. He wished he'd brought something to chew on other than his own tongue but he managed to say "Wow. You look fantastic Lilia!" She smiled wickedly and Vil felt his heart and move in concert with other parts of his body. Vil opened the door for her without fumbling too much. They entered the car and together set off for the city.

Lilia chose the restaurant and Vil was happy to follow her lead. It was in the heart of the city. One of the best, an exact replication of a twentieth century Chinese restaurant from Terra. A slightly androgynous looking man rose from the desk to their left, his ornately decorated uniform pristine.

"May I see your identification cards please." He asked perfunctorily.

Vil and Lilia both slipped out their cards and showed them to him.

"That is most satisfactory, I have a table just right for you." The man gestured for them to follow him into the heart of the restaurant, uttering a few glib pleasantries.

Vil had almost forgotten that being 'an inspector' lent him some privileges. The social system focused on the central government with those in the employ of the administration considered amongst the city's elite, and the tax office was by no means the lowest of the governmental departments. Vil smiled at the waiter, bemused by his obsequious behaviour. He realised that he had not been out properly like this for months and had forgotten some of the more endearing aspects of his job. The power, such as it was, didn't impress Vil although he sometimes wished he had a bit more influence.

The two sat down, Lilia smiled pleasantly at Vil who promptly pulled his ace card. “I hear they do real cheesecake in here Lil. It’s called New York cheesecake”

“If that’s true Vil” Lilia exclaimed, “then you’ve made me a very happy girl.”

Suddenly things seemed okay. It was time to forget about everything else just for a while. The conversation began, slowly and tentatively at first until the drinks started to arrive, followed by some quite delicious food. As the alcohol took hold in they became more animated and forthcoming and unconsciously they drew closer together, hands almost touching on the table.

"Vil, I was concerned about the missing data cards, you know. In fact, I did a little detective work to see what had become of them."

Vil sat back, immediately interested. Things out of the ordinary simply didn't happen in the office. It was virtually unheard of, until now.

"What was the problem?" Vil asked,

"Well, apparently, according to my immediate supervisor, it was nothing, merely a misallocation by the computer of today's workload. It just so happened that you were missed out."

"Is that what you think happened?"

"Well, it *is* possible of course. The computers do make mistakes from time to time. The difference is, this is not the first time it has happened. In fact you're the third person to come to me with the same problem."

"And did those people take you out for dinner as well?" Vil said dryly.

Lilia laughed and said, "No, you're the only one", Vil smiled at her and her eyes smiled back.

Suddenly the waiter bustled up, 'If there would be anything else?'

Vil puffed out his cheeks and gave the man a brief but hard stare. Quickly realising his mistake the waiter nodded and quietly faded into the background.

*****

In the restaurant Lilia and Vil were by now very merry. Vil leaned back in his chair and stretched luxuriously before sipping on an artificially aged Jameson's whisky. Vivaldi's 'Winter' from the Four Seasons played softly in the background. The desserts and coffees followed and the conversation drifted, broadly covering topics and then flitting on. Cassus was always busy and these days especially, there seemed to be less and less opportunities to talk to him properly. There were Vil's friends of course, but Vil knew that he had been neglecting them recently.

The bill came and to Lilia's approval, Vil paid. Slowly, almost reluctantly the two left the restaurant. He felt mildly surprised that time had slipped past so quickly, but also happy because he had had such a pleasant and enjoyable time.

Lilia said, "Thank you Vil, I had a great time."

"It's been an absolute pleasure Lilia. Let's definitely do this again!" Vil, wondered whether he should ask her back to his apartment. His intoxication fuelling his desire on one hand, the more sober part of his

conscious brain urging restraint and good manners! With a small, inaudible, groan Vil decided to let things take their natural course.
They entered the car that had been called from the restaurant's computer.

“So, where to Lil?” he asked and she gave him her address. Vil spoke into the tiny central microphone mounted in the centre of the car's roof from his seat in the back. Calming soft blue lights powered on bathing the occupants in their glow as the vehicle set off.

When they arrived, Lilia turned and kissed Vil fully on the lips. She smiled and said "Goodnight" and left in one movement. Vil closed his eyes and savoured the moment. It lasted for a few seconds and then the microphone buzzed and the strangely tinny voice of the car's vocal programme kicked in, "Your next destination please." Vil grinned to himself and muttered, "Damned annoying aren't you!"

The car merely repeated its message. Vil sighed to himself, stated his destination and they were off. Through the core of the huge city packed with his fellow human beings, sheltered and kept alive by a series of domes billions of miles from their ancestral birthplace. Vil peered up through the window as he slumped, half cut, in the back seat and watched as the stars flitted past above.

CHAPTER 5

Another week passed relatively quietly as Cassus settled into his new role and Vil debated with himself the ethics of the information his brother had imparted. Coldor meanwhile had waited petulantly to put the next stage of his plan into action. On the dawn of the fourth day of the week he decided to move into phase two. He needed to make use of the intelligence room within the core barracks in order to gather data on the arrivals and departures of all the ships over the next few weeks. Coldor had managed to obtain an entire month off work, more than he had hoped for and as such he had plenty of time.

Coldor hoped to find passage on one of the huge cargo ships, which made monthly tours of many of the Federation Planets, by bribery or force if need be. By using the all-access computers at the info-lab, he could check the shuttle service records. If he was lucky he might be able to find a ship piloted by one of his old Academy friends. Most of the star pilots on Acto came from the Academy and it was a long and arduous process to qualify, but as Coldor thought wistfully, that at least got you off the planet.

The spaceport itself was another major problem. The planet had two; a major freight and transportation facility and a much smaller passenger and defence port. Both were within a large series of domes on either side of the city. Originally they had not been part of the city proper, but they had long ago been swallowed up by the expansion of the urban area.

Special modifications had been made to the port domes to allow craft in and out and to withhold the tremendous sound from the jets escaping into the rest of the city. There was of course a central computer department dealing with the requirements of the ports. The passenger port was used for those lucky enough to be able to afford travel away from the planet and the Governor's personal craft. Both the shuttle service and the core security kept an eye open for unwanted inbound passengers and potential 'escapees' and as such was heavily monitored. The cargo port had slightly lighter security, probably because the authorities reasoned that no-one would be so stupid or desperate enough to stow away on a cargo freighter.

Coldor was fervently hoping that he would not have to fit himself into a cargo bay; that would be a last resort as the flight to even the nearest inhabited system could take weeks; if he was lucky! He also wanted to avoid the second port because the planets defence systems were stationed at there. They consisted of four, rather old, 23rd century fighters that could sustain limited space flight. However they were also lethal and inordinately expensive. Acto was one of only two dozen planets to be able to afford such machines. Coldor wanted to avoid unnecessary risk at all costs and hence the fighters were given a wide berth. Coldor eased himself into a transmod and set off towards the barracks. To his left a rank car slid along beside him.

*****

Lucinda watched her squad shuffle off down the narrow dust encrusted hall into the open terrain of Acto. The passage did not have a roof, it had never been finished, but that didn't really matter because everyone was fully covered up in ground suits anyway. These were heavy, rather bulky protective suits with a backpack air supply. They were well equipped and a man could stay alive in one for two days if he had a full air tank, since there was a water supply and even a nutrient hose. They also had short range radio transmitters, sun glare visors, tool pack, and recycler and several other utilities. They were the best bit of equipment the conscripts had and Lucinda made sure that her boys kept them in good working order. She wanted to avoid any more deaths if at all possible.

It was 0600 hours Dome time and the city would still be slumbering, she wished bitterly that she was within the safety of the Dome right now, back in her lab testing indigenous and genetically modified plant life against the planet's natural crust. Unfortunately the secret staff had picked her to work on the mineral fields. This was not because she was deemed incapable for any further practical use within the Domes, but precisely because her knowledge of the Martian landscape made her so useful outside. She had actually been asked if she would like to work for the Core on the mineral depository. She had hesitated but they had taken her anyway. Cold, resigned anger showed behind her protective expressionless visor.

The group soon reached the half-collapsed end of the stone passage and the squad of ten formed up in a ragged line waiting for the day's orders. The eight men and two women already knew what the orders were going to be, since they were nearly always the same and could be summed up quite neatly. Dig. The men would extract the mineral by hand and with the aid of small, motorised machines of limited capability. It would then be loaded onto the sorting conveyor and the women would separate any obvious rocks and impurities from the pile. It was hot and dirty work, but more than anything else it was tedious and the teams all worked nine hours a day, excluding breaks.

Lucinda looked round at the landscape and sighed. It was as beautiful as it was deadly, gently rounded hills and a glorious red dust mixed with jagged out-crops of black rock like broken teeth in the distance. Here at the depository it was mainly black rock that stretched on and on.

*****

Vil was confused, he was pleased for his brother of course. He knew there would be all kinds of benefits for his family because of his new position within the Administration. On the other hand the thought of people being conscripted from the street at random disturbed him constantly. He had spoken to Lilia about the matter in private two days earlier. She had been instantly intrigued and shocked. Vil had debated the prudence of his decision to tell her, but eventually concluded that he trusted her and had relayed the whole story. He hoped he'd made the right decision.

They had thought carefully about whether there was any way to confirm the Core's actions against individuals. The tax data card scenario had seemed the obvious place to start and Lilia had suggested using the city's central library to try and track down any further evidence

. So it was that Vil sat nervously at a grey coloured table, in a hard library chair in-between a row of black computer consoles that were smaller than his head and a large coffee machine, which made an irritating whining sound. Vil absently sipped his black coffee and looked around, anxiously muttering under his breath, "what on Acto am I doing here deliberately searching for evidence to undermine the legality of the State's action. I don't know. I must be mental."

Vil wondered what he could actually do if he could find information confirming what Cassus had told him. He didn't know if was suited for this work and didn't consider himself to be any kind of hero.

Lilia arrived wearing an indescript black top and coat. Behind her, grinning impudently was Vil's Academy friend, Alan Spartan, who was commonly known as Al, perhaps because of his somewhat unfortunate name. Vil had invited Al because he trusted him and was sure that he would be interested in his news. He was right; Al was outraged and spontaneously committed himself to aiding Vil in his investigations.

Vil rose and grinned back at his old friend and greeted Lilia who was obviously excited about the prospect of a little underhand work.

The library was fairly empty; there were only a few old men and women chatting quietly in the library bar and the usual gaggle of Academy students desperately researching for topics which should have been completed the day before. Vil suddenly remembered his own days at the Academy and the time he had spent here in the library. He realised then that he was sitting at the table he and his other friends used to sit at some five years ago.

Al noticed it immediately and said, "Ah, I see you have taken us back to our roots Vil! Good old table." Al patted it fondly and searched closely for any of his old scribbled messages, but was disappointed to see that the surface was clean and unblemished.

"What!" he cried, "what kind of students have we got these days? Where are the amusing jokes, anecdotes, quotes, anything remotely resembling wit?" His scraggly face showed indignation.

"Guess students are too well behaved these days to muck up all the desks like you did Al," Vil laughed.

Al shot him a crooked half smile and replied, "'Maybe this has become a swot table" he said looking round suspiciously. "You just never know!"

"Guys, please, you are making me feel old," Lilia said with mock indignation as she had graduated some years before Vil or Al.

"Sorry young lady, would you like me to get you a nice cushion?" Al said flirtatiously.

Lilia shot him scowl.

"Anyway, we do have something more important to look into, my friends," Vil said. The three of them pulled up chairs around a computer screen at the far end of the row and booted up. Al sat at the controls since his knowledge in this sphere was far greater than either Vil's or Lilia's. He was a scientist specialising in plants and head of one of the hydroponic dome research facilities.

As he logged in he said quietly, "Vil, after you had talked to me on the viewer, which possibly wasn't the best idea, considering the nature of your message, I gave the matter some serious thought. You have had your problem with those tax things, although that's probably nothing to go on and of course Cassus has told you about the Governor's plan but we need hard evidence, not stories. Anyway, I've noticed a few odd things as well."

"Really? Such as what?" Lilia inquired.

"Well, there was the case of my assistant at the dome. Her name was Lucinda and to cut to the point; she disappeared. One week she was happily working away in the lab, the next week she was gone. I was offered a very abrupt message from the authorities saying that she had been transferred to a research facility at City Gens. She had said nothing to me about any transfer, but I had no reason to suspect treachery and sudden transfers are uncommon but not unheard of. However, we were friends and I was a bit puzzled as to why she never bothered to contact me afterwards. Now it looks like we have a reason."

"How long ago was this Al?" asked Vil.

"Oh, not long, maybe five or six weeks," Al told them.

"I'm just trying to figure out how long this has been going on for, Cassus didn't say, or did not know, when I spoke to him."

"Why don't you have another chat with him? See if you can gather any more info," Lilia suggested.

Vil clicked his tongue against the roof of his mouth as he thought about it. "I may do, but not yet. I want Cassus to think that I have accepted the situation and that I'm happy for him. I don't want to arouse any suspicions yet."

******

Coldor, meanwhile, had reached the main barracks building at the centre of the city. A rush of adrenaline coursed through his body and his eyes lit up in expectation. The building seemed curiously quiet and still. Coldor walked around the edge of the ten storey gloomy looking property to the back door. He did not want to bring undue attention to himself; the fewer guards who witnessed his sojourn, the better. This was essentially a tradesman's entrance and led directly to the small kitchen, which prepared some of the canteen's snacks and refreshments. The door was small and partially protected by the rear elevation of the property that hung outwards for two metres from the main building. There was a security code key number panel on the door but no thumb recognition pad. There was a tiny video camera though, which zoomed in on him as he approached it. He knew that there was no way of avoiding the camera and so gave it a pleasant smile and put on a display of officiousness. He hoped that the soldier watching the monitors inside was not paying too much attention.

The captain typed in his pass-code and the door slid open. The interior was, as he had expected, clean and predictably dull. The short passage led to the kitchen at one end and there was a sharp right hand turn just before the kitchen door. There was a possibility that the canteen was in use, but Coldor knew the kitchen wouldn't be open at this time. He entered the slightly cramped preparation area and took a door on the west wall. This led to the central corridor adjacent to which was the intelligence room. Outside the intelligence room door was a single guard. So far no one had actually seen Coldor with his or her own eyes. If he could just provide a distraction to the lone guard he might be able to slip in unnoticed, Coldor thought.

The cameras might know he was in the building, but they wouldn't know what he had been doing, until the log-in records on the computer were reviewed. The captain knew that the records would be checked, but not until the end of the week and he hoped to be off Acto by then. Coldor ducked back into the side passage and drew his blaster. With the metal butt he hit the wall of the passage three times, hard enough for the guard to hear, but not hard enough so that others would be alerted. Then he slid back into the kitchen area and slipped quietly behind the back door.

The guard's footsteps sounded closer. He stuck his head into the kitchen briefly and looking round but seeing nothing out of the ordinary, he continued down the dim service corridor, hip blaster leading the way. Stealthily, Coldor slipped out from his hiding place and along to the intelligence room. As the guard disappeared the other way he quietly closed the metal door behind him and moved to the far end of the room.

He took station at the last computer, which was partially obscured by a cabinet filled with old maps and plans of the city and its buildings, booted up and logged in. He looked around the room and hoped nobody had installed any cameras in here in the last few weeks. He started to formulate a plan for his exit.

Outside the barracks two men leaned against a wall, they were dressed in inconspicuous grey overalls and long blue workman under-jackets; the kind which the city engineers and Dome construction workers always wore. These clothes were a common sight in the city and nobody would give the men a second glance. They were looking at the service door. One of them pulled out a hand communicator and started to talk. The other fingered a blaster inside his jacket.

*****

In the library the three conspirators were making slow progress. None of them had sufficient clearance to access anything other than public records. Their search for missing persons had come up with little but a helpful Government advice line and procedures to follow. Officially there was only one missing person in the entire city. Their exploration of the tax data procedure was an exercise in boredom and told them nothing and even the Dome expansion plans simply provided useful information and some forecasts. There was no mention of external mining, or rapid Dome expansion. The computer just restated the same facts. Al sat back exasperated.

"This is useless!"

"There must be something else we can do, another sort of approach perhaps?" Lilia said irritably.

Al looked pensive for a moment and then started typing. (The library computers were not fitted with vocalisers because of the obvious noise this would cause and 'Think-pads' were simply too expensive).

"What are you up to?" Vil asked.

"I'm checking my own department. Maybe the computer can come up with a reason for Lucinda's sudden disappearance. I'll access the central computer for the hydroponics department via my own laboratory passwords. It isn't really allowed, but nobody's going to know; I should have thought of this earlier."

Vil thought that it wouldn't achieve very much but said nothing. The logo of the central computer department flashed up on screen followed by a list of central computers. Al selected the hydroponics and livestock computer and selected personnel from a sub-directory. A long list of names appeared on screen. Al's name was near the top and next to it were his position, title and a list of his academic achievements. There were only a dozen or so names above his own.

"Getting quite important in your old age aren't you, Al!" said Vil mischievously.

"That's me. I'm grinding my way to the top," he replied.

Al selected Lucinda's name and waited for her information to come up on screen. "It's lucky I am a hydroponics head, this information is restricted for anyone under my level."

The display changed to show a small picture of a very thin woman, bordering on scrawny, with short swept back black hair. Her background details, blood type, academic grades, and other achievements were all listed. At the bottom of the page there was a small box with the title, 'Current Occupation.' Within the box the text said 'Field Research on Acto Outer-Dome terrain.' Al stared at the screen for a moment. Then he said softy, "There. someone has made a mistake, Lucinda is supposed to be in the City Gens, not doing field research."

"It could just be a typing error," Lilia said.

"I thought the CCD didn't make mistakes!" Al replied.

"The real question though is what shall we do now? This is interesting, but hardly ground breaking, and hardly enough to denounce the city-state!"

"No, but it's a start. I suggest we make our way to my dome and see if she left anything of interest behind," Al said. He added, "Vil, even if we do come up with anything worthwhile, are you really going to say anything? No one has ever openly denounced the Core before. The news services may sometimes be vociferous about poor conditions, but it never attacks the Core directly. We are only three people and even if something terrible is happening out there, what can we do?"

Vil looked at Al. He had been thinking pretty much the same thing. He shrugged. "Maybe we can't do anything. We would be crushed or simply removed without wider support. At the moment all we can do is listen, watch and learn. The Core makes mistakes. It is not infallible."

CHAPTER 6

On the very same day the Governor stood behind his glass wall and watched his city go about it tasks. The Governor thought for a few fleeting moments about Cassus working a floor below on the project and regulator Marden and his secret staff plotting to abduct the next wave of workers he so desperately needed to work on the mineral deposit and his other great project. The Governor was pleased with Cassus. During the last week he had proved his ability and efficiency, he was fast becoming a valuable asset to the team, yet he grew increasingly impatient.

Thus far he had been ever so patient; waiting, plotting and biding his time until the moment was right. Now the process was under way he desperately wanted it to be over. He had power, wealth and his health, but Governor Sendrick knew that this was not enough. There was good in his soul too, he knew it. The basis for the deception really had been for the long run benefit of the colony and certainly not just his personal gain. He was not an avaricious man in the conventional sense of the word. Sendrick truly wanted his people to be content and thought they deserved a higher place within the order of the Galaxy. He had little time for the petty squabbling of the so called Planetary Network.

His altruism and generosity were not inconsiderable; he had personally guaranteed the pensions for those working outside the Domes, but his other plans were so much bigger and grander. His obsession with order and hierarchy drove him faster even as his own time dwindled. The Governor wanted more than any other man on the Planet. It wasn't even greed; it was simple ambition and a towering confidence in his own abilities and the knowledge that with matters in his own capable hands he could do so much better than anyone else.

He had a vision of a true galactic order. Harmony between the systems with himself at the head of a proud new Empire of Mankind, thrusting the race forward by the strength of his steel will. His grasp on the long term deliverance for mankind was phenomenal, his vision transcending the trivial issues of the masses. Where the man on the street thought about what to have for dinner, the Governor dwelled constantly on how to conquer the Galaxy. Gradually he had lost sight of the detail and of the individual.

The Governor closed his eyes and indulged one of his favourite daydreams. There was a great hall, vaster than anything else in known history, gleaming with the burnished armour of his Imperial legions and filled with the happy smiling faces of his adoring subjects. Soft lights and bright banners lined the walls and the great marble floor. Mighty doric columns rang with the sound of laughter, hope and belief. He stood upon a lofty burnished silver platform at one end of the hall, hands raised to the incredibly high-vaulted ceiling, giving his benediction to the citizens. Their applause filled his soul with the adoration he so badly needed and so justly deserved.

Sendrick had read the old-world bible, and he could sympathise with much of its content. However, he knew that, given the chance, he could do better than God.

*****

Coldor had easily found the information he needed. There were a number of freighters coming in next week. Indeed, looking at the statistics, it seemed as if the planet as a whole had stepped up the level of trading taking place in the last year. Coldor had not realised quite how many ships visited the freight spaceport every week. To his delight there was also a cargo ship piloted by one of his oldest Academy friends, Harvey Young. He was sure that Harv would give him passage on his ship, which was bound for the recently colonised planet of Cleisthenes. This planet was on one of the perimeter systems and had a population of barely twenty thousand people. Coldor was certain that such a planet would be grateful to receive someone with his skills and experience. He decided to try and contact them that night.

He also noted three other ships with reasonable destinations which he could try and bribe his way onto or, at the very worst, smuggle himself aboard. To that end he needed certain provisions and it was when he accessed the hydroponics and livestock computer that he realised he wasn't the only one using the system. The computer listed the number of people currently logged in to each central computer. Of course, this was not unusual in the slightest; thousands of people could be within each system at the same time. At present there were only 156 people logged into the hydroponics and livestock computer, it being a minor central function with few people in either the food production industry or within the CCD.

What caught Coldor's eye was the fact that a red light was flashing around the box which contained the number of people within the system. This meant that someone had entered the system illegally, through forged passwords or some other means of bypass. Coldor leaned closer, curious. He clicked the flashing box. Immediately an information screen popped up and displayed a map and a few paragraphs of text. The map showed a computer in what was, he was informed, the central public library. The text told him that the information they had accessed had been restricted, or should have only been accessed through a computer linked directly to the hydroponics department at the hydrodomes or one of the massive intensive livestock farms.

“Someone’s going to get in trouble” he murmured and checked the login name. It was Alan Spartan.

*****

Coldor debated his course of action. He was amused that he had caught someone else in the act of a quiet minor illegality. He needed to visit a hydro dome - why not visit the one which he knew, thanks to the computer, was run by this Alan character? He could stock up on his supplies and also do a little gentle probing of his own. Coldor checked the time. It was just coming up to lunch at the barracks. There was a chance the guard had been relieved by now. Coldor was in an intelligence room, which could reach, through its superior access, almost anywhere in the city. Coldor decided to make full use of its capabilities and started a search for the building's alarm controls.

If he could isolate one nearby and set it off, he would probably find the corridor outside the intelligence room empty and be able to make his escape. He hoped the guard did not have strict orders to stay at the front of the door under any circumstance. The impulsive captain decided to find out.

It wasn't difficult. Coldor managed to pull up a plan of the building that highlighted the alarms within minutes. Each alarm had its own serial number and thus all Coldor had to do was select the appropriate alarm and activate it through the standard core computer interface. His rank ensured he had sufficient access through the security system. He selected an alarm on the second floor, pressed his finger to the touch sensitive screen and activated the alarm. He then logged off and powered down. Coldor flung the door open and stepped out into the corridor. It was empty. There were shouts from the floor above, but he paid them no heed. He left the building with half a smile on his face, he was going to get away with it - It had been all too easy.

Minutes later his smirk turned to a grimace as he noticed two men in his peripheral vision wearing inconspicuous grey overalls and blue jackets. They were trained and followed him at a safe distance, but after making a few random turns in the street Coldor was sure. The secret staff were onto him.

“Shit,” he said.

Colder sped up, trying to put as much distance between himself and the staff as possible. After doubling back once and pelting across one of the city’s pocket parks Coldor ducked into an electric vehicle rank, threw himself into one of three identical waiting EV’s and slammed the door shut. The sleek vehicle powered up and silently slipped away.

*****

Vil and company made it back to Al's hydrodome without incident. Vil was curious. He had never seen where most of his food came from. Rows and rows of genetically modified plants sat happily in their nutrient vats. Each quietly growing until it was eventually automatically harvested and tended to by the machinery, which hung in tidy rows from double butted aluminium struts in the small passages between the plants. The overhead space had to be kept clear in order to provide direct lighting from above. The dome itself was 100 metres long at its widest point. Al's tiny laboratory was tucked away at one side of the dome in between supply storehouses. The laboratory, itself, was a two-storey affair, reaching almost half way up the dome's haunches. There were two rooms on the ground floor and one larger room on the first floor. The access to the first floor was through a dull metal ladder set into the outside walls of the annex. The first floor entrance was simply a hole in the wall, although a plastic sheet could be pulled over it from within if necessary. There was plenty of headspace inside but very little in the way of floor-space. Each wall was piled up with scientific instruments and data disks. The floor was barely visible through all sorts of clutter Vil noted, as they entered through the narrow door. This included a small camp bed at one side of this ground floor room and incredibly, an ancient electronic tablet copy of 'Star Wars, Episode 14' lying on the floor beside it.

Al noticed Vil's expression and said, “this was one of the first Domes. It was built along the lines of the inside of one of the space cruisers of the day, you know, so the pioneers would feel at home. In fact bits of it are from the actual ships! It’s something of an antique, but she still serves her purpose well enough." Looking around Vil could suddenly see the history within this space, he had never been in such an old structure, most of the city was relatively new, the original core had been renovated and redesigned and added to a hundred times so that almost nothing remained. The city did have a small museum, but this felt different because it was still in use; it was real.

“Lucinda worked with me in this lab for several months. Let’s take a look around.” Al scurried about; searching for something which Lucinda might have left behind; some clue to help them. Vil and Lilia helped as best they could, but there was so much stuff around it was difficult to know where to look.

"Wait a minute guys, this is silly, we don't even know what we are looking for. Phantom clues at best, and Vil and I might be moving those clues around without even knowing it. There must be a better way than this!" Lilia said after a few minutes.

Al poked his head out from round a wall-mounted monitor, a wry grin on his face.

"No, you're right. I'll tell you what, you and Vil go upstairs, there's a coffee and food machine up there - and it's tidier. I'll continue to poke around down here and join you in a few minutes. I also want to check Lucinda's computer." Al gestured vaguely to a door, which led to the other room in the little complex.

"Okay boss!" Vil laughed and he stepped back outside into the warmer environment of the dome proper. He had just turned to make his way up the ladder, when he caught sight of Lilia's face. He turned around to see what she was looking at and jumped back. Facing them was an athletic looking man, dark eyes staring at them dangerously. In his hand he held a blaster pistol. The pistol's barrel was pointing straight at Vil's chest.

*****

"Don't do anything rash and you won't get hurt," Coldor stated, "I am not here to cause a problem, unless you make one. I need to ask you a few questions and pick up some supplies. Just make sure you keep your hands away from your pockets and remain calm and I'll be out of here in no time, okay?"

"Yeah sure," said Vil, not wanting to argue with a blaster pointing at his chest. He was stunned at the sudden turn of events, a horrible feeling that somehow the Core had found out about the group's activities and plans. Visions of torture and terrible pain flicked through Vil's mind, before he could control himself. Lilia was pale and looked to be in shock.

Al was sat with his back towards them when they entered, reading something on the screen of Lucinda's computer monitor. He turned when the trio entered and was about to speak when he noticed Coldor and a second later the pistol Coldor held raised in his fist. Al raised his eyebrows and his jaw dropped. He managed to say "what the f..." when Coldor interrupted, "there is nothing to fear if you co-operate. I don't want trouble. I am not here to report you, so stay calm and we'll get along nicely. I am not from the Core and I am not a member of the secret police. I only want answers and some supplies, which you can provide for me. Now that you know the rules and we're all friends perhaps you can tell me which one of you is Al?"

Al wished that he could slip away unnoticed into the safety of his dome's soothing green haven of plants but instead he tentatively raised his hand and nodded. Coldor proceeded, in a calm and collected manner, to tell the trio some of the facts leading up to this moment and a list of the items he required. They sat in silence and listened, although there was not a lot else they could do.

*****

Very soon the story was finished and Al had been sent off by Coldor to gather some necessities for him. Coldor turned his attention to Vil and Lilia. "So, my little dissidents, why were you illegally logged on to computer you shouldn't have been? Be quick about it, I don't have time to waste."

Vil wasn't sure what to say - he was alternating between pent up irritation, distrust and fear. "It was nothing, everybody does it from time to time, we were just trying to access information," he managed to say.

"Hmmm," Coldor replied. "That's convenient for you isn't it. You know, you really don't have anything to fear from me. As I've already told you, I am leaving this damn planet. It's the Core you should be worried about. You could have your jobs revoked if they find out."

"The Core won't find us!" Vil pronounced with a certainty he didn't feel. "They can't do this, it's wrong. It's just wrong," he murmured under his breath.

Coldor paused and regarded Vil closely, his expression thoughtful.

"Well kids, I don't know precisely what you are up to, but good luck," he said after a moment.

Just then Al returned with the jars of the nutrient tablets Coldor had demanded and a few other pieces of equipment.

Coldor looked around. "It has been a pleasure." He waggled his fingers goodbye but had walked no further than a dozen paces when the front entrance to the dome burst open and two armed men rushed in.

"Oh no!" Vil cried, "this is getting ridiculous."

Coldor swore and grabbed Al. "Is there another way out?" He hissed.

Fortunately, there were a series of doorways for loading and unloading all around the dome. Al bolted for the nearest one, with Vil and Lilia behind him. The two secret staff agents spotted the fugitives and although they were some distance away at the other end of the dome they both raised black blaster rifles and let off a couple of bursts. Red laser fire sizzled and burnt a neat hole into one of the Laboratory's walls. Coldor returned fire quickly, wrecking a batch of plants, but he was already running for the other door, and his freedom.

Outside the dome it was eerily quiet. The afternoon was waning. Al shut the large metal hatch with a reassuring clang and locked it with his security code.

"That probably won't do you any good you know," Coldor advised him. "Quick, follow me." The companions could only obey the guardsman as he set off at pace down the street.

CHAPTER 7

The Governor was not pleased. 'Useless', he thought. How could they lose such an obvious group? A fresh search was under way even now; they would be flushed out, this Coldor and his accomplices. The secret staff had informed him of the disturbances earlier in the day. The Governor was almost disbelieving that such events had occutred, but quickly realised that such an unheard event was also a potentially dangerous one. Sendrick erred on the side of caution, they would be found and they would be dealt with.

Fortunately, for the present, there were more pressing matters for the Governor to attend to. He had invited, at great expense, an earthbound architect and planner to Acto to aid him in his new plans. The lady, Octavia Brinsmead, was due to arrive at any moment. Putting aside all the irritating details of the day, the Governor prepared himself to receive her. There was a firm knock on the study door and Miss Brinsmead was ushered in. Sendrick bestowed her with his best smile.

*****

Meanwhile the unlikely foursome was sitting uncomfortably in a temporary construction shed at the boundary of the newly reclaimed martian landscape. It was one of the few vacant buildings in the city and even that would not last for long. The reclamation process moved too fast for that. Coldor knew he had to get out now, or else all would be lost.

They sat on crates of building materials around a single low power rechargeable LED lamp. Vil hesitantly filled Coldor in with the rest of the tale, occasionally interrupted by Al and Lilia. Coldor nodded as Vil recounted their earlier vain attempt to retrieve any information about missing colonists in the library, following his brother's revelations.

"So, what happens now?" Lilia asked nervously.

"We wait, until I can find some way out of this predicament." Coldor was thinking furiously. The secret staff were on to him, he did not know how, but he did know that he was going to have to tread carefully.

Licking his lips, Coldor turned towards the colonists, recently turned renegades and said, “Listen, the staff are probably only after me. They do not know you. They do not know who you are and probably don’t care. I would suggest that you quietly go back to your own lives and forget that this ever happened."

"What about you?" Vil queried.

"I'll make it to one of the ports and get out of here."

“And what about the actions of the Administration? Are you going to just forget about that?”

“That’s not my problem. Look, I don’t agree with what they’re doing, but there isn’t a whole lot I can do about it.”

“You could stay here and help us?” Lilia ventured.

*****

Three weeks later the Governor avidly examined his new holo-model city. “This is exquisite Octavia. The detail is simply amazing. You have captured my vision perfectly.” Sendrick gazed at the model as one might gaze at a lover. It was a masterpiece. Octavia, who had conceptualised Sendrick’s vision stood next to the model, eager to show off some its finer points.

The monumental public buildings of the vast central plaza surrounded by a number of double triumphal arches straddling the new boulevards that terminated in the plaza from eight points of the compass and in the centre of the plaza shining like a miniature sun rose a scale holographic image of Acto, slowly rotating on a giant vaulted plinth. All were represented faithfully in great detail on the model.

“I have followed your brief exactly Governor, whilst applying all of my expertise into the creation of this new city.”

“Your skills are not wasted on me Octavia,” Sendrick said almost fondly. “I am most impressed.”

*****

Months passed. The renegades has disappeared. Vil, Al and Lilia returned to their ordinary lives and nobody knew of Coldor's whereabouts. Vil was experiencing a number of newfound benefits from being Cassus's brother. Not only had Vil received the offer of promotion to a rank equivalent to Lilia's but the brothers had moved to a more central apartment. It was twice the size as their previous abode, better equipped and more opulent. Vil was impressed with his newfound status as he was elevated in Actavian society but its superficiality also grated with him. He was now greeted with deference and respect but he was still the same man he'd been a few weeks ago.

Vil still worked in the same building but had been moved to a higher floor in a new office equivalent to Lilia's dealing with another sector of the city. He sat behind his desk, occasionally wringing his hands together. The three of them had agreed to meet in a new restaurant called 'Saturn's Rings and Wings' after work. It was the first time they'd all met since Coldor disappeared and Vil imagined spies everywhere. His new found status and visibility was not helping matters.

At the agreed time Vil met Lilia in the atrium of the office and they made their way to the restaurant by EV. Conversation was sparse, each of them too nervous to indulge in frivolous small-talk.

However, there were no surprises and the pair were warmly welcomed as they entered the restaurant. They'd arrived a few minutes early and Al had not yet arrived. Vil ordered some wine and looked around, trying to appear discreet. There were only a couple of other guests in the dining area though and they didn't appear to be at all interested in Vil and Lilia, or were they feigning their disinterest? Were they drinking or were the bottles just for show? Vil shook his head and tried to ignore his growing paranoia and relax.

"So far, so good," he said, looking at Lilia.

The minutes ticked by. Vil noticed that Lilia was drinking her wine quickly. Fortunately, a short time later Al arrived. Unfortunately, he had someone else with him. Vil wondered who it could be. Someone to aid the cause? The man was wearing nondescript clothes and sported recent facial hair. Vil and Lilia simultaneously realised it was Coldor, albeit with different coloured hair which was now trimmed close to the skull. He'd also changed the colour of his eyes using lenses.

"Fancy seeing you in a place like this," Coldor grinned at Vil and Lilia as he sat down. Vil looked at Al who raised an eyebrow and gave a brief shake of his head.

'Marvellous,' thought Vil; and not for the first time.

Coldor ordered a beer and another bottle of wine. He appeared composed and comfortable. Vil hoped he hadn't taken something.

"To what do we owe this pleasure, Coldor?" asked Lilia.

However, it was Al who answered as Coldor sat back and eyed the three companions. Al sighed. "To my amazement a day after the er, incident, I was back in the Dome, losing myself in the plant cycle. I'd been patching up some of the damage caused by our friend here when I felt a tap on the shoulder and there he was with his hands on his hips telling me that I ..."

Coldor butted in, "I told Al there was nowhere else to go. I told him I needed a place to hide out and where better than a hydro-dome that few people ordinarily visit?"

Lilia snorted, "Oh, that's super for you - but I thought you were leaving?"

"So did I. I'd be in space now if the ports had not been so heavily guarded. At this moment in time there's no way I could get out of the city. I can't even get to a suitable ship. In short, I am stuck here and this being the case, I might as well help you out."

"So, you're only helping because you didn't have any choice!" Lilia said, colour flushing to her face.

"Yes. I don't have anything better to do. I'm here and I'd like to know what you've got planned?"

"Plan? Coldor, I'm afraid that we have taken your advice to heart and returned to our old lives; there is no plan. Nothing is happening," Vil explained.

"I see, so your nascent concern for the welfare of our worthy Citizens has been crushed in its infancy has it? How long did that last exactly? A couple of days?"

"We're concerned, but what are we supposed to do?" Al shot back.

Coldor leaned back in his chair, "That, Al, is where I may be able to assist," he said and grinned at them.

Much later the four of them were still in the restaurant, leaning over the table, picking at left over chicken wings, eyes glassy from too much alcohol. There were still a few other people dotted about at various tables, but the numbers were dwindling. The subsequent conversation had not been enlightening, conducive to a sense of frustration rather than achievement. Coldor had not elaborated further, saying it was too early to get anyone's hopes up.

Eventually Vil bid everyone good night and left the restaurant alone, feeling as though something was missing. Shaking his head slightly he wished that he had never got involved. Coldor, meanwhile, retired with Al, his brow furrowed with thought.

*****

Time passed slowly for the next few days. An almost tangible sense of anticipation hung in the air and tugged at the edges of Vil's conscious thought. Lilia was seemingly immersed in her work and provided no solace for his anxiety. On the fifth day after the inconsequential meeting at the restaurant, Vil decided to take some relief in the games arcade. This brooding dark structure stood formally in the centre of the city, a masterpiece in space gothic revival. Apart from the Core buildings it was probably one of only half a dozen structures on Acto that could claim any real individuality. It was here that many of the University students could be found after lectures engaging in some of the most advanced computer simulations that the galaxy had to offer. Seen as a vital form of escape and means of relaxation, the arcade was funded by the

Administration and was a popular venue for people from all demographics. Vil had spent many a happy hour there during his own study days and eagerly anticipated returning.

He had arranged to meet Al at the arcade and sure enough as Vil exited from the module with another knot of people making for the arcade he spotted his friend idling by the main entrance, leaning casually on a balustrade and drinking a can of AquaCoke. Vil grinned, hopefully this would provide the break he needed.

The interior of the vast multi-sectioned arcade was busy. There were people from all aspects of the city congregated in this mecca to entertainment. The new religion of the State was expressed in the devotion of the masses to its technological prowess; or so some speculated.

Vil knew where the game he wanted to play was located, Star Pilot XIV on the fourth floor. Star Pilot had originally been a military simulation programmed a few years ago for a fighter craft consortium. Years later when that particular craft was being phased out of service, Star Pilot was snatched back by the programmers and a new software games company was born. Star Pilot was marketed across the limited Galaxy. The main selling point was that it was now possible to play the game between people across several different worlds through a long range relay satellite system. The

Star Pilot satellites had been in use ever since and that particular enterprising software company were almost omnipresent across the Galaxy. The latest incarnation of the game was the 14th version and was based on a selection of actual and potential star-fighters throughout the Federation of Planets.

The simulation was used not only for recreation, but by the military and even by some education systems. Certainly Vil remembered his initiation to the game back in a general gal-tech class years ago. He had played the game constantly throughout his University career and was noted as one of the top players from his year. Al had been only a few places behind Vil and was still a dedicated player. Vil himself had not played for several months.

His eyes narrowed slightly as the lift opened onto the dimly lit floor which contained the Star Pilot machines. Fifty of them lined up in five neat rows of ten. The whole place had a palpable buzz of suppressed excitement. There were thankfully a few machines empty and Vil and Al managed to climb up into two next to each other.

The machine itself was some five-foot from the ground, supported by a thin super-steel harness. An advanced hydraulics system allowed for real time movement, so pulling back on the control yoke engaged the hydraulics and moved the pod within its secure and stationary harness. The shape of the pod was very much like the cockpit of a fighter. Once you were in strapped in and the pod's computer introduced itself, the door closed in on you and the lights dimmed to the serene stillness of the interior of a starship.

Vil took one last look at Alan as his door moved into the closed position. Al was already settled in and making personal adjustments to the interior layout of the control console to suit his personal style. Vil smiled to himself and turned back to face his own controls.

The soft harmonic female computer voice was asking Vil which sort of craft he wanted and what nature of game he wanted to play, Vil picked his old favourite; a late 23rd century Earth Fighter called the 'Neotechnic Fighter'. It was for all intents and purposes a similar version of the spacecraft used by the Acto defence authority. Vil keyed in his customary personalisation of the craft; a pure white body with his name emblazoned in a vile *puke* green colour below the cockpit.

He and Al had earlier agreed to sample a scenario called 'The Rock'. In this theme the action took place around a massive slowly moving meteorite and a series of many smaller rocks flying in its wake. There was only a limited amount of space around the rock and if a player flew out of the arena they would be automatically be brought back in from the other side - which was in itself a useful tactic. Vil knew that you could fly from one end of the arena to the other in just over five minutes with the particular fighter he was using today. That left enough room for space combat for a whole swarm of fighters. The rock itself was, in real terms, some seventy by thirty kilometres and contained as part of its attraction a series of deep canyons and craters.

Having told the computer of his choice, Vil asked how many other players were in the zone and was informed that there were twelve others including Al. Vil was surprised, because this zone could support up to one hundred and fifty fighters at the same time. Twelve seemed a little lame, but with a little further examination Vil found out why; Three of the twelve had incredibly high rankings and kill ratios. Between the three of them they had destroyed some forty-four other craft. Vil guessed they must be working as a team, which whilst not against the rules, could be annoying for individual players.

Vil saw his own recorded ranking on the screen and felt half amused, half proud that he was still, just about, in the top hundred in Acto. He even outranked one of the three-team members already in the game. Al was only half a dozen places behind Vil. As Vil went through the motions of powering up the craft he also sent a voice signal to Al; "Listen up Ace, you seen those three with the ridiculous rankings out there?"

Al's voice sounded in the cockpit, "Roger that Vil. You want to team up with me and take them down a peg or two?"

"Sure. Let's get 'em! You in your normal ship?"

"Yep, I take it you're still using that old rust bucket?"

"What else! Let's go!"

Vil hit his engage button and the flawlessly joined screens all around his head blazed into a magnificent star-scape. The meteorite was just visible up ahead, Vil lowered his shields and pumped power into his sub-light engines and powered up his wing lasers. To the right, Vil's radar picked up the signs of two fighters battling it out in a classic dogfight. Vil however, hurried on, sure that the triumvirate he was after would be using the meteorite to their advantage. The computer dutifully warned him of his lowered shields, Vil replied "It's okay. They aren't even going to touch me, whack up the electric deterrent to max and keep as much power as possible in the engines."

"Are you sure you wish to use the deterrent Vil?" Asked the computer

"Yes. Otherwise, it's no fun."

The deterrent was an electrical charge, which was transmitted to the human pilot's body when an opponent's weaponry hit them. Their voltage was low, but even so a continuous barrage of enemy hits was a dazzling experience to say the least. Vil gripped his control yoke softy yet firmly, marvelling at the response of the craft to his slightest movement and the impressions conveyed by the pods flawless hydraulic system. The sounds of a fighter's cockpit echoed pleasantly in his mind and Vil lost himself to the simulation.

*****

Octavia clasped her palms together. The opportunity to partake in the Governor's vision remained as an extraordinary and fantastic opportunity for her to leave some form of legacy in the galaxy for future generations. When people talked about Governor Sendrick she wanted to be the inevitable second character or architect-designer supreme: The Albert Speer of Germany, the Vitruvious of Rome, the

Hausman of Paris; a designer of unparalleled eminence across the galaxy. Textbooks would heave under the weight of analysis of her designs and style, realised in the mighty city of Acto. Whether it failed or thrived, there would be no stopping her rise to fame within the annals of civilisation.

The monumental aesthetic design of the city was under way. Like many architects working to a brief, which could best be summarised as the visual representation of despotism, the monumental style best suited the mood. The soaring towers and symmetrical facades were a contemporary interpretation of classicism, Octavia's interpretation of the Governor's vision was an impressive city indeed. A beautiful city, a timeless city, the city of the future from echoes of the past.

Octavia knocked on the doors of the Governor's suite, which were flung open and she was ushered inside, Sendrick had his back to her facing the window wall. Beside him was a young man Octavia knew to be Cassus.

The Governor turned and bid the guard who had opened the door to leave, "I am glad you are here, my dear. Come, let me introduce you to my right hand man, Cassus Toradon."

*****

Vil's fighter streaked through the starlit sky. A mighty machine thrusting forwards into the darkness, its engines throwing a deep red glow in its wake. Vil imagined this to be how his ship must look. He was by now totally immersed in the simulation, so life like were the sensations and feel of the cockpit that it was very easy to lose touch with reality, if you so wished it. And Vil really did.

The moment was almost upon him. He knew that soon he would engage in combat, Al on his wing, a delicious surge of adrenaline pumped through his veins as Vil twisted his ship through the sky. Suddenly an enemy craft swung into view, tearing across his port window. Vil raked his ship up and left, whilst converting what energy he had reserved for his engines into use.

His view levelled out. The enemy was dead ahead, making for the relative safety of a distant rock cluster. Vil could see, by the blueish haze outside the enemy ship, that instead of engaging his main drive, his opponent had diverted energy to his shields. Consequently his prey was making slow progress. Vil powered up his lasers, his catch was in reach. He could hear the noise of Al's boosters in his left ear, his vision narrowed, his mind focused. Then he was in range and Vil hammered on the fire buttons, sending wave after wave of powerful energy across the gulf of space. The bolts were deflected by his opponent's shield, but the sheer magnitude and volume of Vil's unceasing volley was doing its job. Al joined in from the left, adding his own assault. The haze surrounding the enemy ship flickered, burst into light once and then dimmed.

Vil guessed that either the shield was either virtually destroyed, or that his opponent was diverting energy. Keeping him in his view all the time, never letting him veer off, Vil flicked to torpedoes and let two fly. The two deadly missiles smashed into the enemy ship. It burst into flames and fell out of the sky, disintegrating as it plummeted, Vil grinned savagely and looped his ship in a victory roll, "Yeehaaaaa!" he yelled into the mike.

"One down, a dozen to go!" came Al's cheery response.

The game continued for another twenty minutes with Vil and Al notching up another three victories between them, receiving barely a scratch in return, when Al's voice sounded urgently in Vil's ears.

"Look, three o'clock, three of them coming over the rock in formation at full speed!" No sooner had Vil looked when he saw a barrage of laser fire coming towards him from the right.

"Break, break, break!" He cried and peeled off to the left.

Al was ahead of him. The two ships dived downwards out of the sky. Another voice spoke, "We have been watching your crappy old Neotech ship take our kills. It's about time you paid the penalty for your impertinence!" The voice was strong and confident.

Vil replied flippantly, "Give it your best shot but you'll have to find me first!"

He switched to another communications channel, which they had agreed on earlier. "Al, you there?"

"Yep, just waiting for you. What's the plan? We can't outrun those fighters; they look upgraded to me."

"Turn round, shield full front. Head for the rock. If we can lose them for a minute we can perhaps peel back and catch them off guard. Use a couple of your missiles on the way through."

"Ok, got it."

Al's craft was more heavily armed than Vil's and carried an extra eight torpedoes. Whacking power from his lasers to the front shields and engines Vil pulled his ship around and almost directly into the noses of the three fighters following them. Al released his torpedoes almost immediately and Vil saw one of the enemy fighters shake at the impact. Vil's own lasers fired a couple of times and then they powered down, so much energy had he diverted to his engines. Then the two craft were through and past the three marks, who had not been expecting the daring manoeuvre.

The three enemy ships were not slow to respond however and were soon hot on the trail of Vil and Al. Vil leaned around and checked his back window (screen). The three would not outrun them until they had reached the cover of the rock, he was sure of it. Vil's sweaty hands gripped the yoke, his heart pounding and his blood pumping.

*****

"A delight, I am sure, Miss Brinsmead," said Cassus, inclining his head. The Governor looked on, radiating enthusiasm.

"This is it Cassus," the Governor paused and turned to Octavia. "The atmosphere machines, they have arrived?"

"They have Governor, on the last flight in."

"Atmosphere machines, what machines?" asked Cassus sharply.

"Aah, Cassus, surely you didn't think you controlled everything? I have delegated responsibilities to other people who share your ... approach."

"Of course, I merely wondered what machines we could have ordered?"

"Octavia, would you explain?"

Octavia faced Cassus, all the while thinking what a cute face he had. She smiled demurely and gazed at him with fresh blue eyes, which complimented her light blue dress. Cassus blinked a few times. Her face was plain but underneath her dress she had a figure to make a man weep with desire. He thought it made a change to see a woman in a dress, but then he remembered she was from Earth. He turned away to face the Governor who had watched the exchange with interest. He nodded to himself before moving to the other side of the room and began to fix some drinks from his well-stocked bar.

Octavia began to explain, "Some time ago a system was devised which can be used for temporary periods of time, to make an unbreathable atmosphere tolerable to the human lungs. A certain number of machines are used to create a bubble of a designated size. This bubble, a kind of tenuous plastic, is pumped full of air and a temporary low-level atmosphere created. Standard gravity is assumed by the use of strategic grav-pads of course."

"I see," Cassus looked dubious, "How did you afford these 'machines'. I thought the budget was stretched as it was?"

"We have reserves," the Governor interjected, "We also have enormous credit facilities with certain galactic banks and in truth these sort of things are not really that expensive."

Cassus nodded and took the whisky offered to him by the Governor.

"There really is no need to worry. Everything is under control. This is simply another step on the road to glory!"

Cassus smiled back, but in his heart a thread of unease started to unravel.

*****

"I have you now!" shouted the Dove, one of the three enemy fighters hunting down Vil and Al. The trio had evidently found Vil and Al's second communication channel but things were getting too hot to give too much thought to that. A quadruple blast of laser fire erupted from the Dove's laser cannons, Al yelped and spun his craft away, but his shields still took a hammering.

"Damn it Vil, where are you?" he gasped.

A few seconds later, although it seemed an eternity to the struggling Al, Vil's ship screamed over a high ridge of rock to the west. Missiles followed by bursts of laser fire spewed forth madly. The Dove called for his comrades, but they had been engaged by two other ships, seeking revenge from earlier dogfights. The homing missiles smashed into the ship, blasting chunks of shield and armour. Vil pressed the attack and Al, seizing the initiative, followed him in. Within a few minutes the Dove was obliterated.

"Now we are on a level pegging" exclaimed Vil.

"Let's find them and kick some arse," Al shouted.

They didn't have to wait long. Having dealt with the previous unfortunate aggressors, the remaining two ships sped in low over the same ridge Vil had appeared from.

"You'll pay for that," stated the pilot of one of the ships.

"Come and get it big boy!" said Al, kicking his ship into full throttle and roaring in to engage. It was to be a head to head finale and Vil, laughing with excitement, followed suit.
The four ships covered the kilometres between them in seconds, Vil charged his lasers, diverted energy to his front shield and readied his two remaining missiles. The enemy wavered in his sights; his computer was having trouble locking on.

"Come on, come on," he hissed.

'Targeting, targeting, confirming visual lock. We have a lock...'

Vil did not hear the rest, his fingers had already squeezed the fire button and his deadly cargo shot forwards; A double messenger of death. Vil turned his head and could see Al's craft flying only fifty metres away from him. A moment later two missiles were released from his friend's machine. Turning back to his control panel, Vil just had time to see four red dots closing in on his ship, "Aaagh!" He gurgled and broke right and up furiously. Thud, thud, two of the missiles slammed into his front shields almost obliterating them. Fortunately the other two missiles could not have been locked on and sped past harmlessly. An explosion sounded to the left.

"Al, you okay?"

"Shields, down, received three direct hits, second engine knackered, I'm gonna have to break," came Al's annoyed reply.

"Right, Al, get out and repair and get back ASAP! I will take them... myself!"

Vil scanned the surroundings. One of the ships lay battered and broken on the hard surface of the rock. The other mark was nowhere to be seen. The peace did not last long. Suddenly, from twelve o'clock, the enemy fighter sped almost directly down on Vil, firing wildly.

"Shit!" was all Vil could manage to say and quickly adjusted the controls to redistribute what remained of his shields to cover the whole ship. A couple of shots hit the topside of his ship and Vil received mild shocks from the electric deterrent. He kept going, his enemy's trajectory would surely force him to pull up soon and then he would strike back.

Sure enough, overhead the mark started to pull up. Vil killed the shields and piled power into his engines and lasers. Screaming round in a loop, the enemy ship slowly, very slowly, filled his sights. When Vil was sure that he could not miss he did not hesitate and hammered his fire buttons until warning sirens blared in his ears. The forward screen filled with smoke. Then, through the haze came a shower of sparks, followed by a burst of red. Vil's ship burst though the other side of the smog and Vil pulled his fingers off the fire buttons. To his surprise, behind him, the third ship was going down in a blaze of fire. 'His shields must have been in tatters,' thought Vil. Relief and glee filled him.

The game was won and Vil was satisfied. Overhead flew Al's ship, his wingtips waggling, a flash of powerful machinery through a starry sky.

Vil told the computer to end the simulation and the cockpit faded into black. Vil closed his eyes and smiled.

CHAPTER 8

"Thus, it is imperative that we step up the program of construction Cassus. These new machines will make the job easier, but we still need more manpower!"

Cassus was tired and also slightly diverted by the attractive Miss Brinsmead who sat draped across a chair flicking through a holopad. Cassus was aggravated with himself as his gaze kept returning to her and lingering there for longer than strictly necessary, or decent.

He replied in the positive, "I will see to it personally Governor."

"Yes, yes, I'm sure you will. Now, enough of this business talk. I have arranged for an informal meal for the top staff this evening, and you, my friends," the Governor looked at Cassus and Octavia in turn, "are to be my honoured guests,"

Sendrick moved away to the desk to notify the other guests. A private half-smile on his face. Everything was going exactly to plan.

*****

The drive for fresh manpower was well underway, unbeknown to the other colonists of the city or Vil and his friends. That evening, Vil idly flicked through various news channels at home, before shutting down the view-screen in disgust. He paced the prep area and downed half a pint of water, idly drumming his fingers against the work surface. Restless, he grabbed a light jacket and stole out for a stroll to clear his head. The climate was brisk, a slight wind blew across the darkened and deserted street. He had ventured into the city instead of towards its perimeter and it was here that the artificial atmospheric simulator did its work best. It was almost possible to believe that there was open sky above you and a real breeze cool against your skin. He knew that the Dome was there but it was not conscious in his mind. The Domes had always been there. They were as natural to Vil as the blue sky was to Earth.

Vil avoided the centre, it would be busy and he did not feel like company for a few hours. He travelled on foot and by transport module, from neighbourhood to neighbourhood. So many seemingly 'individual' neighbourhoods were so alike to each other at a City-wide level that it was with some surprise that Vil realised that he had wondered into an area he knew he had never been to before. He wasn't lost, it was incredibly easy to find the nearest transport hub, which was never more than a few minutes away and get back to familiar territory in a matter of minutes.

This district looked older than most Vil had seen, certainly it was far older than Vil's neighbourhood. The buildings were smaller, even more tightly clustered together than the norm and as such of a much higher density. They also seemed shabbier; dirty and stained, their lights emitted a distinctly low energy, feeble glow. A few people were walking down the street where Vil had ended up. A couple glanced at him momentarily and then averted their gaze, quickly, almost furtively and moved on. Vil scowled slightly, he noticed that the people looked tired, gloomy, their shoulders bowed. He wondered if he wore the same expression. Shaking his head slightly Vil turned to go, he'd had enough of this area and felt distinctly like having a quick drink and retiring for some relaxation.

Vil headed off at a brisk pace back towards the nearest transport hub from which he had come with the intention of heading into the centre and getting Cassus or Al out for a drink. Vil clapped his hands involuntarily at the thought, his mood lightening and quickened his pace. He did not see the two shapes detach themselves from a deep entranceway and step into place behind him.

A few seconds later he felt their presence looming up close behind him, but it was too late. Even as Vil turned to face the stalkers there was a heavy thud as one of them smacked a truncheon against Vil's head and he went down immediately. Two men in grey overalls and blue jackets bent over to gather him up. On a signal an electric car pulled up and the door swished silently open. Vil was bundled unceremoniously inside the car. In seconds the men and Vil, were gone.

*****

Vil was not missed that night, nor even the next day although there were some raised eyebrows at work since Vil had given no notification. The next evening Cassus started to ponder Vil's disappearance but made no move, presuming that Vil had reasons of his own for staying away. On the second day an official explanation was sent to the Tax Inspectorate explaining that Vil had been moved to another administration office and would no longer be employed by the bureau. Lilia did not accept that explanation and resolved to ask her superiors exactly where Vil had been moved to. At the same time the insidious thought of their involvement against the Core wormed its way into her mind and she shuddered involuntary.

'If they were onto Vil did they know about her? What about Coldor?'

She decided to contact Al and see if he had heard anything.

It was on this second day that Cassus received a nasty surprise. He had requested the latest figures for the manpower drive and they had promptly been sent to his computer over a secure channel. There were only fifteen names on the list, since to plunder more people from the streets at one time was deemed to be too risky. Cassus read the names to himself as always and as always they meant nothing to him.

Then he read the second to last name on the list; 'Vil Toradon, sector ID', Cassus stammered, rendered speechless for a moment before leaping to his feet and spitting, "What the? No! You utter cretins! I'm the adjutant to the damn Governor! How could this happen? Idiots! His face crimson, Cassus spat expletives in an uncharacteristic tirade. A junior staffer alerted by the noise the office to investigate. One look at his fury stopped her in her tracks. She backed away as Cassus uttered a feral snarl and barked at the computer to print a hardcopy of the list, which he snatched from the slot under his desk and stormed out with the intention of making someone in the control room pay!

*****

By the evening Cassus had caused a large number of headaches amongst his subordinates and retired home to think about his next move. In between throwing things, he had arranged for a party be sent out to retrieve Vil as soon as possible and informed the general staff that they were brainless imbeciles of questionable parentage.

The Governor had not been in the building at the time and Cassus had not yet spoken to him. He was not looking forward to doing so and was unsure how he would broach the matter. No longer furious, he seethed quietly. He was interrupted from his reverie by a repetitive buzz from the living room viewscreen. He hesitated before accepting the call. He did not recognise the number on the screen and the caller had not bothered to enter their name for his convenience, but Cassus was pretty sure that it was not a Core code. He shrugged and said “Accept”. A young woman appeared on screen. She looked concerned and a little upset.

"Oh hi. You must be Cassus.”

"I am, but I don't know you. Confirm your identity please."

"Yes, of course. I’m sorry. I am Lilia. I used to be Vil's superior at the Inspectorate. I noticed that he didn't come to work today and we haven’t heard from him. I wanted to check if he’s okay?"

Cassus leaned back in the chair for a moment as he debated how to deal with this. He knew that Lilia was Vil's friend and ex-boss at the Inspectorate. Cassus thought he had a pretty good idea of the sort of people Vil would form friendships with. He sucked in his breath and wished he had a whisky in his hand. He fingered his stubble thoughtfully for a second or two more, leaving a silence that stretched before he spoke.

"Lilia, hi! I've heard a lot about you. Everything is fine. Vil has just been feeling a little under the weather. I blame it on overwork! He is feeling much better this evening though. He’s even planned a few drinks at the 'Space Rat' bar for 21:00 if you're interested?"

The girl looked slightly sceptical and looked around the room behind Cassus as if searching for Vil, but readily agreed to the meeting. Cassus signed off and looked at his watch. One hour to wait.

Cassus had kept his tone light. If anyone was listening in on this conversation, which was likely, they would detect nothing untoward. Cassus would be upholding his position and calming anxious friends as to a potential disappearance. He could level out the situation at the Core tomorrow with the Governor and explain that he had met the girl alone and reassured her. If she wondered why Vil had not accompanied him, he would say that he had felt ill again. He would elaborate by explaining that he had organised a temporary job transfer for Vil to the tax office at the Gens, which was looking for new Class I management level staff. In the meantime, Cassus would organise the retrieval of his brother with the Governor’s assistance and no one would be any the wiser. Well, except Vil.

This was of course all fine in theory except that he had no intention of lying to Lilia. The lies were starting to wear thin on his tongue. The kidnapping of his brother was a personal affront. He could see the greater good but he now had first-hand experience of the pain caused by a 'disappearance'. The Core's own arrogance was greasing the wheels to his gradual change of heart. A seed had now been planted. The fight for liberty and the protection of all the colony's Citizens against a manipulative central administration would be difficult, if not impossible, but there were other methods to build a better future. Cassus didn't kid himself, he knew that there were many undeserving citizens on Acto, but that did not excuse their exploitation. Cassus the ambitious poured himself a scotch, which tasted nothing like scotch, and started to plan.

*****

The 'Space Rat' was a poor bar. It was not too dirty and the drinks were palatable, but the place was frequented by a rowdy bunch of industrial workers and knots of cargo pilots. There was a lot of hard drinking and a lot of shouting. Cassus had forgotten what it was like and that he loved it. The bar was tucked away between the spaceport and some of the manufacturing plants.

Cassus had not drunk there since he was at the Academy. He'd been too busy climbing the career ladder of the Administration. He could not help grinning as he entered; the thrill of anticipation carousing up his back gave him a tremendous buzz. He was early. Lilia should not be here yet. He pondered whether she would like his choice of venue and thought it unlikely, which made him chuckle.

Cassus ordered a *Tsing Tao II* and edged his way back towards a vantage-point from where he could spy on the entrance. He received a few cursory glances from the patrons. What they thought of him he could not say. It was possible they thought he was a pilot, but at any rate he deigned not to notice anyone else and seemingly poured his interest into his beer. He was left alone, apart from the odd jostle as someone lurched to or from the bar.

The minutes ticked by and Cassus noticed that he was drinking quickly. He contemplated getting another when the door opened. Lilia entered, followed by someone he vaguely recognised and then another more heavily built man with a military style haircut and an angry glare. Cassus weaved his way towards them, trying not to spill his beer on.

******

Vil shuffled along the outbound passage, his head down, trying to summon up some sort of feeling towards the hard day's labour he knew lay ahead. His mind and body refused to co-operate. All that remained was a numb sort of lethargy. A grim acceptance of the situation. Vil had closely examined his work team's routines and looked eagerly for a means of escape. He was not rewarded for his pains. The working zone was sufficiently far from the protective domes to make walking, even in the well-equipped protective suit he wore, an impossibility. The air supply would simply run out. Even if he stole another supply, what was he going to do, knock on the dome's wall and wait for someone to let him in?

The supply vessels that kept the outpost stocked up with food, water and other necessities arrived frequently but they were also equipped with armed guards and Vil could never quite muster the courage to take on a laser rifle. The other members of his work team seemed to feel the same way. Only Lucinda, the team leader, still held an oft hidden gleam in her eye. Vil had been surprised to learn that it was she whom Al had previously worked with and for whom they had conducted the inconclusive research at the library. He was pleased that at least one mystery had been solved even if he couldn’t tell his friends.

The squad reached the rubble that marked the end of the passage. A short distance away they could see the new buildings rising from the ground, a vista of grand monuments. Each sat in its own space, a richly powerful statement of architecture in a classical rather than contemporary style. A physical symbol to the people and the galaxy of the power and aesthetic maturity of its builder. 'A fitting setting for the new dynasty', Vil thought with ill-concealed bitterness, Vil wondered if the slaves who toiled to create the Great wall of China back on Earth felt the same way, or whether the legionnaires who battled to erect the aqueducts of Rome also harboured a secret resentment in their hearts towards the Senate or Emperor. The sun continued its lazy journey and beat down overhead.

******

It was the day after the meeting in the Space Rat. It had been a success, even if an unpolished one. An awkwardness between the parties had manifested itself almost immediately and never quite dissipated. Nevertheless, decisions had been made and they had a plan of action. Cassus alternatively ran his fingers through his hair or tapped his fingernails on his broad desk in his office at the central tower of the Administration. He hoped that he had made the right decision but, in any case, it was almost too late now. Cassus glanced at his computer screen and then at the viewscreen on his wall. He could alert the authorities, foil the plan in its infancy, but then, he knew, he would be a traitor. On the other hand if he didn't alert the authorities he would betray the Governor and the Government and be a traitor. “Some choice,” he said to himself and called the Governor.

The viewscreen in the Governor's study announced the call from Cassus.

“I’ll take the call. Put him on.”

Cassus appeared on the screen. Sendrick peered at him, thinking he looked agitated. Perhaps even a little ill.

"Ah, Cassus, I’m glad you called, I was going to send for you. Can you join me in my quarters in ten minutes, our

Miss Brinsmead has called a meeting and I do not want to disappoint her."

Cassus started to reply but the viewscreen had already shut down at the Governor's command. Cassus raised his eyebrows and let out an exasperated sigh. He gathered a few items that he thought might be necessary and hurried over to the Governor's quarters. He wondered whether this would be the last time he would ever see them.

Minutes later a discussion was under way as four of the most important people on the planet reclined in the comfortable chairs of the Governor's plush study. Octavia was leading the meeting, regulator Marsden was also present, his cold eyes calmly surveying everything. Cassus himself was having trouble trying to keep his mind focused on the issues at hand. He picked up on what Octavia was saying midway through her speech.

"... And so, if we purchase these new construction machines the subsequent need for acquiring new, er, manual labour will diminish to practically nothing, although we will need to maintain existing labour stocks. However, with these new machines in play, the construction speed on the new city will increase by an estimated 1000%."

"That sounds excellent Octavia. Nevertheless, the cost of these machines is astronomical. I need to see and learn more before I can even contemplate acquiring any," the Governor said.

Cassus interjected, "I thought the cost of those things was so vast that we simply could not afford them, certainly not in the short term anyway?"

"That was certainly true. I never expected to be using such automated machinery of this scale so soon. However, if we can secure new financing against the mineral deposits this could allow us to raise the capital to invest."

Octavia turned towards Cassus, studying his face intently. Cassus regarded her stony faced, giving nothing away. When Octavia spoke she kept her gaze upon him but spoke to everyone in the room, "I will show you all the data I have prepared." She glanced at the Governor expectantly who signalled impatiently for her to carry on. Taking a tiny chip from a protective case in her pocket, she slipped it into a port in the Governor's interactive desk and a wall screen lit up. Octavia expertly navigated through the program using the touch sensitive screen. Within seconds a schematic of a constructorbot was displayed both on screen and as a smaller holographic desk image.

Cassus examined it. "It must be huge!" he exclaimed.

"It is. They can extend to over two hundred feet in length without mentioning the assortment of other deployable machinery they carry. These are the very latest models. They have an immense artificial intelligence chip, almost up to 'human-droid companion' levels, with incremental construction intelligence based on virtually all known current engineering, surveying, development, planning and architectural knowledge available to all mankind. They are, in short, masterpieces of design fused with science."

*****

Later that evening, Cassus sat unmoving in his office. He had been impressed by the stats. The boxlike structure of the 'bot moved on a series of caterpillar treads and retractable stabilising outrigger wheels. Octavia had punched up a metre-tall holographic projection of the vast droid on the floor and they'd walked around the projection, peering at it from all angles. Cassus couldn't deny that he had felt his pulse quicken. These machines could speed up the construction of the city and everyone could come home early! Then he'd remembered his brother and all the other colonists forcibly taken from their homes and set to work in what was really nothing more than a modern day forced labour camp. Feeling a little sick, he had excused himself and left the Governor to make plans for an imminent outbound trip to visit the new city.

Cassus stared at his desk's pop-up screen which displayed a list of names on a loop. What had started as hundreds of meaningless, depersonalised names on a list of detainees was starting to appear in his mind as real people, with endless hopes and dreams. There were just so many people, so many dreams. The work camps were reasonably civil places if you conformed, but people still died. Cassus knew escapees had been shot in the back by regulator Marsden's troops or just left to die in the inhospitable terrain. He'd seen those lists too and had quickly mentally filed them away as something distasteful. If he didn't dwell on it, perhaps he'd forget. They were only another statistic anyway and Cassus saw those every day.

Then Vil had disappeared and now those names of the dead kept appearing in his mind's eye. How many family members had died and how many more would die before the city was complete? They'd lingered, floating in the darkness of his subconscious and now they were starting to claw their way free, back to the light. They were there when Cassus closed his eyes at night and he didn't want to live with them, with these dead men's names anymore.

He knew he would get Vil back soon if he brought the Governor into his confidence. The Governor would instantly affect profound shock, apologise extensively and elegantly and probably berate Marsden. His family would be well compensated. The team Cassus had arranged to retrieve his brother would be sent out and they would be reunited within a matter of hours. Then the Governor would move on without giving it a second thought and would expect him to do the same.

Cassus chewed his thumb nail, head down, the computer screen's dim light casting flickering shadows over his face. Could he do that? Part of him could, he knew that. The ruthlessly ambitious, cold-hearted part of Cassus could consign the other conscripts, the innocent men and women to purgatory and eventually he too would become blind to their plight, just like the Governor. His other persona didn't want his soul to slowly choke and wither away to become whatever it was he would transform into as the Governor's puppet. He couldn't wear that mask for the rest of his life. He didn't want to become a mask.

He believed in the Governor's vision and he longed to plunge his planet and society into the limelight through marvellous accomplishments. But the softer, paternal Cassus cared for others and for one in particular. He wanted to spare them all pain.

The Governor had made Cassus into one of the most powerful men on the planet but by the time the Governor returned from the new city, the puppet would have cut his strings. A weary, conflicted Cassus had nonetheless made his decision. Better to make a decision and live with it than live with the fear of it. The Governor's dream was valid, but it was thwarted. His deceptions were unnecessary, his subterfuge pointless, his conceit futile.

CHAPTER 9

Cassus sat behind his new desk in his new apartment close to the Core, a stiff measure of Scotch in his hand and some 22nd century soft Astro-rock playing in the background. His hand was steady. It had been a busy week, the outcome of the meeting four days ago with the Governor, Octavia and Marsden had resulted in a ambiguous promise to consider purchasing one of the constructorbots at a future date, much to Octavia's disappointment.

The main outcome was a planned Core Administration visit to the partially completed new city by the Governor, his personal entourage and a selection of industrialists and guests. Regulator Marsden had also arranged for a full complement of secret staff agents to be present. In total, almost six hundred people, combined with the three thousand workers already situated at or near the city meant that there would be an impressive number of people present. Cassus, however was to remain at the Core and oversee the operation from there.

The Governor had been sincerely apologetic for keeping Cassus away from the 'festivities', as he put it, but he needed someone he could trust back at base. Cassus felt wrong. His mask had slipped, fallen and been crushed underfoot and he lurched from sincerity to hollow words and false promises. He was surprised the Governor hadn't seen through this façade but he supposed the Governor only saw the puppet he had created. The puppet grimaced when the Governor clapped him on the arm and said "We'll be back before you know it. Don't worry Cassus. I'll make this up to you."

In accord with the original plans laid down at the Space Rat, the conspirators were prepared. Cassus had met them all again at Lilia's apartment the day before to confirm their strategy. Coldor had been able to rally fifteen of his former core security force command. Cassus had also inserted a special hand-picked team of three, who combined with Lilia and Al, had been prepared to ambush a transport to take them to the city at about the same time as the Governor's ceremonial visit was taking place.

They had some leeway as the Governor planned to stay the night, his first night, in the new city before returning to Acto. In actuality there had been no need for an ambush, it had been a straightforward matter for Cassus to arrange not one, but three transports. He'd scheduled it with the relevant authorities as the emergency rescue vehicles in case something went wrong with the Governor's expedition.

The external vehicles were mainly used for research and exploration trips or Dome maintenance and construction. These rugged vehicles were always in use and therefore not available to Cassus. There were a few modern commercial vehicles, great tubular cylinders with side-mounted caterpillars and long observation windows for paying tourists or interested citizens to view the planet. These, however, were the most comfortable of the transports and had as such naturally been appropriated by the Governor along with the two dozen military ground vehicles Acto possessed. All were to be used for ferrying staff across to the new city. In fact, all that was left to Cassus were a couple of massive fifty-year-old ground cargo vessels (GCV's) that had been once been used for inter-city trade across the planet. There were also some equipment tugs and an ancient light attack pod.

Cassus intended to make use of the GCVs and the attack pod to rescue as many of the conscripts as possible. It had been decided that the tugs, which could easily drag a dozen big containers behind them were too slow to be of much use. If the GCV's were fully loaded Coldor had thought that they could carry about five or six hundred people each anyway; more than enough for Cassus's requirements. The attack pod itself was a lightly armoured bug like contraption, which sped along on six independent electrically powered wheels and was armed with a roof mounted blaster cannon.

Despite being an antique, Cassus had been assured that it was in pristine condition. Apparently it was the hobby of one of the engineers at the transport depot, which held virtually all of the ground vehicles of Acto, including the city based transmods and electric cars. The main drawback of the attack pod, for Cassus' purposes at any rate, was its size. It could only hold six people. Coldor had commandeered the vehicle along with Lilia and Al.

Coldor and his teams intended to move in on the second day after the planned events were dying down with a lightning raid to grab as many workers as possible, bundle them into the GCVs and make a dash for it back to Acto. If they were caught before they got to Acto, Cassus knew that not only would they be doomed, but so too would he.

*****

The great day dawned and the Governor was on top form, making sure the operation ran smoothly and that the inevitable arguments between different guests and teams were kept to a minimum. This, at last, was his day. Virtually six hundred people from the Administration and across the inhabited galaxy had been assembled to witness this moment. The operation had begun much earlier in the day when the first groups were ferried across Acto to the transport depot and then outwards onto the planet surface and towards the new city. The Governor would arrive in the last batch, delayed to maximise the impact of his entrance. With him were ten of the most important delegates and heads of state from other colonies and a select few journalists, including some from Earth and the ever present Octavia Brinsmead.

It was almost time. He said farewell to Cassus who looked worried. Sendrick was ashamed to have to leave him behind but he needed him in control at the Core. Then Marsden appeared, flanked by four serious, fit looking young men. Muscles bulging under regulation uniforms. The Regulator dipped his head in greeting. "The cars are waiting my Governor. We must make haste if we want to meet the predetermined time."

"Good. Everyone ready to depart?" asked Sendrick looking around at his assembled gathering. Eager nods and affirmative words went round the group.

"Let’s move out then!"

The little troupe headed towards the door and the awaiting cars. Cassus remained in his office, trying not to sweat with anticipation.

The outbound trip to the new city seemed to pass in moments for the Governor. Whilst he circulated and made polite small-talk and dazzled his guests, almost effortlessly, his mind was elsewhere. He was thinking of the future, of the new Capital, of the splendour of his people. When finally the new city did come into view, his audience were not disappointed. The centre of the city, the new hub of a dynasty was virtually complete, evidence of building work was present everywhere, but the centre was the showpiece. A quiet awe spread throughout the transport as one by one the various guests and agents made their way to the long windows to regard the spectacle.

The Governor smiled to himself. This was it! The city, as he had visualised, incomplete, but still discernibly awesome. Something passed through the Governor then, something he'd only felt a few times before. A rare feeling; an almost tangible sense of 'time' itself. The bright new future which would run itself from here, this city; his legacy, The Governor wanted to shout, to fight, to touch the smooth black stone under his fingers. He would carve his name into the galaxy and scream the fact of his very existence unto a complacent universe. The petty hates, the worries and all his fears fell away from his mind and his visage and the

Governor, just a man, stood for one perfect frozen moment as an embodiment of human endeavour and vision. He closed his eyes, savouring this sensation but a minute later they were preparing to disembark and walk into the city itself.

*****

Lucinda had formed up her recently enlarged squad of twenty into a neat line some way behind the work squad in front of her. It had been easier than she had expected as someone had marked the standing positions of each squad on the ground. They were in the great assembly square - a paved stretch of flat ground at the centre of a crossroads and surrounded on all sides by huge colonnaded buildings, which although imposing in their own right, were dwarfed by the size of the square, which was immense. Lucinda could only speculate as to the numbers it could hold. She knew that there was a total work force of some three thousand and that even in the well-spaced lines they had been told to form, the total area they occupied was only the front section of the square facing the largest building yet constructed, the 'Senate House'.

The three thousand workers plus the hundreds of guests that seemed to keep arriving could not have filled more than a tenth of the total space. Still, even that was impressive, rank after rank of neatly conforming conscripts had lined up in their thousands, without fuss, led by their appointed team leaders. They had no protective suits on. There was no need now that the atmospheric bubble was in operation.

Each conscript had been issued with an extremely cheap and itchy white overall. The team leaders wore an equally poor quality pale blue overall. They all stood behind the relatively few volunteer workers who wore a deep blue coverall. Lucinda could not help but postulate whether they were more comfortable than her own chaffing clothing.

In front of the volunteers stood the fully armed divisions of the secret staff. Fully four hundred of them, almost their total number. Their black dress uniforms and caps were pressed and immaculate, at the very front, but still more than hundred metres from the Senate House were the lesser ranked guests, who wore what they pleased and were allowed to mill about their enclosure to some degree. A few dozen regular Core security force troops were dotted about each assembled rank.

The Senate House itself stood over the East Road (the construction of which ended only a few metres beyond the building itself). The twenty metre wide road passed under a mighty triumphal arch that was the base of the Senate House. The building then rose up into a central dome surrounded by a momentous railed balcony upon which stood the senior guests, above this balcony, set higher up in the Dome of the building, was a smaller oratory platform, upon which the Governor would himself stand in but a couple of hours.

Lucinda could not help but feel excited. After so many days of endless repetition, this event had been something she had found herself looking forward to. This would be a welcome pause from her daily regime of back-breaking work. The expressions on most of her squad members' faces told her that they were having similar thoughts. Lucinda knew that recreational events had been organised for later in the evening in the great square. It was to be a day of pleasure to elate the gathered masses.

Vil stood in line in front of Lucinda. He examined the architecture closely and was impressed by how much had been achieved so far. He knew that little else apart from the centre had yet been completed but even the great square and its accompanying Corinthian basilica's were an aweing feat, even though the city construction workers had far more automated equipment than the mineral digging teams. Looking around Vil could see the assembled ranks of his fellow conscripts. Most looked excited, even eager. Vil struggled to share the jubilant mood. He couldn't help but think, 'Why hasn't Cassus got me out of this nightmare yet? Surely family comes first?' His back ached, his wrist was sore. Only his bitter thoughts kept him company 'Where are my friends now?' Vil spat and pushed such thoughts aide, again. At least he could spit again, freed from the confines of the survival suit. He stood silent and alone under the equivalent of a fragile pressurised bubble waiting for the head of the Administration to make an appearance.

A few minutes later his attention was distracted by the events unfolding in front of him.

"It would appear that the Governor has arrived," he heard Lucinda mutter from behind him.

*****

Coldor, Al, Lilia and the fifteen security force troops had assembled in the almost deserted external transport depot only hours before and were even now sheltering behind one of the huge GCVs waiting for Cassus and his specially picked team. They'd had no problem in reaching the depot in three separate teams of six. This part of the depot itself was devoid of any human life. The only guard they had seen on the gate had been sound asleep. It was Coldor's belief that Cassus had something to do with that as well, but he held his tongue, after all it had aided their cause.

The minutes slipped by quietly. A few hushed conversations had sprung up and Coldor had not silenced them since there was no one else in this part of the depot and the conversation probably helped to calm his rag-tag band's nerves. Then one of Coldor's men spotted Cassus. Corporal Rhodes was in look out position on top of the GCV's pilot cab some 50 feet up, chewing noisily on a protein bar. Coldor was below with sergeant Barthan and corporal Lowery. The corporal signalled to Coldor with a spotlight. Coldor in turn peeked out from behind the GCV only to see Cassus and three other men walking brazenly towards them in the meagre haze of the depots energy conserving lights.

Coldor gave a lopsided grin. "So much for all this sneaking about!" The sergeant grinned in return.

"Get the men, I want to be ready to go quickly." Barthan saluted and delved off into the semi-darkness to inform the rest of the company.

"Greetings, Cassus." Coldor stepped out from the bulk of the GCV.

"You all here?" Cassus did want to be hanging about especially when he had so much to attend to at the Core. He had only really showed up, after some deliberation, in order to wish the rescue teams good luck and introduce Coldor to his specially selected trio who had their own mission to attend to. He also wanted to ensure that they all got away safely and had obtained the proper codes and sequences to exit the depot without having to blow it up.

"Ready when you are chief. Who are these three then?" Coldor eyed the men, They were big and looked as though they could handle themselves. They did not look like Core troops or agents though.

"My team, Coldor. Space pilots. They have their own mission and won't interfere with your command or the smooth running of this operation."

Cassus had confirmed Coldor's suspicions. They definitely looked like pilots. "Smooth running eh?

I hope so. Alright, so be it. Sergeant Barthan, get these three kitted up. If they step out of line; they'll know about it." Coldor looked hard at the lead pilot, who nodded back, but appeared unconcerned.

Cassus interrupted impatiently, wanting to get things under way, "right, get boarding then. I'll drive with you to the departure gate and get the doors open. Oh, incidentally, what have you called your operation?"

"Operation Lightning!" Coldor laughed, "Sorry, no time for anything better. I have also split the company. I will lead in the attack pod with Lilia and Al and three of my men under the call sign 'Attack Pack l.' This GCV is under the command of Corporal Rhodes up there." Coldor pointed, and Cassus peered up with some surprise into the gloom at a grinning Rhodes who sat with his legs dangling over the cab roof, which was by now covered in crumbs. Rhodes gave them the thumbs up. Coldor continued, "my sergeant will head up the other GCV. Their call names respectively are 'Rescue Corps 1' and 'Rescue Corps 2'."

"Got it," Cassus replied. Several minutes later the convey was on its way, slowly, cautiously threading its way across the depot floor. Cassus gulped. The operation was really going ahead.

Cassus and Coldor exchanged a few pieces of key last minute information and then they had reached the airlock gates compound. The distinguishing feature of this airlock was its size. It was essentially a very long tunnel, big enough to hold both GCVs and the attack pod, although only just. Cassus scrutinised each member of the crew. Lilia and Al sat hunched up at the back of the pod. They looked nervous. Cassus smiled at them. Coldor was cool and collected, eyes focused on a fixed point. Cassus realised that he was placing his trust in this man perhaps more than Coldor was placing his own trust in Cassus. They clasped hands, Cassus bid them all good luck and then he hopped off from the seat he was sharing with Stoat, another of Coldor's men and jumped through the open hatchway to the ground a few feet below. Each pair of eyes within the pod watched as he went. Each holding his or her own council and private thoughts.

Al voiced what he was thinking. "This is it. There's no turning back now!" Coldor swivelled in his seat and with his customary grin in place replied, "There's still time to go back Al, if you want to." Al had a notion that Coldor was only half joking, but said, "Not a chance - You realise it's dark outside?" Everyone smirked and Coldor sat back in his chair. It dawned on him that he was actually enjoying this. It was certainly better than being a fugitive at any rate.
Down below in an office that looked about hundred years old and probably was, Cassus had figured out the controls with a little help from the voice activated handheld computer he had in his pocket and had the

first gate opening. The heavy super steel portal swung open smoothly in a stately controlled manner and Cassus watched the little attack pod lead the lumbering GCV's into the airlock chamber. Within minutes they were gone and the gate began to close behind them automatically.

*****

The Governor climbed the huge geometrical newel staircase on his way to the oratory platform at the top of the Senate House, higher even than the balcony. The platform jutted out from a set of wooden double doors near the top section of the glistening black rock dome that formed the apex of the building. The platform was lit from its base and incorporated many modern technologies to aid the speaker. The Governor was relying on the setting sun in the East (Acto rotated anti-clockwise on its axis, like Venus around Titan) visible through the bubble to aid the effect of his speech. Only two aides, Regulator Marsden and Octavia Brinsmead now flanked him.

Sendrick reached the top of the winding stair, wheezing slightly. He paused to catch his breath. The double doors leading to the oratory platform stood at the end of a short simple corridor, as yet empty of any ornamentation. Sendrick breathed deeply, eyes closed for a moment. Then h straightened his back, raised his head high and pulled his robes of office tighter around his shoulders as he walked at a regal pace towards those plain wooden doors. Marsden and Octavia followed in an appropriate respectful silence.

The gathered crowd raised its one voice in a roar of appreciation as the Governor stepped out onto the platform. Of course they had been told to, but they had needed no prompting. The moment had been building up for too long. The roar was half in exaltation, half to release pent up frustration. Vil felt himself drawn into the powerful, primeval throats of the assembly. The reactions of the front ranked guests varied from full-blooded participation to bemusement and shock. Certainly they had not expected anything quite like this! The Governor basked in the waves of the voices as they rolled over him,

There they stood; the thousands. This was the moment he had been reaching for all his life. Sendrick's eyes lit up and burned with the fervour of his beliefs. He would not disappoint his subjects today. Raising his arms he gestured for a measure of quiet. The roar died away slowly, but he was not in a rush. The gathered could watch a magnified version of their leader on two floating flat screens that had been unfurled on either side of the Senate House. These were thirty metres square in size and allowed everyone to see clearly. Sendrick's voice was boosted by the speakers inserted into strategic plinths around the great square and even from hovering speakers at the back of the assembly. His speech would be heard in high resolution audio, carefully modulated to produce the smoothest sound.

"Greetings my devoted hosts and most welcome guests, I am truly honoured by your presence. This day will long be marked as the turning point in the fortunes of our colony and our planet. You, the few assembled here today will always be remembered and duly honoured as the dedicated pioneers of the next epoch of our civilisation. We toil now. We break our backs just as our forefathers did to secure a better life for our kin. We shall not be forgotten in our efforts nor shall we allow our society to crumble around us as has happened so many times in the past. The principles we have been taught will remain. Passed on and strengthening our common bond as one people, one community. A society of strength through shared heritage, preserved ideals and above all, the presence of a vision for the future. My vision. I give it to you, my guardians. Together, united with a shared precept and a common ideal shall we triumph over all!"

The pumped up crowd roared their consent. The sound was caught and amplified by the acoustics of the square. Around their heads it rolled, fuelling the adrenaline, the bond that the Governor aimed to secure, he basked in the sound, flushed by the cacophony crashing in his ears.

He looked on as the ordered ranks of his conscripts cheered his proclamations. The square was only partially filled, but already in his mind the Governor could see his legions again, head after head, uncountable in their numbers. The subjects of his new Empire raised their arms in a crashing salute and the Governor basked in the glow of their approval.

Vil had joined in with everyone else. He enjoyed the spectacle. The Governor whipped up the crowd and had them shouting and cheering at almost anything. Truly, the Governor was a master orator. His silences counted for as much as his spoken word. His posture and movements accentuated rather than detracted from what he was saying and towards the end of the speech some part of Vil felt as though he was indeed taking part in something great, something special. The Governor thought his contribution mattered! But as the cheering died and the Governor retired for the last time, his anger crept back, degree by degree, and his nails dug painfully into the flesh of his palm as he clenched his fists, arms rigid at his side.

The Governor had succeeded in binding the work force, but he had already failed in the means he had used to secure them. That thread of resentment remained in many hearts that evening. In some cases the conscripts' train of thought had been subtly altered in the way they perceived what they were doing. More than a few felt pride in their achievements and the great square was a physical reminder of their accomplishments. But the monotony of their grinding daily labour and the physical coercion into being there in the first place, ripped from their homes and lives spawned doubt, resentment a growing anger.

Vil found himself thinking, with some irony, that if the Governor had made a series of speeches like that when he was originally trying to recruit people for the project, he would have found a lot more volunteers.

*****

The small convoy levelled off at the bottom of a gentle but extensive gradient and there it stood, the city loomed up on the horizon, Lit by a thousand lights, several dozen structures were easily recognisable, even at this distance, Coldor eased the attack pod past an outcropping of rock, which thrust its battered visage a hundred feet into the air, and put his foot down as much as he dared. The tension within the little pod started to mount and effect the passengers.

"Is that laser powered up Stoat?" Coldor asked the gunner.

"Yeah, I've looked over it and this baby is ready to discharge."

"Marvellous. Make sure you're ready as soon as the action starts. Let's hope it doesn't."

Stoat nodded and began making the appropriate alterations to the remote control panel that controlled the gun. These were fairly simple. A camera mounted on the weapon transmitted a picture back to a small screen, which displayed the image the gun was seeing, and a target icon. The weapon could be moved around remotely and tilted by a small joystick on the right of the screen. On the left were the power gauges and fire buttons for the twin-barrelled laser. A few other dials and buttons were mounted below the screen for tracking targets, setting up and powering down the laser. Stoat had discovered that the weapon could also be operated manually from a collapsible panel in the roof of the pod.

Some way behind the nimble pod lumbered the great GCVs. Corporal Rhodes sat in the co-pilot's seat of one of the machines, as his number two, Marcus Satchel drove the GCV. The cabin itself was sparse and basic, the GCVs being not much more than mobile freight bins. Even so, the chairs in which Marcus and Rhodes sat were comfortable and fully adjustable in order to make the normally boring job of hauling freight a cosy one.

Marcus commented, "I hate this thing. You don't drive it; you get it started and point it towards wherever you're going. I've had more fun shaving my chest hair."

Rhodes laughed and leaned back almost horizontally in his chair, his head brushing the back wall of the small cabin, "Don't worry Marcus, I reckon we'll be seeing some action soon enough. Then you'll be glad of all the armour this thing's carrying!"

Marcus grunted his reply. Suddenly a light began to wink on the straight panel that formed the front controls. It sent a meagre yellow glow over the men's faces in the darkness of the cabin as the main lights appeared to be broken. Rhodes flicked a switch below the light and spoke at the control panel, which contained a two-way speaker, "Rhodes here."

"Morning Corporal. We are almost there. Attack pack 1 has the target in site, Make ready, over."

Coldor's voice echoed around the room with a metallic ring before quickly fading away. Rhodes looked at Marcus and nodded. "Let's inform the troops. It's party time!"

*****

Back in the city the festivities were in full flow. The fun had created mixed feelings though. For some it had stirred up something akin to gratitude, even from the conscripts. For many, including Vil, as he walked side by side with Lucinda, and another conscript called Adrian Sign, the good times had reminded them that they should be having this sort of fun back in the dome of their own free will; not at the instigation of the Governor. They were all glad, however, of the reprieve.

Indeed, Vil felt a swirling sickness in his gut every time he thought about returning to work the next afternoon. The Governor had bestowed an extra half-day's holiday on them during his speech. When would their next break be after that? When the city was finished? Vil's feared so, even with the aid of new machines it would still take years to complete even the heart of the city.

Vil took a swig of his beer. He could forget about it all tonight at any rate. Tomorrow he would have to face reality. Lucinda and Adrian seemed to have arrived at the same conclusion.

"Another drink?" Adrian asked.

"I think so," Vil replied.

The three of them made their way through several other little groups milling about, some of them drinking heavily, others looking sombre, some irate and others cheerful. Vil shook his head, hoping to reclaim his feeling of stoic resignation.

Two hours passed, Vil and his now enlarged group of drinking partners sat like many of the other assembled people beside one of the four giant plinths that stood in the square. Three were unadorned, one held a fifty-foot statue of a hardy pioneer; His visage determined and paternal. Vil's party however sat beside one of the unadorned stone bases. All were quite drunk and loudly recounting tales of accidents and incidents, even fake ones, which had befallen the work groups. No one had yet broached the subject of home. No one had yet talked about the injustice of it all. Adrian had voiced his theory to Vil and Lucinda earlier that it was probably because they were afraid that there was an informer, a member of the Secret Staff amongst them. Vil looked around at the score of so of men and women around him. One of them could be a spy, who was looking around the most? Who seemed to look the shiftiest? Vil realised belatedly that it was probably himself and he self-consciously stopped looking about and concentrated on his beer.

A drunken giggle sounded behind him and Vil peered round into the hazy light as Lucinda whispered into his ear, "don't worry Vil, I know you are not a spy!"

Lucinda leaned back, resting her whip-thin, lithe body against the cool base of the plinth, watching him. Vil suddenly felt cold and alone and he scooted over to sit next to her. She didn’t pull back when Vil took her hand in his and they sat companionably together, backs against the cold stone and watched the evening fade.

*****

In the Senate House the Governor was sitting at the head of the long table within the principal dining room. The evening was drawing to a close, and a number of guests had already retired, certainly, the majority of the workers had now been ushered back to the camps lining the City, although some were sleeping it off in the square below. Thirty-one guests had had the honour of dining with the Governor. Some remained sipping wine or coffee, wearing the content expressions of well-fed, sated people. Other guests were relaxing within one of the many reception rooms surrounding the dining chamber. Yet more stood upon the balcony admiring the view and spectacular evening lights and the fireworks that now lit the ground. No air fireworks could be permitted because of the danger of piercing the protective environmental bubble.

Nearly every conversation revolved around the events of the day, most of the talk in the refined chambers of the Senate, at any rate, praised the Governor's accomplishments. Sendrick was conversing with one of the most important delegates in the room, Stuart

Bronzemerit, a journalist from Earth who worked for one of the preeminent media groups.

"I nearly didn't come you know. There were other stories I could have covered, but having never tried long distance space flight before I decided to satisfy my curiosity and head out here. It's a long way from Earth Governor."

"I am glad you did Stuart. It's important to us that we receive as much coverage as possible and obviously news from the most important system in the Planetary Network is a priority for us out here, on the edge of civilisation. There are no major systems beyond us you know. Just unexplored space. This is the frontier."

Bronzemerit nodded in agreement. "It has been for a long time. I think you have achieved an amazing amount given your isolation from Earth. I'd like to dive into some more of the detail but from what I've seen to date I am looking forward to sending my report back to Earth Sendrick. When my story is released you can expect a further deluge of inquiries and visits from other media groups. You may even come to dislike the limelight in due course."

"I'm sure I will endure. Our aim here is to receive as much attention as possible, facilitating the eventual visitation from a council member of the Planetary Network"

"If the Network becomes involved you will probably lose some of your autonomy," Bronzemerit warned.

"I think we are too distant to pose any threat to the Network. However, their involvement will draw attention to all of the colonies within the Federation. Attention which should lead to greater and hopefully lucrative relationships!"

The conversation weaved in and out of the intricacies involved in inter-planetary relationships and the Governor found to his delight that the journalist was no novice to politics and they spun their words comfortably, growing in fervour as the champagne flowed.

An hour passed in this fashion before a Secret Staff officer with a nervous face and floppy swept back hair interrupted the pair.

"May I have a minute of your time sir?" said Lieutenant Hill.

Sendrick knew that he would not have been interrupted without good reason, he nodded curtly at the officer and graciously excused himself from Bronzemerit's presence before making his way with the Lieutenant towards the operations control room at the top of the building. The Governor was not particularly worried. He was sure that, whatever the trouble was, it could be dealt with expediently.

The scene behind the dark-panelled wood door was removed from the genteel grandeur of the dining chamber. Soft lights glowed within silver metallic control panels. Screens and pop-up monitors and holographic representations covered the walls and work areas. A small-scale map of the city stood on the table in the middle of the room. Four men operated the consoles following the advice that emanated from the audio synthesiser of the complex's new computer. Softy dilated and soothing the voice instilled confidence and competence. The operations centre was running smoothly. The occupants were sure that the Governor would know what to do. From a small office to one side of the room, regulator Marsden emerged grim-faced.

"We have a situation Governor. Our short-range scanners have detected a small convoy approaching the City. We were unable to detect them earlier because of the interference from the protective canopy."

"A convoy? From Acto? Has Cassus been in communication with you?"

"We think three vehicles sir. One may be a military vehicle. There has been no communication from Cassus and we have been unsuccessful in our efforts to contact Acto." Marsden hesitated and pressed on, "It would appear, sir, that our efforts are either being consciously ignored, or even jammed."

"Jammed? But why? Who would do such a thing? This is ridiculous. There could there be a sandstorm out there interfering with our communications. There may be a fault with the equipment. I cannot accept that someone from the Administration would willingly jam our transmissions."

"The fibre optics are laid' directly to the Core. There can be no fault with the equipment. Either someone is not paying attention to their job, or there had been deliberate disruption at the Dome. I personally checked all comms equipment before we left and we were in communication with the Core earlier today. There is no storm. There is no fault with equipment. I would surmise my Governor, that you have been betrayed."

"What! A coup! By whom? I cannot believe that! This is our greatest day, who would dare to move against me?" A coup was impossible. There were only two people remaining in the entire administration who had enough power to organise such a feat. Everyone else was too carefully monitored for such an event to occur.

Certainly, it could not be organised from the new city, it would have been noticed immediately. Briefly Sendrick suspected Marsden, but dismissed the notion immediately. He was not that paranoid and the regulator had proved his loyalty beyond doubt over the years. That left Core security Commander Perterson and Cassus. The Governor gulped back sour tasting phlegm and was, for once, temporarily at a loss as to what to do.

CHAPTER 10

Time passed all too quickly for those in the convoy. Barely thirty minutes has passed since they had first been spotted by the Secret Staff but Coldor's units were already in position. The atmosphere was heady; the quest for a definitive course of action had reached fever pitch. In the attack pod the temperature had risen steadily and Coldor's face glistened with sweat. He wiped his clammy hands on his already stained trousers, gripped the controls again and clicked his neck. Glancing down he checked, yet again, that everything was running smoothly on green. The soldier looked around at his crew.

'This was it. They were really going to do it. Would anyone die tonight?' He thought.

Their current position was only a few hundred metres away from the camps that lined the outer extent of the city. Cassus had informed the teams that the conscripts were all placed in two massive linear camps in close proximity to each other. Coldor had dispatched one of the GCVs to each of the camps with the pod taking a central position between them to co-ordinate the operation.

The intercom buzzed. "Rescue corps 1 in position Sir," Sergeant Barthan reported in.

A few seconds later Corporal Rhodes confirmed his vehicle was also in position. Coldor acknowledged and gave the signal for the teams to move out. The sudden roar of engines shattered the quiet night and Coldor winced, but he hoped that it might rouse some of the workers from their beds.

The plan was straight forward. Each GCV would drive in as close as possible to the camps. Both vehicles would then switch on their extensive array of external lights to awaken as many people as possible. The squads would move out in pairs and attempt to shepherd the conscripts towards the GCVs. After twenty minutes both teams would move out with maximum speed back to the Dome. They were not going to attempt to rescue everyone and they were not going to penetrate deeper into the City. The huge GCVs could hold perhaps a thousand people between them. A number which could easily be fulfilled by even a partially successful rescue from the conscript camps. Cassus considered this sufficient to mobilise the Dome into resistance against the Governor based on sheer public indignation whipped up by the media. That was assuming they made it back at all.

Cassus had been pretty sure that the camps would be guarded. Probably by Secret Staff and a few regular Security Force Guards. However, it was a safe bet that many of the designated guards would have indulged in a few drinks and would certainly not be expecting any trouble. Coldor hoped that they would not be too alert.

The GCVs rumbled in. The pod darted between the two and checked the perimeter before nipping back in-between the vehicles, which headed steadily inwards towards the camps on a parallel course running about fifty or sixty metres apart, far closer than running regulations would ever permit. The signal came and the carriers ground to a halt, brakes straining to bring the monstrous contraptions to a halt. Almost simultaneously, each switched on its powerful lights. Multiple beams of light fell upon the slumbering workers and lit up the area. The blackness rolled back from the GCVs to reveal two squads running down the egress ramps and darting through the ranked lines of tents.

As the darkness lifted so too did the calm of the night. Shouting erupted as people were woken up by the squads or by the sudden commotion and light. Napping guards raised their heads and grumbled in confusion. They grabbed their rifles, but were unsure of what to do. This was not on the agenda, or was it some special exercise organised by the Governor? In the confusion the only people who knew what they were doing were the rescuers who moved continuously, rousing people directing them towards the GCVs, shouting "Rescue - get towards the ships! Move, Move!"

Cassus's special team of three moved methodically, trying to hunt down the missing Vil. From the other direction approached an army of Secret Staff. They marched confidently. Their weapons were loaded and they were ready for a fight.

*****

The Governor drummed his fingernails nervously onto the table in the control room. Regular Marsden and one other staff member were still present.

The regulator tried to assure Sendrick. "Sir, we have sent over two hundred of the Secret Staff, almost half their number to deal with the intruders. If they are hostile, and I suspect they are, then, with your leave, we will retaliate. Commander Harer and his crew are awaiting your order."

The Governor bit the side of his thumb in anxiety. Reasons for the sudden appearance of the convoy had been running through his mind in a frenzy. He had racked his brain for a logical explanation. He did not have an answer, but he did know that if news of this escapade should reach the Dome it would be problematic. If a coup was being operated from within the Administration, the Governor was in serious trouble. He had hundreds of guests out here in the desert and limited supplies. His only real hope was that the army of Secret Staff would deter or defeat the mysterious interlopers. There was one final item that was causing the Governor immense trepidation.

"I don't want people to die Marsden. Bear in mind what will happen that if news of this gets back to the Dome – Particularly if your men start shooting. There are delegates out here from a score of different systems including Earth. If news of this cock-up should reach them, this colony will be the laughing stock of the Planetary Network. What happens if these assailants are not here to attack but try to rescue the workers? If they get back to the Dome and the news is broadcast throughout Acto..."

"I know, Sir, I know." Marsden looked at a flat screen monitor showing the positions of the army and the unknown assailants. Already the monitor showed dozens of blips, the conscripts, heading towards the two large vehicles that Marsden surmised to be transports. It was a rescue attempt. The Governor was looking at the monitor as well now, his army only a couple of minutes away from their target.

"We need a decision Governor," Marsden prompted.

Governor Sendrick remained silent. Head bowed. The seconds ticked by. 'More time, if only I had more time.' But there was no more time. He nodded briefly at his head of Secret Staff and turned away. Regulator Marsden smiled his approval.

"Signal Commander Harer. We have been sanctioned to use all necessary force." Marsden nodded to himself and thought, 'there is no way these intruders, whoever they are, can stand a chance against my Secret Staff. There will be blood split on Acto tonight.'

On the normally peaceful world of Acto no arms had ever before been lifted in anger against fellow colonists.

*****

The Secret Staff reached the conscript camp to witness scores of workers fleeing into the distance. The two hundred and a supporting ground tank (Regulator Marsden had deemed that one tank only would be more than sufficient) fanned out across the far side of camp, using the numerous half- complete building works as cover. Each agent had a two-way communicator and thus when Commander Harer, directing from the tank, gave the order, two hundred blaster rifles lifted simultaneously and two hundred deadly laser beams cut into the camp. Screams of confusion changed to screams of terror as several conscripts fell to the ground clutching burning wounds.

Then, through the haze screamed the attack pod, with Coldor at the controls. Its limited range ancient scanner had picked out the approaching army seconds before. Through the fallen and blasted tents it screamed, the wheels hissing in protest as the pod swept along the lines of the enemy army, its twin laser cannon blasting bolt after bolt into the hidden ranks of the enemy.

The Agent's return fire came swiftly, but the pod had already veered away back into the camp. A few bolts did strike however causing sizzling black burn marks on the outer hull of the vehicle. The Agent's ground tank howled through the sheltered army and into the camp. Its bulk more than three times the size of the pod. Its fire power thrice as great. A great quad-barrelled laser cannon was mounted on a swing turret above a brooding black hull. Two side mounted single laser cannons completed the armaments. Twin caterpillar tracks thrust the machine forwards through the camp.

Commander Harer held onto a rail in the cab on the tank, standing behind driver Mick Adamson and gunner Dan Galls. Harer's orders were simple, "We must take out that attack pod. It is the enemy's only key armament. Destroy it."

The turret swung round tracking the nimble pod across the terrain. The pod was perhaps slightly faster than the tank and certainly more agile. Harer knew, however, that one good hit from his quad laser would blow the pod sky high.

In the pod Coldor wove and swerved desperately. He had seen the battle tank emerge from the haze of the city into the camp and the size of its weapon gave him no option. The pod fled back into the blackness.

Al was on the intercom, "Rescue corps 1 and 2, withdraw. I repeat, withdraw. We cannot stand against that sort of fire power.

A crackling reply burst from the speaker, "Rhodes here, negative, attack pack 1. Repeat, negative, we cannot withdraw, we're pinned down. Heavy fire coming in from the south!" Rhodes wailed, the sound of battle and a cacophony of shouting and screams threatened to drown out his voice.

"Any casualties?" Al asked, not quite sure of what to do in his new role.

"Not yet. Most of the shots seem to be going too high. But there is still enough dangerous fire to keep us pinned down. Request assistance."

"Okay, Rhodes you hang on," Al urged. To no one in particular he shouted across the din of the full-out engines and the whine of the laser cannon, "Rhodes is in trouble. What do we do?"

"Get Barthan down there!" shouted Coldor. "Here, give me that intercom." Al grabbed the handheld intercom mounted on the front dash and passed it to Coldor. He sat back in his chair, sweat pouring from his face and fear shining in his eyes.

Coldor was saying, "Barthan? You copy?"

No reply came in.

Lilia let out a shriek. She had been keeping a sharp eye on the battle through the canopy and had seen the blast from the battle tank hit the dirt not ten metres away. Coldor pulled the pod around.

"Bollocks to this. We're going in. Get ready boys."

Commander Harer could hardly believe it. "They're moving into attack position! Track them. We'll blow 'em away!"

The turret mounted quad laser swung round divulging a staggered fire from its charged barrels, the ground beside the encroaching attack pod burnt and leapt. Sand sprayed into the air showering everything within a twenty-metre radius. The deadly hail of fire moved steadily closer to the pod.

"Die! Just fucking die!" Screamed Harer.

*****

Sergeant Barthan, meanwhile, had not been idle. He had rounded up his squad as soon as the first wave of enemy fire swept into the camp. Barthan was surprised there had not been more casualties since that first hail of red laser bolts had lit up the black city to the south. Still, he didn't have time to ponder that now.

His handheld comms unit was shattered. It emitted a steady low humming noise. Barthan held it up to inspect the damage and one of the buttons fell off. In disgust Barthan threw it to the ground.

His squad of six hunkered down close to the ground following a slight dip in the terrain towards where he believed Rhodes's squad to be. The firefight was certainly heavier from the other camp. Barthan had left corporal Lowery behind, to supervise a steady retreat of some three score conscripts they had rounded up. That herd of scared people crept along the ground towards the comparative safety of the GCV, picking up many more refugees on their way. Barthan hoped that they would make it. The dip his squad was traversing was levelling out and soon they would be left exposed. The next cover was down in the other camp, only thirty metres away, but thirty metres across the enemy line of fire.

He hissed to his lance-corporal, "Jaris, take one of the men and bear around to the left towards that outcrop of rock. Let's give 'em something to think about. When you see four laser bolts shoot straight up into the sky start shooting. We are going to make a dash for it into the other camp,"

"Wilco Sergeant." Jaris confirmed.

Barthan bid them good luck and the remaining four men crawled off to the edge of the protective ridge that marked the end of the dip. He had barely peeked out when the ground tank lumbered past, perhaps a metre from his nose. It was making good speed, its laser cannons roaring.

"Sweet Jesus" said a private beside him, "Look at the size of that thing."

The sergeant noticed a vehicle coming in the other direction, a much smaller vehicle, its roof mounted twin laser pouring fire at the battle tank.

"Isn't that the attack pod?"

"Shit! Squad, let's give Coldor a hand, shoot that bloody tank!"

The four of them shouldered their laser rifles and let lose a continuous barrage of fire towards the tank.

*****

Jaris and Erantes had reached the rock. They crouched down beside it. Clutching their weapons tightly.

"Where's the signal?" Erantes whispered, eyes wide.

Jaris had no answer. What he had seen was disturbing. The Agent army had gushed out of their protective cover and were charging in behind the tank.
"Er, this doesn't look good, Erantes."

Erantes looked out from behind the rock to see a couple of hundred men bearing down on him.

"Let's get out of here!"

*****

In the attack pod, Stoat was letting loose a withering number of shots. He was sure he had hit the tank several times, but it kept on coming, its armour absorbing or deflecting his shots. The pod's laser was already running on emergency power. Then, inevitably the tank struck back, its quad-laser opened up again and this time it hit the pod. The underside of the light vehicle exploded into a fireball and two of the wheels on the right-hand side rolled off into the desert, fire licking their rubber, black smoke bellowing. The vehicle slumped down onto its side, a small electrical fire spouting from the front control panel. Stoat's gun controls fell off their mounting into his hands.

"Well, that’s just fantastic,” he said from his skewed position between his seat and the floor. Coldor was back up immediately and unstrapping himself. "Anyone hurt? Can you all get out?"

Steve South smashed open the roof exit portal set behind the now silent twin lasers and virtually threw a stunned Lilia out of the vehicle, Al followed next, then Coldor emerged. He scrambled along the roof towards the laser cannon. Heaving it into a firing position, Coldor tried to get his bearings. He scanned the terrain. Laser fire was still erupted sporadically some way in front of him. Green laser fire was shooting at an advancing squat black shape.

Green fire? But the Agents weapons discharged red bolts. The rescue team's older lasers fired green.

Those were his boys!

Coldor lined up the laser with the tank, which was by now only a matter of metres away. He hit the double fire button and his laser spewed death towards the monstrous enemy for the last time. The big weapon also recoiled in his hands, snapping his wrists back painfully and blowing him ten feet away to land on the hard sand of the desert. He fell with a grunt and passed out.

Steve South rushed out from behind the battered pod where Lilia and Al were sheltering and unceremoniously grabbed Coldor's feet. He hauled him back to within the shadow of the vehicle, picked up his blaster and partially stepped out from past the uselessly spinning wheels on the left-hand side to take a few shots at the tank before they were either blown away or crushed.

*****

Gunner Joe Galls had seen the soldier run out and drag his companion back to the comparative safety of the smoking hull of the vehicle he had just blown up. Galls considered the job done. The little laser bolts that kept pinging off his hull were nowhere near powerful enough to stop the beast, although they were ruining the paint work.

Commander Harer spoke again, "Excellent shooting Galls. Now finish them."

"They're out of the game. Sir, should we not return to support our rear lines?"

"I have given you a direct order gunner! Blow them apart!" Harer yelled down at the bewildered Galls.

The gunner looked out of his view port, a lone soldier stepped out firing a few pointless shots at the armoured hull of the battle tank. Galls fingers closed over the quad lasers controls. His fingers tightened around the moulded plastic grip. He wasn't a gentle man, but he also held honour in his heart. He couldn't simply blow them apart, "They're Actavians Sir! Sorry, no can do." Galls squirmed out of his seat to face the Commander.

"What! I will see you pay for this insubordination Galls. You will never work again. Your family will never work again! I am warning you, you had better fire that damn gun or I will have you boy!"

Galls shuddered, he knew the Commander would keep to his word. He glanced at Mick Adamson who looked away, shamefaced. There was no way out now. Galls, who stood over a foot higher than Harer, bowled his way past the man and made for the rear hatch. He never made it. In a rage the Commander shrieked, lips drawn back in a rictus, spit flying as he drew his blaster pistol and shot Galls in the back. The gunner looked round in amazement. Shock registered on his stricken face. He fell where he stood, a foot away from freedom. The smell of cooked meat mixed with the metallic aftertaste of blood started to fill the cabin. Harer breathed in deeply, satisfied that he had asserted his authority and turned back to the driver.

He started to speak, "Any other problems..." his voice died away as he came face to face with Mick's meaty fist.

"Bad move chum, bad move," Gall's friend Mick Adamson smashed Harer in the face twice in rapid succession and then knocked him out with a third heavy blow.

The tank sat motionless on the desert floor as laser fire erupted all around.

*****

Lieutenant Hill led the fourth platoon operating at the far end of conscript camp alpha. His platoon moved squad by squad, laying down an effective field of fire without receiving casualties.

His earpiece crackled and burst to life "Hill. Hill, do you copy?"

"This is Hill."

"Continue the advance lieutenant," ordered the control room.

"Advise proceeding with caution. There is a pocket of resistance from somewhere within the camp."

"Roger that. Hill out."

Hill eagerly led his thirty men forward in open order to present less of a target, using a half-complete apartment complex as cover before breaking into the camp itself, which was in chaos. Flattened tents and discarded gear littered the ground. A scuffed up polycarbonate survival helmet rolled to a stop near Hill's feet.

Hill pressed forward, negotiating a shallow trench in the ground. The officer stumbled over the ripped up body of a conscript and fell face first into the body's cooling life-blood, a pair of dead eyes on a decapitated head regarded the lieutenant frigidly from a few centimetres away. Hill rolled over aghast, trying to get away from the horror. Bile rose in his throat and he had to spit a mouthful of sick onto the stained sands. The fight drained from him. The officer shook his head and backed away from the gruesome site. All around him several other members of his platoon were having similar experiences. Without guidance from their immediate commanding officer the platoon faltered, then the advance stopped.

All around the battlefield men who had not really wanted to kill their fellow colonists and had not been shooting at them with any fervour in the first place stopped in disgust at the sight of those who had fallen. In truth there were not many, a few dozen in total, but combined with the death of some of their own comrades this had proved to be enough. A force of two hundred had set out that night to do the Governor's will. A force of less than fifty continued into the desert to do the dark deed.

*****

In the control room, Regulator Marsden stood rigidly upright in a martial pose but his eyelid betrayed him and involuntarily twitched continuously. He watched the tactical display of his forces fervently. The tank had not moved for some time and Commander Harer was silent. He watched in increasing horror as half the force stopped their advance and some even started to fall back. The army was disintegrating before his eyes! Only fifty or so men had continued the charge and they were still some way behind the stricken battle tank.

The Regulator hoped they would be enough, already one of the enemy transports had started to move.

Time was running out. Marsden looked around, but the Governor was gone. He was alone in the room now, having dispatched the operators to the fight and other duties. His hands shook at the thought of what would happen if the agent army failed. This could be the end of his career. The Regulator steeled himself then. His conviction returned, fifty was enough against a few malcontents. He would win through!

*****

Corporal Rhodes noticed that the deadly hail of laser fire had stopped. He had been out of contact with everyone for what seemed like hours. Now though his intercom crackled to life and he heard the welcome voice of one of the squad.

"Rhodes is that you? It's Lowery here. I'm back on GCV 2 with about three or four hundred of the conscripts. I have you pinpointed on my scanner and we are heading in to pick you up. We cannot contact anyone else, although I know that Barthan has a broken communicator. See if you can find anyone, and let them know we are on our way! Send a man to get back to GCV 1 if possible as well."

"I copy, Lowery, I copy. Well done that man!" Shouted Rhodes jubilantly.

"Just doing my job, sir!"

Rhodes got his still unharmed squad in formation and under the suddenly quiet sky they bolted back towards their transport. To the right Rhodes noticed the smouldering remains of a vehicle, smoke drifted up from several points in its shattered body.

"The pod!"

"Marcus, get back to the GCV. Head back to the Dome. Don’t stop for anyone."

Marcus hesitated, not wanting to leave his corporal.

"That is an order soldier. Move yourself lad!"

Marcus saluted hurriedly and headed towards the distant GCV. Rhodes signalled the remainder of his squad to spread out and head towards the broken pod.

They reached it seconds after Barthan's men. They found Steve South, Al and Lilia sheltering beneath the rear side of the pod. After cries of relief that they were still alive, Steve told them that Coldor and Stoat had set out towards the battle tank shortly after it had ground to a halt. To the companions general relief it had not moved since. The reunited squads were soon joined by Jarvis and Erantes who bundled in, shouting gibberish.

'They are coming! There's a stinking army behind us!"

Rhodes shouted over the din, "Listen, we only have to hold out for a few minutes. One of the GCVs is coming to pick us up!"

"Lowery made it then!" Barthan breathed a sigh of relief.

Rhodes joined Barthan who had set his squad to digging in at the side of the collapsed pod. "Where is this army and where the hell are Coldor and Stoat?" They scanned the dimly lit ground behind the silent battle tank, but everything was eerily calm. Then, seconds later, they appeared.

About fifty armed Agents sprang into view only a score of metres behind the still prone tank. Their laser rifles opened up and the companions were pinned down by the deadly red fire. To make matters even worse, the battle tank spluttered into life again and it turret started to swing towards them.

Rhodes surveyed the scene and nodded once.

"So, this is it men! Honoured to have known you all." Without looking to see if anyone still stood with him the corporal roared his defiance and rose to his knees behind the pathetically inadequate sand barrier Barthan's squad had constructed.

Fourteen other men and women, the total number present, joined him in his show of defiance, but the battle tank's turret and its mighty quad laser continued to turn.

*****

Rhodes's weapon fired repeatedly into the enemy ranks, the green laser fire spurting forth in to the desert, wreaking havoc. Rhodes was in battle frenzy, the adrenaline pumping ferociously. He never felt the shot that killed him. He was blown backwards by the force and hit the hull of the pod, head lolling, dead before he hit the ground.

It all happened so quickly that it took Barthan a moment to react. He looked down aghast at the now prone form of the corporal. In fury and indignation at the unjustness of it all, Barthan raised his rifle. He fired again and again into the ranks of black robed Agents. They seemed to melt before him, his rifle expunging punishment upon them like some terrible disease of old. The tank's turret was now facing him and Barthan expected death and he faced it down. Unconsciously he held his breath and waited for it to happen, but when he looked up again he could see that the turret had continued to turn and was now facing the remaining Agent's, indeed the tank itself had hesitantly reversed direction and was scattering the fanatics across the desert. The mighty quad laser fired once, twice, three times in rapid succession and when the sand finally settled no Agents remained standing.

Everything drew to a standstill. The tank stopped. The firing stopped. There were a few long seconds of peace in the desert as those remaining alive surveyed the situation. Barthan looked around again. The dead intermingled with the living. Rhodes was gone, Jaris was gone, three other companions were gone. Steve sat on the floor bandaging a wound on Al's ear with the aid of Lilia. Erantes's weapon dropped limply to the ground with a clatter and he looked off vacantly towards the tank. From the other side of the pod two other privates emerged, blinking. There they stood, the few, dazed and confused and waiting for something to happen.

They did not have to wait long, the top hatch of the battle tank clanged open, and into the night sky emerged Coldor, closely followed by Stoat and then another brawny man carrying someone over his shoulder, both wore the uniform of the Secret Staff. Stoat waved over to the little group beside the pod. He gave the thumbs up and all they made their way slowly back to the pod. Mick carelessly banging Commander Harer's head against the tank as he descended. Coldor shook his head but patted Mick on the back anyway.

"You made the right call son."

“Aye, hurt my bloody hand though didn’t I!”

A short time afterwards corporal Lowery arrived in the GCV. It was not until everyone had safely boarded and made their way up to the crew's quarters that Coldor realised that someone was missing.

"Where is that team Cassus put aboard?"

Barthan replied. "They disembarked with my squad, said something about finding someone. Vil Toradon, I believe. They started to search for him whilst the rest of us were rounding up the conscripts. Where they got to I don't know. When the shooting started I lost interest."

"Hmm, what to do? We cannot very well wait around here all night for them. We must get back to the Dome with the other GCV to put Cassus's plan into action." Coldor reasoned.

Lilia spoke up; "We can't just leave Vil here! Let's wait a little while longer at least!"

Al backed her up, "I will wait as well, whatever happens. He'll turn up, I'm sure of it."

Coldor had a sudden thought. "He might already be here! Who is to say that we did not round him up before Cassus's pilots even got to him? Can we broadcast something into the cargo area and check the other GCV?" Coldor asked Stoat.

Stoat, the technology expert, looked a bit dubious. "I'm not sure. This equipment is antiquated, but I'll have a look."

They checked both GCVs cargo holds but no one responded to the name of Vil Toradon or indeed any of the three Space Rat pilots. However a couple of conscripts had come forward with information concerning Vil's whereabouts. They had apparently last seen him passed out in the great square, hours ago. Coldor was disappointed. He was impatient to get moving.

"We're picking up new conscripts all the time. The cargo hold is almost full. Perhaps Vil has come in with one of the more recent batches. We are going to have to evac soon and catch up with Marcus and the other GCV."

"Just wait another few minutes, please!" Lilia pleaded.

Coldor muttered something rude, but agreed.

*****

Back in the operations room in the Senate building the guests continued to sleep soundly, the building had been fortuitously soundproofed and they slept in ignorant bliss.

Regulator Marsden was meditating on how long it would last. His scanner now showed only a few blue dots, the milling remains of his glorious army, several dozen had returned to the Senate Building and the Regulator had informed his four remaining guards to notify all stragglers to assemble at the military transports. He had no thoughts of another strike attempt; he just didn't want to personally face any member of the losing side in the battle. Now there were only a few shocked stragglers out there mixed in with the red dots representing the remaining swathes of disconcerted conscripts and workers. Marsden peered absently at the screen for a few seconds more, watching a group of five red dots make their way towards the one remaining transport, before he picked up his comfortingly heavy standard issue blaster from the cold metal table, put it to his head and pulled the trigger.

*****

The special team implanted by Cassus had been informed by some of the conscripts before the battle of a number of people who had remained in the square. One had even thought he had seen Vil slumped against a plinth near the Senate house. The deep space pilots had taken the chance and set off to investigate.

Their gamble had paid off. The great square was still partially lit when they arrived and they had been able to make out that most of the remaining workers had congregated beneath an impressive looking statue. Beneath the shadow of this imposing figure they had eventually found Vil and a woman named Lucinda. It had taken a few minutes to rouse the couple and the five of them had started to make their way back to the transport. They had not gone very far before one of the pilots, Ajax, had spotted the advancing columns of the agent army. The five had run for cover in the building works behind the square and gradually made their way back towards the camps.

Unfortunately the Governor's army had reached the camps before them and formed a barrier between the transports and freedom. Vil and Lucinda's state of health had not been conducive to further sneaking about or stealth and so they had hidden a good way behind the agent army. When the fighting had died down they had taken their chance and started to make a wide detour around the battlefield and towards the transports.

The five companions were lucky. They arrived back at the last remaining transport just as it started its engines and began to turn away. With as much speed as they could muster they charged down the bulky transporter, whilst firing their blasters into the air. Sure enough the signal worked and the transport ground to a halt. From the main hatch sprang a dozen armed men, silhouetted by the light behind them. They advanced with intent, blasters raised.

Ajax shouted, "Woah there! Wait one damn moment. We are friends. Wait you dogs!" Vil peered anxiously as Ajax kept shouting. From amidst the mysterious figures, emerged a face Vil recognised. Al ran forward, his weapon discarded and the two friends embraced each other. Relief flooded him as the reality of the situation dawned and Vil and party allowed themselves to be ushered aboard the overcrowded transported and up in to the crew's quarters.

He vaguely remembered laughing and crying and sitting exhausted next to Lilia and Lucinda whilst wedged into a tiny space on a hard metal bench attached to the wall of a cabin. The lights flickered on and off intermittently, casting strange shadows over human faces and solid machines. Vil closed his eyes and slept. The pain drifted away into a dream filled with course sand and black rock. A red sun beating down on his naked body and a sharp wind chastised it. The taste of bile was in his mouth and his head was hung in submission. He dreamt he watched wearily as a mighty river of sluggishly churning blood flow slowly towards him, the unstoppable red tide lazily rolled over and eventually submerged him, ripping away his hate, fear and suffering and taking them to some place unknown. Vil was left sitting on a rock in the middle of the desert smiling up into the face of the blazing sun.

CHAPTER 11

Cassus had been in communication with the transport commanded by Lowery and it waited for the second vehicle to catch up. Together the two laden machines made their way back to Acto in relative peace. Cassus had not been idle in the few hours since the rescue teams had left, he had organised media from across the planet promising the story of a lifetime. The assembled ranks of journalists now fidgeted expectantly outside the main depot from which the army of conscripts would emerge. The Core Security force and a number of other CCD heads who had remained at the Dome, including Kathryn and even two of the other Administrators, had joined Cassus's cause and aided in the preparations.

Cassus had also made contact with the defeated army of Agents. They had seamlessly accepted the change in regime and were even now starting an operation to round up the remaining conscripts and other workers, of which five or six hundred remained. Many of the conscripts had fortuitously made their way back towards the great square anyway in the hope of getting to the transports there. The surviving Agents did not have a choice in co-operating with Cassus, especially as most of the surviving Commanders, including Lieutenant Hill, did not want any further association with the Secret Staff. Cassus did not have a hard time persuading the staff to do his will, despite a few minor protests. There was no sign of Regulator Marsden or the Governor.

Members of the converted army also calmly collected the waking guests and transported them in luxury back to the Dome, wisely avoiding the battlefield with its broken and twisted bodies. Their blissful ignorance of the events of the night remained intact. Within hours of the dawn breaking in the desert there was only one soul left in the city.

*****

The coup was a success. The media captured the still shocked army of bloodied and weary conscripts on every digital format. Interviews were carried out on the spot and broadcast live across the planet. The shock to the populace was immense and the inhabitants of Acto grew increasingly indignant. Long-standing mysteries concerning 'missing people' were solved. Loved ones were reunited, or not, in some cases. Relatives scanned lists that were drawn up of the dead.

At the climax of it all, hours later, the picture of Cassus appeared on every screen everywhere in the City. His voice was heard on every communicator, every audio instrument. His message was full of hope. The beginning of a better way of life for the populace, a new life, a superior life. He cast aside doubts and pledged a new beginning. He had saved the conscripts from the greed of the Administration and became, in a very short time, a hero of the city; the hero of the planet. The adoring masses watched his face and believed. Together they would work. Together they would triumph.

The new Administration organised a series of street parties in and around the Core. This successfully diverted attention away from the depot, and the guests and other new arrivals started to stream in and were taken to accommodation and the spaceport. Cassus managed to spend half an hour with the off planet guests before they departed, assuring them that they would be welcome back any time and the Governor had been taken ill with food poisoning and that he sent his apologies. The guests offered their concern for his health and wished him well. Cassus accepted these magnanimously on the behalf of Sendrick as he bade them farewell. Then he made all speed back to the dome to finally meet with the other heroes of the rebellion.

*****

Cassus and his considerable escort of officials and Core guards arrived back at the Administration within a short time, their convoy of electric cars passing slowly through the heaving streets towards the central building. There on the steps leading up to the main entrance stood a gaggle of weary looking people, many of whom Cassus did not recognise. But there too amongst them were familiar faces, Coldor, Lilia, Al and Vil.

His brother was there! He looked bloodied and worn, but he was alive! Suddenly everything seemed worth it. Cassus, the new Governor to be, ordered the car to a standstill some metres away from the steps to his new building. Before the car had even drawn to a halt he was out and running. Behind him his security escort made efforts to catch up but he was too quick. The companions on the steps suddenly noticed the swiftly approaching Cassus and turned towards him, but he headed straight towards Vil.

Finally, the two reunited brothers were able to embrace and they yelled joyfully at each other, clapping each other on the back and shaking hands without a care.

*****

A day later and for the last time the Governor climbed the steep stairs to the top of the highest tower, this time there was no mighty throng for him to address; the plain was empty. The protective atmospheric canopy bubble wheezed and shuddered as it started to fail, and the Governor looked out from his platform high above the sandy ground of Acto. Far away he could see the lights of the Dome City twinkling against the enormity of space. Without the automated projection of his voice and image the Governor knew he must look very small indeed.

For some time Sendrick looked out into the distance, he listened to the wind gently blowing amongst the deserted structures, which were to be the beginning of a new and better world. A gentle gust blew sand onto his face and Sendrick could taste its bitter dryness. The tendrils of many smaller surface gusts shifted the sand below, swirling it and blowing it onwards and away.

A deep emptiness filled his being and a compelling melancholy whispered its sweet messages through his mind. The Governor raised his eyes to the stars and smiled. He had fought for his cause with all his being and lost. He thought back to his youth, a long, long time ago it seemed now. He should have enjoyed the moment, lived in the present instead of always looked to the future, because the future had loomed brighter and the present paled into insignificance. He thought of old friends. Now those friends were all gone, lost in the past. Lovers had departed and he could barely recall their faces.

The Governor felt the pain of his mistakes as they intruded onto his consciousness. The feeling welcomed him back like an old friend, smothering him in the comfort of familiarity. Sendrick smiled the same defiant smile, which had come to his face through his long life. This time there was no strength left behind the gesture. Sendrick leaned against a pillar and bowed his head.

An unexpected tear fell slowly down his cheek and splattered on the red dust, which had settled on the blackness of the great rock platform. The Governor looked at it for a time, watched the moisture quickly become absorbed by the dust until it was gone. He could sympathise with the tear, like it, he was but a single speck in time, the future would swallow him up too, until he was forgotten. Until he was just another irrelevant name on a list to a new student at the Academy. Who then would remember his deeds and thoughts? All for which he had fought would be as for nothing. The oval red capsule in his hand would end his days painlessly. Suddenly he felt old and weak and his knees trembled. He realised he was afraid, and he thought about the feeling for a while, considering it like a corporeal entity and eventually he shrugged it away.

Governor Sendrick, the leader of a brave new world, slowly descended empty steps towards the desert. He didn't look back. The shiny red capsule lay discarded on the oratory platform for a few moments before being quickly hidden by the restless dust.

*****

Cassus searched the last of the incoming vehicles frantically for the man who had shown him the future. He hoped desperately that Sendrick had been picked up. He shot questions at Lieutenant Hill as he climbed down from an exploration vehicle and jumped off the caterpillar tracks. Hill shook his head. Cassus cursed and gazed out towards Sendrick's silent city. He knew he had done what had to be done to save the many but guilt gnawed at him. It pushed up like a black stain from his gut. The cost had been high. A single man, a great man, had snatched him from obscurity and raised him up and Cassus had taken that trust and torn it into tiny pieces.

Cassus grimaced, his face twisted. He looked away and spat. He accepted that he had betrayed his mentor. The guilt would remain but he pushed it down into the darkness. Sendrick had made him but that old man was gone and the future passed into the hands of a new Emperor.

And the vision lived on.

Printed in Great Britain
by Amazon